BEYOND FEAR

ALSO BY JAYE FORD

Available in Australia and New Zealand

(Coming soon to US, UK Canada and Germany)

Scared Yet?

Blood Secret

Already Dead

Darkest Place

For news on the international release of these Jaye Ford titles, sign up for her newsletter on her website at www.jayefordauthor.com

BEYOND FEAR

JAYE FORD

To Paul, Mark and Claire

1

They were going north this year, just the four of them heading out again on a cold, winter's Friday night. Jodie smiled as she drove, watching the lights of a small town disappear in her rear-view mirror.

There was a hint of mist in the bush on either side of the road and her headlights cut an eerie passage in the darkness. Like a tunnel guiding her safely through the night.

Or straight to hell.

Jodie knew about taking the wrong tunnel – and the ugly places it could lead you. But that wasn't going to happen, she told herself. Not now. Not with these friends.

'Here, have some chocolate.' Louise held out the broken-up block of fruit-and-nut next to Jodie. 'Ray'll be on his way to swim club about now. I'm eating chocolate and he's running around after both sets of twins. It's great.'

Jodie checked the clock on the dashboard. 'James should be picking up Adam and Isabelle from the birthday party right about now. There was a heap of red cordial and lollies when I dropped them off. He'll be begging them to go to bed in a couple of hours.' She grinned at the thought of the two ramped-up kids her ex would have to deal with and tossed a square of chocolate in her mouth. 'Mmm. Good choice, Hannah.'

'Ta,' Hannah said, leaning over the back of Louise's seat to take a piece. 'Pete's on car pool duty for basketball tonight. That means he gets to cart around stinky kids, shout Macca's on the way home and have dinner with Mum, who's looking after Chelsea. He loves our weekends away, I tell you.'

'Bailey and Zoe are staying with the outlaws. Is it too early to crack the champers?'

Jodie lifted her eyes to the rear-view mirror again and grinned at Corrine and the champagne bottle she was holding aloft.

'I brought plastic flutes in case of an emergency,' Corrine offered.

'What kind of emergency would that be?' Jodie said.

'I'd say no alcohol at six-fifteen on Day One is definitely an emergency.'

Jodie laughed but as she rounded the next bend the sound died in her throat.

A car was in the centre of the two-lane road, lights on high beam, maybe a hundred metres away. Coming at them fast. Its movement was loose and uncontrolled, lurching one way then the other. Jodie's heart banged in her chest. At the speed they were going, if she didn't do something quickly . . .

She took a solid grip on the wheel, remembered her defensive driver training and resisted an urge to slam the brake through the floor. She touched her foot to the pedal, swerved left. The tyres on that side skipped off the road and a hailstorm of stones sprayed the doors. Someone in the back screamed. Beside her, Louise braced herself against the dashboard. The other car roared past so close Jodie could have reached out and touched it. The rush of wind that followed pushed her car further onto the dirt. The tyres couldn't get traction. The rear end fishtailed violently. The front lurched sideways in the start of a fast, wide arc.

Her headlights swept across dark scrub. Then the dirt at the edge of the road. Then the two-lane strip of bitumen. Jodie pulled against the steering wheel, desperate to drag it off its circular course.

Minutes, hours, probably only micro-seconds later, the car tilted out of its spin, reversed direction. The lights swept back across the road. Across the dirt. Then Jodie saw what was going to stop them. The reflective dot on top of the white marker post glowed like a beacon in the headlights for about half a second before it slammed into the grille.

Jodie was thrown hard against her seatbelt as the car thumped to a stop. Her foot was locked on the brake, her fingers held their death grip on the steering wheel. For a long moment, no one said a word. The engine gurgled, the white post was somewhere underneath it and the sound of breathing seemed to fill the car.

'Is everyone okay?' she finally said.

'Oh my God.'

'What the hell?'

'Fuck.'

Jodie rubbed her chest where the seatbelt had cut in. 'Is that a yes from everyone?' She turned off the ignition and looked over each friend to make sure. Louise's mass of curly hair had fallen over her face and she had one hand on her chest, the other on a knee, rubbing gently. Hannah still gripped the back of Louise's seat but she smiled grimly at Jodie. Corrine held the champagne bottle with both hands like she was clutching a lamppost in a hurricane.

'Thank God the champers is safe. We're really going to need it now,' Corrine said without a hint of humour.

Jodie felt a wave of relief before anger charged in behind it. 'What a bastard. What the hell was he doing? He could have killed us.' She pushed her door open, slammed it behind her, stomped around to inspect the damage. 'Bastard! Look at my car.'

It had come to a stop on rough gravel about a metre off the road. Dense scrub was no more than a giant step from the passenger side doors and the glow from the one headlamp still working was the only light on what looked to be a very dark, isolated stretch of road. The car itself was a mess. The front looked as though it'd been hit by a battering ram. A deep cleft was gouged into the left half of the grille, the hood on that side was crushed and the mangled end of the bumper was lying on the dirt.

Jodie looked up as the light came on inside the car. Louise had opened the door, was speaking to Corrine and Hannah. She couldn't hear what Lou was saying but she kept flashing her hand across her face, as though she was reliving the moment the car sped past. Corrine was leaning into the centre of the car, hugging the champagne bottle to her chest and Hannah looked white under the dim overhead light.

Jodie's stomach tightened. She'd almost killed her best friends. Almost destroyed four families. She put a hand to her mouth, swallowed hard against nausea rising in her throat. Her hand started to shake, trembled all the way back to her shoulder and rattled down her spine. Oh God, she didn't want blood on her hands.

Not again.

Her knees buckled and she landed on her butt in the dirt. Someone squatted beside her, put an arm around her shoulders.

'Hey, it's okay.' It was Louise.

She felt Hannah's firm nurse's hand between her shoulderblades. 'Head between your knees, Jode. Suck in big breaths. In and out. That's it.'

Jodie kept her eyes open, her mind in the present. *They are alive, Jodie. All of them.*

The cold hit her then. Suddenly, as though her brain had just got around to processing her physical state. An icy breeze sliced through her sweater, made the nearby scrub shush. She looked up, saw a huge, black, moonless sky. Off to her right, a champagne cork popped.

'I think we all need a stiff drink,' Corrine said. 'The plastic flutes got squashed when we were bouncing around so we'll have to drink straight from the bottle.'

Jodie watched as Corrine, lit up by the headlight in her high-heels and long coat, tossed her blonde hair over her shoulders, tipped her head back and swung the champagne bottle up in one fluid movement for a slug. Only Corrine could stand in the rubble at the side of a dark road after a near-death experience and do that with style. Jodie grinned and held out her hand.

'Pass that thing over here,' she said and wondered for the hundredth time how she ended up with a friend like Corrine. Jodie couldn't do glamour. She was a high school PE teacher and a single mother of two sports-mad kids – what was the point of even trying?

'So where are we?' Corrine asked, handing the bottle over.

Jodie took a mouthful and screwed up her face. Too bubbly, too cold, too much adrenaline already making her head spin. 'Good question,' she said. She stood up, brushed off her jeans and looked in the direction they'd come, to where double yellow lines disappeared around a bend, then the other way to the crest of a hill. 'Somewhere outside Bald Hill, I guess. We can't be too far away. The agent said it'd take about an hour and a half from Newcastle, and we left an hour ago.'

'So what do we do now?' Corrine asked.

Jodie gripped the twisted end of the bumper and pulled on the cold metal. It groaned but held fast. 'Well, we're not going anywhere in my car. We'll have to get a tow.'

'I'll get my phone,' Louise said, starting around to the passenger door. 'I put the NRMA on speed dial the last time my car broke down.'

While Louise walked in circles with her arm up in a looking-for-reception pose, Jodie checked over the damage again. It was going to be a major pain without a car for the weekend, not to mention for the couple of weeks while it was being repaired. At least her insurance would cover the cost of a tow truck.

'I can't get reception,' Louise called from the edge of the road. A minute later, all four of them were wandering around in the dark, mobiles held high.

'I've got one bar,' Hannah called. She was across the road on the edge of the bush, one side of her face lit blue from her screen. 'What's the number?'

The champagne was passed around again while Hannah handled the rescue operation.

'I hope this place you booked has decent heating, Jodie. It's freezing out here,' Corrine said, pulling her coat tighter.

'And a toilet. I need to pee,' Louise said.

'And lights, 'cause it's really dark tonight,' Hannah called.

Jodie handed the bottle to Lou. 'It's got an open fire and two loos and if it doesn't have lights, I'm pretty sure we could ask for our money back.' It had been Jodie's turn to book the accommodation this year and she knew only too well the success of the weekend could turn on the lodgings. Four years ago she booked a houseboat – a leaky houseboat – and it had rained and rained and no amount of red wine and chocolate could make up for an overflowing loo. She was feeling more than a little pressure to come up with something fabulous. 'No, seriously, it looked great on the website. A hundred-year-old barn.'

'Tell me we're not staying in a barn,' Corrine said.

'It's not a barn now. It was renovated six months ago. The pictures are lovely.' Corrine took the bottle from Louise and pointed it at Jodie. 'Okay, but let me just make this clear. I don't care what state your car is in, you're driving me straight back home if I see anything that looks even remotely like a farm animal.'

Their laughter echoed into the cold night as Corrine swung the bottle up for another slug. Jodie shook the tension out of her shoulders as the terror of the last few minutes dissipated. Nice to know a brush with death hadn't ruined the mood of the weekend.

'Okay,' Hannah said, coming back across the road. 'Road service got onto a local service station and they're sending a tow truck out. I hope you've all got your thermal undies on 'cause it's going to take half an hour.'

MATT WISEMAN CHECKED out the Mazda as he swung the tow truck in a wide U-turn across the road. Nice job hitting the post, he thought. As he backed up the truck, he saw through the rear-view mirror a driver and three passengers get out. He pulled the handbrake, checked the clipboard, shook his head. Looked like the new kid his dad had employed needed some lessons in asking questions. He'd obviously missed the one about how many people were stranded with the broken-down car. Hope this lot had some other transport or the job wasn't going to be as easy as he'd banked on.

I'll get this one, Dad, Matt had said after the call came in. *I've been back two months. I know what to do. Go shoot a bullseye.* The psychologist was wrong. Covering for his dad so the old man could play in the Bald Hill darts final did not symbolise an innate desire to save others. It just proved he was a sentimental idiot.

He stretched his bad leg as got he out of the cab and looked across the truck bed at four women standing in the glow of his floodlight. Well, that was something you didn't see every day. Not out here on a cold Friday night. He checked the paperwork for a name, looked up again when they laughed. Stranded on a deserted road in the dark for almost an hour and still laughing – that was even more unexpected.

'Evening, ladies. Everyone okay here?' Matt watched them as he walked around the truck. They were good-looking women. All four of them. Mid to late thirties, probably. One of them was all done up like she was on her way to dinner. The short one on her right had a mop of dark curly hair. The one on the other side had a pretty face and was a little fleshy around the middle, like she'd had a couple of kids and never managed to firm everything back up. The one on the end had funky, short-cropped hair, huge dark eyes and the legs under her short coat looked like sculpted denim.

'So which one of you is Mrs De Crane?' The four of them giggled.

'Jo De Crane?' he tried. More laughing. Then he saw the champagne bottle the dressed-up one was holding. 'You ladies been drinking tonight?' He used a neutral voice – not an accusation, just an inquiry.

'Absolutely,' the one with the bottle said, swinging it back and forth by the neck.

'Purely for medicinal purposes. We didn't want Jodie passing out from shock.'

The one with the sculpted-denim legs stepped forward and

laughed. A low, confident roll of sound. 'Hi. It's my car. I'm Jodie Cramer. You were close. You know, with the name.'

She didn't look drunk and she didn't look stupid enough to drink and drive but you never could tell. 'A breathalyser wouldn't be able to detect whether you had the drink before or after the accident.'

She lifted her chin, held the smile. 'I doubt a breathalyser would even register the single mouthful of champagne I had after the accident. But seeing as the police aren't here and you are, it'd be great if we could start with the towing before we all freeze.'

Matt watched her a moment. It was said nicely but firmly. She was practised at giving direction, that much was clear. At another time and place, he would have pressed her further, breathalysed her for sure. But no one was hurt, they weren't doing any more driving in that car and it wasn't his job anymore. At least that's the way he felt about it tonight.

He made a show of looking at the damage. 'What happened?'

Jodie told him about the driver who'd pushed her off the road and pointed out the post that was lodged under the engine block. She was really cheesed off. It was impressive to watch. He looked under the car, couldn't help checking out her legs as he stood up. They were lean, toned. Maybe she was a runner.

'Where are you ladies heading?' he asked.

'We're staying the weekend at a house just outside Bald Hill,' Jodie said.

Well, they weren't going to be walking then. 'Anyone there to pick you up?'

The dressed-up one answered. 'It's just the four of us. A girls' weekend away.'

'Not such a great start, huh? Well, hate to break it to you but I can only take two of you in the truck.'

There was some muttering and someone said, 'Fuck it all'. He agreed. It was definitely a fuck-it-all situation.

Jodie ran a hand through her funky hair. 'So how far out of Bald Hill are we?'

'About forty k's. Half an hour in the truck.'

'Can we get a taxi this far out of town? On a Friday night?'

Matt raised an eyebrow. 'Bald Hill isn't exactly rocking on a Friday night. I'll radio our one and only cabbie on the two-way. He should be here by the time the car's up on the hoist.' He wouldn't leave them in the dark on their own, anyway. It wasn't a place to leave anyone.

Matt went back to the truck, radioed Dougie and told him not to take his sweet time about it. Told him there were four nice city women pissed at being run off the road and waiting in the cold so he should get his arse out here quick. That guy needed a bomb under him sometimes.

Matt took as long as he could to get the Mazda ready for towing but there was still no sign of Dougie when he was done. As he radioed again, the women huddled together in the cold, the luggage they'd taken from the car in a heap beside them.

'The cabbie said he's about five minutes away. I'll wait till he gets here. You can get in the truck to keep warm, if you want,' Matt said.

Jodie stepped forward. 'We're a bit worried about the time, actually. We have to pick up a key at a shop in town by eight and it's almost seven-thirty already. If you left with two of us now, we might get there before it closes.'

Matt looked up and down the dark road. 'Which shop is it?'

She unfolded a piece of paper. 'Smith's Food Mart.'

That made sense. It was next door to the real estate agent. He didn't know the Smiths well – they hadn't owned the place when he'd lived in Bald Hill as a kid – but everyone knew they liked to close on time. It was a fair drive to their property out of town.

Matt shook his head slowly. 'It's not a great place to be waiting at night.'

Jodie checked her watch. 'Look, you said yourself the cab's only five minutes away. It's probably just around the corner. And a couple of minutes might be the difference between getting our key and finding someplace else that can put up four people at short notice.'

Matt scanned the road again, took his phone out of his pocket. No bars. Reliable reception was a figment of the imagination out here. He looked at Jodie. He didn't like the idea but he could see her point.

He could spend ten minutes trying to hunt down reception to find a number for the shop or getting through to the pub to get someone to make the call for him – or he could hit the road and save them a lot of stuffing around.

JODIE WATCHED the tow truck driver think it through. He seemed like a nice guy, despite the breathalyser crack. Not bad looking, either. Tall, muscled without being beefy. Excellent smile. But he wasn't smiling about leaving them.

She wasn't too happy about the idea either. It was damn dark out here. There was no question she'd stay behind. It was her car. Her fault, really. It was the risk she always took as the self-appointed designated driver wherever she went. Her life was in her own hands that way, with her own overblown sense of caution. But the flip side was that if anything went wrong, it was her responsibility. Staying behind wasn't the problem, though. If they didn't get the key, she'd be guilty of another 'houseboat' weekend and in a year's time they'd be discussing leaking loos versus no roof over their heads.

She smiled encouragingly at the driver, watched him juggle the phone in his palm for a moment. He closed his hand around it, dropped it back in his pocket and looked down at her.

'Okay, let's get rolling,' he said.

Jodie chaired a brief meeting over who was going in the truck.

'We could all stay,' Hannah suggested.

'Don't be ridiculous,' Jodie said. 'A cab won't fit all of us and the luggage. Look, I'm staying. Lou needs to pee so unless she wants to duck behind a dark, creepy bush to relieve herself, she should go into town.'

Lou made a face, a mixture of apology and relief. Jodie turned to Corrine and Hannah. No one was volunteering now – to stay or go. 'Hannah is freezing in that thin jacket so Corrine either gives Hannah her coat or stays with me.'

Corrine bordered on skinny while Hannah was carrying a couple of extra kilos. It was unlikely Corrine's figure-hugging jacket would meet around Hannah's middle.

Hannah looked Corrine up and down, tugged the hem of her sweater over her belly and tucked her short, brown bob behind her ears. 'Well, I wouldn't mind but . . .'

Corrine shrugged and sighed, then stood with her hands in her pockets, looking unimpressed, as Jodie passed luggage up to Hannah and Louise in the truck. When Jodie closed the door, more than half the cases were still on the dirt at her feet and everyone, including the driver, looked unhappy about the arrangement.

Brilliant bloody start to the weekend, Jodie.

'Don't worry. We're fine,' she said. 'See you in Bald Hill.' She shooed them off, waving about the torch the driver had given her and smiling like she and Corrine were already having a ball.

She stood in the centre of the road and watched the truck's head-lights flare into the night sky as it crested the hill, then disappear as it dropped over the other side. She thought of the tunnel her own lights had carved in the darkness not so long ago and felt a chill at the black and lonely place she was now standing in.

2

'Better save the batteries,' Jodie said and flipped off the torch. Night wrapped itself around them like a black shroud.

'Bloody hell, it's freezing.' Corrine's voice sounded deeper than usual in the silence of the wide-open space.

Jodie turned away from the road, strained her eyes in the darkness, thought she could see the faint glow of Corrine's blonde hair. 'And dark. It's bloody dark.'

'The cold's worse.'

'No way. Dark like this gives me the creeps.' She stepped cautiously in the direction of Corrine's voice, not wanting to stumble into the luggage, willing herself not to flinch at the feeling that the night was breathing down her neck. 'We should have borrowed the fluoro vest the tow truck driver was wearing.'

'Are you kidding? That colour would look terrible on you.' Corrine's face suddenly appeared, lit in blue by the screen of Hannah's phone – it was the only one that had found reception. 'Okay, it's seven-thirty-two. If the taxi isn't here in ten minutes, I'm calling the tow truck driver back.'

Jodie grinned as Corrine looked up at her. 'You look like something out of a ghost story. A decapitation victim whose head haunts the highway, terrifying drivers, causing unexplained accidents.'

Corrine moved the phone under her chin so the light made her look like a glowing blue skull. 'Could this face do anything but inspire a lifelong trust in good skin care?'

Jodie laughed, heard Corrine's husky chuckle and was glad her friend had decided not to stick with the huffy silence over having to wait behind. 'Thanks for staying with me.'

The light slid downwards and disappeared as Corrine dropped the mobile into her pocket. 'I guess that's what I get for having a strong bladder and a warm coat.'

She said it laughingly but Jodie got the message – it was the short straw, not a good deed. 'Sorry about all this.'

'It's not your fault that driver tried to run us off the road.'

'Did you get a look at the car?'

'Briefly. I was opening the champagne.'

'I thought it was one of those big, chunky utes. Black or something dark. With lights mounted on top. Floodlights or something.'

'I think it had a sort of frame over the tray section,' Corrine said. 'Fat, silver posts. Or maybe they were white. I only got a glimpse.'

Jodie flicked the torch on, walked the five paces to the edge of the road, looked right to the crest of the hill then left to the bend.

'What are you doing?' Corrine asked.

'I don't know. Just looking.'

'The view's the same from here, you know.'

Jodie swung the torch around, lit up the bags and Corrine and the bush at her back.

'Yeah, I know. But walking and looking feels better than standing still.' She left the light on as she made her way around the luggage, flicked it off, folded her arms tight across her chest. Beside her, Corrine's boots shuffled about on the roadside gravel. She could smell Corrine's perfume. Something far off made a birdlike sound. The light from the phone appeared at waist-height, briefly lit Corrine's manicured hand, then disappeared again.

The sound of an engine began like a whisper in the silent night, grew to a rumble then the bush beyond the bend glowed.

'Thank God,' Corrine said.

Headlights speared the darkness and a moment later a car careered around the bend. It was going the wrong way to be coming from Bald Hill but maybe the cab hadn't started there. Corrine slung her handbag over a shoulder, picked up a suitcase and stood like she was waiting for the bus. Jodie walked towards the road, moving the torch from side to side in a wide arc, letting the cabbie know he'd found them.

The car was almost on her before she realised it wasn't the cab. No telltale taxi light on top, no attempt to slow down. She squinted in the glare of the headlights, glanced a shadowy, lone driver at the wheel as it rushed past, then watched until its red tail-lights disappeared over the hill.

'Shit,' Corrine said. Something hit the gravel. Jodie guessed it was the bag, hoped Corrine hadn't slumped to the ground in a sulk.

Jodie stepped onto the smooth surface of the road and stood in the centre, torch still pointed at the corner. 'Shit.' After the blaze of light, the dark seemed even more oppressive. She didn't like it. Or the way it made her heart hammer inside her chest. 'What time is it?'

The blue light appeared. 'Seven-forty.'

'I'm going to call.' Jodie walked back, took Hannah's mobile, crossed the road and had a shoulder pressed into the bush on the other side before one reception bar lit up. 'What's Hannah's passcode?' She tapped them in as Corrine shouted the digits, then the number the tow truck driver had given her and watched the torchlight dim a little as she listened to the ringtone switch to the cabbie's message bank. She left a polite message – we're here, we're waiting, be great to see you soon. She phoned Louise then the truck driver. No answer on both counts.

By the time she reached Corrine, the torch beam looked like it'd been connected to a dimmer and turned to low. She flicked it off, sucking in a breath at the sudden blackness. 'I can't see a thing.'

Corrine was silent for a moment. 'I can make out the top of the trees against the sky.'

Jodie lifted her eyes, saw shadows materialise as her vision adjusted to the dark – the ragged edge of treetops silhouetted against a starless dome of sky, the looming, solid mass of a gum tree, the white roadside markers. She sensed again the darkness at her back, wanted to turn around, check they were alone. Don't be paranoid, Jodie. You're past that. She pushed her hands into her pockets. 'I can see the white lines on the road, too.'

'I can see you. Your face but not your hair.'

'Your hair looks like a puff of steam.'

'Thanks for that.'

'Any time.'

'Christ, it's cold.'

Corrine shuffled her feet again. Jodie repositioned her weight from one frozen foot to the other, blew on her hands, hitched at the collar of her jacket. It was so quiet, she could hear her pulse thud softly inside her head. Icy tentacles of wind played across her face, rustled the bush behind her – a gentle, shushing sound that was amplified in the eerie, dark silence and made her feel suddenly, irrationally alone.

'Adam said you went all the way back to school for his model plane today,' Jodie said loudly, a little too cheerily. She notched it down a tad. 'He's so forgetful. Hope it wasn't too much of a rush to get packed.'

'No problem. My bags were already waiting by the door. Besides, he looked like his little heart would break if I didn't.'

Jodie smiled, relieved to hear Corrine's voice. 'He really wanted his dad to see it,' she said, wishing she could tell Corrine how thankful she was.

Corrine had banned her from saying thank you two and a half years ago. That was a week after Jodie had gone back to full-time work, still angry and reeling from James' decision to give up on their rocky marriage. She'd gotten stuck in traffic, had been late to pick up Adam and Isabelle from after-school care. The kids were upset, Jodie felt sick with guilt and it'd cost her a fortune in late fees. Then Corrine dropped by to see how the new job was going. She was the most unlikely candidate for childminding – the woman was so perfectly groomed and styled, it was hard to believe she had children of her own – but it was Corrine's idea. Jodie had to stay behind to teach a senior sport class on Wednesdays and Fridays, and Corrine was at the primary school anyway, to collect Zoe, her youngest. So after that, Corrine picked up all three kids two days a week, took them home, fed them afternoon tea and let them play until Jodie arrived. No need for thank yous, Corrine had said. She enjoyed their laughing and shouting and running around. Her late husband Roland had loved a raucous house.

More often than not, Corrine had a chilled bottle of champagne waiting for Jodie's arrival on Fridays. Hannah or Lou might drop by and all the kids would be shooed down to Corrine's huge rumpus room or out to the pool. Sometimes, after Hannah or Lou had gone home to their husbands, Jodie and Corrine would order takeaway or make something easy like cheese on toast, sit around the table with their four children and conjure up some of that relaxed, end-of-the-week family time they both missed about being married.

'Just don't let James think I did it for *him*,' Corrine said.

Jodie knew she'd have that piqued tilt to her chin now. Corrine had never forgiven James for walking away from his family – not when he'd seen how Corrine's had been torn apart by Roland's heart attack only months earlier. If ever Jodie needed company for a bit of liberating ex-husband ranting, Corrine was her girl. 'Won't even mention it.' Jodie heard the scuffle of Corrine's feet, saw her bend over the luggage.

'What happened to the champagne?' Corrine asked.

'Champagne? Are you kidding? It's too cold.'

'Honey, it's never too cold for champagne. I saw it with the bags. Here it . . . what . . . oh, bugger. It got knocked over.' More scuffling. 'Oh. Oh, fuck it all.' Gravel skittered across the ground. 'I've been squatting in a big puddle of champagne. The hem of my coat is soaked!'

Jodie heard the muted sounds of Corrine slapping at her coat, the scrunch of gravel as she flailed about. 'Where the hell is that cab? Give me the phone. I'm going to call.'

Jodie handed her the mobile and the torch. She heard a couple of sighs then Corrine said, 'How do you work this thing? Oh, got it.' The torch came to life and Jodie screwed up her eyes as the beam shone straight into her face. 'Let's see what this cab driver's got to say for himself,' Corrine said.

The cabbie would get a mouthful. Jodie grinned to herself as Corrine lit a path around the bags but as she stalked across the road, the smile on Jodie's face dropped away. The torch beam had wiped out her night vision and the further away Corrine got, the blacker everything became. The jagged edge of sky was gone, so was the looming tree. She thought about running over to her – they could huddle together in the light, make defamatory comments about the cabbie while they waited for him to answer – but she couldn't see her own feet, thought she'd probably do an ankle tripping over the luggage. She pulled her coat tighter, tried to keep her eyes on Corrine, felt her chest tighten, her heart beat faster. Where was the damn cab? And what happened to five minutes away? They'd been waiting fifteen already, freezing their butts . . .

A snap. In the brush.

Jodie spun around, blinked blindly at the darkness. Something familiar and unpleasant fluttered in the pit of her belly. Her hands turned to fists inside her pockets. She stood perfectly still, ears straining in the silence, listening. For footsteps, breathing, whispering. It was like a sensory deprivation tank out here – no sound, no sight. Then behind her, Corrine swore.

Jodie jumped so hard it sent little stones scattering. Adrenaline buzzed in her head, tingled across her shoulders. She turned, saw Corrine in her halo of phone light, stabbing at the screen. Get a grip, Jodie. There was no one out here. No one could be. It was just you and Corrine. The fashion queen and her tracksuit-and-runners friend. Shake it off, Jodie. Take a damn breath.

'Any luck?' She called it loudly, filling the darkness with the sound of her own voice.

'I left a message for the cabbie and Lou's mobile rang out,' Corrine said as her heels clacked back across the road. 'What the hell are they doing? We said we'd call when we were in the cab. They should be waiting to hear from us.'

Jodie felt a flicker of concern. 'Maybe it's the reception out here. I could only get one bar. Maybe the calls aren't even getting through to them. They're fine. I'm sure they are. I'm sure it's just a reception problem.'

Corrine skirted the luggage, came to a stop beside Jodie and clicked the torch off at the end of a long sigh.

'Leave it on,' Jodie said.

'My hand's cold.'

'I'll hold it.'

The torch came back on. Jodie took it from Corrine, ran the light over the bags at their feet, then in a wider circle around the luggage, across the gravel, the skid marks in the stones, the bent-over white post. She turned around and shone the glow into the bush behind them. See, Jodie, just bush. The light was little more than a dim disc now. The batteries wouldn't last much longer. She should turn it off. She didn't.

'So what's the latest on the school dinner?' Jodie said it like the ins and outs of the fundraising committee were prime conversation. She didn't have the time or the skills to organise a classy dinner and Corrine's enthusiasm for table decorations and menu options had, to this point, encouraged her to steer clear of the topic but right now, she'd be happy to hear all of it. Anything to keep them talking, to fill the silence, to take the edge off the darkness.

She huffed. 'The colour scheme has been such a drama this year,' Corrine started. And Jodie listened, mmm'd and oh-lovely'd until she couldn't stand not knowing the time any longer.

'Pass the mobile,' she said when Corrine paused for breath. She checked the glowing blue numbers – twenty-three minutes they'd been waiting – and as Corrine talked on, Jodie took the torch to the edge of the road, looked right to the crest, left to the bend. 'I'm going to try again.'

She jogged across the road and nestled into the bush. She didn't bother leaving a message for the cabbie. He wasn't going to get there any faster if she told him he was a useless, time-wasting jerk.

She phoned Louise then the tow truck driver. Still no answer. Then it didn't matter. Light flared in the sky beyond the crest of the hill before the car roared into sight like two blinding eyes. Jodie stepped out of the bush, had her arms in the air to flag it down when she saw Corrine on the opposite side lit up by the headlights. She'd stepped forward but had already seen it wasn't stopping, stood there with one hand on her hip, one leg jutted out – body language for pissed off.

As it passed, a man shouted out the window in a loud rush of sound that was carried away by the speed of the car. Jodie had no idea what he yelled – it could have been *Praise the Lord* – but she stiffened with apprehension, flicked off the torch, watched the car all the way to the bend, hoping it didn't turn around. Not feeling a whole lot safer when it didn't.

She sprinted back across the road as its red tail-lights disappeared. The dark closed in. She flicked the switch on the torch but got nothing. Tried again, gave it a bash with the heel of her hand. Nothing.

'And?' Corrine said.

Jodie tossed the torch in the direction of the luggage, heard the soft thud as it landed, edged closer to Corrine. 'Still no answer.'

'What are they doing?' It was more exclamation than question.

'Must be the reception.' *They're fine, Jodie.*

Corrine started up a rhythmic rocking, knocking one foot against the other. 'I've been trying to think of something hot,' she said. 'But it's not working. All I get is Brad Pitt and I just can't imagine anything hot with all those kids of his hanging around.'

Jodie smiled, tried to relax. The cab would come. It would be here any second. 'It's been so long since I had anything hot, I'm not sure I can conjure up an image that would warm me up, kids or no kids.'

'I'm with you there. I haven't had a man to cuddle up to since Roland died. Well, except for that one close call.'

Jodie looked at Corrine, saw Corrine's puff-of-steam hair turn in her direction.

'Rob the Sales Rep,' they said together and burst out laughing.

Corrine's tale of her disastrous widow-tries-the-dating-game had kept the four of them in stitches for months. Rob the Sales Rep was a friend of a friend of a friend. He'd asked her out; she'd thought it was time. He was younger; she figured, what the hell. She had her hair and nails done, bought a new dress, wore four-inch heels and he'd taken her for pizza.

'Classy pizza,' Jodie said, glad to have something to take her mind off the darkness.

'Pizza restaurant with a drive-through,' Corrine returned and their laughter cranked up.

The low points of Corrine's big night out had become the punchlines to a running joke that was less about Rob and more about their anxiety over the singles scene. Out here in the cold, poor clueless Rob was the perfect stress-reliever and they cackled through the shorthand version of the tale.

'You're turning *forty*?'

'Your condoms or mine, babe.'

'On a first date?'

'Hey, you're forty. You haven't got time to wait?'

Then it wasn't Rob they were laughing at but each other. Gasping with an increasing hilarity that shook out Jodie's nerves and eased the apprehension.

As the laughter finally wound down, Corrine slung an arm around Jodie's neck, laid her head on Jodie's shoulder and let out one last, long hooting laugh.

The hairs on Jodie's neck stood up. Sweat broke out along her hairline. A thought stirred in the back of her head.

No, a memory.

It wasn't just the last, long laugh. It was Corrine's sudden closeness. Her breath on Jodie's neck. The dark, the cold. The pressing silence of a large, open space.

Then the memory hit like a thump between her shoulderblades.

Images blasted through her head. Crazy, mixed-up images, as though the memory was a reel of film that had been chopped up and stuck back together in random order.

Pink platform sandal.

Man's face. Long hair, stud earring, chipped front tooth.

Breath misting on a laugh. Feet running on gravel. Rough hands on her face.

Blood on her hands. On her clothes. So much blood. So much . . .

3

J odie held her hands up in front of her face, close enough to see pale palms, ringless fingers. No. There was no blood now. She shook her head, heard her lungs suck air in, let it out, suck it in again. As fear surged through her body, a part of her brain recognised the flashback for what it was, even calculated how long it had been since she'd had one. Four years, at least.

It's not happening, Jodie. They're memories. *Old memories.* But it was so hard to hear herself over the terror.

'This is a bad place to be.' She grabbed Corrine by the sleeve. 'Come on. We're not safe here. We've got to go.'

Corrine pulled free, still laughing. 'Where are we going?'

'Anywhere. Away from here. Come on.' Jodie grabbed her arm, tried to tow her along the gravel.

'No.' Corrine snatched out of her grip. 'What do you mean go? There's nowhere to go. And what about the bags?'

Oh shit, the bags. She'd forgotten the bags.

'Okay, we'll take them with us.' Jodie picked up the closest one, hauled its strap over her shoulder, hefted a thermal bag full of food over her other shoulder. Fear was making her strong, Superwoman, she could carry ten of them. She grabbed two more, pushed another one at Corrine. 'Here, take this. Come on.'

Corrine stepped away. 'No. I'm not going anywhere. Over there is as dark as over here. There's no reason why I should stumble around in my new ankle boots just to go stand in another dark spot.'

Jodie's heart thumped in her chest. The tips of her fingers tingled as though the adrenaline racing around inside was about to burst through the skin. They're just memories. Very old memories. Pre-kids. Pre-uni. A lifetime ago. Get a grip. Take a breath.

She pulled in a lungful of air, snapped out the handle of a wheelie bag and leaned on it. Okay, she was freaked out. Infused with pulse-racing fear. But this was still a bad place to wait – and she wanted to get them out of there.

She tried to make her voice even, reasoned. 'The first rule of self-defence is not to be there. And right here, we're sitting ducks. I should have seen it earlier. Look.' She pointed to the right where the crest of the hill met the dark sky then left to the right-angled bend where the lines in the road disappeared. 'Between the hill and the corner, we're totally obscured. There's bush right up to both sides of the road and it's so dark we can barely see each other.'

'But . . .'

'Don't you see? We have to stand on the edge of the road for the taxi to see us but we can't tell if it's a taxi until it's already on us. Some freak could take that as an invitation for a cheap thrill and run us down, or worse, drag us into a car. And unless another vehicle drives through here at that same moment – which is pretty damn unlikely since we've only seen two cars in half an hour – no one will know we're here. We could be dying in the dirt and the cabbie would drive right past us. We have to find a better place to wait.'

'Calm down, Jodie. You've been teaching too many of those self-defence classes,' Corrine said, still not moving.

Jodie pursed her lips at Corrine's tone. Her self-defence course wasn't offered for a fun alternative on sport days. She was trying to save lives. Teaching what she wished she'd known eighteen years ago. 'I'd be pretty stupid not to take my own advice, don't you think?'

Corrine shook her head. 'Okay, look, I know this isn't the pick of places to wait for a cab but surely it's better than wandering around in the dark.'

No, it wasn't. It was dark and creepy and all wrong here. 'Doing something is better than nothing. Moving is better than standing still. I want to start walking towards Bald Hill and I'm not leaving you behind.' She would never do that again. 'So *come on.*' Too late, she recognised the irritating playground tone of her voice, took a breath, tried to lighten the mood. 'Besides, walking will warm us up and we might get better reception when we get over the hill. And if you don't come, I'll knock you out and drag you by your new boots, and you know I *can* do that. Please, Corrine.'

Corrine sighed. 'Okay, okay, if that's what you want, but if I ruin my boots, you can pay for a new pair.'

Jodie passed her a bag. 'Thank you and you better walk carefully because I can't afford a new pair of your boots.'

She helped Corrine load up with as many bags as she would carry and took the rest herself. The high tide of fear began to recede once they were moving. Her eyes adjusted a little more as they followed the white roadside markers. She could make out the long ribbon of road, the line of bush on the other side, the charcoal cover of sky. Her heart slowed and the howling in her head eased a little. She still had the Superwoman strength but dragging two wheelie bags along the gravel with the thermal bag on one shoulder and a pillow under the other made for slow going.

'Do you have to go so fast?' Corrine called from behind.

Jodie tried to ignore the urge to grab Corrine's hand and run for safety, and forced herself to cut her pace.

'Let's cross the road and try the phone again,' Jodie said and veered onto the bitumen. She dragged her wheelie bags over the lip, felt them fall into line behind her on the smooth surface. 'We should walk on the road after I've called Louise. It's a lot easier,' she called over her shoulder as she manoeuvred the cases onto the dirt on the other side.

Behind her, she heard Corrine's boots clomp onto the road,

followed by the bump of her suitcase and a hum of wheels as she crossed the tarmac. Then came a sudden scatter of gravel and Corrine cried out.

Jodie turned, took a moment to decipher the shadows in front of her. Corrine was sprawled on the dirt, a wheelie case up-ended and a smaller bag flung across her. Jodie dropped her baggage and skidded to her side.

'I turned my ankle.' Corrine's voice was tight with pain.

Jodie placed a hand gently under the back of Corrine's boot to support the ankle, took the bag from her shoulder and helped her sit. 'How bad is it?'

'It hurts like hell.'

'Can you move your toes?'

She took a second to answer. 'Yes. Did I break it?'

'If you can move your toes, you've probably just sprained it.'

'I mean my boot. Did I break the heel?'

'Are you serious?'

'Yes. They're Italian. They cost a fortune.'

Jodie felt under the boot, found a dangling spiked heel. 'Yes, you broke the heel.' She looked up at the crest of the hill that now loomed above them, then down the road to the bend and felt the fear rev up again. This was a worse place to be. Too close to the crest, too close to the edge of the tar. The bush was nearer to the road on this side and it seemed darker somehow. They wouldn't need a freak looking for a cheap thrill to knock them down. Anyone coming over the hill too fast could plough right into them. 'Do you think you can walk?'

'Jesus, Jodie. I've just sprained my ankle. Can you give me a second?'

Jodie shut her eyes. Corrine was angry but it didn't change their situation. They needed to move. She gently rubbed Corrine's ankle. 'I'm sorry. I know it's hurting but it isn't safe here. We should at least move off the road a bit further.'

Corrine pushed Jodie's hand away. 'We should have stayed where we were.'

Jodie shot to her feet. 'No, *you* should've been more careful. Why did you wear bloody spike heels for a weekend in the country, anyway? What were you expecting? A nightclub?' Her heart pounded and her stomach tightened like it was waiting for a blow.

She turned sharply, took half-a-dozen steps along the gravel. What are you doing, Jodie? Corrine was just being Corrine. Her narcissistic streak was usually good for a bit of a laugh. Right now, though, Jodie wanted to shake it out of her. Get a grip, for God's sake. Losing your cool will not help.

She walked back to Corrine. She was sitting on the edge of the bitumen, her hurt ankle propped on her opposite knee. Her chin jutted out indignantly. She didn't look up, didn't speak. Shit, she's really mad, Jodie thought. She stood on the edge of the road and stared at the double yellow lines disappearing over the hill.

Jodie hadn't felt scared like this in a long time. She'd worked through all that crap. What was the hell was happening? The near miss and almost killing her best friends had started it. A thing like that would throw anyone off balance. Then there was the hurry to get the keys for the B & B and getting left with Corrine when she was the least likely to be practical in a bad situation. Now Jodie had made it worse by freaking out and dragging Corrine around in her ankle-breaker boots.

Okay, Jodie, think it through. Make some better decisions.

She turned a slow circle. Corrine was still sitting on the edge of the road, still saying nothing. That situation needed mending for a start. Corrine had no idea what was going on in Jodie's head. She didn't need to know – it was Jodie's own private freak-out and she didn't want to dump it on a friend.

The crest of the hill was a dark line in the night sky, a short upward slope. And Hannah's mobile was in her pocket. She took it out and held it up in the air. Not even one bar. Jodie ran a hand through her hair, felt the dampness in it from the cold night air. Okay, doing something always felt better than doing nothing. She squatted beside Corrine.

'I'm sorry I made you walk around in the dark. And I'm sorry I yelled at you. I just don't like it here.' Corrine looked up at her. 'And your shoes aren't stupid. I'd buy a pair myself if I thought I could walk in them.' She tried to inject a smile into her voice. 'How's your ankle?'

'It feels like I jammed it in a car door. I don't think I can walk.'

'Then I think we should try to move you and the bags away from the road. And then I'm going to the top of the hill to see if I can get better reception up there. Are you okay with that?'

Corrine shrugged. 'If it'll stop you prattling on about it.'

Jodie took a second, decided not to comment. She helped Corrine away from the road, made several trips to move all the bags then kept the phone in her hand to watch for reception as she began the jog up the hill. The fear was like a straitjacket now, making her stiff as she ran. Making her breath jerk in and out, refusing to let it settle into its usual running rhythm – but running felt a damn sight better than standing and waiting. Like she had some control. She stopped at the top.

'Hallelujah. Three bars,' she yelled to Corrine and counted five rings before Louise answered.

'Hey, guys. About time you got here.' She was somewhere noisy, sounding happy.

'We're not. We're still waiting for the taxi,' Jodie said.

'What?' It wasn't a shock-horror exclamation but a please-repeat.

'I said . . .'

'Hang on, I can't hear you.'

Jodie squeezed her eyes shut. She'd wanted Louise to cry, 'Don't panic, a chopper will be there to rescue you within the minute', not 'Hang about while I turn the volume down'.

'We're in the pub and there's a bourbon and Coke here with your name on it,' Louise said.

'We're still waiting for the fucking cab,' Jodie snapped, then wished she hadn't. She knew it wasn't Lou's fault but cheery was beyond her emotional range right now.

'Oh my God. I thought you were at the service station.'

Jodie heard Hannah in the background and Louise repeated the 'fucking cab' bit.

'Hang on. Hannah's asking someone about the taxi.'

Jodie heard muffled voices. Then some kind of shocked exchange between Hannah and Louise.

Lou came back on. 'The taxi left ages ago. Someone at the pub's been trying to call him. He's not answering his mobile. No one knows where he is.'

Jodie tried to rein in the panic that was brewing in the back of her head. 'Get someone out here, Lou. Now.'

4

Matt flicked the wipers for a swipe at the mist that was almost a light rain. Bad night for Jodie Cramer and her friend to be sitting by the side of a road. He eased his foot harder on the accelerator, glad he'd brought his car instead of the tow truck this time – it would get him there a lot faster.

He shouldn't have left them. He knew it at the time but their concern about getting the key had made him ignore his instincts.

That was the problem. He didn't trust his instincts anymore. And the problem with *that* was that he'd always acted on gut feeling. The police psychologist called it an emergency reflex but what would she know about being in a tight corner? He glanced at his reflection in the dark passenger window. If he couldn't rely on his gut, he couldn't do his job anymore. *Just a loss of confidence*, the psychologist had said. Matt said *Ditto*: what would she know? She'd never even fired a gun.

Matt topped the crest of the hill and pulled up sharply. Jodie and the other woman were sitting on their luggage at the side of the road. What were they doing there? Why not just stand in the middle of the road and ask to be run down? At least his instincts had left them in a safer place.

His tyres crunched on the gravel as he steered off the road. Jodie stood as he reversed back. So she wasn't the one who'd hurt an ankle. Standing there with her feet firmly planted and her hands stuffed in her coat pockets, he guessed it'd take more than a walk in the dark to knock her off her pins.

'Need a lift?' he called as he stepped out of the car.

'About an hour ago,' she called back and the tone of her voice said they weren't having a party out here. When he'd walked over, she said, 'What happened to the damn cab?'

'A tree.' Matt waited a beat while she opened her mouth and closed it again, as the concept took some of the heat out of her reproach.

'The cabbie hit a tree?'

'Yeah, you're lucky it happened before he picked you up or you'd have more than a tumble in the dirt to worry about.'

'Is he all right?'

'He's on his way to hospital but a broken leg seems to be the worst of it.'

Up close, the two of them looked cold and damp and the cheery mood on his first trip out had definitely taken a hike. The other woman was sitting on a suitcase with one foot propped on a bag. Her shoe was still on and the leg of her jeans was pulled down over the ankle so he couldn't tell how bad the injury was but from the way she was huddled in her coat, she looked like she'd probably die of cold before the pain got her. He knelt on one knee beside her, kept his bad knee angled away. 'What happened?'

She shot Jodie a look – the kind that implied she'd already had a few words to say on that matter. 'Jodie didn't like it back down there. Thought we'd be *safer* if we took a walk.' She rolled her eyes.

Matt frowned up at Jodie. 'Probably better if you'd stayed where you were. You're sitting ducks here. I was lucky to see you.'

'Thanks for that. I'll try to remember next time I'm stranded out here.' She gave him a tight smile. 'Right now, Corrine needs to get to the car. Can you give me a hand?'

He looked back at Corrine. 'How bad is it? Do you need a hospital?'

'A hot spa would be my first choice but Bald Hill will do. I think it's just a sprain.' She held a hand out to him. 'I'm Corrine, by the way, and I'm very happy to meet you again.'

'Matt Wiseman,' he said, taking her hand, lifting her to her feet. 'Nothing like a bit of excitement on a Friday night, hey?'

She curled one arm around his neck, the other over Jodie's and used the two of them as crutches. After half-a-dozen steps, he could see it would take them an age like that.

'I've got a better idea,' he said, hooked an arm under her knees and picked her up.

'Oh, I didn't expect that. Are you sure? You're limping yourself.'

'It's no big deal,' he said, figuring a little more physio wouldn't hurt.

She fastened her arms around his neck, purred into his ear. 'Well, then, you can come to my rescue any day.'

Matt chuckled. The helpless female thing had never really appealed but a good-looking woman in his arms was better than a kick in the head for his efforts tonight.

He helped her into the back of the car, left her arranging her leg along the seat and found Jodie strongarming a suitcase into the boot. He reached in to give her a hand, bumped her as he heaved against the weight and on contact, she snapped her arm away. He looked up in surprise. She took a step back, stood with her feet apart, arms at her sides, fists bunched like she was ready to throw a punch. That was one hell of a defence reflex. As he straightened, she took another couple of steps back, looked away like she wasn't sure what to do, then turned and walked to the pile of luggage.

They collected the rest of the bags and she stayed to the side while he loaded the car. No more nasty bumps that way, Matt guessed. He let her find her own way around to the passenger door, half expecting her to be sitting with her friend when he climbed into the driver's seat. But she was next to him, already belted in. As he fumbled with the keys, she dragged both hands through her hair, ran them over her face, held them there a second as she pulled in a deep breath.

He started the engine and said, 'Everything okay?'

She folded her arms across her chest before she turned her face to him. 'Yep. Great.' She smiled a little. It looked like it took some work, like she had to unclench her jaw before her lips would soften into a curl. The effort was worth it though and made up for her keep-your-distance act outside. 'Thanks for coming to get us.'

'No problem.' He U-turned onto the bitumen and picked up speed on the familiar road. Beside him, Jodie rubbed her hands up and down her arms, crossed her legs. He turned the heating up a couple of notches.

'Thanks,' she said. 'How's my car?'

'It's seen better days.'

'Is there any chance you could patch it up so I can drive home on Sunday?'

Matt shrugged. 'Can't answer that. You'll have to wait till the old man takes a look at it in the morning. He's the mechanic. I'm just the hired help. Depends what parts he's got but I'd suggest you talk to him before you make other arrangements.'

Corrine spoke up from the back seat. 'I'm more concerned about how we get to our cottage tonight. What do we do if there's no taxi?'

Matt ran his hand over the stubble on his chin. 'I could run you over. Where are you staying?'

'The Old Barn On The Hill,' Jodie said. 'Do you know it?'

The barn on the hill. Bloody hell. In his head, he saw its small boxy shape, the unpainted timber frame, the crude steps up to the front door – and his gut tightened. It must have changed some if it was being rented to tourists. 'Yeah, I know it. Hope it's in better condition than the last time I saw it.'

'When was that?' Corrine called.

He glanced at her in the rear-view mirror. 'A few years ago. Actually, I'm surprised it's still standing.'

'Great, Jodie,' Corrine said. 'It's a barn and it's falling down.'

'No, no.' Jodie looked over her shoulder then back at Matt. 'The website said new owners did a major renovation on it last year. It's a B & B. It looked really nice.'

Matt raised his eyebrows. The old barn a B & B. What a joke. 'Did the website say anything about its history?'

'Something about being shearing sheds at one time, and storing feed and machinery,' she said.

Guess squatters and a police search weren't stories that would draw the tourists.

'Well, you don't want to be stuck out there without transport. You better take the loan car for a couple of days. It's a bomb but it'll get you from A to B and back again.'

'What do you mean 'out there'?' Jodie looked concerned. 'The website said it was only a few minutes from the town centre.'

'That would be a few *country* minutes,' Matt grinned. 'I'd say about thirty k's. And I'm guessing that's to the turn-off. It'd be another five minutes to the top of the hill in the dark.'

Jodie turned her face away but he could see her jaw working on that piece of information. She looked back at him. 'The loan car would be great, thanks.'

Guess the weekend wasn't starting too well at all.

They travelled in silence after that. Beside him, Jodie sat like a block of ice, arms still folded across her chest, shoulders hitched. It wasn't cold in the car now. In fact, Matt was starting to sweat in the heat. Her face was turned away but her reflection in the passenger window showed dark eyes as big as dinner plates and she was worrying at a patch on her lower lip with her teeth. Matt took another look in the mirror at Corrine. She was staring out at the night, lips pursed. Annoyed, impatient, not happy.

He glanced at Jodie again. Annoyed and impatient, yes – but there was something else. He watched her reflection in the windscreen a moment. It was some kind of anxiety. Fear was the word that came to mind. He knew what that looked like. He'd seen it make people whimper, scream, ramble incoherently, laugh even. And he'd seen cold-to-the-core fear, too. He turned his eyes to the strip of road lit by his headlights and tried not to think about the scared faces in his head.

He didn't know why Jodie was frightened – or even if that's what she really was. Just told himself he wasn't responsible.

Mist crept across the road in places, clung to the scrub in others. Matt knew every bend out here – it hadn't changed since the thousand trips he'd taken with his dad in the truck as a kid – but he kept his eyes focused on the distance, wary of kangaroos on the road and his own dark thoughts. When the light from the service station loomed in the distance, he broke the silence.

'The loan car needs cleaning up so I'll drop you off at the pub with your friends,' he told them. 'I'll bring it over when it's ready.'

Jodie swung around. 'I don't mind waiting.'

'Are you kidding?' Corrine said. 'I'm not waiting another second. The pub sounds great.'

Jodie shook her head. 'No, really. You've already done more than enough for us tonight. I'll wait and pick up the others from the pub. Then you don't have to go out again.'

It was a nice offer. She might make interesting company for half an hour or so – and he hadn't had that in a while. He eyed her across the car, saw the straight line of her mouth.

Who are *you* kidding, Matt? She didn't want to spend time with him. She wanted the loan car asap.

'It'll take twenty minutes or so and I'm going to the pub anyway. The old man's playing in the darts final.' As he spoke, he drove right on past the service station, head for the pub another two blocks down the main street. He pulled up out front, got out and opened the back door to help Corrine. By the time he had her on her feet, Jodie had come around the car and was standing beside them, staring at the pub, making no move to go in.

'Busy night in there,' Jodie said.

Matt looked at the pub. It was the typical country hotel, wrapped around a corner, a couple of large windows facing each street, tiled facade, balcony above. From the car they could see right into the main bar. 'The darts comp is a big deal.' He looked at Corrine. 'Do you need a hand?'

She draped an arm around Jodie's neck. 'We should be fine. Even better after a stiff drink.' She pushed herself off the side of the car and looked back at Jodie with a frown.

'What are you waiting for?'

5

Jodie pressed against Matt's car, watched the crowded bar through the street window and thought, who the hell made it Scare the Shit Out of Jodie Night?

Even without the crash and being stranded on a dark road, the bar would ramp up her stress levels. She didn't like crowds. Didn't do places where she could get hemmed in by strangers. Couldn't make it through one without looking for that face. Long hair, stud earring, chipped front tooth.

'Well, come on,' Corrine said, impatiently pulling Jodie forward with the arm she'd draped over her shoulder.

Twenty minutes in Matt's car had given Jodie time to tamp down the fear that had overwhelmed her by the side of the road. Now she felt it unfurling its wings again. But there was no getting out of it. Corrine couldn't get there without her help. And there was nowhere else to go. Matt had said half an hour. So, Jodie, have a stiff drink or three and get over yourself. She pushed off Matt's car, wrapped an arm firmly around Corrine's waist and said, 'Let's do it.'

The smell of beer hit them as they stepped over the threshold. Good-humoured crowd sounds led them down a short corridor to a glass door. She saw Louise's mass of crazy, shoulder-length corkscrew curls at the bar, bobbing about as she talked to the barman. Behind her, a group of drinkers raised their arms as one and cheered. Jodie pushed open the door and as Corrine hobbled through ahead of her Jodie saw Lou turn and the 'Oh my God' on her lips.

'Oh my God,' Louise said again, standing on her toes to reach up and wrap them in a hug. 'Are you okay? You must be freezing. You're wet, too. Thank God you're here.' She took Corrine's other arm, talked as she walked them past milling drinkers to the opposite side of the room. 'Your car's fine. It's locked up at the garage. Hannah sorted out the key for the B & B, got directions off the guy in the shop. Bought milk, too. Look, Hannah, they're here.'

Hannah stood up from a tight group of four chairs around a low table and led Corrine to a seat. Jodie was glad to hand Corrine over, glad Hannah's attention was focused on Corrine's sprained ankle. She needed a moment to pull herself together before she could do the fun-girls-away thing. She peeled off her damp coat, hung it over the back of a chair and took a deep breath.

'Lou, pass my jacket,' Hannah said. She'd helped Corrine into another seat and was supporting her injured ankle above the low table. One-handed, she took the jacket from Louise, bunched it into a cushion and tucked it under Corrine's leg. 'Can you move your toes?' she asked her.

Jodie watched as Hannah rolled up Corrine's trouser leg, unzipped the boot, folded back the stiff leather. There was no fuss in the way she did it. She looked like she'd done it a hundred times. She probably had. She'd been a nurse since she left school, had only taken three breaks from the job, one for each child. 'You've got some swelling starting. And a good bruise,' Hannah said. Without looking up from the ankle, she raised her voice, waved a hand about in the general direction of the chairs. 'Louise. Anti-inflammatories in my handbag. Side pocket.'

Lou lifted her eyes briefly to Jodie's. A 'don't say anything or I'll laugh inappropriately' look. Hannah, bless her, meant well and they had all benefited from her ministrations at one time or another but the occasions tended to take on the tone of an intensive care unit.

Jodie figured it was exactly what any of them would want if their life was in Hannah's hands but when it was all for a cut finger or a bad headache, it just felt like overkill. And after listening to Corrine carry on about the stupidity of walking about in the dark, seeing Hannah treating the sprained ankle as a major trauma was like salt in the wound.

Thank God for Lou's sense of humour. She'd dragged Hannah's big, brown leather satchel onto her lap, unlatched a side pocket the size of a briefcase and was looking back at Jodie with a mischievous grin. She pulled out scissors, a roll of tape, rubber gloves, an eyebath, gauze bandages, a syringe, lining them up on the low table like evidence. 'You've got half a hospital in here, Hannah.'

'It's just the basics.'

Lou pulled out a disposable scalpel. 'For open-heart surgery maybe. Hey, you got any of those electrics paddles for jump-starting the heart? I've always wanted to say 'Clear'. Maybe Corrine can go into cardiac arrest for us.'

'Louise, I'm in *pain* here,' Corrine said.

'Can we focus on the anti-inflammatories, do you think?' Hannah said.

Lou looked at Jodie, pulled her mouth down, an 'oops, too far' and Jodie felt the tension in her own mouth soften. Lou found a packet, slapped it onto Hannah's upturned palm like a nurse on a TV hospital drama, said, 'Anti-inflammatories, doctor.'

Hannah cracked a smile then. So did Louise. So did Jodie, at last. Corrine said, 'I need some water.'

Hannah found a bottle of water in her satchel and as she passed it to Corrine looked at Jodie as though she was seeing her for the first time. 'I think Jodie could do with something a little stronger. Lou, you want to get those drinks now?'

'Excellent idea.' Lou took her handbag and headed into the crowd.

Jodie saw the intent as Hannah moved towards her – she was the next patient in line. But she wasn't looking for TLC, she just needed some time and space. And a stiff drink. She made herself smile, tried to look what she didn't feel – calm, relaxed, up for a good ole time. It mustn't have worked because Hannah stepped around the low table, put the back of her hand against Jodie's cheek.

'You're freezing.' Hannah dropped the hand to Jodie's shoulder, gave it a brisk rub.

'You're shaking, you're so cold. Sit down.'

'No, I'm okay.' She was still standing behind her seat. She wasn't ready to sink into a comfy chair. The darts competition was winding up for another round, and the crowd and its sudden, rowdy cheers made her feel the need to be ready to move.

'Come on, you should try and warm up.' Hannah took her by the arm and pulled. The unexpected force made Jodie resist. She snatched her arm away then felt petty for it, moved around the chair, did what she was told anyway and sat.

With the same efficiency she'd used on Corrine, Hannah began a vigorous massage of Jodie's upper arms. The closeness was claustrophobic, the pressure like bindings. She pushed Hannah's hands away. 'No, I'm okay.'

Hannah moved to the low table and sat knee-to-knee with Jodie, took both her hands and rubbed them between her own.

'No, Hannah. I'm *okay*.' She tried to pull away. Hannah held on with her nurse's grip.

'Hannah!' If Hannah had any idea what had turned Jodie's blood to ice, she wouldn't be confining her hands like that. But she didn't know any of it, Jodie reminded herself. Give her a break. Take a breath. 'Hannah,' she managed more evenly. 'It's okay. I'm fine.'

Hannah let go with a pointed sigh, used both hands to tuck her hair behind her ears before taking the woollen scarf from around her own neck. 'Put this on then. You might not *feel* cold but believe me, you are.' She held it out to her, insistence on her pursed lips.

Stubbornness burned in the back of Jodie's throat. Hannah was a force of nature, the kind of friend every working mother needed as proof a woman could divide herself a hundred ways and survive. She had an unflagging conviction in whatever she did, totally there for family and friends and patients. But the conviction made Jodie want to beat her about the head sometimes. Hannah never backed down easily and Jodie hated to be pushed.

Two ways to go, Jodie. Tell the truth or take the scarf. Did she want to sit here in the pub and say, 'Actually, Hannah, it's not the cold, it's something else entirely'? Because once she explained the flashback, she'd have to explain the rest and . . . She closed her eyes, felt that cold, ugly memory snake up her spine. It was just a damn scarf, Jodie, and Hannah was only trying to help. She opened her eyes, took the scarf, smiled. 'Thanks, I'm sure it's just what I need.'

'So, guys,' Lou raised her voice. She was back with the drinks, looking between Hannah and Jodie. 'Now that's all sorted, I want the blow by blow of stranded in the dark.'

Jodie shrugged, glanced over at Corrine.

'We-ell,' she groaned theatrically. 'We were in pitch darkness and Jodie decided to pack-march me down the road with all the luggage. Then I fell over, as you do when you're made to stumble around in the dark in four-inch heels. God, I was in agony . . .'

Jodie took a large mouthful of the bourbon and Coke Lou had bought her and tuned out as Corrine told her version of the story. The pub was all but full now, mostly men, mostly turned towards the back of the room where the darts were being played. She looked at faces, avoided eye contact, checked her watch. How much longer? She was trying to relax. She was. But she was pretty sure there wasn't enough bourbon in her glass to numb the tension in her gut.

'Oh my God, Corrine,' Lou's playful voice cut into Corrine's story. 'It sounds dreadful. Are you sure you just twisted an ankle? It sounds like you ripped off a limb.'

Even anxious, Jodie had to smile. She watched Lou's grin spread to Hannah, saw Corrine close her mouth and think about it. Corrine looked from friend to friend, must have decided it wasn't worth taking offence and laughed. Started them all laughing. 'Okay, okay. Don't think you're going to be using those electric paddles on me any time soon, Louise.'

'Party pooper.'

'How about being nice for a change and getting me another drink?'

'Already?'

'The first one didn't count. It was just to warm me up.'

'Oh, sure,' Lou said and stood up.

'No,' Jodie said. 'The car will be here any minute now. We should be ready to go.'

'We don't have to go straightaway,' Louise said. 'I want to see what all the excitement is over the darts.'

'Yeah, there's way too much cheering going on for just tossing pointy things at a corkboard,' said Hannah.

Jodie looked at the crowd. Large, brawny country men, drinking beer, jeering and cheering. No need to spoil their fun just because she was a mess. She drained her glass, stood up. 'Okay, you check out the darts and I'll go wait for the car.'

Louise caught Jodie's hand as she passed her. 'You all right?'

'Yep, 'course. Just don't want to keep Matt What's-His-Name waiting. Go cheer for blue, or whatever you do with darts,' she said, backing into the crowd, and into a drinker. Beer slopped over her shoulder. She jumped and turned.

He was late twenties maybe, blond crew cut, weirdly pale eyes. 'Hey, they don't give beer away here, you know,' he said, giving her a pub-friendly grin.

'Sorry. I . . . sorry.'

He moved towards her, a kind of swagger. 'I'll forgive you if you buy me another one.'

Jodie looked around for a quick exit. For all she knew, he might be Bald Hill's Mr Nice Guy but her heart was hammering in her throat and she'd had enough of the pub.

'Good try but I can live without forgiveness.'

She shouldered her way past other drinkers, pushed open the glass door then pulled up short in the foyer when a bunch of new arrivals blocked the street entrance. Another crowd of strangers. She looked the other way, saw an arrow to the ladies and followed it.

The small bathroom was empty so she leaned against the basin, taking long, deep breaths, waiting for her legs to stop shaking. *What are you doing, Jodie?* One, out-of-the-blue flashback and she was falling to pieces, back to a place she'd left behind a gazillion years ago. She rubbed both hands over her short-cropped hair, dragged them over her face. *Okay, Jodie, this is getting you nowhere. Remember – you don't have to be in any situation that freaks you out. Calm down, get out of the pub and wait for the others outside. Matt What's-His-Name would be there any minute.*

She sluiced water over her face, used a paper towel to dry off and straightened her hair in the mirror. *Okay, go.* She walked back into the corridor, was halfway to the front entrance when the man from the bar stepped into her path.

'I'm still waiting for my beer,' he drawled.

Jodie's spine went rigid. He was a solid mass in front of her. Half a head taller and in the confines of the narrow corridor, he seemed just about as wide. He wore a red-checked flannel shirt that clung to broad, beefy shoulders and arms. And he was looking at her with a leery smile. Jodie's heart pounded.

As he moved towards her, she turned, hoping to dodge past and keep going for the front door, but he blocked her, stepped closer, still smiling like it was a great lark. She backed up, felt the wall against her shoulders, wondered how hard she could jam her knee into his groin with the wall so close behind her.

'Get two beers,' he said. 'One for each of us. We can have a drink. Get to know each other before we go to my place.'

Dear God, he was hitting on her. Jodie tried to keep her face from screwing up in disgust. 'That's not going to happen.' She pushed off the wall, tried to shove past him. It was like trying to move concrete.

He put a hand on the wall beside her and grinned. She smelled beer on his breath, BO on his shirt, there was a dark splotch on his collar, a rusty smear on his throat. 'I know your type,' he said. 'Practically drag me out of the pub then you want to talk before you fuck my brains out.'

She swallowed hard. Her chest heaved in and out. Fear flared into anger. 'Get away from me.' She braced her arms against the wall, lifted a foot and jammed it down hard on his. As he recoiled, she slammed flat hands into his gut and shoved. He let out an 'oof', stumbled back – more from the surprise of her attack than her strength but it had the desired effect.

She watched him as she turned, saw him start to straighten, eyes narrowed at her. She pushed away from the wall, ready to run, and slammed into another male body – tall, hard and oozing aggression.

6

'She's not interested.' Matt planted himself in front of Kane Anderson, giving him nowhere to go in the narrow corridor but backwards. Jodie looked like she could handle herself but as far as Matt was concerned, no woman was safe with Kane Anderson.

Matt had wondered when their paths would cross. He'd been back in town for eight weeks – it was a small town, you ran into everyone eventually – but he'd only seen Kane from a distance until now. It didn't matter. Matt knew where Anderson had been, he'd made a point over the last seven years of keeping track. Getting promoted to Homicide in Sydney hadn't prevented that. Or leaving the blood and brutality of the city behind five years later to join the detectives unit in Newcastle. He wasn't the only cop who kept an eye on the ones who got away.

Kane was bulkier than the last time Matt had faced off with him. He must have put in some hard physical work, probably spent his two years in prison lifting weights instead of getting an education. He was still shorter, though, and Matt stood close enough to make sure he appreciated that fact. He looked down into Anderson's eyes, saw the flicker of recognition in the cold, callous pale blue – and regretted again that he hadn't been the one to arrest Kane, that he hadn't been locked up for life.

'Fuck you, Wiseman,' Anderson said in a spray of spittle.

Matt ignored the second-hand beer on his face, narrowed his eyes and kept his voice even, an order. 'Piss off and leave the tourists alone.'

Anderson made tough, squared off, bounced about on the balls of his feet like a goddamn prize-fighter. Matt looked him up and down, contemptuous, wary. Kane had always been on the edge but he seemed more demented than he'd remembered. Hyper, agitated. But then Matt hadn't seen him in a while. Maybe he'd had too many kicks in the head in prison.

Matt held his ground, careful to keep Jodie behind him. He didn't have to wait long. A couple of seconds and Kane gave it up.

'Fuck you, pig,' he said in a last attempt at aggression. He gave Jodie the finger and pushed back through the door to the bar.

Matt watched him go with a humourless smile. He wasn't a cop right now but Anderson would always be an arsehole. He turned to Jodie, saw her still up against the wall where he'd pushed her out of the way. 'Are you all right?'

She didn't look good. Not as in hard on the eye – in fact, it was possible she'd never be difficult to look at – but her body was rigid, her hands were clenched in tight fists and her huge eyes were even bigger. She looked up at him suspiciously, edged down the wall a couple of steps. Obviously not the type to fall to pieces in the arms of the nearest safe man. He moved the one short pace to the opposite wall of the corridor to give her some space.

'Did he hurt you?' he asked.

'No, I . . .' She swallowed hard, shook her head. 'Thank you.' The blood seemed to suddenly drain from her face. 'Excuse me.' She turned and ran the last few steps down the corridor and out the door.

Matt watched her to the bottom of the steps, saw her wrap her hands around her head like a runner trying to catch her breath. He checked the glass doors into the main room. Anderson was at the bar, hands on the counter, head turned away as if he was keeping an eye on the darts. Although he wasn't, he was looking down and around, a brooding, cagey, over-the-shoulder scrutiny of the room. Matt quickly scanned for Anderson's brother Travis. Kane was unpredictable – and sadistic, even if Matt hadn't been able to prove that seven years ago – but Travis always had his back and could be brutal in his little brother's defence. Matt figured he'd be stupid to turn his back on both of them after that encounter, at least not without a weapon. It didn't look like the older Anderson was there, though, so he followed Jodie out into the cold night.

She'd walked the length of the pub and was standing at the corner in the light from the windows. She turned as he descended the stairs, crossed her arms over her chest and started the return walk. It was more of a stalk than a walk, her mouth a tight line. Man, she looked steamed up. A gutsy response after having someone like Kane Anderson in her face.

She stopped a few paces from him. 'Thanks again.'

He stayed where he was at the bottom of the steps, let her have her space. 'Nice move in there.' He inclined his head towards the corridor. 'Not easy to pull off with a wall at your back.'

She nodded stiffly. 'Thanks. It seemed to do the job. Although your arrival made a nice follow-up.'

He grinned. 'A good one-two. Nowhere to go after that but inside for another beer. Sorry about him. Not all the locals are jerks.'

She took a long, slow look at him. Matt pushed his hands into the pockets of his jacket and waited until she was done. She'd had a tough night, so he figured she was just working out what she was dealing with now. As her gaze reached his face, the tightness in her mouth relaxed a tad, her shoulders slowly dropped and the anger and whatever else it was that was lurking in her eyes seemed to retreat.

She smiled a little. 'And hopefully all your tourists aren't prone to dire circumstances.'

He gave a 'whatever' laugh. 'I brought the loan car.' He pointed to the clapped-out sedan across the road. The driver's door was a different colour to the rest and there was a dent in the rear fender.

'Oh, wow, you should have said it was a limousine.' She laughed then, that low roll of sound that had caught his attention at the side of the road earlier.

'Most of your luggage fit in the boot. The rest is on the back seat. Where are your friends?'

She gave a tight-lipped cock of the head towards the pub. 'Inside.'

'Feel like going in to get them?'

'Not really. I'll ring.' She went to put a hand in a coat pocket before realising she wasn't wearing one. 'Except I haven't got my phone.' She looked at the pub, winced.

Matt didn't blame her for not wanting to go back. Anderson was in there. 'I'll go.' He took off his coat, tossed it to her. 'Put that on so you don't freeze out here. The car key's in the right pocket. Let yourself in.' He turned to leave then stopped. 'Maybe you should show me that move again before I head in.'

She raised an eyebrow. 'It takes a lot of practice. You haven't got time.'

'My mobile's in the other pocket. If I don't come out in five, call an ambulance.'

She gave him the once-over again. 'You look like you'll do fine.'

He left Jodie on the footpath. It was well lit, there was no one else out there and she was in front of one of the pub's big windows. If Anderson made another appearance, Matt was guessing she'd make enough of a fuss to catch someone's attention. He smiled to himself. She'd probably deck him.

Her three friends had joined the crowd watching the darts, the tall blonde perched on a bar stool. As he approached, he saw his dad shaping up to the board. He looked good tonight. Not so tired. It made Matt feel better about marking time in Bald Hill. He'd have to make a decision about his future sooner or later, and later was a lot easier to think about. Especially tonight, when his impulse to leap to the rescue was so pumped up. Jesus, he'd stared Kane Anderson down without a thought. Not that he would have left Jodie to it but he thought he'd put all that leap-to-the-rescue-without-a-second-thought shit behind him.

He tapped Louise on the shoulder. 'I've brought the car around. Jodie's outside.'

'Thanks,' she said and cheered with the crowd as Matt's dad hit a bullseye. When she didn't make a move to go, he said, 'I think she might need some company.'

Louise turned around then, concerned. 'Why? What's wrong?'

'She got harassed out in the corridor. It got a little physical.'

'Oh my God.' Her eyes went to the window overlooking the footpath then she jabbed the other two women. 'Come on. We've got to go.'

He swept the pub with his eyes while they collected their belongings. He couldn't see either Anderson brother. They hadn't left through the front door but then it wasn't the only way out. He glanced out the window, saw Jodie standing at the kerb focused on something out of view down the street and decided her friends didn't need him to escort them. He crossed the pub in long strides, pushed through the glass doors and out the main entrance. At the top of the steps, he looked right and left. She was still alone on the street.

She turned to him with a puzzled expression. Then Louise and the woman she'd come back to town with were hurrying down the steps, one of them carrying a coat, Jodie's presumably.

'Are you okay?' Louise called. 'Matt said you got in a fight.'

The tall one with the sprained ankle hobbled up beside him at the top of the steps.

'Need a hand?' he asked.

'That would be lovely.'

As he helped her down, the other two crowded around Jodie. He could hear her saying, 'No, really, I'm fine. It was just some drunk trying it on.' Heard one of the others say, 'Do you want me to drive?' As he propped Corrine next to a parked car, Jodie's voice lifted above the others.

'I think that's the ute that ran us off the road.' She pointed across the street. Both Louise and the other woman said, 'Where?'

'You saw it, Corrine,' Jodie said. 'That's it, isn't it?'

'Mmm, I don't know,' Corrine said.

'Did you get a rego number?' Matt asked.

'No, but that's what it looked like.'

Matt looked in the direction of her arm. 'Which one?'

'The one with all the chrome.'

He frowned. 'Which one?'

She looked crossly at him. 'What do you mean?' She pointed down the road again. 'That one. Oh . . .' She'd seen it. Almost every other vehicle on the street had a flat bed of some kind or another, with or without chrome. 'The dark one with the chrome going across the back.'

'Are you sure? There are a lot of utes like that out here.'

She closed her eyes for a second, as though trying to see it again. 'Well . . .'

'It could be,' Corrine said.

Jodie turned to him. 'It *looked* like that *ute*.'

He wondered what to tell her. Looking *like* a vehicle wasn't the same as *being* that vehicle. And how well could she have seen it, coming towards her at high speed in the dark while she was taking defensive action? But, hey, he wasn't investigating the incident. More than likely, she was just pissed off at the turn of events tonight and needed someone to blame. The only comfort he could offer, and for some reason he wanted to offer her some, was the idea that there might still be hope for closure. 'The police station in Dungog is open tomorrow morning if you want to make a report.'

She looked a little embarrassed then, flicked her eyes across the road one more time.

'We could go into Dungog tomorrow,' Louise offered.

'I'm not sure now. It looks like it but . . .' Jodie shrugged, put an arm around Corrine's waist.

'Here, let me,' Matt said, taking her other side.

'Oh, you are a lovely man,' Corrine cooed. He suppressed a smile, held onto her until Jodie opened the rear door and then lowered her inside.

Jodie slid in behind the wheel. As Matt leaned down to the window, she suddenly pushed the door open and lurched out again.

Her cheek collided with his shoulder. He reached out to steady her and heard a sharp intake of breath as she recoiled as far as she could without dragging the door off its hinges. He raised an eyebrow, wondered if her personal space was always the size of a backyard pool.

'I forgot your coat. Sorry.' She took it off, held it out at arm's length.

He gave her his best impression of a nice guy. 'No problem.' He closed the door when she got back in and bent to the window as she wound it down. 'You girls try to stay out of any more trouble this weekend, okay?'

Corrine leaned forward and spoke over Jodie's shoulder. 'Make sure you drop by for a drink if you're in the Old Barn's neighbourhood this weekend. So we can say thanks.'

Matt stood up, looked down at Jodie, thought of the kickarse way she'd handled Kane Anderson and the confident roll of her laugh and how it might be interesting to listen to it over a couple of drinks. 'I'll keep that in mind.'

7

J odie held onto the steering wheel with clenched fists. Getting a grip, literally. Or trying to. She knew if she let go, her hands would be shaking from the adrenaline that was still pumping through her.

'Are you sure you want to drive?' Louise asked. She was in the front passenger seat again.

'I can do it if you're not up to it,' Hannah said from the back.

'I'm fine, really.' She needed to drive, needed to feel in control of something. And after everything she'd fielded tonight, she wasn't going to be comfortable with anyone but herself at the wheel. 'Besides, I've only had one drink, which is better than the rest of you.'

'Okay then. Let's roll on take-two of Fringe Dwellers Weekend Away, Episode Eight,' Lou said and snapped her hands together like a movie clapboard. Jodie could see her grin in the light from the pub. Her derring-do grin, the one that had talked them all into their first weekend away eight years ago, that had goaded them into leaving the kids with their husbands to remind themselves they were people as well as mothers. It was Lou who'd come up with the Fringe Dwellers title for the way they'd all hung back from the kiddie craft table at playgroup. At the time, Jodie had just been relieved to find some other mothers who'd missed out on the scissors-and-glue gene. Eight years and countless coffees and babysitting and family dramas later, these three women were Jodie's best friends.

'Lights, camera, action, Jode,' Hannah called from the back seat.

Jodie pushed the gearstick into first, over-revved the loan car's old engine and shuddered into forward motion.

'Just get us there in one piece, will you?' Corrine said.

Jodie checked the rear-view mirror and winced at the expression on Corrine's face. She'd seemed fine in the pub but maybe Jodie wasn't the only one trying to hide how she really felt at the way the night had gone.

As she steered the loan car away from the kerb, she saw Matt Wiseman raise a hand in farewell. Jodie lifted a hand in return and watched him out her window as she moved past. He was one interesting guy. Lean and fit looking with an athletic way of moving that made his limp seem more like a recent injury than permanent. He had some sort of jaded thing happening, as though he'd seen it all before but, what the hell, he was there so he may as well help out anyway. And there was something else about him, something that made Jodie take another look in the rear-view mirror at him. There it was. He was standing on the kerb, hands in his pockets, and in one brief, fluid turn of his head, he checked up and down the road. He was alert. Relaxed and alert at the same time, if that was possible. And Jodie liked it.

Which made her feel all the more guilty about the way she'd behaved. He'd gone well beyond the call of duty coming out to rescue them that second time – and she'd reacted like he was a prisoner on day release. By then, though, she'd spent an eternity putting up with Corrine complaining about her ankle and listening to a bloodcurdling scream being dragged out of her memory. He could have been Nelson Mandela and she would have treated him like a serial killer. And at the pub, after that guy had bailed her up, she'd been rattled and angry and probably rude. He most likely thought she was a total jerk. She shook her head, wished she could shake off the lingering anxiety as easily.

They turned off the main road out of town onto a narrower country byway. It was potholed and winding and Jodie had to slow to under the speed limit to negotiate it in the dark.

'Fifteen more kilometres down here, turn right at the Old Barn sign then two more k's on dirt and we're there,' Hannah said, reading from the page of directions she'd picked up with the key.

'On this road in this old rattler, we should be there by morning.' Louise grinned at no one in particular. 'So what's for breakfast?'

'I'm glad someone thinks it's funny,' Corrine said.

Louise laughed. 'Oh dear, did someone forget to pack her sense of adventure?'

'I packed it but it broke with the heel of my Italian boots,' Corrine snapped. 'Just in case you've forgotten, I have a sprained ankle. The sooner we get there, the better.'

Jodie flicked a look at her in the rear-view mirror again, reminded herself to feel some sympathy. Jodie had had a bunch of sprained ankles over the years. Sports injuries, mostly. Annoying more than anything because they kept her off the field. But Corrine wasn't the running-around sort. No doubt did something delicate like ballet when she was young and was probably a little distressed at the sight of swelling and a bruise.

Twenty minutes later, they spotted a sign to the Old Barn nestled into the front yard of a weathered timber cottage. Jodie bumped onto a dirt track and slowed the pace even further on the rough surface. Bush crowded in on either side and she crunched the gears back to second as they began a steady climb up what she assumed was 'The Hill' part of the 'Old Barn'. As they crested a shoulder, the bush cleared and the silhouette of a tall barn appeared to teeter on the top of the hill.

A knot of worry nestled between Jodie's shoulderblades. It was more isolated than she'd expected. 'The view should be fantastic from up there,' she said, attempting to find a silver lining.

'It'll be better than the Hilton if it's got a kitchen and a fire,' Louise said.

'Who's doing dinner tonight?' Jodie asked. Every year they organised a food roster. They figured if they all prepared one meal, they each got to put their feet up for three others over the weekend – and as mothers of a total of eleven kids, that was pure luxury. Jodie looked cautiously in the rear-view mirror and hoped Corrine wasn't on duty for Friday night.

'Me,' said Louise. 'Coconut chicken curry and rice followed by my sticky date pudding and cheese and chocolate.'

Jodie groaned. 'That sounds like cholesterol heaven. I just realised how hungry I am. I move that we help Corrine inside, Louise starts dinner and Hannah and I carry in the bags.'

'I second that,' Hannah said.

Corrine let out a sigh, as though being injured was exhausting. 'Well, if someone can find my icebag and someone else can look for glasses, I'll have the next bottle of champagne ready and waiting when you're finished.'

As they approached, Jodie could see the road was really one long driveway leading straight up the hill to the barn. If it wasn't for the undulation of the land, she figured they could turn around and see right down to the house at the turn-off. The headlights bounced across the front of the barn as they approached and she squinted to make out some detail. The dark timber gave away little more than its boxy shape. High external walls were topped with a squat A-frame roof, making it look too tall for its width. A door set in the middle of the facade was bordered with two windows on either side and a low, covered verandah ran across the front and around both sides. It probably met out of sight at the back.

'It looks like something a five-year-old would draw,' Jodie said.

'It looks like a barn,' Corrine said.

'It looks great,' Lou said.

Jodie stopped on a gravel parking pad in front of the building, aiming the headlights at the door so they wouldn't have to fumble with the lock in the dark. It was cold outside and damp underfoot and she reached back into the car for her coat before climbing the half-dozen steps to the door ahead of Hannah and Louise. A row of shrubs along the front had kept the verandah from view but once up the stairs, they saw a cosy arrangement of wicker chairs and a small table.

'You booked, so you get the first look,' Hannah said, handing her the key on a ring. She unlocked the door and pushed it hesitantly. This place had better be as good as it looked on the website or Corrine would never let her forget it. She fumbled for the light and flipped a switch.

'Wow.' She stepped aside for the others to go in and sent a thumbs up to Corrine in the car.

They entered a huge, open space, probably the whole left half of the barn. The ceiling was so high the light fixtures had been hung a metre or so under the crossbeams, which were supported by two massive old tree trunks that stood like sentinels on either side of the room. Three generous sofas were arranged in a cosy U around a fire-place that dominated the far end of the room. Heavy white curtains ran the full length of the back wall, covering what Jodie assumed were windows that overlooked the valley beyond the hill they were on. A large and rustic dining table was placed to take in the view at meal times. Opposite the front door, tucked into an alcove in the rear, right-hand corner of the room, a gourmet kitchen glowed in the sheen of its marble tops.

Jodie opened a door near the kitchen, flicked a few light switches and saw it led to a hallway that ran through the centre of the building to the rooms in the other half of the B & B. At the end was a huge bedroom that, like the main room, spanned the width of the barn.

She guessed the doors on either side of the corridor led to a second, smaller bedroom and a bathroom.

Hannah ran her hand along the smooth, black surface of the kitchen's island bench.

'Nice, Jodie.'

As Louise removed the fireplace screen and began stuffing news-paper in the hearth, Jodie said to Hannah, 'Let's get the bags.'

'Let's get the big one with the sprained ankle first.'

Louise looked up at Hannah from the fireplace, eyebrows raised in surprise. She turned to Jodie and grinned. Jodie put a hand to her mouth and the three of them burst into laughter.

The sound rolled around the room, breaking the strain of the last few of hours. Such a pity Corrine wasn't there to appreciate the moment. Not the 'big bag' line – she might not get the joke – but the laughing with abandon. That's what they went away for. And right now, Jodie needed it.

A couple of minutes later and still chuckling quietly, Jodie pulled open Corrine's door.

'What's so funny?'

Jodie glanced at Hannah over the car and suppressed a smile. 'Just Hannah drooling over the kitchen. Come on, you'll love it in there.'

They walked either side of her, an arm each around Corrine's waist, waited patiently while she hopped up the steps on one foot and led her through the door. She stood for a moment by the closest tree trunk and moved her gaze across the room. 'Mmm, not bad,' she said. 'Is the fire on yet? It's freezing in here.'

Jeez. Jodie pursed her lips, helped Hannah to lower her onto the lounge closest to the fire then stepped back to the door before Corrine could ask her to rearrange the cushions.

'Big bag,' Hannah murmured as they walked outside again.

'We could put her in the boot if she takes up too much room on the lounge,' Jodie said and laughed with Hannah all the way down the steps. She pulled open the driver's door and turned the head-lights off. She didn't want to call Matt Wiseman in the morning to tell him she'd flattened the battery. He seemed like a nice guy but that might be pushing it a bit. The internal light went off as she shut the door. A lamp under the roof of the verandah was on but the beam didn't make it past the steps and the darkness seemed to swell around them.

'How much champagne do you think it'll take for Corrine to pass out?' Hannah asked.

'We couldn't fit that much in the car,' Jodie said.

Their cackles sounded like shots in the night air and white puffs of vapour from their mouths floated in the darkness. The hair on the back of Jodie's neck stood up. She looked about uneasily.

'Come on, let's get this done,' she said.

The gravel crunched under their feet and the low-voltage light in the boot flickered as they unloaded as many bags as they could carry. They heaved them up the steps and deposited them at the door to the hallway. The fire was doing its job and the large open space was noticeably warmer. On the lounge, Corrine had taken off her broken boot and was massaging her ankle by the glow of a log burning and crackling in the hearth. The marble benchtops in the kitchen shone under halogen bulbs and the stove was framed by the bright light in the range hood that was whirring over a steaming pot Louise was stirring.

Maybe they didn't need the rest of the bags tonight, Jodie thought. She could survive without her suitcase – sleep in her undies, swish a bit of toothpaste around. One night of poor dental health wasn't going to make her teeth fall out. Then she could shut the front door, lock out the darkness and the trepidation hanging on her shoulders, have a few glasses of wine and forget everything that had happened tonight.

'Did you find my icebag?' Corrine asked, stretching out on the lounge. Jodie and Hannah checked through the bags they'd carried in. No icebag.

'The old bag needs her icebag,' Hannah mumbled from the corner of her mouth. Jodie was smiling as she stepped out the front door again. Hannah was still rifling through her bag looking for gloves, so she pulled her coat against the cold and stood warily at the top of the steps. The darkness seemed darker after being inside. She lifted a hand to the front of her coat, spread her fingers and pressed her palm against her stomach. It was only a short walk to the car but she waited for Hannah to join her before descending the stairs into the blackness beyond the verandah.

They had unloaded only half the remaining gear when the light in the boot flickered out.

Jodie gasped. The darkness closed in on them and her heart

sounded a drumbeat in her ears. She swallowed hard, bent back into the boot and began grabbing whatever she could feel. She passed each item to Hannah, heard her drop them on the gravel.

'I think that's it,' Jodie said.

'No, the icebag must still be in there,' Hannah said.

Jodie tried to swallow the urge to leave the damn icebag right where it was. Her eyes had grown accustomed to the dark now and she could see the dim light from the verandah around the edges of the open hood of the boot, its rectangle of blackness looming over them like a tsunami.

'There was a bag tucked into the front corner before the light went out,' Hannah said.

Jodie took a breath and bent back into the boot. The spare tyre cover was missing and she ran her hands over the wheel to feel her way, dirt gritty under her palms. There were tools wrapped in a towel and something long and cold, maybe a tyre iron, and some greasy rags. And the icebag. Jodie pulled it out by its corner, was about to hand it to Hannah when a noise behind her made her stop. It was a crack, like hands clapped together or a stick breaking. Beside her, Hannah sucked in a breath.

'Hey, girls. Nice night for it.'

Jodie went cold. The voice was male and its friendliness – out here, at night, on the top of a deserted hill – sounded like a threat.

8

Jodie spun around, saw two figures. Both men, for sure, but in the blackness she couldn't make out any detail. The faces were lighter but their mouths and eyes were just shadow. They were a couple of body lengths away, side by side. Same height, same stocky build, thick buttoned-up jackets, beanies – like the same person in double vision.

The one on the right spoke. 'Need a hand?' She saw the silhouette of his head nod towards the gear at their feet.

Jodie felt a rush of blood. She didn't want them anywhere near her. Or Hannah. Or the barn.

She raised her voice, tried to sound firm. 'No, thanks. Just trying to get the luggage sorted out before our husbands get here.' The message was simple – *you guys are about to be outnumbered.*

Hannah's shadow looked at her then turned back to the two men.

'You just staying the night?' the one on the right asked.

Where had they come from? They didn't have torches. Maybe there were more of them. Jodie looked quickly left and right. Couldn't see anything but deep, dark night. 'No, we're all here for the whole weekend.' *There's a big group so don't bother coming back.*

The man on the left pushed his hands into pockets, hunched his shoulders inside his thick jacket, took a step closer.

Jodie edged away and felt the car bumper against her thighs. Don't panic, Jodie. Keep your wits about you. She took a breath. Okay, don't answer any more questions. It felt wrong, like it was giving too much away.

'Where did you come from?' Her voice sounded small and frightened. She cleared her throat, raised the volume. 'What are you doing here?'

The one on the right spoke again. 'We're camping over the ridge.' He pointed in the direction of the long drive but up and over the other side of the hill. 'Came to see where the lights were coming from.' When she looked back, he'd stepped forward, level with the other guy.

His hands were in his pockets now, they looked like they were just having a casual chat. But there was nothing relaxed about the way they were standing. Their bodies were squared, torsos erect, feet apart, ready to move if they wanted to. And they were way too close. Not quite within the two arm's lengths Jodie taught in her self-defence class – two arm's lengths was too far away for grabbing, enough distance for a heads-up if an attacker moved – but here, in the dark, it was too close for comfort.

The bumper on the back of her thighs told her she couldn't do anything about the distance between them but she could improve the odds. She sat on the edge of the trunk like she needed to take a load off and let her left hand drop into the boot. 'Is there a camping ground over the hill?' she asked as she slid her hand over the dirty base.

'Nah, don't need a camping ground to pitch a tent around here.' It was the guy on the right again, inching forward as he leaned his weight on one leg. Jodie heard the gravel shift, realised he'd reached the parking pad. They were boxing her and Hannah in.

Jodie touched the cold metal pole she'd felt earlier, closed her fingers around it. 'Hey, look, Hannah. I found the tyre iron,' she said loudly, holding it up high so the dim light from the verandah could catch it.

Hannah turned her head towards her briefly.

The one on the right nodded with his chin. 'What do you girls need a tyre iron for?'

To beat the crap out of you if you come too close. 'Oh, I don't know.' Jodie tried to keep her voice steady as she swapped it to her right hand. She gripped it low and firm, like a tennis racquet. 'Maybe a bit of indoor hockey. After twenty-five years running around a pitch, I reckon I could do as much damage with this as your average hockey stick.' She hoped they got that message.

Hannah turned her head towards Jodie again. Jodie wished she'd look back at the two men. They both needed to be on guard, needed to be ready to move. Jodie's mind spun through the options. If she moved to her right, around the car, the two guys could go for Hannah. If she moved to her left, towards Hannah, she'd be tripped up in the luggage stacked at their feet and they'd both get grabbed. The car was behind them – not a rock but definitely a hard place and difficult to get under or over in a hurry. Okay, if you couldn't talk your way out of it or run away from it, the only thing left was to fight. Fast and hard, like she taught her students. It was what an attacker least expected.

'Jodie.'

It took a moment for Hannah's voice to register. Not the fact that she'd spoken but the way she'd said it. Her tone was low and quiet, like she was sending Jodie a message. But Jodie didn't get it. It wasn't, 'Jodie, be careful' or 'Jodie, watch out' or 'This is getting serious, Jodie'. It had a question mark at the end. Like, 'What do we do now?' No, that wasn't the question. Jodie replayed Hannah's voice in her head. It didn't make sense. It sounded like, 'What the hell are you doing, Jodie?' She let her eyes leave the men for a second. Hannah's face was in darkness but she was looking Jodie's way. And she was shaking her head.

'It's cool, Jodie,' she said softly then turned back to the two men. 'We've got to get inside before we freeze our buns off. Enjoy your camping.' She bent over, began picking bags up off the ground.

Jodie studied the two visitors. They were watching her. Hands still in pockets, feet still planted. Ignoring Hannah picking up the bags, just watching her. Waiting maybe or assessing. Jodie straightened, squared her shoulders, raised the tyre iron a little, shook it about a bit, like she was testing its weight. *Two men against two women, one with an iron bar that she knew how to use – assess that.*

Hannah nudged her along the car. Jodie took a few stiff steps, kept her eyes on the two men while they kept their eyes on her.

'Don't forget the icebag,' Hannah said and pushed it at her empty hand.

Jodie gripped its handle, thought about how best to swing it if she needed to. She took another sideways step, cleared the back of the car, heard Hannah drop the boot hood and waited until she'd slipped in behind her before she started moving towards the barn.

The two men watched her all the way to the verandah. She paused at the bottom of the steps, the iron bar still clutched at her side. The man on the right nodded to the other one. They turned and walked in the direction he'd pointed to earlier. Jodie climbed the stairs and waited until she could no longer see their shadows in the dark then went inside, shut the door and turned the deadlock.

JODIE LEANED against the front door and closed her eyes. She was out of breath, the thin cotton singlet under her winter clothes was damp from sweat and her spine shook like a tuning fork.

'What are you doing?' Louise asked.

Jodie opened her eyes, saw Louise at the kitchen island with a big spoon in her hand. Hannah was standing amongst the bags they'd deposited at the hallway door. Corrine was half reclined on the lounge in front of the burning fire. And they were all looking at her. No, they were staring, frowning, perplexed.

'Is that a tyre iron?' Louise asked.

Jodie looked down at her hands. She was still gripping the tyre iron in one hand, the icebag in the other. She wasn't sure she was ready to let either of them go yet. 'Yeah.'

Corrine shifted, getting a better view over the lounge. 'What are you doing with a tyre iron?'

'Scaring the shit out of a couple of campers.' Hannah cut in from across the room. She let the last of the luggage fall from her shoulder, tossed it onto the pile already on the floor then walked wordlessly to the door, took the icebag out of Jodie's hand and delivered it to Corrine. 'Don't take too long with the champagne. She scared the shit out of me, too.'

Corrine and Louise turned in stereo to Jodie, clearly not sure what to make of the moment.

Jodie ignored them. She was still focused on Hannah. '*I* scared the shit out of you? What about the two men who appeared out of nowhere, like they were taking a nice stroll in the middle of a cold, dark night?'

'What men?' Louise asked.

Hannah stood in front of the fire, crossed her arms over her chest. 'There were two guys walking around out there. They offered to help us in with the bags.'

'Offered to *help* us?' Jodie heard the pitch of her voice climb. 'Like your average porter leaps out of the bushes in the middle of the night.'

'For God's sake, Jodie,' Hannah snapped. 'It's not the middle of the night and they're camping just over the hill. You carried on like they'd been hiding out up here waiting for some handy, unaccompanied women they could rape and pillage.' She looked at the other two. 'She told them our husbands would be here any minute. I hope not 'cause mine would be bringing the kids with him.'

Jodie felt her mouth drop open. She couldn't believe it. Those two men may not have been hiding out up here waiting for women, but rape and pillage had definitely been an option.

'Where did you get the tyre iron?' Louise had moved around the kitchen bench and was standing in the centre of the room.

All three of them were looking at her again. She still had her back to the door, still stood on feet slightly apart, ready for action. It seemed out of place now. Self-consciously, she lowered the bar and relaxed her grip.

'It was in the boot. I got it out just in case we needed a weapon.'

'She threatened them with it,' said Hannah.

'No, I didn't. I just made it clear I'd use it if I had to.'

'Yeah, right. 'I've played hockey for twenty-five years. I know how to use this thing'. If that's not a threat, I'd hate to see what is.'

Corrine and Louise turned surprised faces to Jodie.

'I didn't say it like that. And besides, *they* were threatening *us*.'

Hannah made a scoffing sound. 'They came over to see where the lights were coming from. They looked about as threatening as a couple of campers hunting for firewood.'

What was she talking about? They could barely see them in the dark and menace had just about pulsated off them.

'Two big men appearing without warning in the dark wanting to help two women, who, for all they knew, were alone up here. That's a threat. And frankly, I don't care if I did scare the shit out of them, or you, Hannah, it's better than at least one of the alternatives. She shuddered involuntarily, a quick, rolling tremor. 'Believe me, it's a whole lot better.'

9

J odie stared into the silence that followed her declaration. Hannah looked down. Corrine fingered the icebag on her lap. Louise cocked her head to one side and watched her across the room.

By the fire, Hannah unfolded her arms, tucked her hair behind her ears, tried to look conciliatory. 'Okay, it's been a strange night and we're all hungry and tired.' She sent Jodie a small, charitable smile. 'And after everything you've dealt with tonight, you're probably suffering from a bit of shock. I'd overreact too if I'd been through what you had. Why don't you come and sit down.'

Been through what you had. It was her ex-husband James all over again. Anger burned up from Jodie's belly like indigestion. Hannah was wrong. And Jodie was glad she hadn't told Hannah about the flashback. She was not being paranoid. 'You're not listening and you need to for your own safety. Damn it, Hannah, the girls I teach at school could have analysed that situation better than you. I didn't *overreact.* Every instinct told me it was a threatening situation and if you'd paid attention, you'd be thanking me for averting what was pretty obvious danger instead of telling me I'm going over the top.'

Hannah looked away and sighed. A great, big she's-unbelievable kind of sigh. Jodie gripped the tyre iron hard. This situation was unbelievable. She needed to leave the room before she said something she regretted. Before the adrenaline that had been pooling inside her for the last couple of hours exploded in a nasty, weekend-wrecking argument. She stalked past the pile of bags, turned into the dark hallway, took the door on the right and shut it behind her.

It was the second bedroom. Two big single beds, thick white comforters, timber floors, timber walls, large window overlooking the front verandah. No way. She stepped across the room and pulled heavy white curtains across the glass. Chest heaving, jaw clamped tight, she looked around the room again. Aged set of drawers, bedside tables, soothing photos of misty countryside. Damn the soothing. She was mad. Hannah was wrong. She was not freaked out. She'd followed her instincts. She . . .

Jodie noticed the mirror above the set of drawers. Actually, what she noticed was her reflection *in* the mirror – arms out at her sides, eyes wild, still holding the tyre iron. Not holding, brandishing it like a weapon.

Okay, maybe she was a little freaked out. Maybe more than a little.

She flung the metal bar onto the closest bed, put a hand to her mouth and sucked in a long breath. Then another. She'd been scared tonight. All night. She could still feel it. A rock in the pit of her gut, an ache in the ridges on her belly. She moved her hand down, rubbed it across her stomach, sensed rather than felt the markings under the layers of clothing. Tears welled in her eyes but she batted them away. Come on, Jodie. You don't cry. Not over something like this. What is *wrong* with you?

The whole night was what was wrong. It was a litany of scary moments. Each one on its own would have been unsettling but they'd come one after the other without a breather in between. And now Corrine had a sprained ankle, she'd yelled at Hannah, caused a scene and pretty much screwed up Day One of their weekend away.

She sat on the end of the other bed, legs folding with sudden exhaustion. A post-adrenaline slump. It had been flooding her system since that car ran them off the road. She must be drained of the stuff by now. She put her elbows on her knees, looked over at the tyre iron and the black mark it had made on the white comforter. Frowned at it. Thought about what had happened at the boot of the car – the two men appearing, the over-friendly conversation, the way they'd moved slowly closer, watched Jodie while Hannah picked up the bags. She shook her head. Where had she overreacted?

There was a knock at the door.

'Can I come in?' Louise asked, opening the door and coming in anyway. She sat on the bed next to Jodie. 'You okay?'

Jodie shrugged. 'Aside from ruining the night for all and sundry, including the nice guy from the service station, yeah, I'm fine.'

'Corrine and Hannah will live. They've almost polished off a bottle of champagne already, so they're feeling pretty happy now. They need some dinner before they pass out so if you've finished beating yourself up in here, come out and join us.'

Jodie smiled at her. 'Yeah, I'm finished.'

Louise opened the door, then turned. 'And just to refresh your memory, that guy from the service station wasn't just nice. He was *exceptionally* nice.' She walked backwards into the hallway, grinning.

'Very nice, maybe,' Jodie said. 'Not exceptional.'

Louise, still grinning, reached the kitchen island, picked up two glasses of champagne, handed one to Jodie and clinked the other against it. Then she pulled her by the sweater sleeve over to the fire. 'Okay, girls.' She looked pointedly at each of them.

'Cheers.' She held up her glass. 'Here's to the weekend.'

Jodie eyed Corrine on the lounge, stocking-clad feet resting on a cushion, and Hannah on the next lounge, feet in footy socks crossed at the ankles and propped on the coffee table. Both raised their glasses with a distinct lack of enthusiasm.

This dour mood was her fault, Jodie thought. So fix it. Massage it back into shape before the weekend becomes a total disaster.

'Okay, it's official. I'm responsible for the worst start ever to our weekends away.' She held her hands up. 'But I've given my trusty tyre iron a good talking-to and it's having some time-out in the bedroom. So do you think we could start over, have a take-*three* of Fringe

Dwellers Weekend Away, Episode Eight? Pretend Corrine sprained her ankle *before* I picked her up, that she didn't even bring her gorgeous, expensive Italian boots, and that Hannah doesn't really think I'm a raving lunatic.' She looked back and forth between them.

'We-ell,' Corrine said. She took a sip of champagne then pointed at Jodie with her glass. 'You know, I think I remember tripping over Bailey's soccer ball this afternoon. I was lucky I didn't break my ankle.'

Hannah was shaking her head. 'I don't know, Jode. It'll be pretty hard pretending you're not a raving lunatic.' She raised an eyebrow.

Louise let out a huff. 'Oh, don't kid yourself, Jodie, you can't claim the worst start. That undisputable honour belongs to Hannah. Remember when she locked her keys in the car?'

Hannah frowned. 'No.'

'Yes,' Lou said. 'It was our third year. We went to the Hunter Valley and did some wine tasting on the way then we couldn't get back into the car. We were close enough to home that Pete could have driven out with a spare key but he was on a conference in Sweden.' She cocked her head. 'Or maybe it was Switzerland. Whatever, Roland climbed through a window in your house, got the key and brought it out to us.'

Hannah put a hand to her cheek. 'Oh God, I remember now. And it was Sweden.'

'We asked Roland to stay for dinner,' Corrine said. 'But he didn't want to intrude on our time away. Gorgeous man.'

Jodie smiled – at the happy memory of Corrine's husband and at Lou's ability to lighten a mood. 'How do you remember all that stuff, Lou?' She asked and not for the first time. Louise was like a walking, talking memory bank. Hopeless with phone numbers but could recall reams of useless information at will – which was great when you were on her team for Trivial Pursuit but a real pain if you were discussing politics. 'You've got way too much stored in your head.'

'It's a gift, I tell you, a gift.' Louise raised her glass again. 'Cheers, ladies.' And Jodie knew then that the mood was on its way up. Not quite at cooking temperature yet but definitely out of the freezer.

After a feast on Louise's fabulous curry then dessert with buckets of cream followed closely by an indecent amount of cheese and chocolate, all ingested with a steady supply of wine, they were indeed cooking. On a rolling boil, actually.

All four were sitting on the floor, having toppled there one by one during numerous fits of laughter. The hilarity had blown off Jodie's fear, helped by the fact they were locked safely inside the barn. Corrine even seemed to have forgotten the pain in her ankle as she cackled at Louise's story of chewing on near-putrid goat meat in the Afghan desert, where she'd been a foreign correspondent some time between the first and second Iraq wars.

Jodie hadn't known her then. They'd met a few years later at playgroup before their children were old enough to go to school – after Louise had had two sets of twins fifteen months apart, realised she couldn't have it all and retired her hot-shot reporter career. Jodie suspected the jaw-dropping stories Louise occasionally popped out with were only partly entertainment. The other part was to remind herself she hadn't always been knee-deep in nappies and school lunches.

They'd met Corrine and Hannah at playgroup, too. Actually, it was Lou who'd met them, found them really, hanging back from the craft table – Corrine trying to keep the paint and glue off her designer clothes, Hannah too impatient to deal with a three-year-old sprinkling glitter on an Easter Bunny cut-out. Corrine and Hannah already knew each other, were playgroup veterans with older kids at school. Lou introduced them to the new girl Jodie, hauled the three of them back to her house for coffee, let the kids run wild and for some reason only known to Lou, decided they were all going to hit it off. She was right, of course, despite their differences – careers, money, marital status, age (Corrine quietly cracked the big four-oh last year, Lou celebrated with a boozy barbecue three months ago, Hannah would make the milestone next year while Jodie was the baby at thirty-five). And eight years later, the friendships – both collectively and individually – were all the more precious to Jodie for the fact that she'd thought she'd never have close friends like that again.

'By the way, Jodie,' Louise said, tossing a scorched almond at her. 'I think that guy from the service station is perfect for you.'

Jodie rolled her eyes as she laughed. Louise was drunk. Not passing-out drunk, just very funny drunk. They all were. Still no excuse for matchmaking. 'Let's not do this again.'

'No, really, he's hot. If I wasn't married and prematurely aged by the ravages of twinology, I'd consider some serious flirting.'

'Oh, yeah, totally,' Hannah said and caught a chocolate-coated peanut in her mouth. 'Not a patch on my Pete, mind you, but totally hot in a non-Pete, non-medical, non-I-only- fall-for-doctors kind of way.'

Corrine nodded slowly. 'You might think this surprising, considering the type of man Roland was, but I find that slightly scruffy, buffed-up, blue-collar thing quite attractive. And the way he picked me up with no regard for his own limp, just enhanced his whole man's-man thing. It could just be that I haven't had real sex for three hundred years but I was quite turned on by some very appealing muscles I felt under his shirt. Yes, I'd say he's hot. S-s-sizzling, even.'

That brought on another round of chocolate/alcohol-fuelled laughter. It was no wonder Corrine found the blue-collar thing attractive, Jodie thought. She'd spent three years after Roland's death fighting a nasty legal battle for his share of the solicitors' firm. Corrine could probably do with some s-s-sizzle, too. Three hundred years was a long time to go without sex.

'Wait a minute.' Louise held up her hands, like she was about to make an announcement. Jodie covered her ears. 'No, no, hear me out,' Lou said. 'He's hot and strong and kind and generous . . .'

'And lives in Bald Hill and has a good Samaritan complex,' Jodie finished the sentence for her. 'No way. I don't need someone else who wants to save me. James tried that for ten years and I'm done with pretending I can be something other than this. If I ever get involved with a man again – and it's a big if – it'll be with one who wants me for who I am.' She jerked her thumbs at herself. 'Tough and controlling and bossy and every other thing James says is wrong with me.'

Corrine raised her glass to her. 'You go, girl. Be as controlling as you like.'

'And just to let you know, the next time you try to fix me up, I'd like someone who's sexy and vulnerable and can handle a weapon. Like James Bond – the Daniel Craig version. You know, totally hot, totally armed, totally unrealistic and totally unlikely to be found anywhere outside a Hollywood movie. Oh, yeah, and he'll have to live a lot closer than an hour and a half's drive away.'

Louise laughed. 'You don't want much, do you?'

'No, but here's to hot.' She held up her wineglass. 'Good to look at, best not to handle without oven mitts.' She took a swig and realised her glass was empty. And so was the bottle. 'Is it too late to open another?'

'Nooo,' was the chorused answer.

She stood a little unsteadily. Hmm, maybe it was a little late for another – she didn't want to spend the rest of the weekend with a hangover. She went to the kitchen, ran a hand over the marble on the island counter on the way to the fridge. Aside from the dirty dishes that hadn't been stacked in the dishwasher, it was pretty much a to-die-for cooking space. The stand-alone bench was all that could be seen of the work area from the front door. Recessed in the alcove was a deep U of timber and marble cabinetry housing a double-door fridge, stainless-steel stove and roomy pantry. So different from the dingy fifty-year-old kitchen in her small house in Newcastle, the one she'd been lucky to afford after she and James split up.

She opened the fridge. Wow, four women really knew how to provide for a weekend. It looked like her fridge after a two-week grocery shop. She had to shuffle a few items around – two lettuces, a huge wedge of cheese, punnets of strawberries, the tender, little Wagyu steaks she'd brought – before she found the wine. The last cold bottle. Probably just as well or they might be drunkenly tempted to drink another.

As she shut the fridge door, a light flashed briefly on the cabinets under the island bench. Odd, Jodie thought. She opened and closed the fridge again. No flash of light. She glanced around. The almost double-storey ceiling made the bank of curtains covering the back wall appear quite short but as Jodie stepped over and stood at one end of the run of heavy fabric, she realised they were taller than the average household door. She ran a hand along the folds to find where the first pair of drapes met. She was right. They didn't quite join and the gap between them was opposite the island bench.

She stood to one side of the narrow opening, hesitantly pulled the right-hand curtain open an inch and peered through the window behind it. Nothing but darkness. She repeated the move with the left-hand curtain and gasped. She snapped the drapes together, held them closed with a tight fist. There were lights out there. Small, low-voltage, *moving* lights. Her chest tightened and her fuzzy drunkenness disappeared like a bubble bursting. Definitely not house lights – too round, too dim and they were *moving*. Not car headlights because one had moved up when the other had gone sideways. And not bike headlights either – motor or otherwise – unless someone was swinging them around on the end of a short rope. She felt her pulse quicken as she opened the curtains again. Just a touch, just enough for one eye to get a look.

Two dim lights. Torchlights. Moving separately. There were people out there.

And they were playing torches over the back of the old barn, just a stone's throw from the end of the verandah.

10

Jodie yanked one curtain end over the other to make sure the gap between them stayed closed then backed up to the island bench.

Okay, the torchlight wasn't penetrating the heavy curtains. That was good. It meant whoever was out there couldn't see in. Unless there was another gap between the drapes further down the wall. She fingered her way urgently along the fabric, trying not to disturb the folds in case the torchbearers outside saw the movement. No need to let them know the element of surprise had changed hands.

There were five breaks between the curtain drops and Jodie peeked out each one, reconfirmed she wasn't imagining things before securing one drape firmly in front of the other.

'Hey, Jodie, have you tried your phone in here?' Louise raised her voice across the room. 'We can't get reception.'

Jodie moved to the shorter curtains on the window beside the fireplace. 'No, it's still in my bag.' She peered out. She couldn't see around the corner to the source of light but a glow played across the edge of the verandah.

'I'm going to see if it's any better outside,' Hannah said and stood unsteadily.

'No!' Jodie bunched the curtains together in one hand. 'There's somebody out there,' she said in a stage whisper.

All three friends looked at her.

'Two people. Or one person with two torches,' she whispered.

'What?' Louise said, clambering up off the floor.

'Where?' Hannah said as she and Louise stepped over to the side window.

Jodie parted the drapes a crack. 'They're around the corner. You can just see the tail end of the light from here.'

Hannah pulled the curtains further apart. 'Where?'

Jodie snatched them closed. 'Don't let them see us.' She peered out again. The light was gone. 'They must be further around.' She went back to the long curtains, inched apart the drapes halfway along the wall.

'Where?' Hannah said again, peering through a gap in the fabric on Jodie's left. Louise put her nose to the curtains on Jodie's right. 'I can't see anything.'

'They must have gone,' Jodie said, still looking out. 'Or maybe they saw us and turned their torches off.'

'It's probably just the two campers who were here earlier,' Hannah said.

'Exactly.'

'Let's not go there again.' Hannah flung open a stretch of curtain. 'I'm going to try my phone.'

Jodie grabbed the billowing fabric, yanked it back across the window. 'Don't go out there.'

Obstinacy flashed across Hannah's face. She took a sideways step to move around Jodie.

'Don't, Hannah. Somebody's out there. Watching us.'

'Oh come on, Jodie.' Hannah said it with a half-laugh, almost a scoff. 'It's just someone going for a walk. If there really is someone.' She moved past Jodie trying to find the next break in the curtains. 'I'm going out to ring Pete.'

Jodie felt a surge of panic. What was with Hannah? Why push the issue? 'It's not safe out there.'

'Fine, then I'll go out the front door.' Hannah turned on her heel, marched across the room. Jodie had seen Hannah leave hospital staff in her wake with a march like that. Had been thankful for it the day she'd rushed into Emergency after Isabelle came off her bike. But now there was plenty of reason to stop her.

As she moved to go after her, Louise grabbed her arm. 'Leave her. Whatever was out there is gone now.'

'Don't you believe me?'

'I don't know what you saw but whatever it was, it's not there now.' She shrugged apologetically. 'Come back and sit down. Where's the wine?'

'I don't want any more wine.' Jodie looked over to where Hannah had left the front door open. Bloody Hannah. Be safe out there. She crossed the room, stood by the open door.

As Louise watched her with concern from the curtains, Jodie poked her head cautiously out the door, looked left and right along the verandah. Hannah was nowhere in sight. Shit.

She stepped back inside, unsure what to do next. She wanted to go find Hannah but if she was just around the corner having a private chat with Pete, Jodie's appearance might make her even more annoyed. On the other hand, if she didn't, whoever had been out there might silently grab her off the verandah and whisk her away before they even knew she was gone.

She looked around for something she could arm herself with. There was a writing desk by the door – dried flowers in a large glass vase, a small brass Buddha, a pair of wooden candlesticks. Jodie picked up the Buddha, held it in her palm like a cricket ball. *How determined are you to defend yourself?* That was the question Jodie asked her students. Or, in this case, how determined was she to defend a friend? Enough to throw a lump of brass at someone's head? Hell, yes. She stepped back to the door and collided with Hannah.

They both gasped.

Hannah said, 'Not the bogeyman, Jode. Just me.' Jodie pulled her inside, shut the door and locked it.

'No reception out there, either,' Hannah told the three of them. Her cheeks were rosy from the cold and she was slightly breathless. 'I went all the way around on the verandah. Nothing. I was going to walk up the hill a bit but Jodie scared the crap out of me with all the 'someone's watching you' stuff. I'll call in the morning.' She put her mobile on the writing desk and noticed the Buddha in Jodie's hand. 'What are you doing with that? Planning to beat up someone? That could be bad karma.'

Jodie laughed stiffly, feeling a little stupid. 'Oh, ah, no. I was just looking at it. It's kind of cute, don't you think?' She put it down, rubbed sweaty hands on her trousers.

Hannah looked at her for a second, concern mixed with the irritation. 'Try to relax a little. Everything's fine. See if you can have some fun with the rest of us.' She turned and joined the others around the fire.

'Wine's open. Are you having another?' Corrine called to her.

Jodie looked at the three of them sprawled on the lounges, Corrine sipping, Hannah popping chocolate in her mouth, Louise with her feet on the armrest, and knew she'd had enough. She was wound up, her stomach felt vaguely nauseous, her shoulders tight, her mood even tighter.

'No, thanks. I think I'll go to bed.' She saw their faces, knew what they were thinking. It was bad form to go to bed early on the first night of their weekend away. Not that midnight was early. In fact, on an average Friday night she'd be thinking how late it was. But when they were away, it was a ritual to stay up late, get drunk, sleep in, be stupid, swear a little – a salute to all the stuff they couldn't do at home. But she needed some time out. She couldn't tell anymore if she was overreacting or if everyone else was being reckless. 'Sorry to ruin the party but I don't seem to be in the right frame of mind tonight. Don't worry, I'll sleep it off and be more fun tomorrow. Promise.'

Jodie claimed the bed that gave her the best view of both the window and the door. She slid the tyre iron underneath it and looked briefly behind the curtain before climbing under the covers. It took her a long time to fall into a restless sleep. Her head spun with a combination of alcohol and angst. She dreamt of being strong and athletic, repelling threats with her bare hands, then a second later was aggressive and paranoid and Lou and Hannah and Corrine were laughing at her.

Some time after two am, she heard the girls moving about in the hallway. Louise climbed into the other bed in the room not long after.

Later still, when the barn was quiet and dark, Jodie woke again. Thunder rumbled and growled in the distance and she imagined storm clouds gathering and jostling over the hill. As she listened, the thunder grew louder. More regular, more mechanical. Then it didn't sound like thunder at all but like the guttural rumble of a large car engine. A souped- up motor or a big V8. The kind the boys at school drooled over when an older friend pulled up.

She checked the time on her phone beside the bed – three-thirteen – and lay with her eyes open, listening in the darkness. The rumbling got closer. Very close. So close it sounded like it was outside the barn. She sat up, ignored the sudden chill, kept perfectly still, straining her ears.

Yes, it was a car. Or a vehicle of some sort. Big, throaty. And it was outside the lounge room.

No, it was moving along the back of the barn. Past the kitchen, past the bathroom across the hall. Her breath was so loud in her ears it was hard to pinpoint the position. She thought she heard a pause and a change in gear as it rounded the end of the barn. She held her breath, opened her eyes wider in the darkness.

It turned the corner and the noise was instantly clearer – a deep, throaty gurgle. Jodie watched the wall, following the sound with her eyes at it moved slowly past her bedroom. No lights, no voices. Just guttural rumble. Then the soft crunch of gravel as it passed over the parking pad below the front door.

Jodie stood beside the bed, her heart thumping against her ribs. She couldn't remember actually getting out of bed or when she'd picked up the tyre iron but she must have been there a while because her arm ached from holding it.

Who the hell just drove around the barn?

She swallowed in a dry mouth. Okay, Jodie, don't overreact. Think it through. The campers? The people with the weird lights?

At this time of night?

It didn't make sense. And that scared her.

What scared her more was the rumble inching up the revs as it turned the corner and started down the back side of the barn for a second time.

Her feet did a small, undecided dance on the floor. She was cold, she was more than a little anxious but she wanted to see what was out there.

She tiptoed across the hall to the bathroom, stepped into the spa bath. Her finger shook as it tilted a blade on the Venetian blind over the window. Blood pounded in her ears as a formless patch of darkness moved past the window.

She prayed for it to keep going, right on out into the bush. It didn't. It paused, changed down a gear, turned the corner. She tiptoed back across the hall to the bedroom, flattened herself against the wall beside the window, slipped a finger behind the white curtain, inched it away from the glass and waited for the rumble to come around the corner.

The vehicle was big and chunky and dark coloured. She couldn't make out any more detail than that as it prowled slowly past the window a few metres beyond the verandah.

Shit, shit. Was the front door locked? She'd locked it when Hannah came in but maybe someone went out afterwards. What about the back? She hadn't checked all the glass. Were they fixed panels or windows and doors? Security glass or the kind you could break with a quick tap from a spanner?

She sprinted on frozen toes to the lounge room. All the curtains were closed. She dashed to the front door, tried the locks – one on the handle, a deadlock above. Both engaged. She pressed an ear to the solid timber, heard the crunch of gravel, then just rumbling again as it drove back onto the grass. She waited, trembling, for it to round the corner.

It didn't. It stopped. The engine gurgled. She held her breath. What? What are you doing now?

The answer came thirty long seconds later when it started moving again. Away. The rumble got louder as the vehicle picked up speed, then quieter as the distance grew.

Jodie stood by the door a few minutes more, her pulse racing, her mouth dry as paper. Then she went to the kitchen, pulled a bottle of water from the fridge and drank it dry.

What the hell was that all about?

She checked every window and door in the barn, tiptoeing into Hannah and Corrine's bedroom then back out to the hall. A few steps into the narrow space and she froze. A loud growl reverberated around the barn. But this time it was thunder. Rocking and rolling up the valley.

As she climbed into bed, lightning flashed briefly then heavy rain hit the metal roof, roaring overhead like a plane. She pulled the quilt up, listened with her eyes wide open and thought about the coincidence of two men followed by two torches followed by a deep-throated car.

Who was out there?

11

J odie's wrists hurt. The skin is tearing. She can feel it. But she keeps pulling on the rope. Hurting and pulling. She knows Angela is alive. The whites of her eyes keep disappearing in the dark then reappearing. Large, round, scared. Angie is blinking. Jodie is crying.

'Angela,' Jodie whispers. 'Angie. I got my hands free.'

Angela whimpers.

'We've got to run, Angie.'

'I can't.' Angela is crying. And bleeding. Her hands are sticky and wet with it. Something is wrong with her leg.

Jodie is too frightened to breathe. Too frightened to stay. Too frightened to go. 'The road's just through the trees. I can run that in under a minute. Flag someone down. Get help.'

'I tried to fight.'

'I know. You fought real hard, Ang.'

'Run, Jodie. Before they come back.'

Jodie runs. As fast as she can. Her feet pounding. Over dirt and grass and rocks. Men are shouting behind her. Feet are pounding. Angie's screaming.

'No,' Jodie cries. Hands grab her. Pound her. She can't breathe. 'No. No!'

. . .

'Jodie. Jodie, wake up.'

It was Louise. Standing over her, shaking her awake.

Jodie wiped her face with trembling hands. She was sitting up in bed, the quilt was on the floor, her pyjama top was wet with sweat.

'Are you all right?' Lou asked, looking worried.

'God, yeah, sorry. Wow.' She swung her legs over the bed and shook her head. 'That hasn't happened in a long time. Did I wake you up?'

'No, I planned on having only five hours' sleep.' Lou grinned and yawned and sat on the bed beside her.

'Sorry.' Jodie tried to smile, checked the time on her mobile. Eight minutes past seven. 'You should go back to bed.' She felt bad about waking Lou but more than that, she needed some time to pull herself together.

'Now that would be an idea if I thought there was any chance I'd get to sleep. Once I'm awake, I'm awake. It's the by-product of four kids in two years.' She shrugged. 'Coffee sounds good, though, doesn't it?'

'Fabulous.' A hit of caffeine would be great and if she had to have company while she came down from one of those nightmares, she'd choose Louise any time – even though she didn't know about Angela or that night. Jodie had never seen the point in retelling her hideous memories when they were all trying to create lovely ones for their kids.

In the kitchen, Jodie left the coffee making to Lou and pulled up a stool at the bar. She put her elbows on the cold marble and her chin in still-trembling hands.

As Lou poured boiling water over the coffee grounds, she said, 'Who's Angela?'

Hearing Angie's name made Jodie's breath catch in her throat. 'What?' she feigned, not wanting to talk about her.

Louise opened the cupboards under the bench, spoke as she

rummaged around inside. 'Angela. You called out Angela in your sleep.'

'God, did I say that out loud?'

'Yes, you called out Angela, then Angie, then you said 'No' a couple of times. It was really clear. Not like the kids when they're dreaming. I can never understand anything they say.' Lou kept talking as she found sugar, fetched milk from the fridge, placed a hand over the coffee plunger, then looked up at Jodie. Twice, actually. A fast double take. The first a casual glance, the second one a look of concern. 'Jodie?'

Jodie stood up, put her hands on her hips and took a gasp of breath. This flashback thing was wearing thin. This is not me, she thought. She didn't do this anymore.

'Jodie?' Louise said again with more concern.

Jodie held up a hand like a stop sign, sat back down again. 'It's okay. It's just some weird thing that happens sometimes. Hasn't happened for ages. Caught me by surprise, that's all.'

Louise passed her a mug of coffee then pulled it back again. 'Should you be drinking coffee? You don't look too good.'

'Coffee is exactly what I need.'

'Me, too,' said Corrine. She was leaning against the hall doorway, satin wrap around a matching nightdress, eyes puffy, face pale without make-up. 'What's with all the noise?'

Hannah appeared from behind her in flannel PJs and fluffy slippers, took the stool at the end of the bench and yawned. 'Yeah. What happened to sleeping in? Who was doing all the shouting?'

Jodie raised a guilty hand as she sipped the strong, hot coffee and felt the caffeine start to smooth out some of the edginess.

'She had a nightmare,' Louise said, reaching back in the cupboard for two more mugs. 'Very cool, actually. She sat up in bed and yelled. Frightened the life out of me. Then she wouldn't wake up. I was about to get a jug of water to throw over her.'

Hannah chuckled. 'Really? What did she yell?'

Louise shot a quick glance in Jodie's direction then shrugged. 'Something unintelligible.'

Jodie smiled her thanks. At least the mood in the barn seemed more congenial than when she'd left them last night – tired, yes, but not tense. 'Sorry to wake everyone. Why don't you go sleep in for a while?'

Hannah used two fingers to rub a spot on the centre of her forehead. 'I've got a drummer playing up a storm in my head. I don't think I could sleep through that.'

'Nothing a little hair of the dog won't cure,' Corrine said, pushing herself off the wall and taking up a spot at the bench. When she saw the look on their faces, she said, 'What? I can't go back to bed. I'm making breakfast.'

Jodie watched her take a sip of coffee, wondering when Corrine started drinking so much champagne. Then Corrine pointed at her.

'Hey, we'll have none of that yawning from you, Jodie, the piker who went to bed hours before the rest of us.'

Jodie covered her mouth, yawned again anyway. 'Sorry. That car woke me up then I couldn't sleep through the storm.'

'What car?' Hannah asked.

'There was a car driving around outside. About three o'clock, before all the thunder.'

'Are you sure it wasn't just the thunder?' she said.

'No, it was a car. I'm surprised no one else heard it. It drove right around the house. Twice.'

'Thunder can sound like it's moving around.'

'It wasn't thunder. I *saw* it.'

'What did it look like?'

Jodie stopped a second, tried to ignore the scepticism in Hannah's voice. 'I couldn't see much in the dark but I saw it drive past the bedroom window.'

A look passed between Hannah and Corrine. It was only a brief turn of the head for Hannah and a sideways flash of the eyes for Corrine but it was enough for Jodie to guess the rest. She'd been the subject of discussion in the other bedroom. Her and the events of last night. And the conclusion wasn't too flattering for Jodie.

'There *was* a car,' Jodie said, annoyed at the defensiveness in her voice. Corrine raised her eyebrows as she stared into her coffee mug.

Hannah shrugged doubtfully. 'Well, it was pretty stressy last night and we all had a bit to drink. I heard the thunder rumbling around the house too. I listened to it for ages and I didn't hear any car.'

Here we go again, Jodie thought. She put her mug down a little harder than she intended, heard it crack against the marble. 'So what are you saying? *You* didn't hear a car so it wasn't there?' She looked at Hannah then Corrine. Both looked back but neither answered. 'I didn't have as much to drink as you guys and I can tell the difference between a car and thunder.'

'Okay, so what would a car be doing out here driving around the barn in a storm?' Hannah said. 'It doesn't make sense.'

'It wasn't during the storm. It was before the storm. And it doesn't have to make sense. A car is a car. I know what I heard.'

Hannah and Corrine still said nothing. Jodie turned to Lou, who shrugged her shoulders. They didn't believe her. Again.

'Okay, fine, whatever.' Jodie's stool made a loud scraping sound as she pushed it back from the bench. She needed some fresh air, needed to burn off the frustration. And she needed to see the barn in the daylight, look around for herself without alcohol or darkness clouding her judgement.

Jodie felt their silence behind her as she went down the hall to the bedroom. She was never organising the weekend again. She'd double up on all the other chores, buy all the food if she had to, just so long as she didn't have to pick the venue. It was a disaster.

She stripped off her pyjamas, pulled on trackpants and looked down. The puckered, raised scars on her stomach were as familiar to her as any other part of her body. She ran the tips of her fingers over the keloid lines and wondered. About the car. About the lights and the men. About the jerk in the pub and waiting with Corrine in the dark. About the dream and the flashback.

It wasn't unusual for the dream to follow a flashback. The one that had woken her this morning was gut-wrenching but there was nothing new in that. The flashback was another story. Last night's was one of the more vivid she'd ever had and it was the first in years. Maybe that was how it went – the more time between them, the more intense they got. The question was whether it had distressed her enough to skew her perception. It had distressed her, that was for sure, but enough to make her believe thunder was a car? Making two circuits of the house?

She pulled on a T-shirt and zip-up jacket, thought about how she'd stood in the spa bath. She walked to the bedroom window, peered behind the curtain and thought about what she'd seen last night. No, she was not imagining things. She may not have seen what kind of car it was but there had definitely been a chunky, dark vehicle with a deep-throated motor out there.

The girls were still sitting around the island bench when Jodie sent them a token wave as she went out the front door, trying to ignore the thought she might be under discussion again. It was bitterly cold outside, the sun too low to do more than cast long shadows past everything it touched. The sky was a mottled grey with one small, pale patch of blue. She hoped it grew a whole lot bigger. She didn't want to be trapped inside the barn for a wet weekend, fending off scepticism about what she had or hadn't seen. Next they'd be questioning whether she had, in fact, put a log on the fire or brewed the coffee.

She trotted down the steps to the gravel parking pad, skirted around the loan car that was covered in watery dew, and walked around the barn. It was a wide rectangle, the front and back making up the long sides, the short ones taken up by the fireplace end of the main room and the large bedroom at the bottom of the hall. The timber verandah wrapped around all four walls, its simple crossbar handrail interrupted only for a staircase at the front door, another one beyond the glass doors in the back and a third on the narrow end outside the bedroom. The owners obviously had comfort and leisure in mind when they'd decorated, thoughtfully leaving rustic coffee tables and padded recliner lounges at regular intervals along the decking.

The land had been cleared to a rough, grassy moat that circled the building, considerably wider at the front than the back, where the land sloped gently away before dropping into the valley. Jodie stopped for a second to admire the distant view of lush, green farming land and untouched scrub. Her runners and the hem of her trackpants were soaked from the grass that was still wet from the storm – and too thick, she noted, to hold wheel tracks. Any other indication of a vehicle, if there was one, had probably been washed away.

After completing the circuit, she stood beside the car with her hands on her hips and looked along the ridge of the hill towards the road they'd driven in on. The men last night said they were camping over the other side. Were they, she wondered?

The area didn't hold the same daunting sense of isolation she'd felt last night. In broad daylight, it looked open and cared for. The barn looked secure and well positioned for spotting approaching vehicles. It was quiet, except for the occasional chirp of a bird. And she wanted to see what was over the ridge.

She jogged along the crest towards the long driveway. The single, unsealed road ran down the incline to the left, disappearing beyond the hump in the track. The other side dropped off steeply into the valley.

Warmer now, she picked up her pace a little, ran past the road for a couple of hundred metres and peered down into the vale. A few gum trees grew in the scrub line and she stood for a minute trying to find signs of a camp. Maybe the two men left when it started to rain, she thought. Or maybe they were lying about the camping.

She headed back the way she came, the exertion and her investigation taking the edge off the frustration and anxiety. It wasn't as creepy as she thought out here. And if the men had been camping over the ridge, they weren't there now. She stopped at the top of the drive, took out her phone and flipped open the cover, smiling as she always did at the screen-saver photo – nine-year-old Isabelle and her six-year-old brother Adam choking Jodie in a bear hug. She looked at the time on the display. Adam had an early soccer match today. He'd be warming up like he was Harry Kewell and Isabelle would be giving him last-minute instructions. Jodie grinned. She was meant to enjoy a little kid-free time but she always missed them.

She checked the reception bars. Even up here, she was out of range. She raised a hand to her brow and squinted in the morning sun at the barn. The peak of the hill looked like a monk's tonsure from where she stood – bare of anything but rough, native grass and ringed by a neat, dense line of scrub. She turned and cast her eyes along the ridge again, then down the driveway. She wasn't ready to sit down to breakfast with the others yet. The running had felt good. It always did. It was what had got her on her feet when the flashbacks were a daily occurrence, made her feel strong and in control. And that was what she needed right now.

She ran for three-quarters of an hour along the sealed road at the bottom of the hill – not as long as usual but still a good work-out – and thought about the last time she'd had a flashback. It was four years ago, after Isabelle had fallen off her bike and Jodie had driven her bleeding and crying to hospital. As she'd waited outside the X-ray room, the horrible, vivid pictures of that night with Angie had rushed through her head. By the time Isabelle was wheeled out, Jodie was sitting on the floor, a shaking mess. The dreams had woken her up every night for a week. After that, they just stopped.

She turned onto the unsealed driveway and pulled out her phone once more. The reception metre was full but half-a-dozen steps up the hill and it was empty again. She started up the lower half of the incline, breathing hard, feeling her thighs burn. As she topped the hump in the road, she checked the mobile again. No reception. It looked like they'd have to drive down to the road to ring their families tonight.

She took a couple of long breaths and started on the final slope. Then heard a sound that made her skin crawl – the deep-throated rumble of a car engine.

12

M att heard the gunshots and opened his eyes. The ceiling above him swam into focus and he ran a hand across his damp forehead. When was he going to stop hearing it? He let his hand drop onto the back of the lounge and readjusted himself awkwardly around the throw cushions. Behind him, little feet pattered down the hallway and a second later three- year-old Sophie jumped on him.

'Uncle Matt, Uncle Matt.'

'Morning, Matt.' His sister-in-law Monica took one look at him and held her arms out to Sophie. 'Easy, honey. I don't think Uncle's Matt's ready to play trampolines just yet. Go tell Daddy his hangover has company.'

Sophie frowned at her mother. 'Huh?'

'Tell Daddy to get his butt out of bed or I'll force-feed him bacon and eggs.'

Matt groaned and sat up gingerly.

'Big night, hmm?' Monica said, picking up his jeans from the floor. 'I hope you and Tom didn't let your dad drink too much.'

'Dad went home after the darts so I felt it was only right that I drink his share.'

'Yeah, right,' she said and pulled the blanket off him.

'Hey!'

'No time to sit around. I need wood for the fire. A fair exchange for breakfast, don't you think?' she grinned and tossed him his jeans. 'How's your knee?'

Matt pushed his feet into the legs of his trousers and grimaced at the tightness in the joint. Surgery had patched up the torn ligaments almost five months ago. That was four weeks after the leap from the balcony that preceded the gunshots he heard every night. It still hurt – the knee and the memory. 'The doctor says it's doing great but *he* doesn't have to walk on it.' He limped as he followed her into the kitchen. Last week, the doc had said it'd be another three months before he'd be running regularly again. On cold mornings like this, it felt like it'd be a lot longer.

He found his shoes at the back door and stepped into the frigid morning. A thin mist hung in the trees behind the shed and he could hear the distant low of cattle. As he walked around the side of the house, he pulled in deep, long breaths and watched the steam drift away as he blew out. His mouth tasted like stale beer, his head ached and the sound of gunfire still echoed in his mind. At the woodpile, he stacked pre-cut logs into a box and thought about Jodie Cramer. Again. There was something intense about her. Even her laugh – that confident roll of sound – hinted at something beneath the surface. He hefted the box and wondered what she was doing this morning. He shouldered open the back door, saw his brother Tom standing in the kitchen in a dressing-gown and grinned – partly because he looked worse than Matt felt and partly because he knew what Tom would say if he told him he'd been out by the wood stack fantasising about a customer. *A truly desperate act, man.* He'd be right, too.

By the time he got the fire started, Sophie and her older sister Bree were shooting Uncle Matt questions. 'Uncle Matt, do you like peanut butter and honey?' 'Uncle Matt, what's your middle name?' 'Uncle Matt, can you spin me around?' Being Uncle Matt was the best cure he knew for a hangover. He carried a niece under each arm and plonked them at the breakfast bar. 'I've done my bit. How's the coffee coming?'

Monica shooed the girls off to watch Saturday morning cartoons and plied Matt and Tom with toast and coffee. She was perched on the other side of the kitchen bar when the landline rang. As she jumped up to answer it, Tom said, 'You still okay to take the Beast into town, Matt?'

The 'Beast' was the 1975 Holden Tom had bought when he was in high school. He'd done up the V8 engine under their father's tutelage way back when he wanted to be a mechanic. Now, after six years on a cattle property, there was no time to play under the bonnet, but he couldn't bring himself to part with it. Just dropped it into town for Dad to tinker with every now and then.

Matt raised an eyebrow at his brother. 'Wasn't that why I slept on your couch last night?'

'That and the fact you couldn't get to *your* couch under your own steam.' After fulfilling his job as designated driver, Tom had shared a few too many more drinks with him on the lounge, until Monica had told them to shut up and dragged her husband off to bed. 'Just checking you can still handle all that V8 grunt.'

'Wanker.'

'Smart-arse.'

Monica held up a hand for them to be quiet. 'What?' she said into the phone. 'Oh God.' She put the hand to her chest and looked over at them, her mouth open in shock. 'When?' A pause. 'What are the police saying?' Another pause. 'Oh no, it's terrible.'

Matt watched her talk for half a minute more, dread gathering in his chest. He knew what kind of call got a reaction like that. He ground his teeth, telling himself it wasn't his job anymore. When she disconnected, he said, 'What?'

'John Kruger's dead. Mum said he was beaten to death.'

'Jesus,' Tom said.

Matt's hand tightened around his coffee mug. 'Where?'

'At his home. His son Gary found him at the back of the house.

Someone hit him with a piece of timber from the frame for his new verandah.'

'Maybe he fell,' Matt said, not wanting to jump to conclusions.

'Gary told Dad his face was smashed in and there was blood everywhere. Oh God, it's awful.' The reality of it seemed to hit her then and she burst into tears. Tom took the phone from her hand and held her.

A pulse thudded in Matt's temple as he watched them. John Kruger and his family were old friends of Monica's folks. Matt and Tom had gone to school with John's three boys before the Krugers had gone to board at a high school in Sydney.

'You've got to *do* something, Matt.' Monica held onto Tom as she wiped her eyes with a tissue.

'It's not my job anymore.'

'You could go out and help the local police, couldn't you? You know what to do and they know you, don't they?'

'Mon, it's not my job.'

'You're a bloody homicide detective, Matt, and it's John Kruger, for God's sake.'

Matt ran a hand through his hair, the coffee in his gut threatening to come back up as the urge to help clashed with the urge to close his eyes and get as far away from the situation as he could. Simple fact made the choice easier. 'I'm not a cop anymore.'

'Bullshit.' Monica yanked a couple more tissues from the box on the microwave. 'You haven't resigned yet. You're on leave. That still makes you a cop, doesn't it?'

Did it? Stress leave would count him out of any investigation and one call to his counsellor in Newcastle would make sure of it. Even without that, the condition of his knee right now would rule him out of anything that wasn't behind a desk. 'I wouldn't be allowed near the case. I'm sorry.'

The phone rang again. She grabbed it from Tom and took it out of the kitchen.

'Sorry, Matt,' Tom said. 'She's just upset.'

'Sure.'

'So there's nothing you can do?'

Matt looked at his brother and felt like shit. The tough detective with the stellar career was too much of a coward to do his job. It was pathetic. But the thought of fucking up another investigation, getting it all wrong, getting people killed, made him want to . . .

He pushed away from the breakfast bar with more force than he'd intended. The stool toppled over, crashing into the clothes basket behind it.

'Shit!'

The girls' little faces appeared over the back of the lounge.

'Naughty Uncle Matt,' Bree called.

'Sorry, honey.' To Tom he said, 'I'm sorry, man. I'm really sorry. John Kruger didn't deserve that. I gotta go.' He bundled up his sweater and coat. 'Where are the keys to the Beast?'

Tom pulled them off a hook by the back door. 'I'll walk you out.'

'No, don't. Look after Monica and the girls.' Matt shut the door on his brother and headed to the shed, breathing hard.

Four minutes later, he gunned the Beast out of the driveway and took off fast down the country road. It was a hotted-up muscle car, totally pointless on a farm, even more considering the price of petrol these days, but there was something macho about being in control of a powerful vehicle. And God, he needed that right now.

Six months ago, Monica and Tom wouldn't have had to ask him to help with the investigation. He'd have jumped in the Beast and headed straight over to John Kruger's house without a second thought. But that was before Somerset Street. Before he fucked up the hostage situation. Before three innocent people died to prove his instincts weren't always right.

Their son had had a gun. When he made a run for it, Matt told the family to stay inside, that they were safe where they were. The gunshots went off in his head again. The first two. The swift twin blast he heard from outside the house. The other three shots were always overlaid in his memory by the screaming, the terrified, hysterical wailing. And his own desperation to get to those people.

He rubbed his knee. He should have gotten them out. He should have secured the site. He should have made the jump off the balcony, intercepted the son and got off a shot before the bastard doubled back to the house. But he misjudged the landing, tore his knee apart and let a nightmare loose on that family. Killing the maniac after the fact didn't make up for Matt's mistakes. A husband and wife and their teenage daughter were still dead.

He sensed the gum trees on either side of the road start to flash past faster. Getting involved in the Kruger investigation wouldn't do the cops or John's family any favours. They needed someone they could trust. And Matt couldn't give them that. Not anymore.

'Fuck! *Fuck!*' he roared.

He tightened his hands on the steering wheel. He'd been the guy who always ran in to help, the one who knew what to do in a tight situation. He had instincts, he'd thought. That was why he became a cop. To put them to good use. His superiors had been sucked in by his confidence, too. He'd been fast-tracked into Homicide, trained for tactical response support. And now it didn't matter how much bloody specialised training he had or that his instincts were screaming at him to do something – anything – because he didn't trust himself to do the right thing.

He saw the bend in the road up ahead. It was a tight left-hand turn that you had to brake through to negotiate safely. If he kept his foot on the accelerator . . . at this speed, in this car . . .

It'd stop the gunshots in his head. Stop him thinking about the goddamn hero he'd thought he was.

How bad was it, Matt? Bad enough to write off the Beast? Bad enough to . . . His mobile sounded the first chords of 'Mr Bojangles'.

It was his dad. The old man loved that song.

Matt jammed his foot on the brake, way too hard for the corner and the speed he was going. Tyres squealed and the rear end spun out. Scenery flashed past in the wrong direction and he knew he was spinning – one full turn then another half before the car finally stopped, stalled in the dirt beside the road, facing back the way he'd come.

He sat for a moment in the cloud of dust, his heart pumping hard and a hot shame filling him up. His dad didn't need a cop knocking on his door telling him his son had topped himself. Matt had seen what that could do to a man. What kind of idiot was he to let a thought like that go through his mind?

The phone was on the last few notes of the 'Mr Bojangles' ring. He picked it up with a shaky hand. 'Hey, Dad.'

'Hey there, Matty. You and Tom have a good night?'

'Yeah, Dad, we had a good night.'

'You okay, son? You sound a bit groggy.'

Matt let his head drop back on the headrest. 'Hung-over is all. What's up, Dad?'

'The Mazda you brought in last night. It's not too bad. Should be right to go this afternoon. I tried the phone number you wrote down but I can't get through. When did the woman say she'd be in to collect it?'

Matt thought about Jodie in the hallway of the pub again, stomping on Anderson's foot and pushing him clear across the corridor. He smiled a little. 'I told her we'd call. Give me the number and I'll try again. She's staying not far from here so if I can't get through, I'll head out there.'

He found a pen and took down the number.

'Are you bringing the Beast in?' his dad asked.

'Yeah. On my way.'

'Take it easy, then. Tom said she wasn't handling too well.'

'She seems to be handling just fine.'

THERE WAS no logic to mobile reception in the area. A phone could be as clear as a bell in a deep, forested gully then useless on flat, cleared, open road. Matt would have thought the Old Barn on top of its hill was perfectly situated for good reception but he couldn't get through to Jodie either. Not even to her message bank.

Matt started up the Beast, the adrenaline still racing in his veins. His dad would never know how much Matt had needed to hear his voice. He smiled to himself. The old man would probably kick his arse if he told him. Then wrap a tanned, sinewy arm around his shoulders in his version of a parental hug and tell him to go find something to do. It was his dad's solution when the going got tough. Find something to do until something better finds you.

That was why Matt had come back to Bald Hill. Once he was off the crutches and the pain in his knee was manageable, all he'd had left to think about were the gunshots and the screaming. Seeing his cop mates had only made it worse. He didn't want to talk about it or see anyone and he was going stir-crazy holed up in his house in Newcastle. When his dad said he could do with some more help at the garage, he'd meant a new junior but Matt had packed a bag and turned up anyway, taken up his old room with the bunk beds in the flat above the shop. And for eight weeks he'd been pumping petrol, driving the truck, cleaning and stocking the workshop and marking time until he found something better.

Which was why he wasn't unhappy about going out of his way to the Old Barn. The fact that Jodie Cramer was there was an added bonus.

He hung a left at the T-junction at the end of Tom's road and headed away from town. From memory, the turn-off to the barn was about five or ten kilometres further down the road. He hadn't had a reason to come out this far since he'd been home. The flat, winding road looked like it hadn't been resurfaced since the last time he'd been here.

That was seven years ago. The same day he'd squared up to the Anderson brothers at the barn. Depressing, how his first and last big cases had ended on a sour note. The first, he'd been sure it was the Andersons and hadn't found the evidence to charge them. The last, he'd been sure that family would be safe and hadn't been able to save them. For years, he'd kept track of Travis and Kane, as though knowing where they were would keep some other young kid safe. Now, six months after Somerset Street, he wasn't sure he knew how to keep anyone safe.

Matt raised a hand to a passing motorist, thought about the strangeness of seeing Kane Anderson last night, only to be heading out to the barn hours later. Stranger still that the arsehole had hit on Jodie, the person Matt was going to see. He shook his head. Coincidence, surely. Anderson wouldn't know she was staying out there. What would be the point if he did? Jodie wasn't a lonely runaway. And the barn wasn't the derelict squat it used to be – isolated yes, but hardly useful now for the sadistic games the Andersons went in for. Christ, he couldn't believe the place was a B & B.

He turned onto the dirt track that led up to the barn, noted it was a little neater now for the nice city folk who wanted to visit. He took it slow up the incline, not wanting to damage the underside of the low-slung car, smiled at the sweet, guttural purr of the engine.

He and Tom had lusted over that sound for hours in the old garage. His brother would kill him if he wrote the Beast off. He changed back to first gear and gave it an extra couple of revs as he powered over the hump in the road. Up ahead, he saw the barn perched on its hill and a jolt of memory made him roll to a stop.

Seven years ago when he'd gone up there with the search team, the Old Barn had been like a rotting wound on the countryside. There'd been rats' nests and fleas had crawled all over the cops. It stank of putrid garbage and mould and soot from a fire that had burned up one wall. Probably not much worse than the house Travis and Kane had left, their father's dump out on the Dungog road.

That whole family had been a prison sentence waiting to happen. Bill Anderson had clocked up a couple of stretches before he was wiped out by a cattle truck. No great loss. He'd been a vicious drunk, a brawler, more likely to smack a man in the teeth or beat up a woman than say g'day. Taught Travis and Kane everything they knew. Just to prove it, Travis got kicked out of the army and Kane served time in Long Bay.

Travis signed up for the military about a month after the search was called off. Matt had been promoted to detective by then and moved to Sydney but according to Dad, word was that Travis wanted to make a new start. Matt figured it was more than likely Anderson's quickest way to get out from under police scrutiny. Three years later though, he was back as a person of interest, rounded up in a sting on a military weapons racket. From what Matt could find out, a stock of rifles had gone missing from training bases over an eighteen-month period. Nine personnel had been pulled in. Travis was one of three dishonourably discharged when there wasn't enough evidence to charge them.

Kane wasn't so lucky. Matt had been working in Sydney for six months when his name popped up on the computer. What a crock that had been. Kane knifed a guy in a pub then got only two years because some idiot social worker claimed Travis's absence had left him without a steadying influence, that he had anger issues because he'd suffered abuse at the hands of his father. It was the only favour Bill Anderson ever did his son.

Matt sat in the idling car, looked at the new roof on the barn, the wide verandah, the garden, the decay traded for charm. If he'd had his way seven years ago, the place would have been torn down. Now it seemed the Old Barn was doing better than any of them. Go figure.

Out of the corner of his eye he saw something red move in the bush. It was off to the right, a few metres up the track. He eased the car forward, stopped beside a rock platform. It formed a natural clearing, five or so metres deep, bordered by native scrub except where the road ran past. And someone in a red top was crouched at the far end. He watched as the person stood up and faced him, felt one side of his mouth curl up as he wound his window down.

'Hey, Jodie.'

'Matt?'

She said it like she wasn't sure so he pushed his sunglasses up on his head and contemplated the way she was looking this morning. Great legs in trackpants, red top, a sweatshirt tied around her waist – and a baseball-sized rock she was gripping firmly in one hand.

'You're up early this morning. With all the wine I loaded in the car last night, I thought I'd have to wake you.'

She studied him for a couple of seconds, moved the rock about in her hand. 'Is that your car?'

Matt hung an arm out the window and patted the chassis. 'She's a beauty, isn't she? But no, it's my brother's. I'm driving it into town for him.'

'Does he live around here?'

He hooked a thumb over his shoulder. 'About fifteen k's that way. Just a hop, skip and a jump out here.'

'Was he driving it last night?'

'No.'

'Were you?'

He tapped the window frame with his thumb while he tried to figure out where the conversation was heading. He'd hoped for a friendly chat with the cool girl at the B & B but it felt more like an interrogation. 'No. Why?'

She took another second, repositioned the rock around in her hand again. 'We heard a car like that driving around the hill in the night. Was it you? Or your brother?'

Matt turned his head and looked out the windscreen at the barn on its hill. Yep, Jodie Cramer had a laugh that could knock a guy's socks off and she could body-slug a hundred-kilo man. It was also possible she was a little paranoid. But, hey, who was he to criticise? He'd just considered wrapping himself around a tree. He turned back to her.

'Okay, I admit it, my brother and I have been guilty of hitting on the occasional tourist in our younger days, but stalking,' he shrugged, 'it's never really been our style.'

It took a moment for her to return his smile. 'Yeah, sure. Sorry.' She lifted the rock and held it on her palm like she was testing its weight.

'So what's with the rock?' Matt asked.

She cocked her head, watched him a moment, like she was deciding what to say.

'Well, you see, I can hit a bullseye at ten metres with a baseball. It's a very handy skill when you're a PE teacher. Not much use for anything else, now that I don't play baseball. But when I heard your car, I figured it might come in handy.'

Her voice and words were casual, jokey, but she looked tense and she still gripped the rock. Maybe he was being optimistic but he decided casual was the one to go with.

'Is that right? What were you planning?'

She shrugged loosely. 'I'd aim for the driver's window. Not good for you, now that you've wound your window down.'

His mouth curled up in a slow smile. He'd got it right. 'Okay. Then what?'

'I'd call the police.'

'No mobile reception out here.'

'There is at the bottom of the hill.' She raised an eyebrow.

He nodded, said, 'So what if you miss?'

She put one hand on her hip, tossed the rock up and caught it. 'According to one of my students, who also happens to be a maths whiz, I have a ninety-four per cent success rate. I wouldn't miss.'

'I don't want to underestimate you but it's a *rock*. Heavier than a baseball, not perfectly round and I'm not ten metres away. Maybe you aren't as accurate over five or six metres. And you'd be throwing under stress. You'd know you only had one shot. That can make a person miss. What then?'

He saw his question pull her up. Her smile faltered for just a moment before she conceded with a shoulder shrug.

'Okay, it's possible I could miss. But I'm going to get damn close. I'd hit the car somewhere, make one hell of a noise, enough to give me a second or two while you worked out what happened. Then I'd run into the bush. You'd never catch me with that bad leg.'

Matt's hand went instinctively to his knee. She had him there. If she was half as fit as she looked, there was no way he'd catch her. 'But can you run to the top of the hill faster than I can drive it? Fast enough to warn your friends that the lunatic in the car was on the doorstep?'

He raised an eyebrow with a look he hoped was kind of cute then saw it was the wrong move. Her casual attitude disappeared and she was suddenly tense. The hand had dropped from her hip and her fingers were tight on the rock. He waited for her to say something, not sure where he'd gone wrong.

'No, you're right,' she said. 'Anyway, Corrine's invitation to drop round was for later in the day. Now isn't a good time.'

He was pretty sure that meant piss off and don't bother coming back. 'Actually, I'm not here on a social call. I came to tell you your car will be ready this afternoon. If you bring the loan car back around three, we can do a swap.'

'You drove all the way out here to tell me that?' Her eyes narrowed in suspicion.

What was with her? 'As a matter of fact, yes. I couldn't get through to your mobile and I thought you'd want your car as soon as possible.'

'Oh.' She gave her head a bit of a shake. 'Oh, I'm sorry.' She took a couple of steps towards the car, trying to do casual again but not quite getting there. 'I forgot about the phones. Thanks, that was nice of you. I didn't expect it to be ready so soon.'

'It's not as bad as it looked, apparently. Dad's doing a patch-up job, a little panelbeating here and there. It won't be an oil painting but it should get you home without the police pulling you over with a defect notice.'

'Well, that's good to know. I'm pretty sure I couldn't claim that on insurance,' she laughed.

She was just a couple of steps from the car now, smiling, like maybe she was trying to make up for the weird glitch in the conversation. He smiled back, enjoying the sight of her. The athletic body and those big, dark, way-too-intense eyes. School would have been a whole lot more interesting if he'd had a PE teacher like that. Well, don't just let her run away. 'So how's the old barn? I see it hasn't fallen down.'

She glanced up the hill and back again. 'Nice.'

'It looks like they've done a good job. What's it like inside?'

Her smile was still there but it seemed a little forced now. 'Comfortable.' Her eyes flicked around the car, the clearing. 'Well, gotta go. Breakfast is waiting. Thanks again.'

So soon? 'Can I give you a lift up the hill? It's pretty steep.'

She took a step away from the car. 'No.' She said it firmly. 'It'll be a good work-out.'

Great, she thinks you're a dickhead trying to hit on her. Well, you are, aren't you? Give it up. You're embarrassing yourself. 'Sure. See you this afternoon, then.' He pushed his sunglasses down onto his nose, hit reverse, backed into the bush on the other side of the narrow track and waved briefly as he drove off.

Face it, Matt. Your instincts are shot to hell.

13

Jodie smelled bacon and fresh coffee as she ran up the steps to the verandah. She took a second to pull herself together. She was puffing from the world record time she'd just run up the hill and felt edgy and spooked. Bursting through the door and announcing that Matt Wiseman, the nice guy who'd rescued them last night, was more than likely a stalker would not be the best method of describing what had just happened. Corrine and Hannah wouldn't exchange glances, they'd politely tell her to bugger off and let them enjoy the weekend.

But she had to tell them. Forewarned was forearmed.

Corrine looked up from the island bench as Jodie walked through the front door.

'Breakfast is on!' she called. She'd changed out of her silk pyjamas, gone from stylishly sleepy to stylishly casual in white trousers and pretty blouse and had secured her hair in a spectacular swirl on top of her head. The big, rustic dining table was just as chic. She must have brought the white tablecloth with her and picked the spray of flowers from the bush outside.

Louise sat up from one of the sofas, tossed a paperback on the coffee table in front of the refreshed fire, stretched noisily in her PJs and said, 'Were you running all that time?'

Jodie thought about Matt. She wanted to just blurt it all out, point by point, how it all fitted together. But she was red faced and sweating, still breathing hard. Not a good look when you want to convince sceptics of a possible new threat. Better to wait until she'd had something to eat and pulled her thoughts in line, do it calmly, logically. 'Pretty much,' she said, kicking off her runners, turning the lock on the front door. 'I thought you might have started without me.'

'Absolutely not,' Corrine said as she limped around the bench into the kitchen. 'One for all and all for one and all that, right?' She smiled, held out a bottle of champagne. 'Have you got enough energy left to open the bubbly?'

'I think I can manage.'

'You're meant to be putting your feet up, you know. Running around the countryside is not putting your feet up.'

'I enjoy it.'

'Don't be ridiculous,' Louise said, pulling out a seat at the table. 'No one enjoys running. Runners just say that to make the rest of us feel guilty.'

'It's not good to do it after a lot of alcohol,' Hannah said as she came into the room, showered, dressed sensibly in jeans and a thick sweater, and her short bob neatly blow- dried. 'You should drink plenty of water this morning so you don't get dehydrated.'

'Yes, doctor,' Jodie said.

Hannah put a hand on Jodie's bare arm, gave it a little rub. 'You should put something warm on, too, before you start cooling down.'

'Already onto it.' Jodie kept the smile on her face until she'd turned away, then rolled her eyes as she headed down the hall. She'd been running most of her life, she knew how to do it without drying up or catching pneumonia.

Breakfast started with fresh fruit and kiddie talk. Louise said, 'Let's do one round of parent news before we ban the domestic conversation for the day.' So they talked about the twins' reading success, the pros and cons of Hannah's oldest staying at home alone while she was on afternoon shift, Corrine's shock when her newly teenaged son dropped the f-bomb, and Jodie's daughter Isabelle being selected for regional athletics.

There was no bragging, no trying to outdo each other with my-kid's-better-than-yours stories. The conversation was honest and open, a safe place to air worries and mistakes and joys. It's what came after eight years of sharing sleepless nights and terrible-twos, tears over first days at school, learning difficulties, braces and brewing puberty. As usual, there was plenty of laughter amid the advice and Jodie was relieved the morning's sharp words seemed to be forgotten.

When Corrine brought eggs Benedict to the table, Lou clinked a spoon against her coffee cup.

'I hereby declare the family discussion over. Time to move on, ladies, or we'll talk about the kids all day. Now, any preferences on how we entertain ourselves today?'

'I don't want to do a single thing that requires me to be on time,' Hannah said.

'I saw a nice homewares shop in town last night,' Corrine said.

'I'm reading,' Lou said.

They looked at Jodie. She hadn't thought past bolting the barn doors. She shrugged, tried to look unconcerned about it.

'What's it like outside? Worth a walk?' Lou asked.

It was an opening, a chance to ease into telling them about Matt Wiseman on the driveway. 'It's cold.' Between mouthfuls of egg, she told them about the mist hanging low in the valley, the kangaroos she'd seen in the paddocks along the road, the mobile reception and how they'd have to go to the bottom of the hill to call home tonight. Then she told them about Matt. How he'd apparently been somewhere close enough to drop by and tell her the car would be ready later. And how his deep-throated engine sounded just like the one during the night, how he'd trapped her on the rock platform with his car and how he'd tried to prod her for information about the barn.

There was silence when she finished. A long, uncomfortable moment of nonplussed, vaguely amused silence. Then a burst of laughter. Corrine mostly, as though Jodie had cracked a joke and it had taken her a couple of seconds to get it. Hannah's laugh was a little harder, a little over it. Louise smiled uncomfortably.

Jodie bristled. 'It's not *funny*.'

'Oh, come on,' Corrine laughed. 'The man was just trying to flirt with you. You're so paranoid, you can't tell the difference between a come-on and an attempted abduction. It's no wonder you haven't had a date since James left.'

Heat rushed to Jodie's cheeks and she looked down at the toast left on her plate. Is that what Corrine thought? Is that what they all thought? Isn't that what she'd thought herself at times?

'Jeez, Corrine,' Louise said then smiled back at Jodie. 'Besides, she doesn't want to date a revhead. They're so not in touch with their feminine side.'

Corrine lifted a piqued chin at the rebuke. Beside her, across the table from Jodie and Louise, like the captain of the other team, Hannah raised a single eyebrow, as if to acknowledge Corrine had a point.

Jodie felt a flash of anger. 'So, Corrine, do you think if you drank another bottle of champagne, you could say what you really thought?'

'What's that supposed to mean?' said Corrine.

Jodie took a breath, about to snap back, but bit down on the words at her lips. Getting personal wasn't going to make them pay attention. 'Nothing. I didn't mean anything. The point is there were two men snooping around last night and at least two people shining torches around the back verandah and a car driving around the barn at three in the morning. It's weird at best, pretty damn suspicious at worst.'

Hannah opened her mouth to say something but Jodie held up her hand. 'Let me finish. I've been thinking it through and the one explanation that makes any sense is that the snoops came back with torches for some reason, got interrupted doing whatever they were doing and returned during the night. That means if Matt Wiseman was driving the car, he may also have been outside with a torch, which means he may be as suspicious as the two snoops.'

No one said a word. Hannah looked off into the kitchen shaking her head, Corrine used a fork to poke at a crust of toast on her plate and Louise sat back in her chair and watched Jodie with an expression she couldn't read.

Jodie crossed her arms on the table. 'Look, I'm just saying we shouldn't trust anyone we see out here. I mean, we're probably perfectly safe but if anyone shows up, we shouldn't necessarily take the situation at face value, you know?'

'There is another explanation,' Hannah said, looking pointedly at her. 'That the two guys were actually campers and they took an evening stroll with a couple of torches before bed. *Or* they were safe and sound in their sleeping bags by the time you saw what you *believed* to be torches but which may, in fact, have been anything. Or nothing. And that the mysterious car driving around the barn was actually thunder and that Matt Wiseman is, in fact, a nice guy who came all the way out here to let you know your car was ready. Yes, I know, your version is way more exciting and dramatic but I prefer mine.'

Why was Hannah being so damn contentious about it? 'So we're back to "I didn't see it so it doesn't exist"?' Jodie said.

'It's better than leaping to wild conclusions at every bloody bump in the night.'

'Give me some credit, Hannah.'

'Actually, what I want to do is enjoy the time we've got left here without any more of your *Nightmare on Elm Street* scenarios.'

'Hear, hear,' Corrine said.

'Come on, guys. Can we move on?' Louise said.

Jodie pressed her lips together. She felt annoyed and patronised and, worst of all, unsure. Hannah's version of events had set off a sickening pulse in her head. It made sense, too. There might be campers around here, she hadn't actually seen people with torches, and yes, she had had a lot to drink last night. The car . . . well, had she *actually* seen and heard it? She felt like she'd held Angela's bloody hands this morning, too, and her screams sounded like they'd come from the next room. Maybe the car was as real as the flashback and the nightmare.

Jodie held her arms tightly across her chest, unsure what to do next now the conversation had come to a screeching halt. She turned her eyes to the big windows that stretched along the back of the barn. The curtains were open and the view was lush and green, not dark and threatening like it had been last night. She thought about it again – the men, the lights, the car, Matt Wiseman. It didn't *feel* right. Something was telling her it was too weird, too coincidental. She told her self-defence students to follow their instincts. If they thought there was a threat, there probably was.

The stubborn, scarred, control freak in her wanted to stand up and yell at them. Make them listen, argue the point until they saw sense. Tell them they needed to be careful, that danger could come from anywhere, that being prepared could keep them alive.

But the faces around the table mirrored how she felt herself – frustrated and fed up and cross. And she thought, what if her instincts *were* wrong? What if the flashback had screwed her perspective? Worried for their safety or not, did she really want to ruin the weekend arguing a point she couldn't prove? A point that might turn around and bite her on the butt later?

She stood up, gathered together her dishes, said, 'Great breakfast, Corrine. Sorry my table conversation didn't do it justice.'

No one said anything as she stacked her tableware in the dishwasher. The plates clanged like cymbals in the tense silence and her footsteps as she walked down the hall sounded, ironically, like thunder. She shut herself in the bathroom, stood under a hot shower and gave a little humourless laugh at how she'd thought this year's weekend away was going to be such a blast.

In the bedroom, she stood in her underwear in front of the closed curtains, rubbed her wet hair with a towel and went over it again. And again. She tossed the towel on her bed, edged the curtain to one side and looked out. It was sunnier now. Peaceful, inviting. The winter light was warming the timber verandah, the scrappy native grass beyond it looked lush and clean after last night's storm and a couple of wallabies were grazing lazily near the edge of the bush.

She should be soaking up the tranquil, country ambience. That's what she was here for, wasn't it? To chill out, not freak out. Not fight with her friends. She rolled her shoulders, one way then the other. Shake it off, Jodie. Get dressed and get on with it. Like you always do. She turned around as Louise walked through the door.

'Hannah and Corrine are talking about driving into town. Feel like going?' Louise dropped onto Jodie's bed, tucked up her legs and leaned on an elbow beside the open suitcase.

Jodie stopped halfway across the room, conscious she was wearing only a bra and knickers and that the scars on her stomach were both unattractive and unmissable. She wasn't ashamed of them – they reminded her she'd survived – but the random, jagged slashes told a story of violence and brutality that right now, she didn't want to talk about. Not while she was edgy and unsure. Not while she could still feel Angela's bloody hand in hers. She thought about turning away but with Louise settled on her bed, how long could she talk to her with her back turned? Stepping closer would only bring the scars into focus so she stayed where she was and folded her arms across her waist, knowing it would take more than that to cover the damage. 'I think I'll pass. I've got to take the car back this afternoon so I'll wait till then.'

Jodie watched as a frown grew on Louise's face. Sitting on the bed, her eyes were at the same level as Jodie's stomach but it still took a couple of seconds for the view to make sense. When it did, Louise sucked in a breath.

'Jesus, Jodie, what happened to you?' She looked up at Jodie's face then back down at her stomach, eyes moving from the top of her knickers to the opposite hip where the scar over the bone was wide and puckered.

Too late to hide it now, Jodie thought, and stepped to the bed, grabbed a shirt from the top of her suitcase and angled away from Louise as she pulled it on. 'It's just from some surgery I had when I was a kid.'

Louise said nothing as Jodie turned back to her bag for the rest of her clothes. She was watching her with a crease between her brows and her mouth open like she was deciding what to say next.

'It looks a lot worse than it was,' Jodie said as she pulled on a pair of jeans.

'Sure,' Lou finally said and nodded noncommittally. She suddenly swung herself upright and pushed off the bed, as if to move right along. 'You know, I could do with a couple of Corrine-and-Hannah-free hours, too. I think I'll hang out here with you.'

Jodie shot her a grateful glance, realising the journalist inside Louise was probably dying to know more. 'And I thought it was just me having a problem.'

Louise shrugged as she stepped to her own bed, pulling out toiletries for her turn in the shower. 'I love them both but Hannah can be hard work when she decides she's right. And Corrine's champagne supply is giving me a headache.'

'To quote the lady herself – hear, hear.'

Louise kept her head down as she lifted clothes from her suitcase. 'But maybe we should cut her some slack. It would've been Roland's fiftieth birthday next weekend. I think that's what the champagne guzzling is about. Her way of trying not to be sad.'

'God, I'd forgotten his birthday was so close to our weekends,' Jodie said. She knew what those anniversaries were like, felt bad for the crack over breakfast, forgave her for what she'd said about never having a date.

'Mind you,' Lou added, still busy with her clothes, 'the way she's been drinking the stuff like water is a bit of a worry.'

'I thought the same. Do you think she's got a problem?'

Lou looked up, shrugged again. 'I hope not. Maybe we should see how she is after the birthday.' She smiled awkwardly and her eyes slid away from Jodie's face. Downwards, to where her scars were now covered by clothes. Lou's lips parted and she took a breath, as though she was getting ready to say something.

'It's lovely outside now,' Jodie said, cutting her off. 'I'm going to curl up on one of those lounge chairs on the verandah with a magazine. Enjoy your shower.'

Lou cocked her head. 'Yeah, I'll do that.'

Half an hour later, Louise joined her on the verandah with two mugs of coffee. She sat on the lounge next to Jodie's, took a sip and gazed out across the late-morning view. The clouds were clearing and the valley looked crisp and clean like a glossy photo. 'Well, it's been interesting so far.'

'That's one way of putting it.' Jodie flipped a couple of pages in her magazine, tried to ignore the way Louise was watching her.

'So what's going on?' Lou finally asked.

Jodie lifted her head, surprised. She'd expected an interrogation about the scars. 'I gave my opinion on that at breakfast and got the impression I'd said more than enough.'

Louise took another sip of coffee. 'I mean you. What's going on with you?'

Jodie looked into the concerned eyes of her best friend, not sure how to answer. She didn't want to shut her out completely but how much could she tell without having to tell it all? Without putting an even grimmer mood on the weekend? She shrugged. 'I'm . . .' Her answer was interrupted with a loud crash in the kitchen followed by a scream and a laugh from Corrine and Hannah.

'Oh my God, the scary men are back,' Corrine wailed in mock fear. Jodie turned away, embarrassed, irritated.

Louise grabbed her arm. 'Let's get out of here. Go for a walk.'

Jodie nodded. 'Probably best if *you* let Hannah and Corrine know.' She raised a cynical eyebrow. 'It'll sound like a conspiracy if I do. And if they take the car, remind them I've got to be back in town by three.'

Jodie took Louise in the opposite direction to the path she'd run earlier, wanting to explore a little further, set her mind at ease – either way. The ridge continued level for about a hundred metres then began a descent into the valley. They found a narrow track of beaten earth and started to follow it down the incline.

They were quiet for a while, watching their feet on the rough ground and taking in the view of the valley. As the ground evened out and the path widened, they walked side by side again and Louise broke the silence.

'I don't know if I ever told you,' she said. 'But when I was in Afghanistan, I was caught in gunfire. There were four of us in a car, stopped in a queue at a roadblock. It wasn't about us, we were just caught in the middle of it. We couldn't go anywhere so we just got down on the floor and crossed our fingers. The windscreen was hit and glass went all over us. A couple of tyres were shot out. It was terrifying. Anyway, about a year after I returned from Afghanistan, when I was pregnant with Lilly and Alice, I started having nightmares. I'd dream I was in the back of a car and someone was firing a gun through the windows. I was on the floor trying to get as low as I could but my pregnant stomach was in the way. I couldn't get low enough and broken glass would drop all over me and I could feel the bullets passing over my head.' She shivered a little, as though she could still see it.

'It was worse after I had the girls. I'd dream they were in the car with me, crying and screaming and I'd be trying to cover them with my body, expecting a bullet to rip into me any minute.'

Jodie thought of Angela's screams in her nightmare this morning and her stomach tightened. 'It must have been horrible.'

'Pretty hard to deal with when you've got newborn twins. You'd think I'd be too tired to dream but no. Ray shuffled me off to a psychologist who said I had post-traumatic stress disorder. Talking about what happened over there helped a lot, you know.'

Jodie nodded a couple of times, waiting for Louise to go on. When she didn't, Jodie looked over, saw her face and frowned. 'What?'

Lou shrugged.

'Are you trying to tell me I need professional help?' Jodie said.

'No, I'm saying it worked for me to talk about it. So if you need to, I know how to listen.'

Jodie's heart beat a little harder and, without meaning to, she picked up the walking pace. 'I'm fine. It was just a bad dream.'

Louise matched her step for step. 'If it was just the nightmare, I wouldn't be saying anything.' She looked at Jodie, raised her eyebrows.

'What?'

'You're so wound up, Jodie. It's like you're on a caffeine drip.' She grabbed her arm and pulled her to a stop. 'Can we slow down? You're killing me.' She puffed a couple of times. 'God, I'm so unfit. Look, you're one of the most together people I know but you're stressing about everything. And so tense.' She held out a hand to emphasise her point. 'And fighting with Corrine and Hannah, waking up screaming, carrying weapons, for God's sake. Like I said, what's going on?'

Jodie slid her hands into the back pockets of her jeans. She hadn't realised the drama in her head had been quite so obvious.

'Who's Angela?' Louise asked.

Jodie sucked in a breath, suddenly angry. 'The reporter in you just can't help it, huh?'

'Don't be ridiculous,' Louise snapped back. 'I'm trying to talk to you. I'm worried about you.'

Jodie was starting to worry about herself. She ran her hands through her hair.

Who's Angela?

Jodie saw Angie's eyes blinking at her in the dark again, felt the slime of blood on her hands, heard the echo of her scream reverberate around her head, and the air in her lungs evaporated.

14

'Jodie?' Louise sounded worried.

Not surprising considering Jodie had just bent double at the waist. She had her hands on her knees, was trying to suck in air. It was no good. She straightened up, clasped her hands around the back of her head and squeezed her eyes shut.

Okay, Jodie, maybe you need to say it. The memory had worked its way up from the bottom of her psyche. Maybe if she let it out it would go away. If nothing else, she'd get another opinion on her perspective. She took a deep breath. God, saying it out loud always felt like she was pulling her heart out with a piece of string. She opened her eyes, looked at her feet and kept them there as she talked.

'Angela was my best friend in high school. We were followed from a bus stop one night. Three vicious bastards beat her up, raped her and cut her throat. One of them chased me when I got away and stabbed me in the stomach six times.' She breathed in and out, felt the anxiety ease up a little, as though the vice holding her body tight had loosened. She looked up at Louise. 'I'm sorry. It's a horrible story.'

'It's okay.' Lou smiled gently. 'I've heard lots of stories.' She waited a beat before asking the next question. 'How long have you been dreaming about it?'

Jodie shook her head. 'It wasn't the dream that freaked me out.'
She told her about the flashback, how she hadn't had one for years,
how she couldn't shake the edginess it had left her with. 'I keep
thinking through everything that's happened since then, the two
men, the lights on the verandah, the car in the night, trying to figure
out if I'd feel this anxious if I hadn't had the flashback. And I just
don't know. All I know is that it feels wrong. It feels like a threat.' She
held Louise's eyes. 'Tell me I'm not nuts.'

Louise took a deep breath like she was deciding how to respond.
It wasn't a good start, Jodie thought.

'To be honest, I don't know what to think. The guy in the pub was
bad timing. You just happened to cross his path at the wrong time.
The two men outside sounded a bit creepy, I'll give you that.' She
shrugged. 'But for all we know, people could camp around here all
the time. The lights and the car – well, I didn't see or hear either of
them so I'm undecided there.'

Jodie took a step away, stuffed her hands in the pockets of her
jeans. 'Bloody hell, Louise, don't tell me you think I made them up,
too.'

'I'm not taking sides, I'm just trying to be objective. Only one
person saw the lights and heard the car, the same person who admits
to having some kind of uncontrolled reaction to a flashback.' She
cocked her head to one side. 'Logically, it doesn't make sense for
anyone to be prowling around here in the middle of the night. On the
other hand, I've written a ton of stories about strange things
happening in unlikely situations. And generally I'm writing them
because they don't have a happy ending.' She shrugged again. 'So, in
the interests of having a good weekend and staying out of the head-
lines, I'd prefer to think something unexplainable happened during
the night but it's not as bad as you think.' She raised her eyebrows, a
prompt to go with the positive spin.

But Louise had said nothing to dispel her unease. '*Preferring* to
think everything's okay doesn't actually make it okay.'

'Look, I know what it's like to have a bunch of crap running
loose in your head but you've got to try to get a handle on it.' Louise

folded her arms across her chest. 'The whole point of this weekend is to give yourself a break and at the moment you're stressing yourself and everyone else out.' She looked away, turned back. 'We're meant to go home on Sunday feeling like we've recharged our batteries and had a few laughs. But if you can't do that here, then . . .'

Jodie frowned. 'You want me to leave?'

'*No.* I meant, maybe we should *all* leave. The weekend is meant to be for all of us. We could go somewhere else. The pub in Bald Hill is pretty big. Maybe we could stay there. It might be fun. We could play darts.' She laughed a little, as if she was trying to convince herself. 'Or maybe we could just go home. Do it another weekend. Somewhere else.'

Jodie saw the valiant smile on Lou's face and hot tears burned behind her eyes. She couldn't believe Lou would offer to leave – for her. She knew how much Lou looked forward to their weekends. How much she needed them. And even though a part of her wanted to run with the idea, to pick up and leave and start again somewhere else, she knew she was never going to do that. She wasn't going to ruin the weekend, wasn't going to ask Louise to go home or make Corrine bunk down in a country pub. Not when she wasn't sure, not really sure, what was real and what wasn't.

'No, we're not leaving,' Jodie said firmly. 'I'm sorry I worried you but I'm fine. It's all fine. I'll have a nap this afternoon and everything will be okay.'

'You sure?'

No question. They were going to stay. They were going to talk and laugh and chill out. And Jodie was going to do it with them. She was going to have a great time or win an Academy Award convincing them she was. She made herself smile. 'Absolutely.'

The distant burble of a car engine drifted over the ridge. They both turned and looked up the hill but couldn't see the barn this far down in the valley. Jodie strained to hear it but it was too brief and too far away to match it with the rumble from last night.

'Come on,' Louise said and hooked an arm through Jodie's. 'The others must be back from town. Maybe they bought something for afternoon tea.'

Jodie watched the top of the hill a moment longer. 'Yeah, it's probably just the others.' She blew air out through her mouth. Everything was fine, Jodie. 'Are you hungry already?'

It was more or less lunchtime – a late lunch – but they never actually ate it on the Saturday of their weekends. After Friday night's foodfest then brunch, no one felt much like a meal during the day.

'No, but I consider it my duty to support the communities we visit by tasting their locally produced yummies,' Louise laughed as they started back up the hill.

Jodie let Louise set the pace then dropped in behind her when the track became too narrow to walk side by side. Her friends were lucky, she reminded herself, that violence and danger weren't the first thoughts on their minds when things didn't add up. She needed to sort the facts from her fears. If it still felt wrong, she'd pack them up herself, drive them home and put up with the consequences later. But until then, for the sake of a good weekend – and perhaps for the sake of a couple of friendships – she had to keep her damn mouth shut.

THEY APPROACHED the barn from the bedroom end, climbing the steps that took them onto the stretch of verandah outside Corrine and Hannah's room.

'Hey, they've got French doors,' Louise said.

The sun shone through the open curtains, casting bright squares of light on the bedroom floor. 'Nice.'

Their shoes clomped hollowly on the timber decking as they turned the corner and looked down the length of the barn. It took a second for Jodie to realise what was wrong with the view.

'The car's not here,' she said, her feet starting to slow.

'Maybe they parked around the back.'

Jodie looked at the gravel pad in front of the barn and thought of the grassy slope on the other side. Out front was the obvious place. She looked quickly around. 'Maybe the car we heard wasn't ours.'

Louise continued along the verandah and stopped several paces short of the front door. The way she stood there, one hand on the railing, just looking at the door, made Jodie's heart thud. She walked carefully, trying not to clomp on the decking, and her hair stood on end when she saw what Louise was looking at.

The front door was open.

Not wide open. Not just ajar. Somewhere in between. More closed than open. As though it hadn't been pushed hard enough to carry it all the way to the jamb. Or wide enough for a quick exit.

Jodie looked hesitantly at Louise, held a finger to her lips then stepped up to the door, blood thumping in her head like a drum as she peered through the gap. She could see the writing desk, the lounges, fireplace and half the dining table. But it was what she couldn't see that worried her. Like what was behind the door.

She slid a hand through the open doorway and silently picked up a wooden candlestick from the writing desk. She pulled off the candle, put it on the deck, looked briefly at the inch-long spike it had been attached to and slowly pushed the door wider. If Hannah or Corrine popped out and sang 'surprise', she'd beat them over the head with the damn candlestick.

As the door opened further, she saw the rest of the dining table, the full run of curtains covering the back windows, the island bar, the open doorway to the hall. The front door touched the wall behind it and she let out a relieved breath.

Louise moved into the doorway beside her and they stood and listened to the silence for a long moment.

'Hannah?' Louise called lightly. 'Corrine?'

If they'd parked the loan car around the back and were catching up on some sleep, Jodie thought, she and Louise would look like bloody idiots turning up at the door with a candlestick in hand. Then a soft shuffling sound came from somewhere at the rear of the barn and her mouth went dry. She glanced at Louise, who returned her look with wide eyes. They moved towards the hall, were just through the door when a loud thud made them both jump. It was on the verandah. At the bedroom end.

Jodie moved first, bumping into Louise in the narrow space. They fumbled about a moment then burst out of the hall and made for the front door. Their feet clomped unevenly on the decking as they ran the length of verandah, spilled around the corner and pulled up short.

There was no one. Nothing. Just empty verandah and the same lush, green view.

Still holding the candlestick, Jodie looked over the railing, walked all the way to the other corner, then halfway along the rear run of deck before turning back.

'What the hell?'

Lou was halfway through shrugging when a car engine revved into hearing range. She reached the front corner of the barn first, held Jodie back with a hand as it approached.

'Wait till we see who it is,' she whispered.

Jodie pressed up against Louise, edging around the corner of the barn, adrenaline flooding her veins. She gripped the candlestick a little firmer. Then the loan car drove into view.

'Shit.' Jodie breathed out forcefully, let the candlestick drop by her side. 'Come on.' She grabbed Louise's elbow, pulled her along the verandah and waited at the top of the steps while Hannah parked on the gravel pad.

'What's wrong?' Hannah asked as she got out of the car.

'We just got here. The front door was open,' Louise answered.

Corrine got out of the car and Hannah repeated what Lou had told her. Jodie waited impatiently for understanding to dawn on their faces. Surely this was enough to make them rethink the events of the previous night.

'Did you shut the door properly when you came out the second time?' Hannah directed the question at Corrine over the roof of the car.

She shrugged. 'I don't know. I just pulled it behind me.' She looked at Jodie's incredulous face. 'Well, I had to go back for my diamond studs and I was trying to be quick. It's not easy getting down the steps with a sprained ankle.'

'Good one, Corrine,' Hannah laughed as she pulled a shopping bag from the car. 'Nice you made sure your diamond studs were out *before* you left the front door open.'

Jodie wanted to yell 'Don't you see it now?' but she clamped her mouth shut. Don't piss them off, she told herself. She shook out her fingers and paced between the front door and the steps.

Louise picked up the candle from where Jodie had put it beside the door. 'You scared the shit out of us. We thought someone was inside.'

'It wouldn't take much to scare the shit out of Jodie at the moment,' Corrine said as she limped up the stairs.

Jodie registered the comment was made with more humour than her final words at breakfast but she ignored it. She was thinking of the soft shuffling sound from the rear of the house and the thud on the verandah. 'There was someone inside. We heard them.'

Hannah walked past her into the barn. 'Don't tell me. It sounded like thunder.'

Jodie followed her in, wanting to throttle her, and paced around looking for signs of disturbance. The room seemed a little off kilter, as though objects had been picked up and put down in slightly different positions. The corner of a rug was flipped up, a chair at the table was out of place, an overhead cupboard in the kitchen was ajar. And there was a faint tang in the air, like old fruit. Or sweat.

Across the room, Hannah pulled the curtains wide.

Jodie remembered how the drapes had been open when they'd eaten breakfast and sucked in a breath. 'Were the curtains closed when you left?'

Hannah gave a not-this-again kind of sigh. 'I don't know.'

Jodie had wanted to keep her damn mouth shut. But she couldn't. She was filled up with anxious, nervous energy that made the blood pump so hard in her legs she couldn't stand still, kept moving back and forth between the two old tree trunks. 'If someone broke in, they'd pull the curtains closed so they couldn't be seen.'

'But no one broke in. Corrine just left the door open,' Hannah said, securing the drapes with tie-backs.

Jodie walked to the island bar. 'No, someone was in here.' She paced to the lounges. 'Louise and I heard them.' She ignored the way the three of them were looking at her and thought about the sound. 'They were in the bedroom.' She turned to Hannah then Corrine. 'Your bedroom.'

Neither of them said a thing, just looked perplexed. Okay, so violence and danger weren't their first thoughts, but who comes home to an open front door and says 'oh, dear, silly me'? What was wrong with them? 'Someone *has* been in this barn.'

She marched down the hall, all the way into Corrine and Hannah's bedroom. The room was neat and organised, both beds made, suitcases stowed somewhere out of sight but the curtains were ... wrong. Sort of messed up and the pattern of sunny squares on the floor was bent out of shape. She took three quick steps to the double doorway, stopped and stared at the inch gap where one side was open, remembered how she'd seen it from the verandah – closed. She slammed it shut, locked it. Locked the windows, too. Then she turned, saw the en suite and walk-in wardrobe on either side of the bedroom door and felt a twang in her gut.

Maybe someone was still here.

She'd been a little afraid before but now she was just mad. How dare someone intrude on their weekend? Force a wedge between them all? She was still holding the candlestick, she realised, and gripping it tight at the base, she held it high and gave the en suite door a shove. A quick look left and right told her it was empty. She did the same to the walk-in robe – apart from a few of Hannah and Corrine's things, it was empty. She went back into the hallway, stood at the door to the second bedroom and felt the hackles rise on her neck. The curtains were haphazardly closed there too, her suitcase on the bed had been opened and she knew – she just *knew* – the stuff on her bedside table had been moved about.

Louise, Hannah and Corrine were standing together at the island bench, heads together, talking quietly when Jodie hustled in from the hall.

'Someone has definitely been here.' She opened the fridge, took out a bottle of water and drank straight from the neck. It was wrong. It was all wrong. She shut the fridge then opened it again. 'Where's all the food?' She pulled the door wide to show the others. 'We had more than this.'

Corrine frowned. 'I used a lot of it for breakfast.'

'What about the orange juice and the fruit and the bread? There was more bread.'

'Okay, so we pigged out,' Corrine said.

'And what about the steaks I brought? Where are the steaks?'

'Are you sure you brought them? Maybe you left them at home,' Louise suggested.

'Like a Freudian slip,' Hannah added.

They all knew the only decent meal Jodie could cook was a steak. They ribbed her about it every year. But this wasn't funny. 'No. Someone was here. Your French doors were ajar, the curtains are messed up in both bedrooms, my suitcase is open and food is missing.' The three girls stood shoulder to shoulder on the other side of the island bench.

There was something different about the way they were watching her – the irritation wasn't there, or the mockery. Or any agreement either. 'I'm not making this shit up. Someone has been in the barn!'

'It's okay, Jodie,' Louise said.

Her voice was calm and soothing and it made Jodie want to scream. 'No, it's not. We should call the police. You should check through your things. Make sure nothing's been stolen.'

Louise smiled gently, a sentiment that seemed so out of place with Jodie's aggravation. 'Try to relax a little, Jodie.'

'What?' Jodie looked at Louise, then at Corrine and Hannah. All three of them seemed concerned and . . . something else. Then slowly, like a camera being pulled into focus, she saw it. A pulse started up in the base of her throat and the temperature of her blood started to rise. 'What have you been saying, Louise?'

15

'They didn't understand what was going on,' Louise said. 'They needed to know.'

Jodie clenched her fists. '*What* did you tell them?'

Louise took a moment to answer, as if she was suddenly not so sure about what she'd done. 'Just about Angela and the flashback.'

Jodie felt sick. A hot churning high up in her stomach. 'Jesus Christ, Lou. You had no right.' She turned away from them, braced herself against the bench on the opposite side of the kitchen, the marble cold against her hot hands. She felt like her friends had just trampled through her deepest, darkest, most shameful memories. Corrine's exclamation of mock fear she'd overheard this morning came back to her – *oh my God, the scary men are back* – and she cringed. She didn't know what was worse – the mockery or the pity she'd just seen in their faces.

Louise spoke to her back. 'I didn't think it was right for them to be pissed off with you when there's a reason you're going over the top about everything.'

Jodie turned around and glared at her. 'You had *no right* to tell them anything, Louise. I get to choose who and when I tell that story.

And you're wrong. This has *nothing* to do with what happened almost *twenty years* ago.'

'I think it does,' Hannah said, lifting her head in a challenge. 'I've done some psych training and I think the crash last night set something off and the flashbacks and the nightmare and paranoia are symptoms of some kind of breakdown.'

A sarcastic laugh escaped Jodie's lips. Her years in therapy beat Hannah's semester of uni psych. 'I don't know how much Louise managed to tell you in the minute it took for me to check the bedrooms but I think you're talking out your arse. And by the way, I've had self-defence training and I think the fact that the front door was open and the curtains were closed and some things have been moved are symptoms of someone breaking in.'

Hannah shook her head. 'You're not well, Jodie. You need help.'

If it wasn't so hurtful, it'd be hilarious. 'I'm *not* nuts. Believe what you want to believe about last night but someone was in here just now.' She looked across their faces and her blood boiled at the sympathy she saw. 'Louise, you were here. You heard the thud on the verandah. What made that sound, if it wasn't someone getting out in a hurry?'

Louise shrugged apologetically. 'I don't know. It could have been anything. A possum, maybe.'

'A possum? It'd have to be a fucking big possum to make that kind of noise. Why are you doing this, Louise?'

'Jodie, it's okay,' Lou said.

'No, it's not okay.' She stepped up to the island bench, faced them over the barrier between them. 'It's not okay for my friends not to believe me.'

'It's not like that,' Louise said.

Hannah frowned. 'We're worried about you.'

'Jodie, honey, I know what it's like to lose someone.' Corrine inclined her head in empathy. 'It takes a long time to get over it. Maybe we never will. It hurts to talk about it, I know, but it helps to share it, too.'

Jodie stared at her caring, sanctimonious smile. Corrine didn't have a bloody clue. Jodie turned away, ran her hands through her hair, fighting the urge to throw something. Don't lose it. Don't give them another reason to think you're losing your mind. She looked back at them. 'I know you've done it tough the last couple of years, Corrine, and I respect that. But, not to put too fine a point on it, Roland died of a heart attack on the squash court. You got a phone call from a friend. I was tied to a tree a couple of metres from where Angela was beaten and raped. I heard her screaming until they cut her throat. And someone stuck a knife in my gut. Do you want to *share* how it feels to be covered in your own blood? Or how it feels to leave your best friend behind to get murdered?'

'That's horrible, Jodie. You're just trying to upset me now.'

'No, I'm not. I'm being straight with you. You have no idea. And I hope you never do.' Jodie was shaking. Damn them for making her think about it. Like it made any kind of difference. 'And now that I've *shared* all that, guess what? I still think someone broke into the barn. So does that make me nuts, Hannah?' She looked at the concern on Hannah's face and decided not to wait for a reply. 'Actually, I've heard enough of what you all think and, frankly, I'd prefer my own conversation right now. So who's got the car keys?'

'What do you need the keys for?' Hannah challenged.

Why was she making this so hard? 'To get my car from the service station, which at the moment sounds a whole lot more fun than hanging out here.'

Hannah lifted her chin. 'Perhaps you shouldn't be driving at the moment.'

'What the hell is that supposed to mean?'

'You're very upset, Jodie.'

'Just give me the damn keys.'

'No, don't,' Louise said. 'She shouldn't be driving like this.'

'Lou's right,' Hannah said. 'What if you have another flashback while you're behind the wheel?'

Jodie felt the air leave her lungs. Something heavy and hot filled them up again. She stared at them for a long moment, her mouth clamped. 'Oh my God,' she finally said and even to Jodie her voice sounded strangely calm. 'You just reminded me why I never told you about Angela. You're just like James. Once you know the story, you can't listen to me without hearing the horror of it all. But try to hear this. I have lived with what happened for eighteen years without needing your advice on whether I should drive a car. So give me the keys so I don't have to listen to any more of your psych-trained, editorialising, caring- sharing ideas about how I should handle my life.'

For a moment, it looked like Hannah might make a stand and refuse to hand the keys over. Jodie glared at her, hoping she didn't have to physically take them from her.

Then Hannah reached into her jacket pocket and dropped them on the counter with a clatter.

Jodie swiped them up, grabbed her handbag from where she'd stowed it beside a lounge, checked quickly for signs of tampering – it seemed fine, but that didn't prove anything – then stormed through the front door. She was so angry, she wanted to kick something. Her hands were shaking and her legs were like jelly and by the time she'd driven to the full length of the unsealed driveway, tears were welling in her eyes. At the bottom of the drive, she was batting them away with the back of her hand. A kilometre down the road, she was crying so hard the view through the windscreen was a blur and her breath came in jagged gasps.

She was in the bend before she knew it and pulling the steering wheel to the right too late. Her left-hand tyres thunked off the tar and scrabbled in the rough surface on the shoulder. She hit the brakes, the bush at the side of the road scratching along the paintwork as she came to a jarring stop more off the road than on. The flood of tears halted in its tracks, adrenaline tingled in the tips of her fingers. She stepped shakily out of the car, went around to the passenger side and checked for damage. It was fine. She was fine.

Goddamn it, *she was fine!*

She wasn't having a breakdown. She wasn't. She stomped around the car and kicked a tyre. Okay, she probably shouldn't have been driving after all but her friends had pulled a damn intervention on her. What was wrong with *them*? Someone broke into the barn and they thought *she* was nuts. Well, she wasn't. She was mad. Angry. Pissed off.

She kicked the tyre again. They'd decided she couldn't cope because she had a flashback and a bad dream. They didn't have a fucking clue what she could cope with.

Jodie rubbed at the dried tears on her face. She was hurt and sad and angry *at herself*. After Angela, she hadn't wanted any more friends. Didn't want the responsibility of another friend on her conscience. If she hadn't run that night, Angela might still be alive. The bastards might have left her alone if they'd been able to rape Jodie as well. Or maybe she could have fought them off – she was fit and fast back then, under-eighteen state hockey captain and she had three brothers, she knew how to throw a punch. But she hadn't stayed with her friend. She'd made the wrong choice.

Jodie leaned against the warm hood of the car and closed her eyes. Louise was the first real girlfriend she'd had after Angela, and only because Lou had refused to take no for an answer. Then Hannah and Corrine had come along and Jodie eventually let them in, too.

'I'm better off without them.' She said it out loud, as though she'd believe it more if she heard it. And she had to believe it because if she wasn't better off without them, if she needed them around, if they were the good friends she'd thought they were, then she had to consider there might be some truth in what they'd said. And that scared the hell out of her.

She hauled herself off the car and got back in. Wiped at her eyes, started the engine and pulled onto the road. Was she having a breakdown? Was it possible she'd invented everything out of fear? Her reactions had been intense but she'd thought it was because the others wouldn't believe her, their denials only making her more determined to convince them they needed to protect themselves.

She tried to think it through from their perspective – the tyre iron, not letting Hannah onto the verandah, following her with the brass Buddha. Then the car in the night and telling them Matt Wiseman was suspect, freaking out because the front door was open. They hadn't seen her crying so hard, she'd run off the road – but they'd predicted it.

A pulse started up in her temples, a loud hammering that made the blood rush in her ears. If she'd got it wrong, if she was having some kind of belated breakdown, then they'd won.

The filthy, murdering bastards had won. They'd got her, too.

A single tear worked its way down her cheek. 'I'm sorry, Angie. I should have fought them for you. I'm so, so sorry.'

16

'Hey, Wisey, you're a fucking mechanic.'

Matt took a second to compose a smile before glancing up from his desk. 'Christ, look what the cat dragged in.' He pushed back his chair and held out his hand to the man in the doorway. 'Dan the Man Carraro.'

Carraro ran a judgemental eye around the small room at the side of the mechanics bay. 'You left the cops for this? You *must* be nuts.' He laughed like he was a real blast.

'Suits me fine.' Matt sat on the edge of his desk and waited while Carraro smoothed down his tie, pushed his hands into his pockets. Matt had wondered who'd turn up. Had thought about it more than he'd wanted to. All the way to town this morning, his mind had kept going back to John Kruger and the wheels that would be turning. Bald Hill's single officer didn't have the resources or the skills to conduct a murder investigation. He'd call for extra uniforms from Dungog to help set up the crime scene and detectives from Newcastle would be sent to handle the investigation. Six months ago, Matt would have been the obvious first choice – head of the squad and former local. As Carraro eyed off trade magazines on top of the filing cabinet, Matt felt a certain sense of relief. The smart-arse knew how to do his job, which meant one less thing he had to feel guilty about, even if he couldn't escape it.

The rumours had started early. Someone at the post office said John's face had been smashed beyond recognition, his skull crushed. The cashier at the mini-mart said she'd heard there was no sign of a fight, that maybe he'd walked in on intruders. Reg, who ran the pub, who knew everything that happened from here to the Queensland border, said he had it on good authority there was no evidence of robbery, that the local cops thought it looked like someone had just walked right up to him and beaten him to a pulp, poor bastard.

After that piece of news, Matt had worked his arse off at the service station but cleaning and stacking and sorting and lifting hadn't stopped his brain from worming its way back to it. And the buzz had started up – the tick-tick in his head, the hum down his spine – that he got when he knew something big was happening. He used to think of it as instinct, some kind of intuitive adrenaline rush. But that was bullshit – he knew that now.

More like some egotistical urge to get in on the action. It was dangerous, it got people hurt. Killed. And he was mad as hell it was back.

'So what d'ya reckon?' Carraro said.

Matt shrugged, tried to make it look casual. He didn't want to be drawn in. 'I'm out of it, Dan.'

'Yeah, right. As if Matty Wiseman wants to take a back seat.'

Matt pushed himself off the desk and distractedly shuffled papers about as he spoke. 'No, seriously. I'm out of it.' He held up a bunch of bills with a tight fist. 'Got plenty to do here.'

A beat passed before Carraro pointed a finger at him like a gun. 'Hey, good one. You almost had me convinced. Wait till I tell the others.' He laughed loudly. It was hilarious. 'So what about this Kruger bloke?'

Shame and anger burned in Matt's chest. He didn't want to be asked what he thought. Didn't want to think about it. Any of it. 'Look,

I hardly knew him. His family knows my sister-in-law's family. Go ask them.'

'You're the guy who reckons he can *read* people. What's Kruger's story? What's the go with the builders?'

Matt tossed the papers back on the desk, crossed his arms over his chest, tried to contain his temper. 'You're the detective. You figure it out.'

'Come on. You know you *want* to.'

What Matt wanted was Dan the Man out of his office. 'Piss off, Carraro.' He said it with a tight smile as he took two strides across the room and got into his face in the doorway. Carraro backed out into the mechanics bay and Matt put a firm hand on his shoulder, turned him towards the exit. 'I told you, I'm out of it.'

'Hey, take it easy.' Carraro shrugged him off as he stepped into daylight. 'Don't kid yourself, Wiseman. You can't stay away from it.'

Matt followed him all the way to his car. 'Just leave me out.' He made it sound like a warning. He didn't want to be anywhere near the investigation. Didn't want to be tempted.

He watched from the driveway until the unmarked cop car disappeared down the street. Arsehole. He rubbed a hand through his hair, dragged it down his face, turned around and stopped in his tracks. Jodie Cramer was standing in the afternoon sun outside the mechanics bay, wearing a hot pair of sunglasses and knock-out jeans. He stood still for a second, thought his heart might've stopped.

'Everything okay?' she said.

How much had she heard? He hooked a look over his shoulder. 'Just my past catching up with me when I was stupid enough to think it was history.'

That seemed to amuse her. 'I know how that feels.'

There was something different about her this afternoon. The boldness was gone, as though whatever it was that held it in place had been sucker-punched. Maybe everyone was having a bad day today.

'Your car's not ready yet,' he said, nodding to where the vehicle was up on the hoist. 'You're earlier than I expected.'

He stood by the front bumper as she pushed her sunglasses up on her head and inspected the repairs. The paintwork was a mess where the dent had been beaten out and the headlight was still waiting to be replaced. She ran a hand over the scratched bonnet and looked over at him. He saw then that her eyes were a little puffy and kind of reddish around the rims, like she'd been rubbing them. Or crying.

'It looks better than I thought it would,' she said. 'How much longer do you think it'll be?'

'Dad said another hour or so. He's just gone up to the flat to take some medication.' He watched her check her watch. 'If you're in a hurry to get back, you can take the loan car for another night.'

She gave a short, sarcastic laugh. 'There's definitely no hurry.'

Should he ask? He didn't want to reduce her to tears. But then she didn't seem the type to go all girlie. 'So the Old Barn doesn't cut it as a B & B?'

'No, the barn's great. The company's a little . . . taxing.' She shrugged, tucked her hands into the pockets of her coat. 'You put four women in an isolated cabin and you gotta take a break some time.'

He thought of how she'd handled herself last night and the fear-less way she'd told him she'd chuck the rock at his car if she needed to and thought it seemed unlikely a spat was enough to jag the mood she was in. 'Sure.' It wasn't his business.

She walked back out to the driveway then turned around, like she'd had another thought. 'Hey, um, about this morning. I'm sorry if I was a bit abrupt. You've been really nice. Gone way beyond the call of duty, really. I guess I'm not the best company before a morning coffee.'

Her smile was more embarrassment than apology. Kind of cute for a tough girl. He thought briefly about the invoices he'd been about to tackle and how he hadn't thought about John Kruger since he'd been talking to her. 'You know what? I really need to take a break for a while. How about we do each other a favour and go get an *after-noon* coffee? The bakery in the main street does a mean cappuccino.'

She looked him straight in the eyes for a long moment then down at her feet. For a good five seconds, the toes of her leather boots seemed to hold her undivided attention. What the hell? He hadn't asked her to drive to Perth with him. When she finally lifted her face, her big eyes were dark and determined. 'Yeah, sure, coffee sounds good.'

Turning away from her to hit the button for the bay's automatic door, he tried not to smile too much. A hot babe takes an hour to decide whether you're worth a coffee break and you're overjoyed. Matt Wiseman, you *are* a desperate man. He fell into step beside her on the driveway, aware that she was walking with her arms crossed over her chest like she was worried her lungs might fall out.

'You can be my excuse for not stopping at the pub for something stronger,' he said.

'Maybe we *should* have something stronger.'

'Believe me, when life gets crappy, coffee is a much better road to take.' He'd been determined not to be a cliché – the cop who drinks his life away to avoid the truth. These days he only drank in company. It was harder to blow your brains out when someone was sitting next to you.

'Are you speaking from experience?'

'Let's just say I've had my fair share of hangovers. Today being no exception.'

'Coffee's great for that. Today being the proof.' She gave a shortened version of her low laugh.

Yeah, Jodie was an excellent distraction.

From a block away, he could see the two police cars still parked outside the pub. They'd been there a couple of hours, at least. John Kruger was a regular in town, so Matt guessed they were doing a door-to-door down the main street. No point canvassing neighbours for a possible witness when the nearest one is five kilometres away.

As they drew level with the pub, Jodie said, 'Are there usually this many police cars here on a Saturday afternoon?'

Don't get into it. 'No, they're up from Newcastle.'

She looked at him then back at the cars. 'Why are they here?'

He shrugged. 'There was an incident out of town last night.'

'What kind of incident?'

'A farmer was . . . found dead.'

'What kind of dead?'

Geez, another interrogation. 'Dead is dead. Does it matter?'

She glanced over her shoulder at the cop cars now behind them. 'They're *investigating* the death, aren't they?'

'Yeah.'

Her lips were pressed hard together, her shoulders suddenly upright and rigid, and her voice was low and grave when she spoke. 'It's a murder, isn't it?'

He frowned, not sure how to read her reaction. He'd expected horror – a hand to the mouth, a gasp of surprise, maybe – disbelief, sadness even. Not grim understanding. But he knew from experience, not everyone fitted the mould on how to react to shock and he should have guessed Jodie would come at it from a different angle. From what he'd seen so far, she came at everything from some unpredictable cue.

'Yeah, it's a murder.' He stopped walking. 'What are you having? Cappuccino?' He hooked a thumb at the bakery.

She pulled up a few steps in front of him, took a second to register what he was doing. 'What? Oh, right, cappuccino. Yes. Thanks.'

He opened the door, checked out her butt as she walked in ahead of him. Don't even think about it. She's got a mood swing like a ping-pong ball and she's *leaving tomorrow*. And you're a train wreck. You don't need any more debris on the rails. She stood in front of the counter, slid her hands into the back pocket of her jeans. But she did have a great jeans.

She turned around suddenly. 'How do you like it?'

He smiled. There was no way he was going to have the right answer to that question.

She waved a twenty-dollar note about. 'My shout. You've done more than enough already.'

'He always has a large take-out, double shot of coffee and full-cream milk,' Rhona answered for him from the other side of the counter. 'Predictable as ever, just the way I like my men.' She gave a bawdy laugh and Matt grinned. Rhona had been married to the same man for nearly thirty years and had worked in his bakery for more than that. Matt remembered buying cream buns from her on the way home from infants' school. She took Jodie's order and fronted up to the coffee machine like she was landing a plane. 'I'm so upset about John,' she said over the noise of the steam jet. 'How's your dad now? He didn't look too good when he was in this morning. I didn't want to say anything then but I hope that teacake he bought doesn't upset his diabetes.'

Matt smiled to himself. Eight weeks back home and he was still getting used to the country town no-privacy rule. 'He's fine, thanks, Rhona.'

'Have the police been to see you?' she asked.

Jodie's head snapped around to him. Had she heard Carraro's conversation? 'Yeah, we had a chat.'

'They were in here about half an hour ago,' Rhona said. 'They're talking to all the shop owners.'

'Is that right?' He tried to look interested in a vanilla slice under the counter.

'I told them they should be talking to you seeing as you're a detective and you know John and all.' She stopped pouring milk for a moment and looked at him. 'And I told them not to bother asking you all their questions. I said *they* should be asking *you* for advice.'

A hot tightness gripped Matt's chest and he had to force himself to breathe.

Rhona kept talking as she put lids on the cups and took money from Jodie but he wasn't listening. And he avoided Jodie's big, dark eyes watching him while Rhona rambled on. He wished they had gone to the pub for something stronger.

Jodie watched him as she passed through the door ahead of him, took half-a-dozen steps before saying anything. 'You're with the police?'

'Not *with* the police. I'm on leave.' He braced himself for another interrogation but she didn't ask anything more, just watched him for a moment then kept walking. He was more than thankful for that. At the corner, he stopped and pointed across the street to the park. A picnic table sat under a huge, old tree, its bare branches leaving it bathed in dappled afternoon light. 'Is that okay with you?'

'Perfect.'

They sat on bench seats either side of the table and sipped in silence for a minute or two, the winter sun warm on their faces. Matt watched a ute as it drove three sides of the park before turning away.

Jodie took her sunglasses off and laid them on the table. 'Where did it happen?'

The sun was behind her and he had to squint to look at her. 'What?'

'The murder. Was it near our barn?'

'No, it was on the other side of town, about forty k's out.'

She tapped her thumb against the side of her cup. There was a small frown between her eyebrows. 'Have the police arrested anyone?'

'No. That's why they're in town asking questions.'

'Do they have any suspects?'

Jeez, twenty questions again. 'I have no idea. I'm not involved in the investigation. Look, it's been a bad day. Do you mind if we change the subject?'

She shook her head a little. 'Yes, sure. I'm sorry. It must be very sad for everyone.'

He took a sip of coffee. Then she did. He heard a vehicle pass along the eastern edge of the park behind him and watched Jodie's eyes follow its progress left to right, then as it made the corner and came down the southern side.

JODIE WATCHED his eyes pick up the progress of the four-wheel drive as it passed them, the green-brown flecks of his irises angled slightly left as he watched the car into the distance. She liked his alertness. It made her feel like she wasn't the only one paying attention. Relaxed and alert, like last night outside the pub, like this morning on the track. Maybe it was a cop thing.

The news that he was a police officer had made her feel a whole lot better about her decision to have coffee with him. When he'd suggested it, her first impulse had been to say no – after the last twenty hours, everyone within a hundred kilometres of the barn seemed suspicious. But Hannah's words about symptoms of a breakdown were still ringing in her ears and even though she couldn't tell if he was a threat or she was delusional, she'd decided she needed to ask some questions and Matt was the only person she had to talk to.

Although now she wasn't so sure she wanted the answers.

A murder. Practically on their doorstep. Forty kilometres out of town. The barn was another thirty from town. Would a person drive seventy kilometres to the Old Barn after killing someone? The thought sent a chill down her spine and she pulled her coat a little tighter around her. No, she didn't want to change the subject. She had questions to ask.

Like whether the police had mentioned a car with a deep-throated engine and was the man she'd seen with Matt at the service station a policeman and what was it he'd said Matt couldn't stay away from? And if she went back to the barn and told the others there'd been a murder, would they pack up and leave like she wanted to now or would they escort her to a padded cell?

'So what have you been doing up at the barn?' Matt's voice cut into her thoughts. She looked up quickly, the suspicion at work again. Why would he want to know what a bunch of mothers were doing on a weekend in the country? He swirled the remains of the coffee in his cup then lifted his eyes to hers – relaxed, alert, interested. *Can't tell the difference between a come-on and an attempted abduction. He's a cop, Jodie. He's just being nice, you idiot.*

'Well, last night we ate a lot of chocolate and drank a lot of champagne so today we're pretty much fat and hung-over.'

He chuckled at that. 'So what have you been doing today?'

The morning's melodrama played in fast forward through her head. 'Nothing much. Just stuff.' She took a breath, told herself to tread carefully or he'd think she was nuts too.

'Are people allowed to camp on the properties around here?'

'You thinking of coming back with a tent?'

'God, no. It's just . . .' She stopped, tried to phrase it like a casual query. 'We saw some campers on the ridge last night and I . . . *we* wondered what they were doing. Not your average camper, obviously. They'd use a proper camping ground. I thought they might have been hunters or poachers or . . . whatever.'

He frowned a little.

'Do you get hunters around here?'

'Did you see them hunting?'

'If you mean did we see them actually pointing guns at the wildlife, then no.'

'They had guns?'

'No. No, they had torches.'

'They were pointing torches at the wildlife?'

'No, they were walking around with torches.' Of course they were, it was dark. 'I mean, we had a bit of an argument about what a couple of blokes would be doing camping out there in the middle of winter.'

He shrugged. 'They could work on the property and be sleeping near their worksite to save travelling out in the morning.'

Well, that seemed plausible. 'Would they be working at night?'

Matt took a moment to answer, watching Jodie as though he was considering her, not the question. 'There could be problems with animals damaging fences at night.'

Of course there could. It was a perfectly reasonable explanation for what she'd seen last night, wasn't it? The skin on the back of her neck felt hot. But what about today? The front door being open, the thud on the verandah. She turned her coffee cup slowly in her hands, thinking about what to ask next. 'What . . . Do you think . . . I mean . . .' She took a breath, looked up at him. 'How big do the possums get around here?'

One corner of his mouth turned up, just a little, like he wasn't sure if she was being funny. 'Where are you going with this?'

He didn't laugh but a hint a humour had crept into his voice. One that said 'what the fuck is she talking about?' Then she knew she wasn't going to ask any more questions – she didn't want to see that look in his eyes, too. The same one in the eyes of the girls back at the barn. Especially after the way he'd looked at her right up until this moment – like she had a clue, like she wasn't just a middle-aged single mother, like there was something in her damaged self that was worth taking a second look at. It had been a long time since anyone had looked at her like that and right now, with everything suddenly crystal clear, she needed to hang onto that.

Because she saw it now. How she'd imagined everything. How there was a rational explanation for it all – torches, farm workers, damaged fences. And she saw how the flashback must have sparked her paranoia. That maybe Hannah was right, that she was teetering on a steep and slippery slope to some kind of breakdown.

'Actually, I'm not going anywhere with it. Just, you know, making conversation.' She ran a hand through her hair, picked up her cup and tipped it way back to finish the dregs of her coffee, hoping it would hide the embarrassed flush on her cheeks. 'Anyway,' she said, looking around for something else to talk about. 'It's really nice here. I've never been to Bald Hill before. I'll have to bring the kids out some time.' The what-the-fuck look was still there in his eyes so she stood up, wanting to go, feeling like a fool. 'Do you think my car will be ready now?'

She pushed her hands into her pockets while he watched her for a long moment. 'If it's not, it'll be close.'

As they walked back to the station, he asked about her kids and her job, whether she had a husband waiting for her back home. He said he lived with his dad above the station, joked that it wasn't as pathetic as it sounded. She was flattered at the singles questions, the kind people asked when they were checking out the territory, working out how much baggage a person had. She should probably tell him she had so much baggage she was sinking under the weight of it. But she figured she didn't have to. When she drove off in her battered car, he'd remember the what-the-fuck moment and figure it out for himself. As far as she could tell, it's what most men did when they met her.

'Thanks, again,' she said as she started her car. 'I'm sorry about your friend. I hope your weekend gets better.'

'Yours, too.' He smiled and she let her eyes linger on him for a moment. She liked his smile. And his eyes.

She turned the car around on the driveway and waved briefly as she drove off. She liked a lot about him. And she wondered, as she did on occasion, what different decisions she might make in her life if she hadn't had a knife plunged into her belly at the age of seventeen.

17

J odie stopped at the mini-market to buy four more steaks for dinner, wondering where she'd left the other ones. It was cold now but she cracked the window open as she drove out of town, worried she might fall asleep at the wheel. The adrenaline rush of fear and anxiety she'd been riding for almost twenty-four hours had caught up with her. She was exhausted and, sitting in the warm car, painfully aware that it was more than likely the result of her own demented imagination, she was overwhelmed with a bone-aching, head-pounding tiredness. She imagined slipping between the crisp, white sheets on her bed at the barn and drifting into a deep, dreamless sleep – and let out a long, tired sigh, knowing it wasn't going to happen.

She had to sort things out with Louise and Hannah and Corrine. She had to apologise for her behaviour and the awful things she'd said before she stormed out. She wasn't looking forward to rehashing everything – it was tough enough admitting to herself she had a problem without having to explain out loud that three filthy, sadistic men were still holding her hostage, eighteen years after she'd torn the ropes off her wrists.

Tired as she was, she had to cook dinner, too. It was her turn and even though she was pretty sure the others wouldn't hold her to it under the circumstances, she wanted to. Like a make-up meal.

And she'd have to find a way of managing the anxiety that had lodged inside her. Even though she understood it was her imagination, the sense of fear was still there, burning in her gut like indigestion. She guessed a doctor would want to talk to her about that, probably give her some pills to help deal with it – she'd think about whether she wanted to go down that road later – but none of that was going to fix it tonight.

It was almost five o'clock when she got back to the barn and the winter sun was well on its way down. A long, distorted shadow of the barn stretched across the gravel parking pad out front. A light was on in the main room and the glow from the two windows spilled onto the deck.

She parked nose-in to the house and took a few deep breaths before gathering up her handbag and the parcel of meat and stepping into the cold evening air. Halfway up the front steps, she stopped, frowned. The voices inside sounded wrong. She took the last two stairs and listened from the edge of the deck. Corrine's laugh was a girlie giggle and Jodie guessed the champagne was flowing again. Louise said something she couldn't catch and Hannah chuckled. There was silence for a couple of seconds then the muted voice of a man said, 'I just love what you've done with the place.'

The hairs on Jodie's arms stood up. Despite the fact she'd just driven thirty kilometres convinced her fear was a delusion, the anxiety in her stomach welled up and squeezed the air out of her lungs. Whose voice was that?

She stood in the shadows of the early evening for almost a minute, trying to breathe, wondering what was going on in there. Get a grip, Jodie. Get a goddamn grip. No one inside sounded the least bit worried. Stop being so bloody paranoid. She rubbed her hands down her jeans, took the four steps to the front door and pushed it open.

The big, main room was bathed in soft lamplight, a log burned gently in the fireplace, an opened bottle of wine was on the coffee table and no one was there. Voices drifted up the hallway – male and female. They're in the bedroom? Then Louise stepped in from the hall.

'Jodie.' She looked relieved and concerned and unsure all at once. 'Are you okay?'

'I'm sorry about . . . I'm fine. I've got my car back.' She didn't want to get into her apology yet, not when there were other people in the barn. 'Who's here?'

Lou ignored her question, walked over and hugged her. She had a glass of wine in one hand and Jodie could feel it press into her back as Louise spoke in her ear. 'You were gone for so long. I thought you might have driven home. I'm really, really sorry. Are you sure you're all right?'

'She's back,' Jodie heard Hannah say from the hallway and her tone suggested she wouldn't be running up for a group hug.

Jodie glanced across the room as Louise stepped away and saw Corrine limp into the room behind Hannah.

'I told you she'd be back,' Corrine said but Jodie's eyes were on the man leaning against the doorframe.

Short-cropped dark hair, work-style shirt, jeans, solid boots, vaguely familiar – or perhaps just another version of almost every other man she'd seen in Bald Hill. He had one arm out, leaning on the jamb, filling the doorway – casual, comfortable. Cocky. The smile on his face made her stomach tighten. She looked around at everyone else in the room. They were holding glasses of wine. So was he. He lifted it to his lips and watched her over the top. No one was worried, Jodie. Don't be crazy.

'This is our friend Jodie,' Hannah said to him. Hannah smiled at Jodie, eyebrows raised. 'Everything okay, Jode?' She spoke the way you do to the kids in front of guests, an 'I'm interested but can we deal with it later' tone of voice.

'I'm fine. We have a guest, I see.' She copied Hannah's tone, smiling and meaning, 'Who the hell is he?'

Hannah looked back at him. 'Two, actually. Travis and Kane lived in this place when they were kids. They were just driving through and they didn't know the place had been done up so we're giving them a bit of a guided tour.'

The man in the doorway lifted his glass in a salute and sauntered into the room. She saw then there was someone behind him. Maybe she *was* crazy. Maybe she'd always been crazy because, flashback or no flashback, she would never have let two strangers into an isolated B & B late in the day for a bit of sightseeing and a chilled glass of chardonnay. The second man stepped into the room and her heart stopped.

Blond crew cut, broad beefy shoulders, red-checked shirt, pale eyes. It was the creep from the pub. The one who'd pinned her against the wall.

She took a pace back, wanted to yell it out loud but he was smiling. For one brief moment, the smile was aimed right at her then it morphed into an all-inclusive, nice-to-be-here grin. The aggression from last night wasn't there; he was polite, making nice. So was the other guy. So was everyone. Sweat prickled at her spine. She watched them, rooted to the spot, as they wandered back through the room. The girls took a sofa each, the guy from the pub rested an elbow on the mantelpiece, the other one sat cosily next to Corrine.

'Get yourself a glass, Jodie,' Corrine called cheerily across the room. Jodie could tell she'd had one too many already.

'Actually, you can get another bottle while you're at it.' Hannah smiled, holding up the first one. 'This one's almost empty.'

Jodie moved her gaze from Corrine to Hannah to Louise and back to the two men on either side of the fire. She didn't know what to make of it. Anxiety was burning a hole in her stomach and her feet felt like they were rooted to the ground but everyone else in the room seemed entirely comfortable. Having a lovely time. The guy from the pub watched her across the room. The one on the sofa turned his head and did the same.

'Jodie?' Louise was looking at her, too. So were Hannah and Corrine.

They'd been here before – Jodie freaked out, everyone else mystified. She realised she was still standing at the front door, meat parcel and handbag clutched to her chest.

Hannah's words pulsed in her head. *Symptoms of some kind of breakdown.* But she had good reason to be worried this time.

Didn't she?

That guy had groped her at the pub. The others couldn't know that, they hadn't seen it happen. She needed to tell them. And they needed to get both men out. She wanted to fling open the front door, tell them to fuck off and not to come back. She shook her head. Pull it together, Jodie. No one will believe you if you go nuts.

'Wine. Yeah, sure. A wine.' She walked stiffly to the kitchen, put her stuff on the island bar, opened and closed cupboards, searching for a glass, trying to figure out how to let the girls know who he was.

'The glassware is beside the fridge, Jodie.'

She saw Hannah twisted around on her sofa, frowning at her.

Hannah wasn't her first choice to explain the situation to but she had eye contact with her and there wasn't time to wait to get Louise's attention. She lifted her chin and cocked her head in a come-over-here gesture. Hannah frowned impatiently. She did it a second time with a more pointed expression and this time Hannah rolled her eyes but put her wineglass on the coffee table.

'I think we need some food with the wine,' Hannah said and as she moved towards the kitchen, the man next to Corrine, the dark-haired one, put his glass on the table and stood up, watching Jodie.

Her mouth went dry. That small move, from sitting to standing, felt like a threat. It shouldn't, she told herself, he was just getting up. But it did.

As Hannah moved past her to the fridge, Jodie looked from one man to the other. They were standing side by side now, the fireplace between them. Corrine was talking, blathering on, tipsy. The blond guy from the pub, Kane, was watching Corrine with eyes so pale that from across the room they appeared almost colourless. Travis, the dark-haired one, was watching Jodie. Pub Guy's shirt was tucked into work-style trousers, the other's was hanging loosely over jeans. They both had their hands in their pockets. Feet apart, chins angled forward. Something snagged in Jodie's gut. Two stocky bodies, short necks, thick shoulders pushed slightly forward as though the bulk of their muscle stopped them standing completely upright. Like mirror images of each other.

Oh, shit. They were the two guys from last night. The ones in the dark. At the car. She was sure of it. And she wished to God she had the tyre iron handy.

'What did you want?' Hannah put cheese and olives on the bench. 'Jodie!' Jodie jumped, looked down to the spot on the bench Hannah was frowning at, where her own hands had a white-knuckled grip on the edge of the marble. She let go, grabbed her friend's arm, relieved that she'd got Hannah's attention. She'd seen them last night, too. 'What are *they* doing here?'

Hannah shucked her hand off. 'Keep your voice down.'

Jodie turned her back to the room and leaned close. 'They're the men from last night. The ones out at the car.'

Hannah stepped away from her. 'Don't be ridiculous. They said they were just passing through.' She unwrapped a wedge of cheese, placed it on a plate, not evening bothering to look up.

'Hannah. It's them. *Look.*'

She sighed and tipped olives into a bowl before lifting her head to glance at the fireplace. 'I don't know what you're talking about.'

Jodie watched them over her shoulder. Kane was talking about the barn – rats in the rafters, snakes in summer. It must have been a dump back then. The dark-haired one turned towards her as if he'd heard them talking. She leaned towards Hannah again. 'It's them. It's *definitely* them. And the blond one is the guy who harassed me at the pub last night.' Hannah abruptly pushed away, took a wineglass out of a cupboard and put it down hard on the bench in front of Jodie. 'Have a drink, for God's sake.'

'What? No. We have to get them out of here.'

Hannah seemed to be making an effort to stay calm. 'Look, Jodie, I don't know what going on with you, but if you have to lose your mind can you do it somewhere else for a while? See if you can *not* insult our guests and embarrass the rest of us.'

Jodie straightened, stiffened, as though a brick wall had just appeared in front of her face and she'd had to pull up short. She couldn't remember the last time she'd been slapped down quite so effectively. She watched silently as Hannah finished her plate arrangement, scattered crackers around and found a cheese knife.

Lose her mind?

The whirl of fear and urgency inside her stilled suddenly and she felt her mouth drop open. Was this the breakdown Hannah had predicted? Her hands were sweating, her knees shaking, blood was pounding in her head. The fear felt real, the situation felt all wrong – but now she wasn't sure. She looked around. It wasn't just Hannah. No one else seemed in the least perturbed. She swallowed, the tiredness she'd felt in the car swept over her again and tears pricked at her eyes.

They did look like the men by the car last night but Hannah didn't see it. Be honest, Jodie, how much could you see out there? They were really just shadowy figures in thick coats and caps. She wiped a hand over her face, ran it through her hair. The one on the right had definitely breathed beer fumes in her face last night. But hadn't that happened just after the flashback? When she was off balance, scared out of her wits. Maybe he hadn't been as threatening as she'd thought. Maybe she'd jammed her hands into his stomach and stomped his foot without cause.

The other one was angled a little towards the kitchen now, attention focused on her across the room. His face was hard and expressionless, his jaw squared, his eyes unwavering in the way they watched her. Or was she imagining that, too? Whether it was real or imagined, it made her skin crawl.

Without taking her eyes off him, she put a hand on Hannah's arm, squeezed it firmly. She wanted Hannah to study him properly, needed to see her reaction.

'Have a drink, Jodie.' Hannah brushed off her hand and picked up the plate. 'Have a lot to drink, would you? Please.' She pushed past her into the room. 'Cheese and crackers anyone? Jodie, bring a bottle with you.'

Oh God, she was cracking up. Eighteen years after that knife was thrust into her, she was bleeding out. Hannah was right. She needed a drink.

She got a bottle from the fridge, poured wine into the glass, her hands shaking so much she slopped it onto the floor. She carried both across the room, glad to have something solid – real – in her hands. She could have done as Hannah suggested, gone to the bedroom to lose her mind out of sight, but she didn't want to be alone, didn't want to sit on the bed having no clue what was real and what wasn't. So she stood beside Louise who was perched on the arm of the sofa – furthest from the fire, closest to the front door – and took a gulp of wine. It tasted like vinegar but she made herself take another. Hold yourself together, Jodie. Just try to figure it out. See if you're sane enough to do that.

Travis, the one who kept watching her, dropped his eyes at last and helped himself to cheese and a cracker. As he chewed, his eyes slid around the room. Up close, Jodie saw they were blue, navy, like solid discs, as dark as the other guy's were pale, and they moved from the front door to the kitchen to the glass at the back of the barn to the women around the U of sofas. 'So is it just the four of you up here?' he asked.

'Yes, just us,' Corrine said. 'Having a bit of girl-time.'

'Is that right?'

'Oh yes, we go away like this every year. Leave the kids and husbands behind. Have a ball, don't we, girls?'

Hannah nodded, Lou smiled in agreement. Jodie swallowed hard.

Travis used his wineglass to point across the room. 'We saw what you ladies have got in your fridge there. Thought you might be waiting for friends.'

'Oh no, we just like to eat well,' Corrine laughed, a little embarrassed, a little proud of their catering abilities.

He flicked a look at the blond guy. 'So you won't have any problems feeding a couple of extras then.'

There was a beat of silence, as though the room was considering the way he'd phrased it. Jodie concentrated on breathing in and out. It felt wrong but apparently her instincts were nothing to go by.

'Oh, hey, don't worry. We won't eat much, will we, Kane?'

The one from the pub, Kane, grinned like their food consumption was an inside joke. 'Nah, me and Travis won't eat much.'

'We had a good lunch, didn't we?'

'Sure did.'

'Cooked up a couple of nice little steaks. Two each.' Travis looked at the four of them in turn, one side of his mouth turned up in a sly smile. 'Cooked up real nice, they did.'

Jodie went cold. *Four* steaks?

'Yeah, real nice,' Kane said.

'Not big enough to feed a small dog. Probably not as good as you girls would cook 'em but you can make up for that, can't they, Kane?' Kane laughed. A nasty, mocking sound.

Jodie looked quickly at her friends. Louise was wearing a polite, uncertain smile. Hannah had raised an eyebrow. Corrine tucked a strand of hair behind her ear, swinging her sprained ankle back and forth, smiling coyly, tipsy.

'So what's for dinner?' Travis grinned like he was cute, like his cuteness would get him a free feed. Maybe it would. Corrine was tittering. Hannah's head was cocked to one side, undecided.

Kane laughed again. 'Got any more steaks?'

The spike of fear that shot though Jodie was like an electric current. It *was* them. In the house. This afternoon. Words were tumbling out before she could stop them. 'It was you. You took our steaks. You came in here and took our steaks?'

'For God's sake.'

'Jodie?'

'Why are you being such a bitch?'

The girls had spoken together, on cue, like a joint rebuke. She felt

Louise's hand on her leg and sensed Hannah and Corrine staring at her across the room but all she saw were Travis's unwavering eyes on her and the amusement on his ugly mouth.

Beside him, Kane finished his wine, put the glass on the coffee table and looked up at Jodie. 'You *are* a bitch.'

18

J odie felt the tension shift. Louise and Hannah redirected their focus to Kane, anger overlaid now with apprehension. Only Corrine let it slide.

'Oh, dear, that's not nice,' she said to him. 'I can call her a bitch but you can't.'

Kane kept his eyes on Jodie. 'You're the prickteaser from the pub.'

Jodie's heart pounded. She was angry as well as frightened now. She had no idea what her friends were thinking, couldn't pull her eyes away from him to gauge it, but it didn't matter. Breakdown or no breakdown, no one spoke to her like that. 'You can leave now.'

'Oh, come on, Jodie. Can't you take a joke?' Corrine tittered.

'No, I can't and they need to leave.'

Kane smiled slowly. 'But we haven't had our dinner yet.'

No one moved. Fear squeezed her chest. If they chose not to leave, how would she get them out.

'Fuck dinner.' Kane stepped casually out of the U of sofas.

From the corner of her eye, she saw Travis do the same from the other side of the fire.

'Oh, dear. That's not nice,' Kane said, smiling, copying Corrine's words as he walked behind Hannah.

Jodie moved back a pace. She looked quickly across the room, saw Travis moving behind Corrine. She took another step and stood behind Louise, the wine bottle and glass still in her hands.

Kane stopped a couple of metres from her, smiled, like they were great mates, like she hadn't just told him to fuck off. His pale eyes were flat and cold. 'Come on, Jodie.'

'A meal isn't too much to ask, is it?' Her head swung around as Travis spoke. 'Then we'll get our stuff and get out of here.'

Kane let his arms drop to his sides, took a step closer. 'Unless you're interested in a bit more fun.'

'Look,' Louise stood up. 'I think...'

Jodie didn't hear what she said. It was just background noise as she reversed even further, her eyes moving between Kane and Travis. They took a couple more steps towards her, still smiling, genial. They were solid, muscular men. It felt threatening. But she wasn't sure.

Then Kane laughed. Not like he thought it was funny or awkward, not like he might if he was trying to take the heat out of the situation. He laughed *at* her. She saw him flick a look at Travis and two thoughts flashed through her head – she was right and it was too late.

Her fingers tightened on the wine bottle. She had a weapon in her hand. She could defend herself. But she'd hesitated too long. As she raised the bottle, Travis smacked her hard across the face with the back of his hand.

An explosion went off in her head. Her feet came off the floor and she dropped hard. Pain shot up her arm, the air was knocked out of her lungs. It took a second for her to think past the burning on her face, the roar in her ears, the fact she was sprawled on the timber desperate to draw breath. She opened her eyes, saw two dirt-crusted workboots and jerked her head up. A second later she moved with a speed she hadn't thought possible the moment before.

Travis had a gun and he was pointing it at her face.

It was a handgun and it looked huge. He must have had it the whole time. Did they both have guns? She wanted to see if Kane was pointing a gun at her too, but all she could do was scrabble backwards, reverse crawling, her shoes slipping on the polished timber, something sharp crushing under the palm of her hand. She kept going until the wall was at her back, her knees on her chest and the heels of her boots pressed into the right angle between the floor and the skirting board. Her breath came in short, sharp gasps as Travis lowered the weapon and touched the cold metal to the cheekbone he'd just hit.

Her body went still. She closed her eyes. And she was no longer in the barn. She was seventeen again. Waiting to die.

It wasn't her life that flashed before her eyes but the night she'd waited for death. As though the vacuum pack that had compressed those memories into a tight, almost unreachable package had been ripped wide open. A strobe of pictures and sounds flashed through her head. Angela's terrified eyes. Cruel laughter. Feet scuffling on a gravel path. Dirt grazing her face. Brutal, guttural grunting. Angie sobbing. *Run, Jodie, run.* The pounding on her stomach. Blood dripping on her bare feet.

'Fucking bitch!' Kane shouted the words inches from her face, the wet spray of spit on her face dragging her from the nightmare of her past to the nightmare she was in. She opened her mouth and air rushed in on a huge gasp. There was movement close by. She squeezed her eyes tighter, hearing for the first time Corrine screaming, and waiting for another blow. Or for the shot that would rip her head apart.

'Get the others,' Travis said.

There was an edge of excitement to Kane's voice. 'Jesus fucking . . .'

'*Get the others*,' Travis bawled, pushing the gun harder into her bruised cheek.

No. *No.* 'No!' She tried to shout the word but it came out as barely more than a whisper. Memories flashed in her head. Louise and Hannah and Corrine mixed up with Angie and the blood and the terror.

She forced her eyes open.

The gun was silver with a black handle and pushed so hard into the flesh of her face that the bulge of her cheek half blocked the vision from her left eye. She could smell Travis's sweat and stale cigarette smoke and alcohol, something a whole lot stronger than their white wine. Whatever it was, he'd drunk enough to make his clothes reek of it. And now he had a gun on her face. Stone-cold fear lodged itself in her chest. She made herself look past it, to find her friends.

Pressed to the wall somewhere between the front door and the hallway, Jodie could see Louise and Hannah over the top of a sofa, huddled together near the fireplace, in the safety of the U of furniture. She couldn't see Corrine but as Kane moved across the room towards them, Louise stepped forward and pulled her up off the floor, dragging her limping to where they stood.

Jodie watched helpless as Kane stormed towards them. They clung to each other, shrinking past the mantelpiece, up against the window. Louise held out a hand. 'No,' she cried.

Kane grabbed a handful of Corrine's long hair and pulled so hard her head snapped sideways. She shrieked, stumbled forward to the floor, disappeared from Jodie's view again. Hannah bent to help her but Kane shoved her roughly away.

'Get over there!' he yelled. He pushed Louise in the back. 'Move!' He reached down and Corrine let out a short, sharp scream. 'Get up, bitch!'

Louise and Hannah helped Corrine to her feet then the three of them hurried forward, trying to keep clear of Kane. He shoved Louise again and she staggered, taking the other two with her as she fell.

Kane rammed his heel into her shin. 'Get over by the wall.'

Lou held her leg, shuffled back, the other two pulling her in by the arms, by the collar of her shirt. Then Jodie couldn't see them. They were right beside her, a metre away, pressed in tight against the wall but she couldn't see them. Her head was pinned to the wall, face forward, the gun on her cheek like a tack holding a page to a corkboard.

She wanted to see them. Wanted to fill her vision with them before she died. The argument didn't matter now. They were her best friends. She rolled her eyes as far as she could to the right, till the muscles behind them felt like they'd tear. Corrine was crying, mascara running down her cheeks, her face crumpled and trembling. Hannah was ghostly pale and she looked back at Jodie with a sickening mix of horror and realisation. Louise was still, frozen, knees hugged to her chest, gripping the shin Kane had kicked, her green eyes wide open and moving in short, sharp jerks from the gun to its owner and back again.

Jodie's vision blurred with tears. She blinked hard and fast, frightened of the images in her head. Frightened of the ones in front of her. She should have ignored Hannah. She should have done something before it got to this. She'd trained for this, taught others what to do. Shit, shit, shit. Think, Jodie. What are you meant to do? She should know what to do. She breathed hard through her nose. Her cheek hurt. She wanted to cry. Focus, Jodie. But she couldn't see past the horror replaying in her mind or the fear that paralysed her. Travis didn't need a gun to hold her against the wall. She couldn't move if she tried.

'Four bitches!' Kane was strutting back and forth in front of them, hyped up, a wild energy coming off him. 'We've got our work cut out for us now, bro.'

Bro? Were they brothers? Or was it street slang, like the boys at school used? She wanted to think about it, figure it out but she couldn't get two thoughts in line. It was all happening too fast. Beside her, one of the girls whimpered and Corrine let out a long, wailing sob.

'Shut up!' Travis yelled at Corrine, pushing the hard metal further into Jodie's cheek. One of the others shushed her urgently and she fell silent. He adjusted his stance, moved over Jodie a little more, brought his other hand up to the handle of the gun in a double-fisted hold. 'Find something to tie them with.'

Kane bounced from one foot to the other. 'It's no fun if they don't fight.'

'We tie them then we do what we came for.' He shot Kane a brief, hard look. 'Move!'

Still leering, Kane turned and headed towards the kitchen.

'And find something better to drink than this wine shit,' Travis called.

Kane disappeared from Jodie's field of view. He was going to tie them up. Deep in her belly, something shifted, like the epicentre of an earthquake, and her body shook violently.

'What do you want?' Louise's voice was clear and firm and angry.

'Shut up,' Travis snapped.

Jodie looked up, past the muzzle of the gun, along the powerful arm that held it, saw Travis's dark eyes dart tensely to the other side of the room and back.

'There's nothing valuable here. We just came for the weekend,' Louise said. She was still hugging her legs to her chest, her eyes were wide but her lips were pressed tight.

'Shut up, bitch.'

'We would've given you all the damn food if you'd asked nicely.' Louise's voice sounded dangerously sarcastic. One of the other girls whispered a shhh.

The side of Travis's mouth turned up in a nasty half-grin. 'Oh, we're not just after food, ladies. We're going to take whatever we goddamn want. And you're not going to enjoy it. All you need to know is that you chose the wrong fucking weekend to come here.'

Jodie's spine turned to liquid. The barn was her idea. An isolated cabin on top of a hill, kilometres from anywhere and anyone. She should have known better. This was her fault.

'Hey, Trav,' Kane called from the other side of the room. 'I found their phones.' Jodie swung her eyes to the right. Kane must be at the island bar. She couldn't see him from where she sat but Hannah in her obsessive-compulsive tidying had put the phones in a bowl on the marble bench last night after they'd discovered there was no reception. They were all gone after breakfast when Jodie put hers back in her bag. Maybe the girls had walked down to the road to call home when she was out and Hannah had tidied up again. Kane came back, the mobiles in his hands.

'There's only three,' Travis said. 'Whose is missing?' He looked over at Louise, Hannah and Corrine then back at Jodie. '*Whose is missing?*'

Oh God, it was hers. It was in her handbag. She tried to open her mouth to say something, to own up to it. But there was a gun pressed to her face. Would he just pull the trigger if she said 'it's mine'? Would they be her last words?

19

A phone clattered to the floor. 'Whose is this?' Kane said.

'It's mine,' Corrine's voice was tiny. Unlike the phone with its oversized six-inch screen and fake jewel-encrusted cover.

'Nice,' he said and smashed it with his heel.

Jodie flinched at the casual destruction. It felt like a demonstration of intent.

'Whose is this?' He dropped a sensible, silicone-cased one on the floor.

'Mine,' Hannah said.

He slammed his boot down and ground the ball of his foot into the debris. 'Whose is this shit-box?' He dropped a cheap model with a starburst crack in the screen.

No one spoke. Jodie looked at Louise. She was staring at Kane, eyes blazing, mouth set.

Jodie took a deep breath, squeezed her eyes shut and thanked whoever it was that gave her a friend like Lou. 'It's Louise's.'

In the moment Kane broke it apart, Travis changed the angle of his gun and pushed so hard on Jodie's bruised cheek that she cried out in pain. He bent to her face and shouted.

'Did you think we wouldn't figure it out, you stupid bitch? Where's your phone?'

'In . . . in my bag. My handbag.'

'Where?'

She couldn't think where she'd left it. She swung her eyes towards the front door. It wasn't there.

'*Where?*'

'I . . . I . . . on the bench. On the kitchen bench.'

'Get it,' he told Kane. Over at the bench, Kane up-ended the bag and the contents spilled across the floor. Purse, keys, lipstick, camera, loose change, a couple of tampons. No phone.

A small choking sound escaped her lips.

'*Where's your phone?*' Travis shouted.

'I . . . I don't know.'

'Where?'

'I put it there this . . .'

'Where?'

'It was there when . . .'

'*Where?*'

'I don't know. *I don't know.* If it's not in my bag, I don't know where it is. Maybe it fell out. It must have fallen out. It might be in the car. I don't know.' Travis loomed over her, dropped one hand from his gun grip, raised the weapon as though he was readying to
...

'I DON'T KNOW! *I don't fucking know.*'

Kane laughed, bouncing from foot to foot. 'I think she doesn't know, bro.'

Travis lowered his elbow and the pressure eased a little on her cheek. 'If that phone turns up later, I'll put a hole in your head. You got that?'

Tears stung Jodie's eyes. 'Yep. Sure. It won't. I promise.'

'Kane, did you find something to tie them with?' Travis said, without taking his eyes off her.

'No.'

He turned and looked at Kane. Thick veins down the side of his neck were swollen with anger. 'Then do it,' he shouted. 'And find me something to drink.'

Jodie watched Travis follow Kane with his eyes. She pushed her tongue around her mouth, feeling bruising on the inside of her cheek and the metallic taste of blood. Her legs ached from squatting against the wall. Her ribs throbbed. The palm of one hand burned. And she was so scared she couldn't think straight. On the other side of the room, out of sight, Kane knocked something large and heavy over.

Louise's voice cut into their terrified silence. 'Let Hannah look at her hand. She's a nurse.'

Jodie rolled her eyes to her. What was she doing? The guy was ready to put a bullet into her brain. What did he care about someone's hand?

'There's glass in it. I can see it from here,' Louise said, releasing her legs from her arms.

'Move again and I'll pull the trigger.'

'Just let her take the glass out.'

'Shut up!'

'She's going to bleed all over you if the glass doesn't come out.'

Jodie felt a rush of heat to her face. One of the girls was hurt. And Lou was going to get herself shot. Or Jodie shot.

'I've got a wad of tissues in my pocket,' Louise pushed.

'Shut up, Louise,' Corrine hissed.

'She'll just get the glass out, give her the tissues and sit back down again. It'll take five seconds. The blood on your jeans would just look like mud then. You know, when you leave.'

Jodie rolled her eyes to the other side and saw his jeans. There was a dark splotch at the front, below the knee. Suspended above it was her left hand. It was red with blood.

Her body jerked as though she'd been zapped by electricity. She saw her hands on another night. In the headlights of a car. Wet and red, blood dripping through her fingers onto her bare feet.

'God. No.' She pressed both hands to her stomach, hard, pulling in the sides, pushing against the muscles under the flesh. She couldn't look down. Her head was still jammed against the wall by his gun. How much blood was there? When had he cut her? She felt pain. A sharp, intense burning. In her stomach. No. In her hand.

'Five seconds,' Louise said, loud and urgent.

Then Hannah was beside her, trying to take her hand away from her stomach. Jodie pulled against her. 'No. I need to keep the pressure on.'

'It's your hand, Jodie. There's glass in your *hand*.'

'What?' She let Hannah take her hand and spread her fingers open. A piece of glass protruded from her palm just below the base of the thumb. It looked like one of Corrine's acrylic nails, as though she'd pointed at the back of Jodie's hand and accidentally pushed it all the way through. Where had it come from? Her eyes slid around, saw on the floor the bottle of wine on its side, a wet stain around it and the shattered pieces of her wineglass. She must have fallen on it.

Then her head was jammed harder against the wall, the side of her mouth pushed up by the muzzle of the gun.

'Five seconds are up.'

'Oh, God.' Hannah was pale, her lips scrunched together, tears in her eyes.

'Do it, Hannah!' Louise yelled.

Hannah bent her head, tried to grip the glass between her thumb and index finger. She was shaking, trembling so hard she couldn't get the sliver between her fingertips. Jodie had never seen Hannah shake. Not even when her own daughter Chelsea ran through Lou's glass door and was cut to pieces. But she was shaking now.

'Fuck!' Jodie snapped her hand away as the glass came out with a sharp sting. She held it up to her face, looked at it along the side of the gun, saw a bubble of blood brew quickly from the hole and run down her wrist.

Travis shoved his foot into Hannah's shoulder, knocking her away. 'Time's up.'

'Bastard!' Louise yelled as Hannah scrabbled to her knees and pushed a wad of tissues into Jodie's hand.

'Get over there,' Travis shouted. 'And *you*,' he glared at Louise, 'keep your fucking mouth shut.'

'I know what'd shut her up.' Kane was back and he'd cupped his hand around his crutch. 'She won't talk with this in her mouth.'

Oh, God, it was starting. Their backs were against the wall. There was nowhere to run. They were going to be raped then die. Jodie's lungs felt as though her chest had been crushed. She squeezed her eyes shut, heard a brutal, guttural grunting from somewhere inside her head.

'Tie them,' Travis said.

She opened her eyes and her fear took on a new, terrifying edge.

Kane stood in front of the others with a bottle of bourbon, the one Lou had brought from home. In his other hand was a bundle of curtain tie-backs. He took a long gulp from the bottle, held it out to Travis then stretched the white, twisted-satin cords between both hands and snapped them straight. He leered at Louise and Hannah. 'You two. Get up.'

Jodie watched with growing panic as Louise's left hand was bound to Hannah's right, the satiny rope wrapped around and around then knotted tightly. 'You,' he said to Corrine. The skin on Jodie's wrists burned with the memory of another rope and she shook uncontrollably as Corrine's hand was tied to Louise's. When Kane turned to Jodie, panic roared.

'No. No!' she screamed. She pulled her hands behind her, tried to shake her head free of the gun pushed into her cheek. Kane stood in front of her, shouted.

'No!' she yelled. The tie-back filled her vision. The smooth, white cord hanging loosely through Kane's meaty fist, a soft, feathery tassel swinging on one end. The sight of it pushed a surge of hot blood through her, making her recoil with every ounce of energy she had. She forced her head sideways, rolling her skull along the wall. Travis shouted, pushed the gun into her ear, mashing the other one against the wall. She squeezed her eyes tight, heard a loud wail come from deep inside her.

Someone grabbed her arm, yanked her to her feet. It was Kane and she pulled against him as he tried to drag her over to the others.

'Nooo!' They were shouting. Her. Travis and Kane. Yelling at her.

Screaming. Her friends were screaming. But she kept pulling back. Her shoulder was tearing, it was going to pop out of its socket. Something inside was telling her to fight but she didn't. Couldn't think how. Could only think about getting away from the rope. It was all over if she was tied up.

She was wrong. It was over when Travis slammed his elbow into her stomach. She went straight down, bent in the middle, gagging for air. Above her, the girls were screaming. Louise was yelling a stream of abuse that, even curled in a foetal position on the floor, made Jodie wonder where she'd learned to cuss like that. Then she was being dragged along the timber boards. One hand was pulled above her head, slapped against Corrine's and the smooth cord wrapped around both. Kane sprayed spittle in her face as he called her foul names, told her what he was going to do to her but the words meant nothing to the sight of the cord being wrapped over the fine, pale scars left by that other rope. He tied her to Hannah, secured them in a circle, facing outwards, like a human X, no one able to move without taking three others with them.

Jodie tried to stand, tried not to be the one that made them more vulnerable. But she couldn't. Her knees collapsed. She banged her head against Hannah's hip, wrenched her wrist painfully around Corrine's as she went down. The others struggled around her, staggering and lurching about, trying to stay upright. But she couldn't help them, couldn't even hold her head up any longer. Just slumped forward onto her knees and cried.

Travis paced in front of her. 'Not so tough now, are you, *bitch*?'

He was right. She wasn't. She didn't have the energy or the arrogance anymore to look up at him. She stared at his legs, watched the bottle of bourbon swing up out of view as he took a drink – and felt fat tears make tracks down her face.

'I told you they were just housewives.' Kane said it as though housewife was the equivalent of useless. He caught a handful of Jodie's short hair, yanked her head up. Needles of pain shot across her scalp as his pale eyes bored into hers. 'Where's your tyre iron now, bitch?' He laughed in her face as he slapped her head back down.

The skin on the top of her head felt like it had been ripped away. She wanted to press a hand to it, stop the stinging but she didn't dare move, not while Kane was still in grabbing range. No, she wasn't tough at all.

The girls sank to the floor. Beside her, Corrine pulled her legs in tight as Travis began pacing. Up and down the length of the lounge. Taut, aggressive steps, his boots making hard rubber sounds on the timber floor. Over near the island bench, Kane was bouncing about – jumpy, edgy, excited. Travis stopped near Jodie's shoulder. He had the gun in one hand, the bourbon in the other, used the fist of his drinking hand to swipe across his lips.

'Okay,' he said, like he was pulling his thoughts together. 'Okay.' He looked over at Kane. 'Now we check it out properly.' He pointed at him with the bottle. 'Start out the back. And don't screw around. We've already wasted enough time making nice with the wine.'

Kane grabbed the bottle from him, took a quick swig. 'Fuck that. I'm staying here. Got work to do.' He hooked a thumb at the girls and snorted a laugh.

Travis lurched forward, smacked an open hand across the side of Kane's head, ripped the bourbon from his hand and shoved him hard up against one of the old tree trunks. He lifted his index finger from the neck of the bottle and pointed it at Kane. '*You* don't get a fucking say.'

Kane bristled, balled a hand into a meaty fist.

Travis took a menacing step forward, pulled his gun arm across his body, ready to hit him with it.

'This is *bullshit*,' Kane spat. 'Kruger was a prick.'

'And you're a fuck-up. You should've waited till we were paid before you beat the shit out of him. Now we got *nothing*.' Travis got closer, lowered his voice to a growl. 'So you're gonna do what I tell you or I leave you for the cops. *Got it?*'

Kane glared at Travis for a long moment, his flat, colourless eyes narrowed in anger. 'We do the bitches first.'

'We do them *after*.'

Neither man moved. A small muscle pulsed in and out at the

side of Kane's jaw. Travis's gun arm was rigid at his side, still ready to strike. They were inches apart. Same stocky build, same bulky upper-body muscle, same belligerent aggression. But Kane was fair – Scandinavian blond, ice-blue eyes, lashes so pale they looked like they'd been dipped in peroxide. Travis was his negative – black hair, deep, deep blue eyes, skin tanned dark enough to suggest something more than just the obvious white European heritage. Brothers, Jodie thought. Or at least one common parent. Maybe cousins. Whatever it was, there was a blood tie – and some kind of power struggle.

'So get the fuck outside!' Travis roared.

Kane finally moved, pushing himself away from the tree trunk and slamming a fist into the big bowl on the counter as he made his way to the back door. The huge glass basin slid across the marble and smashed to the floor.

On Jodie's left, Corrine whimpered and jerked away from the sound. That one small movement pulled Jodie backwards, tipped Hannah sideways and made Louise grunt from the weight of the bodies on her. Jodie looked at the door Kane had disappeared through, turned fearful eyes to Travis. Two vicious men had made Jodie and her friends more in sync than they'd been all weekend.

'*Fuck.*' Travis barked the word after Kane. He used the back of his gun hand to wipe across his top lip, ran it over his short, dark hair. He stood facing the glass at the rear of the barn for a long moment, body rigid, breathing hard, gun in one hand, bourbon in the other. Then he turned, studied the women across the room and, like before, his eyes found Jodie. They stayed there as he stalked towards her.

She kept her face down as he stopped in front of her, listened to his hard, angry breaths. He took a step closer. *We do them after.* What did that mean? Maybe he'd changed his mind. Please don't shoot. Not while I'm tied to my friends. Don't leave them with that memory.

He lifted his knee and drove the sole of his boot into Jodie's shin. Pain rocketed up her leg.

'Where's your *husband*, bitch?' he yelled. 'You fucking wasted our time. We coulda been fucking miles away by now.' He slammed his boot into her shin a second time. She cried out, pushed back against the others as she tried to get away from him.

'Thought you were real tough, didn't you?' He loomed over her, raised his arm, gun butt aimed at her face. She squeezed her eyes shut, let out a whimper. 'Oh, yeah. You're a real tough bitch.' His leg came down again but this time it was a painful, desultory shove.

Jodie's leg felt like it was crushed. She hoped to God it wasn't broken, struggled with Hannah to get a hand to it. Travis watched her with a sadistic sneer as she felt for damage, cautiously moved her foot. Then he stepped slowly to her right, stood in front of Corrine. Her shoulder trembled against Jodie's. Slowly, silently, he made his way around their circle of bodies, stopping in front of Louise then Hannah, the only sound the sloshing of alcohol as he lifted the bottle to his mouth one more time. If he was trying to scare them, he was wasting his time, Jodie thought. They were already terrified beyond belief.

'Try to get up and I'll shoot the first person I see. Got it?' he boomed.

Louise's voice rang out. 'Oh, we got it, Travis. Got it loud and clear. We got the whole damn picture, you bastard.'

Jodie held her breath. What was she doing?

'Shhh,' Hannah hissed.

'Shut up,' Corrine whispered.

He walked around to Louise's side of the circle. Her head snapped back, cracked against Jodie's. Then she was pressing against Jodie, being pushed backwards, breathing in sharp gasps. No one spoke. No one moved. Jodie couldn't see Travis, could only imagine him holding the gun to Lou's face like he'd done to her. Hoped that was all he was doing.

His voice was calm, almost quiet. 'You got it?'

Don't say anything, Lou. Don't open your mouth.

Seconds passed. Three, four, five. Lou's breathing slowed, the pressure against Jodie's back eased up. A moment later, Travis's boots thumped on the timber as he stormed towards the other end of the barn.

The bodies around her loosened up just a little. Travis was in one of the bedrooms, throwing stuff around. Jodie strained to hear him, frightened he'd find something that would make him come back and kill them.

'Jodie, are you all right?' Louise whispered.

She should be the one asking Lou. She should say something. But she couldn't. Her lungs were wracked with sobs, her face ached, her hand stung, her shoulder felt like something was loose and she was as scared as she'd ever been in her life.

'Jodie? Jode, try to take some deep breaths,' Louise said.

She tried. It helped a little.

Lou whispered. 'Are you hurt?'

Jodie pushed her tongue around her mouth, moved her leg around. 'Just bruised, I think. How about you?'

'Just terrified,' Lou said.

'Me, too,' said Hannah.

'Me, too,' Corrine repeated.

It was better than dead. 'Don't talk back to him, Lou. He'll hurt you.'

'I can't help it. It just comes out.'

Jodie thought about Louise's Afghanistan nightmare and wondered what kind of hell she was in right now. Guilt drummed in the back of her head. Lou had stood up to Travis, yelled at him, tried to protect Jodie – and all she'd done was cower against the wall.

'How's your head, Jodie?' Hannah whispered. 'Did you lose consciousness when he hit you?'

Jodie thought about the numb, spinning sensation in her head when she was on the floor. 'I don't think so.'

'What about your leg?'

It felt good to hear Hannah's nurse's voice, even with a frightened tremor in it. She wished Hannah could do that double rub of the shoulders that she'd pulled away from last night. She wouldn't pull away this time, she'd lean right into it, wrap her arms around Hannah and hold her tight. 'It hurts but I don't think it's broken.'

'What about your hand?'

Jodie looked down. 'It's started bleeding again. Oh, sorry, Corrine, there's blood on your trousers.' Tears filled her eyes. The state of Corrine's trousers was the least of their problems but it felt like another way Jodie had failed her.

'Don't worry,' Corrine sniffed. 'I'll sue them for it.'

Her words hit Jodie like a blow to the gut, as though she'd been winded all over again. Corrine thought they were getting out. She thought they were going home. She thought they were going to get back to their kids.

20

All Jodie felt was the weight of defeat.

Eighteen years of training herself, of staying fit and strong, of trying to make sure no one would ever hurt her again and she'd fallen apart at the very first moment of aggression. Travis had hit her and her armour had crumbled. She hadn't done anything. She hadn't fought, hadn't assessed, hadn't even kept her eyes open. She'd only panicked and reacted. Huddled against the wall and cried like a child.

Face the truth, Jodie. Eighteen years was long enough to deceive yourself. She squeezed her eyes shut and shame consumed her.

The truth was, Jodie, that the real you, the *core* of you – melted down and forged in one horrifying night – was just pure fear. Hard, cold, lonely fear.

A cry pushed its way out of her mouth.

'Jodie? What's wrong?' Louise asked.

Jodie couldn't tell her. Because the thought that was going through her head was so appalling she had never been able to say it out loud.

That maybe all she had ever been was frightened. That eighteen years ago she hadn't run for help. That eighteen years ago she'd just run.

And left her best friend to die.

Down the hallway, Travis slammed a door. Jodie jumped. She wanted to run again. She wanted to drag the others to their feet and get them all the hell away from there. But it wasn't going to happen. None of them could get a hand to the tethers, let alone undo a knot. To get anywhere, they had to move as a group. It was worse than a three-legged race, even before Corrine's sprained ankle was added to the equation. They wouldn't get two metres before Travis or Kane caught up with them. And if Jodie herself miraculously broke free . . .

She looked up. Travis was back in the hallway, stomping down the corridor.

'Shut the fuck up,' he roared.

He was waving the gun in her face. He meant her. She was crying. Hiccuping and snivelling and she hadn't even realised. He kicked her again – same leg, one great big pain – then laughed as he turned towards the kitchen. Dread throbbed inside her like an open wound but she forced herself to remember.

Eighteen years ago, she'd stood by Angela's freshly dug grave, put her hand on her heart and vowed she would never, ever leave a friend behind again.

'Jodie,' Louise whispered. 'Are you okay?'

No. 'Yes.'

'What's he doing?'

In the kitchen beyond Jodie's view, cupboards were being opened and closed. She had a side view of the island bench, was maybe two metres away from it. If she tipped to her right a little, she'd be able to see around it, into the alcove. But she didn't want to. If she couldn't see Travis, maybe he wouldn't see her. Wouldn't want to blow her brains out.

'Jodie? Can you see?' Lou said.

Jodie took a deep breath, leaned a little to her right. She could see past the island to the big windows at the back of the barn. She leaned a little more, snapped her head back as he moved to the fridge, listened as bottles rattled in the door, as crockery clunked and plastic wrap crackled.

What *was* he doing? She leaned over again, saw him bent at the waist, head silhouetted in the fridge light, gun tucked into the back of his jeans, bottle of bourbon now on the island bench. He was munching on chips from a packet in his hand and pulling out the apple pie Jodie had brought for dessert.

'He's eating,' she whispered.

With one hand, he lifted an edge of crust off the pie plate and took a huge, gluttonous bite. A spark flared in the pit of her stomach. He was eating *their* food. The indulgences they'd planned and bought and baked for each other.

She watched him take out a plastic-covered bowl, a tub of dip, a carton of cream.

He kicked the door closed, dumped the food on the island bench and took another hunk out of her apple pie. The small flame of anger edged its way through Jodie's fear, all the way into her consciousness. It felt like a whiff of eucalyptus through the haze of a head cold.

Choke on it, you bastard, she thought.

The guy had smacked her in the face and held a gun to her head but what really ticked her off was that he was helping himself to the contents of their fridge. It didn't make sense but she didn't care. It was good to feel something other than fear. And anger was better than fear any day of the week. Even a tiny spark of it. She closed a mental hand around it, felt its heat, its weight, its texture. She took a deep breath. Then another one. The fear was still there, still strong, still pounding in the back of her head but anger had given her new eyes.

She wiped the tears from her face with her shoulder and looked around. They were sitting about halfway between the front door and the marble-topped bench. On her right was the hall doorway, on her left, the back of a sofa. Ahead she could see the kitchen, the island, the dining table and most of the windows.

The curtains were pulled across the glass now but she could tell it was dark outside. Cold air drifted under the front door and from the hallway. The halogen bulbs over the bench were on and a couple of lamps either side of the fire were spreading a soft glow up the wall. Down on the floor, the light was muted and the air was thick with a fearful silence.

In the kitchen, Travis was pulling open drawers and banging them shut. Crockery rattled and two dinner plates landed on the bench, followed by glassware and cutlery.

What *was* he doing?

He was scavenging food, that much was clear. And with the amount he'd taken out of the fridge and the equipment he'd tossed on the bench, he and Kane were obviously planning to stuff their faces. Were they here for food? She shook her head. No, it wasn't *what* he was doing but what he *wasn't* doing.

He wasn't raping and killing Jodie and her friends. At least not at the moment. And neither was Kane, wherever he was. And from her experience, raping and killing didn't require a full stomach.

What had Travis said to Kane when he told him to go outside? *We do them after.*

After what?

Jodie jumped as something heavy clattered on the gas hob. Travis swore loudly and suddenly he was looming over them again.

'Get up.' He waved his gun around and the anger Jodie had felt was snuffed out by fear. 'I said *get up*. You're cooking our dinner after all.'

'Piss off. I'm not cooking anything for you,' Louise shouted.

'Not you, you loud-mouthed bitch. You.' He pointed the gun at Jodie. 'The tough bitch can do it. Get up. All of you. *Move.*'

Hannah and Corrine scrabbled about, trying to get up. Jodie pulled her legs underneath her, wincing as she put weight on her shin. Travis yanked roughly at the cord binding her to Corrine, kept the gun in his hand as he untied them. He freed her from Hannah the same way, then held out the rope.

'Tie her hands together,' he told Hannah. She glanced fearfully at Jodie.

Travis lifted the gun, pressed its muzzle to Hannah's temple. 'Do it.'

Hannah's body stiffened. She gasped and closed her eyes, as though she was waiting for him to pull the trigger. He didn't, he just prodded her with the muzzle of the gun, jolted her head sideways, forced her eyes open and the cord into her hand. She took it, looked at Jodie through tears.

'It's okay,' Jodie said. It wasn't, she was terrified, her whole body quaking in fear, but she put her wrists together, raised them towards Hannah, saw one palm was smeared with blood from the cut under her thumb.

Hannah tied the rope with trembling fingers, her head tipped slightly to one side from the pressure of the gun at her temple.

When she was finished, Travis pushed her with it. 'You three. Back on the floor. Try to get up and I shoot someone. And I don't care who. Got it?' He didn't wait for an answer, just hauled Jodie away from them, shoved her into the kitchen. 'You, over there and cook.'

She looked back at her friends. She'd been released from their circle but she was still bound to them. Whatever happened.

'Do it!'

Jodie glanced at Travis. He had his back to the island bench, the gun trained on her. She turned to the opposite wall of the kitchen, saw a frypan on the unlit jets of the stove, a carton of eggs and a plate of bacon beside it. She walked on unsteady legs, lifted the pan with her bound hands. It was top-quality cast iron, not the sort of make-do equipment you expected to find in a holiday house. She felt the weight in its thick base, tightened her hands around the solid grip. It would make a perfect steak – and it could do some serious damage to a person's head.

'Cook, for fuck's sake!'

She looked at him again. The gun was angled down this time, aimed at the others out of her sight now. No, Jodie, a frypan was no match for a gun.

Sweat gathered on her forehead as she turned away from him. She fumbled the automatic ignition with both hands, lit the jet, dropped in the bacon then scanned the bench for a tool to cook with. In the corner, out of reach, was a knife block. It had slots for three blades. Two were missing, probably in the dishwasher, but the stainless steel handle of the smallest one shone under the halogen lights.

A paring knife could cut through her bindings, could hurt Travis.

Something cold and hard touched the base of her skull. His voice was a whisper in her ear. 'What are you waiting for?'

Jodie's lungs seized. 'I need a . . . a tool. A spatula. To cook the food.'

'Then find one.'

Her eyes flicked to the knife block. Could she do it? Could she even get to it? When she was shaking like a leaf, with a gun to her head? She'd have to move all the way along the bench just to reach it. Then what? Slash at him before he shot her. Or one of her friends. There was no chance. Not while the others were tied together. Not when Kane was somewhere outside.

She pulled open drawers beside the stove, found tea towels, placemats, a can-opener, a whisk. Nothing that would protect anyone. As Travis paced the kitchen behind her, she pulled out tongs, used both hands to push the bacon around, break in the eggs.

Then suddenly he was shoving her. 'What the fuck are you doing?'

She winced, waited for a blow.

'You're getting blood in it,' he yelled.

She looked down, saw blood from the cut on her palm had dripped onto the white of the eggs. She snatched her hands away, knocked the pan, made it clatter across the cooktop. Hot bacon fat splattered her arm and as she cried out, Travis crowded in behind her, pushed the gun into her skull again.

'Do it *properly!*'

She heard Louise's voice loud and angry. 'She can't do it with a gun to her head.'

'Shut up!' he yelled, then leaned in harder on the gun. 'Do it properly!'

'She can't like that,' Lou shouted.

'Shut up!'

'You bastard!'

Jodie closed her eyes, felt Travis's breath hot in her hair. *Lou, be quiet.*

A beat passed. The bacon sizzled. Then the back door slid open.

Kane's voice cut through the tense silence. 'No can do, man.'

The gun fell away from Jodie's head as Travis turned around. She scuttled out from behind him, saw Lou, Hannah and Corrine had slid along the floor to the island bench, had no chance to meet their eyes before Kane pushed through the curtain across the doorway. His shirtsleeves were rolled to his elbows and the buttons of his flannel shirt were undone to below his chest, a blue singlet underneath. He stopped when he saw her in the kitchen, glared at Travis.

'What the fuck's going on? You were going to keep them on the floor.'

'I put them to work,' Travis said. 'She's cooking our dinner like a nice little housewife.'

'Oh, yeah.'

They both laughed, like it was an added bonus.

'So shut the loud-mouth up.' Travis cocked his head at the women on the floor. 'Give the tough bitch something to think about while she does a proper job, hey?'

Jodie's stomach tightened at the grin on Kane's face as he turned his eyes on her friends. He was the scary one. Travis had done the hitting and the gun pointing and she had no doubt he'd use it on any one of them but Kane had a craziness about him, as though he was just waiting for the go-ahead to lose control. Scarier still was that Travis seemed to be the one who kept him in check – and he'd gulped down straight bourbon, was pissed off and had some kind of agenda that didn't include protecting her and her friends from Kane.

She watched as Kane stalked to her friends, grinned at them one by one then honed in on Lou.

21

'Try anything and I'll break her neck,' Kane said. His arm was wrapped around Louise's throat.

Jodie saw the way he held her – pushed down under his armpit, his other hand at the back of her head – and knew it wasn't guesswork. He hadn't watched a few movies and copied the bad guys. Kane knew how to break a person's neck.

She pulled her eyes down, looked at Lou. Her mop of hair was wild, her face streaked with dried tears, her mouth was pressed closed and she was breathing hard through her nose. She raised her eyes to Jodie's and they were filled with tears.

The sight of them drove Jodie into action. She found a cloth napkin in a drawer, wrapped it around her bleeding hand, got back to the frypan, pried the food from its base. When it was done, she spoke tersely. 'It's ready.'

'Well then, tough bitch, bring it over,' Travis said.

Was it 'after' now? Were they going to make them watch while they ate or were they going to shoot them all in the head as an appetiser? She wanted to be sick. She wanted to drop her head and sob but she took a deep breath and hoisted the frypan off the stove. She walked across the kitchen, stood at the island bench opposite Travis, put the pan down in front of him and turned to Lou.

Up close, she was so pale her freckles looked like splats of mud. Kane's forearm was around her throat and as Jodie's eyes took in the tattoo on its pale underside, the scars on her stomach tightened in horror. Stretching from the crook of his elbow to his inner wrist was an elaborately drawn, thick-handled, double-bladed knife. It was in full, brilliant colour, a lethal piece of art, and it was flecked in dirt as though he'd been digging in the garden. There was more dirt in Lou's curls where he'd pushed his fingers into her hair and a smudge of black along her jawline. Jodie could smell the stink of his sweat over the aroma of the bacon and eggs. And Lou, her best friend Lou, was pushed into his reeking armpit.

The spark of a new, stronger flame flared inside her.

She tightened her fist around the handle of the frypan, thought about the kind of damage a hot, cast-iron pan could do to a man's face. Could she? If she kept her wits about her, if she stayed alert, if she didn't let fear rule her, yes, she could do it for Lou.

Jodie looked up as a band of light moved across the lounge room.

Car headlights.

'Someone's here!' Travis said and his aggression seemed to shrink just a little.

Kane let go of Lou, moved quickly to the curtained front windows.

Travis kept the gun aimed at Jodie as he backed into the room. 'Who's here?' His voice was low, agitated. '*Who is it?*'

No one spoke.

'Tough bitch. Who the fuck is it?'

'I don't know.' She watched the light move across the curtains and felt her heart rate pick up. It was a double-edged sword. Whoever was out there could help – or get dragged into the nightmare.

Kane opened up a gap in the curtains, pulled his face back fast. 'Shit! *Shit.* It's Matt Wiseman's car.'

Jodie's mouth dropped open. *Matt Wiseman?*

'The fucking cops are here,' Kane hissed across the room.

Travis swung his head to the window, took a couple of edgy,

furtive steps then stopped, narrowed his eyes at Jodie. 'No, it's not the cops.'

Kane shouted, 'Trav, it's the cops.'

'It's not the cops, bro,' he said calmly. 'Wiseman's not a cop anymore, is he, tough bitch? He's a grunt at his old man's service station.' He raised the gun, aimed it at Jodie. When he spoke again, his voice was hard and flat. 'What is Matt Wiseman doing here?'

'I don't know. I swear I don't know.'

On the floor, her friends turned fearful faces to her. Outside, the car scrunched to a halt on the gravel parking pad.

Travis took a step closer, tightened his hand on the gun. 'He's been sniffing around you like a dog on heat. What the fuck's going on?' Then, as though an idea had dawned, he smiled slowly. 'Oh yeah, I get it. Hey Kane, I think the loser cop's got the hots for the tough bitch.'

Kane sneered, 'Oh man, Wiseman wants a piece of her.'

'What's your missing husband gonna think of that, bitch?'

A car door opened.

'Maybe Wiseman's already done her. Is that why you pissed off with him this afternoon? Did you screw him for the car?'

Jodie said nothing as a hot flush burned her cheeks. She remembered Matt smiling at her in the driveway of the service station and felt dirty for the way it'd made her feel. Had Travis seen them? How long had he been watching them?

'Is he back for more, tough bitch?' Travis said. 'Did you promise him some more tonight?'

Jodie's eyes flicked to the front window and back. 'I swear I don't know why he's here.'

Kane held out his free hand. 'Gimme the gun. I'll get rid of him.'

'Oh, please, no,' Jodie cried, holding her bound hands out to him.

Travis said nothing for a second, kept the gun on Jodie, slid his eyes to the door, then to Kane.

'C'mon, bro! I'll do him now.' Kane had an urgent excitement in his voice.

'No. We're not doing a cop. Even an ex-cop.' His eyes moved back to Jodie. '*She* can get rid of him.'

A car door slammed shut.

'Get the rope off her,' Travis ordered.

As Kane hauled on her hands, the crazy look on his face made fear pulse in her veins. When she was free, she ducked away from him, dropped to the floor and hugged the first friend she could get to.

It was Lou and she whispered in her ear. 'If you get a chance, run.'

Then Travis was grabbing Jodie's arm, hauling her up and across the room. His hand was a vice on her upper arm, the muzzle of the gun a prod in the small of her back.

At the front door, he pulled her close, spoke into her ear. 'Get rid of him. Try anything stupid and I'll kill him and I'll kill your friends then I'll let my brother finish you off. Got it?'

So they *were* brothers.

Footsteps crunched on the gravel. Oh, God, Matt. Why are you here?

Travis flattened himself against the wall behind the door. 'I'll be watching you. Stay where I can see you or I'll put a bullet in him. Got it?'

Jodie's heart pounded and her lungs forgot how to breathe. She could see Matt's face in her mind. Mussed hair, wary eyes, casual and alert. He was a nice guy, probably taking up Corrine's offer for a drink. She didn't want to get him killed.

A footstep sounded on the timber stair.

'Tell him anything,' Travis whispered, 'and your friends are dead. And it'll be *your* fault. Got it?'

Jodie looked at him then over her shoulder at Louise and Hannah and Corrine tied together on the floor. Lou was bent forward now, her face on the timber, Kane's workboot on the back of her neck.

Louise and Hannah and Corrine were her best friends. And Matt Wiseman was a cop.

Travis pulled the door open a crack. 'Get rid of him. Fast.'

. . .

TRY NOT TO LOOK DESPERATE, Matt told himself. If it looks like she thinks you're a try-hard for driving all the way out here, then leave. Do your good deed and wave goodbye. It would be a lot better if she laughed and asked him inside, though.

He stepped onto the verandah, the sound of his boot on the timber reverberating through the deck. It was quiet out here. Strangely quiet for a house full of women on a weekend holiday.

The door opened before he got to it. Just a fraction then a moment later, like a second thought, it was pulled wide and Jodie stood in the doorway. Her arms were folded across her chest and the expression on her face was grim. As though he was the last person in the world she wanted to see. Okay, not exactly the reception he'd hoped for. Do your deed and get lost. But be nice about it. She might change her mind.

'Hey, Jodie.' He smiled. The one she sent back looked like an effort.

'Hey, Matt. What are you doing here?'

He laughed to himself. You idiot. There would be no anything. He pushed his hands into his pockets, felt for the phone and took a couple of steps closer to her. As he moved into the light from the windows, he saw something on her face, a swelling, high on her cheek. He leaned in for a closer look and she backed away. It looked recent. And painful.

'What happened to your face?'

She pulled a hand from her folded arms and waved his concern away. There was some kind of makeshift bandage around her hand and blood on her fingers. 'It's nothing.'

He caught her hand and pulled it closer, palm up. 'No, it's not. You're hurt.' There was a dark stain on the bandage at the base of her thumb and her hand was freezing. 'What happened?'

She tugged her fingers back and tucked them into her other arm. Her eyes flicked to her left. Quickly, like an involuntary movement. 'No, really, it's nothing. Just an accident. So silly, really. I dropped a glass of water and slipped over and hit my head on the kitchen bench on the way down. It's all right, though. Hannah's a nurse, she fixed it up. A bit of a rough job but we didn't have a first-aid kit. It's fine. Really.' She smiled thinly, avoiding his eyes.

He watched her for a second. The nervous eye flick was a tip-off but the giveaway was in the detail. It was the classic mistake people made when they were lying. They thought if they talked a lot, no one would notice the lie. For someone clearly not in the mood to chat, Jodie just did a lot of talking. Hannah probably was a nurse but Matt guessed the rest of the story was horseshit. The question was: why lie about getting hurt?

'Why are you here, Matt?' she asked again, looking past him as though she wished he'd hurry up and leave.

'I found your mobile in the loan car.' He pulled it from his pocket and held it out to her. 'I thought I'd drop it in on the way to my brother's. In case you needed it tonight.'

She used her undamaged hand this time, went to take it then pulled back. Flicked her eyes left. 'It's not mine,' she said. 'Mine's ... That's not mine.'

He frowned. 'Okay,' he said, looking to her left. The front door had drifted halfway closed and soft light from inside cast a glow on the deck. Behind her, he could see timber floors, half of a sofa and a fireplace. No girlfriends. 'Maybe it belongs to one of your friends.'

'No,' she said quickly. 'No, they've got their phones. Definitely not one of theirs.' Her eyes moved left again but it was different this time – a downwards glance that only made it halfway to the door. 'Yes,' she said and for the first time since he'd got there she looked him straight in the eye. 'Yes, we all sat on the deck this afternoon and phoned home.'

So the mobile wasn't theirs. He got the point. 'Well, I guess that's it then.' The point was that he needed to get it through his skull that his instincts were seriously shot to hell. He thought she seemed interested this afternoon. Maybe not so overwhelmed by him in his jeans as he was in hers but enough to flash a real smile and chat for a moment somewhere out of the cold. He'd obviously been way off. 'Have a good weekend, then. Give me a call if you have any more problems with the car. Otherwise, well, it's been nice meeting you.'

He held out his hand. May as well be professional about it 'cause there wasn't anything else happening.

She took it, just held it for a moment without shaking it. 'The brakes are fine now. You did a great job on them. Thanks.'

He kept his face still while he thought about that. There'd been nothing wrong with the brakes and she knew that. He'd walked her through the repairs on her car in the shop and he'd gone over the bill with her. Brakes had never been mentioned. She was looking him in the eye again, chin tilted upwards, mouth set firm. She was making a point – he got that – but what? That he should have fixed the brakes?

He frowned a little. Okay, Matt, what next? He could stall and try to figure it out – if nothing else, it was an excuse to spend a little while longer with her before she fobbed him off for good. Or he could quit while he was ahead. Take up Tom and Monica's invitation for dinner. Yeah, and listen to the latest on the John Kruger investigation and feel bad about it all over again. No, stalling was good. 'Hey, no problem. You need brakes if you're going to make a habit of running off the road.'

Something passed over her face. A private laugh? A scoff? Relief? It was too fast, too veiled, he couldn't put a name to it. Her hand tightened briefly on his then she pulled it away, tucked it across her chest and her eyes looked down to the left again.

Matt frowned some more. She was injured and lying about it, talking about brakes and worried about something. The house? Something *in* the house? Someone . . .

'Look, Matt.' Her voice was suddenly loud and hostile. 'You can't just turn up like this. What happened last night was great, the best. But it's over. We're finished.'

Last night? 'I don't . . .'

'No, Matt. I told you this afternoon. I've got a husband and three little girls waiting for me at home. Remember?' She slapped a hand on the side of her head, as though he couldn't be more stupid. Her big eyes were wide and pressing. 'I'm not *with* you. You said you were *with* someone, Matt. What about who you're *with*?'

22

Part of him instinctively bristled at her aggression while his brain worked furiously to figure out what the hell was going on.

What had he missed that was 'the best'? And what about the 'Who you're with, Matt?' Like he was an idiot.

Okay, wait, nothing had happened between them so this was about her, not him. He looked at her grim face, dark eyes burning into his. What, Jodie? He went over it again. She was hurt but lying about it, she thanked him for something he hadn't done and she was picking a fight and telling him to leave. He looked back at the front door. The swelling on her face was the kind of injury you got from being shoved around. She'd said a husband was waiting for her. This afternoon she'd said she was single. Divorced. Had her ex turned up? And where were her friends? Had they left them to talk and it turned rough?

'Jodie, if you're . . .'

'Matt, it's over. Don't you *get* it? If you had a brain, you'd figure it out.' She dragged the last three words out as though each one was a sentence in itself. 'You need to go. *Please.*'

Matt was paralysed with indecision. Should he do as she asked and leave, or stay and protect her from whoever she was frightened of? The decision was made by Jodie.

'Get out of here, Matt,' she yelled, backing away from him to the door.

'Okay, okay,' he said, hands up like stop signs. He took a couple of steps towards the edge of the deck then turned back to her. 'Hey, Jodie. If you don't want your husband to find out about us, make sure you pay for your damn brakes before you leave town tomorrow.'

'You can count on it,' she said and the urgency in her eyes softened a little before she turned around and went back inside.

Matt stood at the top of the stairs for a moment, listening for sounds from the house but it was silent. Too silent. As though she was standing right behind the door. He stomped down the stairs like she'd really cheesed him off, slammed his door, spun his tyres on the gravel as he drove off and tried to figure out what had just happened.

Whatever it was, she wanted him to play along. She'd told him to go, so he'd gone. He didn't feel great about it but she hadn't given him much choice.

She wanted it to look like an argument, that much he'd figured. Her eyes before she went back in the barn told him he'd been right about the lies. And when he'd thrown one right back at her, she'd caught it on the full, no hesitation. She wanted him to know she was lying. Okay, he did – but *why*?

He pointed his brother's car down the hill to the road, took it slowly over the rough trail. A violent ex-husband was the obvious answer. It would also explain the wariness Jodie had about her, maybe even why she knew how to pull out a punch. But why make up some bull about an affair?

Matt slowed the car further at the hump in the track. He remembered her standing there this morning, the way she'd told him she'd throw a rock through his window if he looked suspicious. It didn't seem likely she'd take a beating from anyone. He shook his head. What was it she'd said? That she'd throw the rock at his head and there'd be lots of blood. *Yours, not mine.* And he'd said, *Then what?*

And she said she'd call the police. *There's reception at the bottom of the hill.*

Matt sucked air in through his teeth. There was no reception at the barn. That's why he'd driven out there this morning. But she'd just told him they'd all sat on the verandah and phoned home. It was another lie. Was she telling her ex she'd tried to call?

Okay, if her ex was still inside, she was in danger. If Matt went back, he could put her in more danger. But it didn't have to be him. He could get someone else to go up to the barn. There were probably a couple of uniform guys still in town.

As he reached the sealed road at the bottom of the hill and turned left, he pulled his phone from his pocket. Only it wasn't his. It was the one he'd thought was Jodie's. Whose was it? He put it on the seat beside him, wrestled his own mobile from his other pocket and hit speed dial for the pub.

'Reg, it's Matt.' He flipped the cover on the other phone as he talked.

'Yeah, mate.'

'Are any of the uniforms still around?'

'No, mate. Left an hour or so ago. One of the detectives was looking for you though. The short one in the fancy suit.'

Dan Carraro. Would he handle a suspected domestic thirty k's out of town? Unlikely. He was a star detective and it was a job for a uniform. 'Is he there?'

'Nah. He and his offsider went for a bite at the Chinese. But he was pretty keen to talk to you. Said he needed to pick your brains about a couple of blokes.'

Matt felt anger brewing in his gut. Carraro didn't need him to do his job. As he hit a pothole, the other mobile lit up and he took his eyes off the road to look at it.

'Shit.'

'What?'

He hung up without answering.

The phone's screen was lit with a photo – Jodie in a three-way hug with a little boy and an older girl. The boy had both front teeth missing and the girl had the same big, dark eyes as Jodie. Her kids. Matt remembered now. She'd told him this afternoon she had two kids, a boy and a girl. *I've got a husband and three little girls waiting for me at home.* She wasn't lying to cover her tracks with someone inside. An ex-husband would know how many kids she had. She was lying for Matt.

The thought hit him like a sledgehammer. His breath turned hard and fast and his heart felt like it was lodged in his throat. No, Jodie. Don't count on him. Not Matt Fuck-up Wiseman. 'Damn it!' She was asking for his help. She didn't know his speciality was getting innocent victims killed. Dread churned in his gut. Whatever was going on up there, he'd probably made it worse by turning up on the doorstep. Which made him responsible, at least in part.

He heard the gunshots in his head. Loud, abrupt reports. He squeezed his eyes shut. Don't go there, Matt. Don't think about it. Think about the barn. Think about Jodie.

She needed help. She needed a cop.

He slowed to make the turn at the intersection to Tom and Monica's road, dialling the pub again as he did. 'Reg, did he leave a mobile number?'

'Got cut off before, huh?'

'Yeah. Did he leave a number?'

'Who?'

'The detective.'

'Not that I know of. I could ask Marg. She only left about ten minutes ago.'

Matt slammed a hand against the steering wheel. He could talk Carraro into going up there. Make a deal with him – give up what he knew about the locals for the John Kruger investigation in return for Carraro checking out the barn. Tonight. Now. 'You got a number for the Chinese restaurant, Reg?'

'Somewhere here.' Matt could hear him shuffling through paper. 'Last time I looked at the local business board it was here.' He chuckled. 'Got three numbers for plumbers, if you're interested. Shit, that guy died two years ago.'

Matt gritted his teeth, forced himself to breathe slower. Focus on Carraro. He could handle a tight situation. He could handle the Kruger investigation, too. He didn't need Matt's help, for Christ's sake. Anger flared as he thought how Carraro had badgered him at the service station. *What's Kruger's story?* he'd said. Matt frowned suddenly. Carraro had said something else. At the time, he'd been trying not to listen. What was it? He forced his mind back. *What's Kruger's story?* Then, *What's the go with the builders?*

The old, familiar buzz started up in his head. More snippets of conversation jumped out at him. Jodie had said there'd been a car on the hill during the night. And she'd asked him about poachers.

'Reg?'

'Still looking for the number, mate.'

'Reg, listen. Do you know who was doing the building work at John Kruger's house?'

'Pretty sure Warren Puller had that, put the Anderson brothers on to help with the heavy stuff. He asked . . .'

Reg was still talking as Matt hung up. He pulled over to the side of the road, yanked on the handbrake and sat very still. His hands gripped the steering wheel and his heart beat hard.

Instinct was telling him something. About the barn. About Carraro. The Andersons. He didn't trust his instinct, he wanted to tell it to get stuffed – but Jodie's voice rang in his ears.

Don't you get it? If you had a brain, you'd figure it out.

So figure it out.

If Jodie was lying for his benefit, what else was she telling him?

He focused on the dark road ahead, the gum trees looming in on either side like a murky tunnel, letting his thoughts get into a familiar rhythm – listing facts, sorting and sifting them. He kept coming back to the few moments she'd done most of the talking, when she'd been ranting at him.

You can't just turn up like this.

It's over. We're finished.

What about who you're with?

Not Jodie, that was for sure.

What happened last night was great, the best.

What *had* happened last night?

He'd gone out to their crash site. He took two of her friends into town. He went back for Jodie and the other one. Took them to the pub. Got rid of a letch. Lent her his jacket. Saw them off in the loan car. Wait. Back up.

The letch. Kane Anderson.

His stomach tightened. Would he . . .?

Matt remembered the old barn back then, the Andersons' filthy squat. It was just him and Kane there that afternoon. Seven years ago – three weeks after the teenage girl had gone missing, two weeks since the search team had left. They'd scoured the entire hill, found nothing. All they'd had was the girl seen bumming a cigarette off Kane Anderson. *She was here. I know she was*, Matt had roared, a forearm pressed against Kane's throat. Kane had grinned, blood from the cut lip staining his teeth red, and said, *You'll never find her.* Matt had a black eye for a week but not enough to charge the bastard with murder. Knowing and proving were two different things and the detectives had let Kane go.

What about who you're with?

In the bakery this afternoon, Rhona had said he was a cop. *You're with the police?* Jodie had said afterwards. *Not* with *the police. I'm on leave*, he'd said.

Who are you with, Matt?

The cops.

23

J odie kept her face to the front door, heart pounding, too afraid to turn around. It was stupid, *stupid*, to think Matt would drive off, put two and two together and come up with vicious bastards about to rape and kill four women. And it was stupid to put her friends in more danger trying to get a message to him. Now Kane was going to snap Lou's neck under his boot.

But the sound she heard wasn't bones breaking. Beside her, Travis let out a soft chuckle. 'Wiseman's a fucking loser.'

Jodie looked at him, turned all the way around when Kane whooped, realised then that she'd gotten away with it. Travis and Kane knew nothing about her kids, thought she had a husband, thought she had something going with Matt. She'd said nothing to dispel that.

Kane lifted his foot from Lou's neck. She scrabbled out from underneath. He grinned at his brother. 'Wiseman was born a loser.'

Travis laughed again, quietly, like it was some kind of personal victory. He grabbed Jodie's arm and dragged her towards the kitchen.

Kane's wired, hyped-up energy had returned. 'Wiseman misses out again. Yeah, we got four sluts this time. He doesn't get any. Loser.'

At his feet, Hannah, Lou and Corrine were scuttling back along the floor on their butts. There was nowhere to go in the small kitchen but up against the cupboards. 'Hey, bro, we should leave him something this time.'

'Tie her up with the others,' Travis growled and pushed Jodie at him.

Kane caught her hand, held it up and grinned. 'Let's give him the finger. One of theirs.'

Jodie wrenched her hand away, curled her fingers into a tight ball, was shoved hard to the floor by Travis. Louise hauled her back by the shoulders, embraced her tight from behind.

'Tie her up,' Travis ordered.

Kane ignored him, danced about in front of Jodie. 'Four. Fucking *four* we got.'

Travis grabbed him by the shirt front and slammed him up against the island bench. Kane didn't react, just grinned, flicked his eyes back and forth from the floor to Travis.

His brother shoved him again then just dropped his arms to his sides. 'Yeah, we got us four sluts. So tie them together.' He walked to the front window, looked out through a gap in the curtains.

As Kane tied her to Hannah, Jodie took in the shock on her friend's face. Beside her, Lou's knees were pulled defensively to her chest and Corrine, last in the row of hostages, was crying softly. Jodie turned to Kane, watched his pale eyes, the tattoo on his forearm and hoped Matt came back with a damn army.

'Which one you wanna do first?' Kane called across the room.

Travis pulled the curtains closed. 'We eat first.'

'Jesus, Trav, come on. Wiseman's not coming back. We got plenty of time now.'

Travis stalked back across the room. 'You want to go into town for supplies? You think you're going to just stroll past those coppers and pick up a couple of bags of groceries before we hit the dirt?'

Jodie couldn't see Kane's face now, only the stiffening in his neck as he held his ground and said nothing.

Travis kicked at something under the island bench, sending it clattering across the floor, and stared at his brother. 'You think it's going to work like that, Kane? Did you think of anything before you picked up that piece of timber?'

A beat of silence. 'Nah, bro.'

'Then shut up and listen.' Travis laid the gun on the bench, kept his hand around it, looked at Jodie and her friends, at his brother, at the front door. 'We eat while we got food and give me some time to figure it out.' He looked over his shoulder to the glass wall. 'Then we do what we came for, shut the bitches up and hit the road. In that order. You got it?'

'Yeah. I got it.'

'Then get it started.'

Kane hauled the women to their feet. 'Do the food,' he yelled.

So they did. Jodie and Corrine, the only ones with an untied hand, piled food onto plates then Travis held the gun to Hannah's head, made them all walk to the big dining table and serve it up.

They were pushed to the floor against the island bench while Travis and Kane shovelled food into their mouths. It was cold now, overcooked and greasy, but it didn't seem to matter. There was no talking, just gulping, huge mouthfuls of egg and bacon and bread and apple pie – Kane's focus moving back and forth from his plate to his prey, Travis's eyes on a continuous circuit around the barn: lounge room, front door, back windows, kitchen.

Watching them at the table, Jodie saw the differences between them went deeper than colouring. Travis seemed to have some level of cognitive ability that had bypassed Kane. Travis was getting a kick out of terrifying them, Jodie had no doubt about that, but not like his brother. Kane was an animal straining at a leash. Travis was more controlled. He was there for a reason, he was holding some kind of plan together and he had Kane on a short chain.

The chain got a whole lot longer when Travis went outside. He'd finished eating, pushed his plate away, scraped his chair back from the table and announced, 'I'm going out to see for myself.' He tucked the gun in the back of his jeans and left them alone with Kane.

Kane was laughing before the glass had slid shut. A high, feral, girlish sound. Like he was in the middle of a joke. It made Jodie's blood go cold.

'You're a fuckin' prickteaser.' He looked at her as he stood up. She shrank back, prayed he wasn't going to 'do' her now. He took his time walking to her, laughing to himself. 'Get up.'

It was an order for all of them. They could have refused – he didn't have the gun. But Jodie had seen how Travis handled him, didn't dare cross him and she guessed the other girls felt the same. They struggled to get off the floor with their hands tied. Kane grinned and waited until they were upright. 'You're a fuckin' prickteaser,' he said again and slammed a fist into Jodie's stomach.

She doubled over, gasping in pain and shock, the blood in her head roaring as she tried to fill her lungs with air. Louise yelled obscenities, Corrine's voice pitched high in a wail. Beside her, Hannah didn't utter a sound but Jodie could feel her trembling violently. Kane laughed and pointed like they were putting on a goddamn show.

As she straightened up, she steeled herself for another beating, hoping she might be able to defend herself with her one free hand. But Kane had finished with her. His awful eyes were on Corrine. Then his hands. He was pawing her face, her neck, her breasts, laughing, telling her she was going to scream, it was going to be great.

He shoved her sideways, pushed her up against the dining table. She was crying and begging him to stop. Jodie watched in horror from where she stood at the island bench – and thought about knocking Kane to the floor with a shoulder tackle. She could do it, she knew how. But she was tied to Hannah and Hannah was tied to Louise, Lou to Corrine and there was no chance of winning any kind of fight with three terrified, untrained women attached to her.

MATT SPUN the tyres through a tight U-turn, pushed the accelerator to the floor and fishtailed down the road as he picked up speed. He was around the intersection before thought kicked in.

It was crazy. *He* was crazy. There was no logical reason for Kane Anderson to be up at the barn. If he *had* killed John Kruger, why would he go there? Any idiot would leave the area. Revenge for Jodie rejecting him at the pub? Now you're clutching at straws, Matt. Jodie wouldn't be the first to fob him off.

No, it wasn't Anderson. No way.

But Jodie's pleading face flashed in his head again and he kept driving. It was someone. Or something.

His phone rang.

'Hey, Matty. I found that number. You still want it?'

He eased his foot off the accelerator as he thought of Dan Carraro eating spring rolls and telling war stories with his junior detective. What would he tell him? 'Hey, Dan, this hot woman I met yesterday had a bandaged hand and just told me a bunch of lies. How about you drive the thirty k's out there and check it out for me 'cause I don't think I can handle it on my own.' Matt rubbed his head. 'No, just tell him I called. Thanks, Reg.' He hung up and tossed the mobile on the passenger seat.

Shit.

The big engine growled under him as he coasted down the road. He didn't want to go back to the barn – not after Jodie had told him to leave, not if there was a chance he'd fuck it up and have another tragedy on his conscience. But there was no way he could just drive out to Tom and Monica's and pull up a chair for the evening. Not if he wanted to live with himself afterwards.

So what are you going to do?

He had no weapon, no police ID, not even his own car. He couldn't go to the barn, knock on the door and ask what was going on. Jodie had made that clear.

But he could scout around in the darkness up there without being seen. And if it turned out he was inventing reasons to spy on Jodie, he could just leave, go to Tom's and no one need ever know how close he'd come to making an idiot of himself.

He could see the lights in old Wally Taylor's run-down shack at the bottom of the track. He slowed and swung the car across the road.

It was just after seven pm – twenty minutes since he'd left Jodie on the verandah. He pulled the car off the road just beyond Wally's cottage, searched the boot for a torch without success then took off at as fast a walk as his knee could bear.

24

It didn't take Matt long to find the old stock track that ran along the boundary fence. He'd been part of the search group that had combed that area on the hill in the first days after the girl had gone missing. It ran parallel to the dirt road he'd come down earlier, went up and over the hill, cutting through bush at the top and passing the barn at its narrow end.

As the incline levelled out, he stopped. It was a long time since he'd walked this fast, this far. His lungs were working hard, pushing gusts of steam into the cold air, and his knee felt hot and heavy, a sharp pain burning in the cruciate ligament he'd torn apart six months ago. He flexed the joint as he looked towards the old barn.

It was silhouetted against the dark sky like a gothic castle. The only light on the hill spilled from the windows at the far end, the lounge room he'd seen through the door when he'd spoken to Jodie. From this end, he'd be able to move around most of the building without being spotted from inside.

He pushed on through the bush to the edge of a clearing that circled the barn like a moat and started on a wide arc around the end of the building. Limping, trying to ignore the pain, he kept close to the shadow of scrub, heading for the back. He'd already seen the front, knew he wouldn't be able to look inside without stepping onto the verandah. And he wanted to avoid that until he had some idea of what, if anything, was going on in there.

He rounded the corner and saw the scrub was closer at the rear, maybe twenty, twenty-five metres from the verandah. He stayed in the shadows of the brush, watching the barn across the clearing as he edged his way along its length. Up ahead was a bank of glass, curtained, he guessed, judging by the dim light coming through.

A quarter of the way along the verandah, he froze. Just ahead, in the garden, a shadow moved. It backed out of the garden and stood up to the full height of a man. A single word broke the silence. 'Fuck!'

Matt's body tightened as his first questions were answered. Jodie and her friends weren't alone. There was a man with them. And whoever he was, he was angry.

As the figure walked away along the garden bed under the verandah, Matt looked for something that would tell him if it was Kane Anderson – but it was hard to tell at this distance in the dark. The guy's shoes sounded like thunder as he took the steps two at a time and clomped three more paces to the bank of glass. He slid back a panel and the curtain behind it.

'The fucking garden . . .' was all Matt heard before the door was rammed shut. The curtain was pulled back in place and when it settled, a bright, narrow stripe of light shone through a gap in the drapes.

Matt moved fast but cautiously, keeping close to the scrub until he was in line with the stripe of light. He squatted on his haunches, breathing hard from exertion, wanting and not wanting to know what was going on.

He couldn't see a thing from this distance. He watched the door, wiped his hands on his jeans and, for the first time in six months, wished he had his service automatic. It's now or never, Matt. Go look or go home. He stood and ran, limping and low, to the garden bed, stopped a couple of metres to the left of the steps and windows.

He listened, mouth dry, breath jagged and knee hurting like hell.

Rough male voices. A brief squeal. An angry female voice. It sounded like Jodie.

He looked along the length of the deck – new timber, four or five metres deep, waist-high handrail. He swallowed hard, closed his eyes briefly as he braced his hands on the rail then silently lifted himself over and onto the verandah.

He crouched beside a small wrought-iron table and counted two panels of glass before the door and the gap in the curtain. Shit. He hunkered down as low as his knee would allow and crept along the deck, hoping the curtains were thick enough to obscure his shadow.

Keeping his body away from the gap, he leaned against the door-frame and rolled his face towards the source of light. It took a moment to understand what he was looking at.

On the other side of the door, about a metre in, was a kitchen bench. White base, dark top, food and cooking equipment scattered on the work surface. Jodie's friend, Hannah, the nurse, was standing next to it, her back to the door, her arms out straight and slightly raised, like she was making the shape of an arrow with her body. Tied to her right wrist and standing in the same position was the short woman with the curly hair, Louise. Matt moved his face a fraction further and saw the tall blonde. She was half turned towards him, making a semicircle with the other two, her left hand tied to Louise, the other one pulled tight across her chest. And she was crying.

A pulse drummed in his ears. Where was Jodie?

'A fucking meat market.' The voice was coarse, manic, muffled a little by the glass but unmistakably Kane Anderson's.

Shit. *Shit.* Matt rolled his face away from the glass. Where was Jodie? He rolled towards to the door again, searching frantically. He moved further into the gap between the curtains, risking being seen. Then he saw her. She had her back to the kitchen bar, one arm outstretched towards Hannah, their hands out of sight under the bench. He couldn't see her other hand, just the tight, tense way she held her body. And her lips pressed together under huge dark eyes.

Blood pounded in his ears. Anger and fear in equal amounts. He automatically reached for his gun holster. But he had no holster, no gun, no weapon. Just empty, shaking hands. He saw Jodie turn her head towards something out of his sight, saw her eyes widen in fear.

'You can fuck one up now and do the rest later.'

That wasn't Kane. It *sounded* like him but it wasn't. Deeper, no lunatic menace. Was it *Travis* Anderson? Were they both here?

It didn't make sense.

He heard Kane laugh again, saw Hannah turn her head. Matt looked past her, past Louise and saw Kane grinning, his crazy-man eyes hard and cold as an ice floe. He grabbed a handful of the blonde's hair, snapped her head back and wrapped a meaty hand around her throat.

'Leave her alone, you animal,' Louise yelled.

Then Travis Anderson stepped in front of Louise, his eyes dark with intent, a pistol in his hand, pointed at her head.

No. Please, no.

Gunshots went off in his memory. Five loud cracks.

Two, a beat, three more.

Bam-bam. Bam-bam-bam.

He tasted bile. Sweat was cold on his face. He was breathing so hard, his head spun.

'No!' The word came from Jodie. It was loud and firm and angry. Matt shook his head. Stay with them. Do that, at least.

Travis's eyes were still on Louise. 'Shut up, bitch.' He straightened his gun arm and pulled himself up into a firing stance – turned slightly to the left so his gun shoulder was forward and braced. 'Leave that one, bro. I'm over of this loud-mouthed bitch. She goes first.'

Matt could see four of them – Travis, Louise, Hannah and Jodie. He held his breath as their reaction unfolded. A sneer turned up one side of Travis's mouth. Louise's knees buckled and she swayed a little. Hannah stood like stone. Beside her, Jodie's chest heaved in and out as she breathed hard. Her eyes flicked around the room. She turned to the raised bar. She reached across her body with her free hand, wrapped her fingers around a heavy- based glass tumbler.

'You weak, sadistic bastard!' Louise shouted.

A voice from out of sight cried, 'Shut up, Lou.'

'Yeah, *Lou*,' Travis said. 'When are you going to *shut up*?'

'I'm not, you piece of shit. I've got four kids. I'm going to make sure you know what a waste of space you are before you shoot me.'

Jodie lifted the tumbler off the bar. Her lips were pressed tightly together, eyes hard and focused. On Travis.

Matt heard her voice in his head. *I can hit a bullseye at ten metres.* He pulled his eyes from the window, looked quickly around the deck. He wanted a weapon. Anything to hold in his hands.

When he turned back, Travis was lifting his thumb, pulling back the pistol cock.

ANGER CHURNED in Jodie's gut. She was not going to stand there and do nothing while Louise got shot in the head.

The tumbler was smooth and cold in her left hand. It was an easy shot with her right hand. She could crack Travis's skull at this distance – with her *right* hand. But her right hand was tied to Hannah's.

'You *coward*!' Louise yelled.

Jodie had only one chance at this so she had to make it count. She pulled back her arm and unleashed the tumbler. It crashed into the glass behind Lou, opened up a spider web crack and made Travis's head snap around.

Now. She pulled her unbound hand to her chest, braced her shoulders and threw herself forward.

In the moment she slammed into Travis, the instant her shoulder crunched and the air was crushed from her lungs, the barn exploded around her.

A thunderous crashing filled the air. And full-force screaming. Then a deafening blast of sound overrode it all, made her hands fly to her ears as it pounded her eardrums. Sharp needle-pricks of pain rained over her face and something hard rammed into her legs, taking them out from under her. Sudden, forceful grappling was all around her, shoving her sideways, sending her headfirst into a tangle of dining chairs.

A single sound cut through the confusion. A hoarse mewling, barely more than a murmur, but Jodie heard it. It came from somewhere over her shoulder, made her lift her head free of the chairs, turn fearfully in its direction. As her eyes moved across the room, she registered the debris, overturned furniture, a wrought-iron garden table, shouting – but couldn't process it. Not once she'd seen Lou.

Louise was on her knees, her arms raised and outstretched to where she was tied to Hannah and Corrine, and her face was angled down to a patch of bright red blooming high up on the front of her shirt. She looked up at Jodie, confusion and terror in her eyes. 'I . . . I'm . . .' Her eyelids fluttered and she tilted forward, only stopped from tumbling to the floor by the ropes binding her to her friends.

Jodie crawled the short distance to Louise, caught her as her dead weight pulled Hannah and Corrine to their knees.

'Oh fuck, oh fuck, oh fuck,' Lou whimpered.

Jodie pressed her free hand to Louise's shoulder, felt the thick wetness of blood on her palm. She saw shards of glass on the floor, remembered flashes of pain on her face.

'Are you cut? What happened?'

'He shot me, Jodie. He fucking shot me.'

It took a moment, maybe half a second, for the words to sink in – half a second of holding her best friend in her arms, of listening to Lou's tremulous moans, of fear and anger running riot inside her. Then, like a gasp, like a nuclear explosion, the panic was blown away, replaced with a clear, urgent, compelling image of what she needed to do.

Jodie lifted Lou from her lap, lowered her to the floor, yelled, 'Hannah!' Both Hannah and Corrine were on their knees and motionless, staring open-mouthed and white-faced across the room.

Jodie could hear voices behind her – loud and angry and male – but she couldn't take her eyes off Louise. Just hoped Travis and Kane beat each other to death.

'Hannah!' Jodie dragged on the tether at their wrists, pulled her closer. '*Help me.*' Hannah turned, saw Lou, let out a shaky, drawn-out 'oh' as she stared at the growing spread of red Jodie was trying to hold back.

'*Come on.* You know what to do.'

Hannah looked at Jodie, looked down at the blood. She didn't move, didn't do anything. What was wrong with her?

'Help me stop the bleeding.'

Hannah's eyes filled with tears, her lips quivered and she shook her head as though she couldn't make sense of what she was seeing.

It was so completely unlike Hannah that for a moment Jodie didn't know what to do. But she couldn't wait. She hauled on their tether, pressed Hannah's hand to Louise's bloody shirt. 'Keep pressure on it.'

Lou's face crumpled in pain. 'Oh God, it hurts,'

'I'm sorry, Lou. I'm so sorry,' Jodie said.

She wanted to hold her, to let her know she wasn't alone. She lifted her free hand and froze. Something cold and clammy slithered up her spine. She turned her palm up, uncurled the other hand, held them side by side. And her throat closed over.

Her hands were covered with bright, fresh, red blood. As though she'd been washing in it.

As though she'd been holding them to her own stab wounds.

Her heart crashed against her ribs. Terror was a fist in her gut, squeezing, twisting, making her head spin. She looked down at her stomach, expecting to see more blood. A waterfall of it. Running down her thighs, dripping onto her bare feet.

But she didn't. Her shirt was hanging open, torn down the front. The flesh underneath was white, clean, intact. She looked back at her hands. Looked at Lou.

'Oh no. *No.*' It's not *you*, Jodie. It's Lou. Lou was shot and bleeding and crying. 'No, no.' She thrust her free hand onto Hannah's, made her push harder on Lou's wound. '*Not* Lou.' She gritted her teeth, breathed hard, fought to ignore the coppery smell of blood in her nostrils. 'It's okay, Lou. You're okay. It's going to be okay.'

Lou *had* to be okay. Because Jodie wasn't going to lose her.

She wasn't going to run and she wasn't going to lose another best friend. It was going to be different this time.

Jodie would *make* it different.

She had to.

'Jodie, look,' Corrine hissed.

Corrine's face was still turned to whatever was happening behind them. But Jodie didn't need to look. All she needed to know was that Travis and Kane were beating each other up instead of pointing a gun at them. 'Help me get the ties undone.'

'*Look*, Jodie.'

'For God's sake, Corrine. Help me here.'

'*Jodie*. It's Matt.'

Jodie lifted her eyes, not sure she'd heard right.

Corrine's gaze didn't move from across the room. 'He came through the window.'

Jodie glanced at the back wall. One of the huge panes of glass was smashed, its curtain was torn from the track, the one next to it billowing gently in a draught of cold night air. *Matt* came through there? She swung around to the frantic sounds behind her. Two men were flailing and grunting on the floor. Above them, Kane lifted a knee, dropped a kick into the fray. One of the men on the floor raised a fist high and drove it into the other man's gut.

Oh God. It *was* Matt.

Matt had come back. He'd understood.

Jodie couldn't take her eyes off him as he wrestled Travis's arm to the floor, slammed it against the timber. 'Drop it, arsehole!' he yelled.

The gun fell from Travis's hand. Matt grabbed it, rose to one knee, held it with both hands, aimed it at Travis.

Matt was a cop. It was over.

Relief flooded her like a cup of sweet tea. Tears welled in her eyes. Louise was going to be okay. They were going to go home. She looked at Corrine, saw fresh tears. Maybe she'd never stopped crying.

She turned back to Matt, saw Kane raise his arm. She ordered her brain to scream, felt the sound welling up from deep inside but it was jammed in slow motion. 'Noooo!'

Matt turned his head. The poker from the fireplace made contact just below his right ear. The momentum carried him to the floor.

Travis scrambled out from under him as Kane raised the long, lethal spike of metal above his head.

'No!' Jodie yelled again – this time in stereo.

'No!' Travis shouted, and from the floor threw himself at his brother, buried a shoulder into his thigh, knocked him down.

'Get off me,' Kane roared. Travis punched him in the face.

It silenced him and sent a wave of horror through Jodie. He did that to his own *brother*?

Travis pushed himself to his feet, not taking his eyes off Matt's prone body. 'Fuck.' He reeled away. 'Fuck.' He ran both hands through his hair, struck a foot out at his brother, connecting hard in the ribs. 'You killed a *cop*.'

'No!' Jodie screamed. *She'd* killed him. He'd come back for her and she'd got him killed. Oh God, no. She tried to stand, to go to him. Louise cried out as the movement jolted her injured shoulder.

'Get up.' Travis dragged Kane to his feet, shoved him towards Matt. 'Go through his pockets. Get his gun.'

Jodie watched Kane use the toe of his boot to roll Matt over then closed her eyes. Shut out the sight of Matt's lifeless body on the floor. She remembered the look on his face when she'd yelled at him on the verandah. Surprise, irritation but underneath it, that alertness. She thought he'd never see past her words – so few people in her life had. Now she wished she hadn't taken the chance because he had understood her. And he'd been killed for it.

So look at him, Jodie. He'd taken a risk for you. Burn his face on your brain. You owe him that.

Kane was kneeling beside him, shoving him about as he went through his pockets. She ignored him, concentrated on Matt's face. It was turned towards her now and she committed to memory his soft mouth, the lines around his eyes that she'd liked. She tried to remember the colour of them. She'd liked that too. Green, with a lighter shade that sparked in the sun.

And then she saw the colour she remembered was bronze. Because his lids were open and he was looking right at her.

25

The room swam into focus. Matt saw sparks of light glittering off shattered glass on the floor. Then the legs of the wrought-iron table he'd thrown through the window. Then Jodie. She was on her knees, leaning protectively over someone lying by the kitchen bench. Two others were partially hidden behind her but he'd have to look away from Jodie to work out which of her friends were where. And he didn't want to do that. Not when she was looking right back at him like that.

Her face was pale, her eyes were almost black and the relief in them was like an echo of his own. When he'd smashed through the door, he'd seen Jodie shoulder charge Travis Anderson. Like a movie at half-speed, he'd seen Travis slide sideways, the garden table knock him forward, the gun track around towards Jodie. When the blast went off, he thought Jodie was shot. Thought the next time he'd see her, she'd be dead.

Someone was patting him down, pulling his wallet from his back pocket. He wanted to move but when he tried, his head spun and his eyes rolled woozily away from her. When he looked back, she made a small side-to-side movement with her head, then quickly, discreetly lifted a hand to her face, two fingers up in a V, and pulled them down over her lids, telling him to close his eyes. As he did what she wanted, his insides went cold at what he'd seen on her hand. Blood. Enough of it to run through her fingers and stain the cuff of her shirt.

You're in the middle of it now, Matt. Four hostages. Two cold-blooded thugs. Killers. And he was lying on the floor like a stunned fish. He was pushed roughly to his other side, patted down again. His head roiled nauseatingly.

'Two phones and car keys,' Kane said from above and behind.

Matt cracked an eye, saw the evidence clatter to the floor in front of him. The phones were smashed under the heel of a work boot and meaty fingers picked up the keys.

'Chuck 'em in the bush,' Travis said from above and in front.

Matt heard the chink of keys being tossed and caught above him. Heard feet walking away, a door swung open.

'Get the gear while you're out there,' Travis called.

'What about more cops?' Kane said.

There was a pause. 'Nah. They'd already be here if there were more. Wiseman thought he could handle us himself.'

'He always was a prick,' Kane said and they both laughed.

From the floor, Matt could see Travis in front of him. Part of him, anyway. Jeans from the knee down, worn boots. Close enough to reach out and grab an ankle. He heard Kane take a step on the veran-dah. *Get the hostages out.* The words roared up from deep inside him, riding a wave of fear and rage. He couldn't tell if it was instinct or training or bitter experience. It didn't matter. He just knew it was the only chance Jodie and her friends had to survive.

Matt saw in an instant how it would have to go down. He'd have to be fast. Have it over and done with before Kane got back. Wrap an arm around Travis's legs, drive up and forward with his shoulder to knock him down. He heard Kane start walking, loud footfalls on the timber decking outside. How long would it take him to get 'the gear'? Even as he braced for action, prepared to drive off the floor with his good leg, he knew that wasn't the only question he needed an answer to. How much would the crack on his skull slow him down? And where was the gun?

He was barely off the floor before Travis lifted a foot and jammed it into Matt's ribs. Pain curled him into a ball. The boot came back, swung like a wrecking ball, slamming into his bad knee. Matt cried out as the impact of it flung him over. His leg felt like it had been ripped off. He wanted to howl in agony but he forced himself past it. He might survive the beating if he knew where the next hit was coming from. Matt looked up at Travis and knew then it wasn't a beating he needed to worry about. It was the gun pointed at his face.

'Move and I'll blow your head apart,' Travis said. He was standing over Matt, knuckles white on the weapon, a sneer on his face. A door banged open. Travis flicked a look across the room. 'Hey, bro, you're not a cop killer yet. Look who woke up.'

Matt felt the timber boards under him shudder as something heavy thudded to the floor. He saw two pickaxes – big, solid and well used. On the other side of the room, one of the women wailed loudly. Then Kane was over him, grabbing him by the collar of his jacket, hauling his shoulders off the floor.

'I owe you this one,' Kane snarled. He pulled back an arm and smashed a fist into Matt's face.

Light strobed behind Matt's eyes. The room lurched and rolled. He heard yelling. The floor was hard and cold against his cheek. He tasted blood. The floorboards were smooth and glossy and pitching under his eyes. Someone was shouting. Hard, angry words he couldn't make out. He thought it was Jodie. Hoped it was. Thought she'd be good at it. He was jostled and then someone was trying to haul him up. He wanted to move but his limbs wouldn't cooperate. Then Jodie's voice was in his ear.

'Try to walk, Matt.' Her words were whispered, urgent. Her breath was on his face.

'I can't do this on my own. Matt, please.'

Her shoulder wedged itself under his arm. She felt slight and lean. He dragged his good leg under him, pushed up, heard someone groan as his bad leg hit the floor. Maybe it was him. He couldn't tell in the confusion of sound and movement around him. The women were crying and crying out. Both the Andersons were shouting. Swearing, bawling orders, shoving, crowding. Matt hit a wall, back pressed flat against it for a second before he was thrust forward. Jodie dragged at his shirt, propelled him onwards, arm at his waist, hand like a vice around his wrist, taking his weight across her shoulders. Damn she was strong. Then his shoulder rammed into something and he was falling...

MATT DIDN'T MOVE. It took a few seconds for the spinning in his head to follow suit. It was dark. So dark he had to blink a couple of times to be sure his eyes were actually open.

Someone was crying. A mixture of hiccuping and wailing. Someone else was breathing hard, forcefully. Big breaths in then blowing out again. He felt movement near his feet.

'Where's the light switch?' It was Jodie. She was whispering. 'Hannah. Where's the switch?'

Someone said through a break in the hiccuping, 'There isn't one. The light comes on when the door opens.'

There was a burst of light, like an extended flash from a camera. In that fraction of time, Matt saw Jodie kneeling up at his feet, one arm outstretched into a small room, the other towards the door at his side, the pads of her fingers pressed against it. Her shirt was torn down the front, her face was white and her eyes were wild. In the pitch blackness that followed, the image of her crucifix pose was burned on his retina in negative.

The light came on again. Her torso leaned a little more towards the door this time, her eyes narrowed in effort and determination. Then it was dark again.

'Wait,' he said. The pain in his knee flared as he moved. He pulled his good leg out from under the other, pushed his foot against the left side of a double door. Something was holding it closed but the slight shift in its position was enough to activate the light. A bare bulb in the ceiling filled the room with harsh light. Jodie looked at him and they squinted at each other for a moment in the sudden glare.

'Are you okay?' she asked quietly.

Concussion was a definite possibility. 'Yeah.'

He flicked his eyes around. The room they were in was maybe two metres square, no windows, one double door, a long metal clothing rail along the wall opposite, a couple of coats and shirts on hangers, a suitcase in the corner. He was lying in front of the doors, Jodie kneeling at his feet, wiping one bloody hand down her jeans.

Her other hand was still outstretched, tied to Hannah. She was propped against the wall under the rail, her face ashen, her legs out straight almost touching him. The blonde had her back to the wall at his head. Between them, tied to both of them, was Louise. She was the one breathing hard. Her head was on Hannah's lap, her eyes were closed and one side of her shirt was covered in blood. Matt's heart thumped at the sight of it.

Jodie shuffled quickly to Louise's side and pulled her free hand from the sleeve of her torn top. With a jagged, tearing sound, she ripped the shirt open down the other sleeve, pulled her arm out, balled it up and pressed it gently to her friend's shoulder.

Matt wanted to check the door – sometimes the best means of escape was the most obvious – but his eyes stayed on Jodie. She was lean and athletic. She was wearing a black bra. Lower down, stretching across her flat stomach like a belt, was a thick, uneven line of scars.

She looked up at him. 'Matt?'

He cleared his throat. 'Yeah.'

'Can you move?'

'Yes.'

'Can you get close enough to untie me?'

He pushed himself into a sitting position, waited a second for his brain to stop rolling about and shifted as far as he could without taking his foot off the door. Jodie angled her hand towards him, pulled Hannah forward as she did so, shifting Louise's head on her lap. She groaned.

'Hang in there, Lou. It'll only take a second,' Jodie whispered.

Matt tried not to bump her as he worked on the rope. It was in

208 | JAYE FORD

some kind of complicated knot that was fastened between their wrists.

'I'm so sorry, Matt,' Jodie whispered to his lowered head. 'I shouldn't have got you involved.'

He lifted his face and the guilt and fear in her eyes made him look back down again. He should have called Carraro. He should have figured it out faster. He should have done a lot of things. 'You took a chance.'

'I should have just told you to leave.'

He should have got them out. 'If you want to blame someone, blame the arseholes who locked us in here.'

There was a loud thump from the other end of the house followed by a smash and raised voices. The blonde woman, the one doing all the crying, squealed. The others jumped. Matt looked in the direction of the noise, waited for more, a pulse pounding in his ears. When nothing came, he got back to the rope with more urgency.

The scars on Jodie's stomach were right there in front of him as he worked. Centimetres from his face. He couldn't not see them. They were raised, stretched, knotted in places, faded to the colour of the skin on her stomach. Clearly not recent. Probably years old. Too uneven to be anything but random and, without a doubt, the result of extreme violence. Matt imagined the type of weapon that could cause that sort of damage without killing a person. A wide, short-bladed knife. It explained her attitude better than his abusive husband scenario. And it said a whole lot more about her. He'd seen plenty of brave people live in a shadow of fear after the kind of violence she must have survived. It took courage to come out of something like that and be ready and willing to body-slug a thug in a pub or throw a rock through a stalker's car window.

When he finally unravelled the rope, she pulled her hand back, rubbed off the blood on her jeans. He raised his eyes and saw she'd seen the line of his gaze. Something passed over her face. She half turned away, said, 'Thanks,' opened her mouth to say more but didn't. She just twisted away and started in on the tie binding Lou and Hannah together.

If Jodie was embarrassed by her scars, she had no need. He was impressed. The woman had guts to have all that in her head, take on a couple of gun-toting attackers and still be upright and functioning when she was chucked in a dungeon.

He slid back, put the flat of his hands on the doors and tested his weight against them. There was a little movement lower down, none at all higher up. There wasn't a lock, so something must have been jammed up against the handles on the outside. Which meant they'd have to break through *both* doors to push their way out. Which meant they wouldn't be getting out that way.

'Where are we?' he asked.

Jodie pulled the tie free. 'In a walk-in robe off the main bedroom.'

There was another thud, more voices – loud but Matt couldn't tell if they were angry or just strident. He pressed an ear to the gap between the two doors. 'Where in the house are we?'

Jodie held Lou's head, said, 'Slide out, Hannah, so Louise can lie down.' Hannah seemed stunned into inaction, didn't move until Jodie tugged at her arm. As she clambered stiffly out from under Louise's head, Jodie answered his question. 'At the opposite end to the lounge room.' She stepped across her friend to squat in front of the blonde.

'Did you hear where they went?'

She pointed over her shoulder at the wall opposite the doors. 'In that direction. Back towards the main room. I think they're still inside.'

The blonde stopped crying. 'Oh my God. Jodie, your scars are . . . Is that . . .? Are they . . .?' She never finished, just started sobbing again.

'Shhh,' Jodie said gently. She put a finger under the blonde's chin and tilted her face up. 'Corrine, honey, don't look at them.'

Jodie sounded unbelievably calm but Matt could see the tightness in her shoulders and the thin line of her mouth as she tossed Corrine's rope. Her movements were fast, staccatoed, as though too much energy was being put into simple activities.

Matt tried the doors again – leaned back on his hands, pulled his good leg up and smacked the sole of his foot hard against it.

Corrine let out a brief squeal. Above her, Jodie hauled a coat off the clothing rail, rolled it up and put it under Lou's head.

'Is it bad, Hannah?' Jodie asked. She gripped Hannah's shoulder, made the woman look at her. 'Hannah? Is Louise going to be all right?'

Hannah shook her head, eyes wide, filling with tears. 'I don't know. I don't know. She needs a doctor. She needs a *hospital*.'

Dread felt like a cold hand on Matt's neck. No. Louise wasn't going to bleed to death. He kicked the door again, shoved it with his hands. He wanted to shake the fucker off its hinges but there were no handles on the inside. 'Goddamn it!' He ran a hand through his hair, met Jodie's wild eyes as she did the same thing.

She stood again and walked stiffly to the clothing rail. There wasn't a great selection, a couple of shirts, another coat. She yanked it down, draped it over Lou, tucked it in around her hips like a blanket. Got up, pulled a shirt off a hanger, bunched it into a ball. She squatted beside Matt this time, pressed the cloth to the back of his head, took it away and looked at it. Breathed hard. There was a patch of fresh blood on it. She held it against his head once more, her other hand on his forehead, her eyes squeezed tight.

Matt watched while she fought to hold herself together. He wanted to reach out and touch her, give her some kind of reassurance. But he guessed she needed something to do more than she needed a tender moment right now. And besides, what kind of reassurance could he give?

When the bump on his head started to ache from her grip, he cupped a hand around hers, eased it away. 'It's okay. It doesn't hurt much.'

She opened her eyes. They were big and dark, shiny with unshed tears. She refolded the bloody shirt, lifted it to his mouth, dabbed at something sticky there, pulled it away with another blood stain.

Matt smiled with the other side of his mouth. 'He owed me more than a cut lip.'

Jodie was about to say something but Corrine got in first, speaking through sobs. 'When are the police coming?'

All four of them looked at him. Their faces were pale with shock and fear but there was a glimmer of hope in their eyes. And he was about to snuff it out.

'They're not. No one else knows what's happening.'

'No one?' Corrine said.

'No.'

'Have you got a gun?' she said.

'No.'

'A radio?'

'No.'

'*No?*' Corrine's voice was shrill. 'What kind of a policeman are you?'

Matt's hands curled into fists. It was the question he'd been asking himself for the last six months. 'I'm *not* a cop.'

'What? *What?*'

'Shut up, Corrine,' Jodie said.

'I thought you were here to save us. And no one *knows?*' Corrine wailed.

'It's not his fault,' Jodie hissed at her.

Corrine wrapped her arms around her chest. 'We're never going to get out of here. They're going to rape us. And kill us. They're going to make me go first then murder us all.'

Jodie got to her haunches, as though she was ready to jump at her. 'Shut up, Corrine.'

'We're all going to . . .'

'Shut up!' She took a couple of breaths, looked quickly about the room. 'We're not. We're just *not*. We're going to get out of this and we're going to go home.'

Corrine was crying again, tears rolling down her face, barely able to speak through the sobs. 'But . . .'

'*But nothing!*' Jodie glared at her, eyes ablaze.

No one argued with her. All three of her friends looked at her like she was Moses about to part the Red Sea – with dread and wonder and hope on their faces.

Then it all fell apart.

26

Without warning, Jodie's control disintegrated. She screwed up her face, mashed her lips together and in an explosive movement, fell forward, a raw howl flung from her lips.

The sound made the hairs on Matt's neck stand up. Her knees were on the floor and her head was on her knees. She clutched at her stomach, her fingers pulling at the flesh on her hips as though she was trying to hold it together. What the hell kind of memories was she trying to push back into place?

Matt glanced helplessly at her friends. They were like cardboard cut-outs. They didn't move, didn't make a sound, just stared in horror. Every group had a leader, someone who took control when the going got tough, who made decisions and gave orders. They'd just lost theirs and it looked like they suddenly felt a whole lot more alone.

When he turned back to Jodie, something had changed. She was still curled in a tight ball but her muscles were tenser, her spine straighter, her shoulders flexed.

'We're all going to die,' Corrine wailed.

Beside Matt, Jodie's fingers formed a fist. Then, in the same explosive motion she'd gone down with, she sat up and swung her hands free of her torso.

'No, we're not!' She said it resolutely, the wildness gone from her eyes. Replaced with something steely and hard. She faced her friends. 'You hear me, Corrine? Hannah? Whatever else you think of me, however crazy and in need of help you think I am, know this – *I am a survivor*. I survived before and I'm going to survive this time. And I'm not leaving anyone behind. You got that? We are *all* going home.' Jodie looked at each of them in turn, daring them to contradict her. She turned her eyes on Matt. 'That means you, too. I got you into this so I'm making sure you get out of it. We stay together and no one gets left behind. You got that?'

Her conviction was impressive. *She* was impressive. Her voice was solid, commanding, like a teacher reading the riot act. Not a sign that five seconds ago she was falling apart. Matt wanted to jump right on board her motivation train. Shit, he wanted to say they were going to walk right out of there. But he knew it wasn't going to happen like that. Knew it was going to get a lot uglier before anyone had a chance to go anywhere.

She was right about one thing, though. The hostages were going to get out this time. Jodie and her friends would go home or he would die trying. His priority – his only priority – was to get all four of these women out alive.

Whatever Jodie saw in his face made her narrow her eyes. 'You got that, Matt?'

'Yeah, I got that.'

'But . . .' Corrine sobbed.

Jodie pointed at her. 'No buts, Corrine. Your kids can't lose another parent.' She aimed her finger at Lou. 'And Ray can't handle both sets of twins.' She locked in on Hannah. 'And Pete would forget where he'd left his head if you weren't around.' She dug a nail into her own chest then, closed her eyes a moment. 'And I am *not* going to let my kids live with the legacy of a murdered mother.' She swung her finger around to Matt. 'Have you got kids?'

'No.'

'A girlfriend?'

'No.'

'Well, you've got a father and a brother and . . . and . . .' She stopped, looked like she wasn't sure how to go on.

There wasn't anything to go on to, Matt thought. He was thirty-five years old and no one needed him to come home. He'd screwed up more than his career in the last six months.

'And you haven't had one of my steaks.' She said it with more resolve than it deserved.

He frowned. 'Did you just tell me the only thing I've got to live for is a steak?'

She lifted her chin a little. 'No, I said *my* steak. I do a great steak. My steak is a damn good reason to stay alive. You got that?'

'Not just any steak then?'

She paused a second. 'You have to survive so *I* can cook you a steak.'

Well, that was unexpected. 'You mean like a date?'

She nodded tersely. 'Yeah, okay, it could be a date.'

Definitely better than the alternative. 'That could be an incentive.'

'Make sure it is.' She said it firmly, like an order, but her eyes gave her away. She looked down a moment then back up at him. Gutsy and coy at the same time.

He felt the corner of his mouth curl up. 'That thing you said on the verandah before, about last night being the best. Did I enjoy myself, too?'

She smiled then. Not a big smile. Not a grin, either. Just a small, bold upturn of the lips. 'Yeah, Matt, you had a great time.'

'For God's sake!' Corrine almost howled the words. 'We're not in a bloody singles bar.' Then she screamed as a thud shuddered through the barn.

'WHAT THE . . .?' was all Jodie managed before the walk-in robe vibrated with another tremendous thump. Corrine was wailing again. Hannah was cringing, Lou was trying to lift her head. Jodie saw the perplexed look on Matt's face and tried to rein in the fear that was ricocheting through her. Don't give in to it, Jodie. That's not how to survive.

She could still feel the surge of energy that had pulled her on course. Corrine's desperate declaration that they were all going to die had pushed her to the edge. She'd come so close to falling apart, to letting every ugly memory fill her up and shut her down. Then she'd heard Angela.

Run, Jodie.

The words that had woken her sweating and shaken this morning. The same words that for years had filled her with terror and shame. But the voice was different this time. Not tremulous with tears but hard and tough and angry. It was the voice Angela had used that last hockey final they'd played together, when they were one point down in the final quarter. Angie had belted the ball across the field at her. 'Kill it, Jodie!' she'd yelled. And Jodie had – she'd smashed it right past the keeper into the back of the net. They weren't meant to win that day but they'd equalled the score then totally demoralised the opposition.

Run, Jodie. Maybe she'd remembered it wrong all these years. Maybe Angie had been angry and defiant that night. Maybe her words had filled Jodie with the same raw, intense energy that flooded through her now.

Run, Jodie. The game wasn't over yet.

Jodie was on her haunches as a third thud was followed by a screech. Voices hooted from the other end of the house. She had no idea what it was but she was on her feet and stumbling over her friends' legs as the fourth crash reverberated. The light went out. Then came back on. Matt was scrambling to get up, one hand on the door, the other gripping his bad knee.

'Corrine,' Jodie said. 'Move over and hold the door.'

Corrine pushed herself along the wall, away from the door. 'No way. I'm not going anywhere near the door. I'm not getting any closer to those awful men than I have to.' She flinched as another thud shook the floor.

She was scared, probably still drunk unless terror had sobered her up, but Jodie wanted to slap her. Like in the movies when the panicking character is brought back to earth with a loud clap across the chops. Except the shock of it would probably make Corrine cry more.

'Come on!' Jodie said through gritted teeth. 'We need the light and Hannah's looking after Lou.' If it could be called 'looking after'. Hannah's hands were on Lou's shoulder but it seemed to be more by chance than choice. Something was wrong with Hannah. Her eyes were flexed wide, she was shaking and every move she made was like slow motion. She'd been that way since Travis had held the gun to her head. And it scared the hell out of Jodie.

'What about you?' Corrine said.

Jodie unzipped the suitcase in the corner of the wardrobe, threw open the lid. 'I'm looking for weapons.'

'Hey, that's my bag. I don't do *weapons*.'

'Then do something useful and hold the door.'

Corrine complained but crawled across the small room and propped herself against the door. Matt was on his feet, holding onto the wall with one outstretched arm as he limped across the wardrobe. There was a fat graze on his left cheek and his bottom lip was swollen on one side but it had stopped bleeding. His eyes looked wrong though, as if he was having trouble focusing. Concussion for sure, but at least he was conscious and on his feet. And the sudden noise had obviously given him the same injection of urgency as it had Jodie.

The crashing continued from the other end of the house. Short, sharp thumps that rocked the floor of the barn and echoed in her head.

Jodie pulled Corrine's belongings out of the suitcase. Sweaters and trousers, a massive bag of bathroom supplies, the boots with the broken heel. She dumped the ruined shoe back in the case, put the other one on the floor beside her. It wasn't called a stiletto for nothing.

She looked up as Matt yanked on the clothing rail above her, trying to break it out of the metal cups holding it to the wall. It ran the length of the room, secured to an overhead shelf halfway along. It was probably in two halves. That would give them two metre-long pieces of steel – not a weapon they could hide under a shirt but it could inflict some damage if they got a chance to use it.

'What do you think they're doing out there?' she asked him.

He looked down with eyes that were grave but more focused, as though the effort to shake the rail had cleared his head somewhat. 'It sounds like they're smashing up the place.'

He heaved his weight against the rod again, his jaw squared with determination. A ripple of fear ran through Jodie's spine. She wanted to grab him by the shirt front and tell him he had to get out of this, too.

He'd said he wasn't a cop anymore but he was kidding himself. She'd seen it on his face when she'd been ranting about getting out. And she saw it now. He wanted to do his job. He wanted to save them. But Jodie didn't want a hero. She wanted him alive. She wanted to cook him that steak. She wanted to sit in a park and drink coffee with him again. She wanted to get hot and sweaty and passionate with him and she hadn't felt like that in a long time. Most of all, she wanted to have enough time to discover what it was that she recognised inside him.

As he pulled down, one half of the rail bent in the middle and came cleanly out of its metal cup. Matt dropped it to the floor, the clatter disguised by the crashing from the other end of the house. The sound had a rhythm to it now – thump-thump, thump-thump. Like Travis and Kane were working as a team. Like a giant piston crashing against the barn. As Matt moved on to the other half of the rail, Jodie pulled a white sweater from Corrine's case and put it on. It was stuffy in the wardrobe but she didn't want to be half naked when Travis or Kane came back. She unzipped Corrine's bathroom case and up-

218 | JAYE FORD

ended it. Amongst the make-up and hair goo, she found spray deodorant, a metal nailfile, tiny scissors. Weaponry.

She crawled to Louise, pushed the deodorant into the palm of Lou's hand, curled her fingers tight around it. Lou looked awful – her skin was pasty, there was a sheen of perspiration on her face and the blood on her shirt was slick and bright – but when she opened her eyes, Jodie saw the anger that burned in them. 'Aim for the eyes,' she told her.

'Here.' She passed the scissors to Hannah, the nailfile to Corrine.

Hannah looked at the small scissors with a blank expression. Jodie wanted to snap her fingers in front of Hannah's face. Come on, girl. You can't run for your life if you're paralysed by shock.

Corrine held the nailfile out on the palm of her hand and thrust it back at her. 'What am I meant to do with this? Grind my way out?' There was panic in Corrine's voice and she was on the verge of hyper-ventilating.

Jodie felt it infecting her. Louise was hurt, Hannah was a statue and Corrine was losing it. She grabbed Corrine by the shoulders, shook her. 'Stop crying. You can't help yourself if you're crying.'

'Help myself!' Corrine repeated, her voice high and incredulous.

Jodie saw the terror in her eyes, knew there was no point telling her not to be scared. They were all scared. But panic would make her useless. And terror might make her too frightened to act. Anger, on the other hand, was a different story. Corrine needed to get mad. She needed that slap across the face.

Jodie shook her again. 'Remember what Roland's partners did to you? Do you remember that, Corrine?'

Corrine frowned, her panic interrupted by the sudden change of subject. 'What?'

'Remember the day they came to your house and told you that you weren't getting any of Roland's money? Tried to tell you he'd been having an affair?' Jodie saw the jolt of memory, the hurt in Corrine's eyes. Wasn't sure if it was the bitter three-year court battle or the fact Jodie had brought it up that had upset her. Either way, it didn't matter.

All four of them had been there that day, had watched in horror at what followed. Corrine had refused to talk about it ever again but right now she needed to dig it up out of her memory and roll around in its stench. 'Remember how angry you were, Corrine? That dinner set was worth the price of a small car. And you smashed every damn piece of it. One by one. All over the kitchen. Remember that?'

Corrine tried to pull away from her. 'Why are you bringing . . .'

'They were going to take your children's inheritance away. The future Roland had wanted for them.'

'Stop it,' Corrine said.

'Jodie, don't,' Hannah said from behind.

Jodie turned, relieved to see a sign of life from her. Hannah still looked stunned, pale, but she seemed cross, too. Good, Jodie thought. Two for the price of one. She pushed Hannah a little harder. 'You're in no position to tell me what to do.' Yep, Hannah was cross now. Jodie turned back. 'You need to remember it, Corrine.'

'No, I don't. I sued their arses off. I don't *have* to remember that.'

'Yes, you do. Because you have to be angrier than that. A hundred times more angry. These guys want to take your children's *mother* away. They want to make Bailey and Zoe orphans.'

Corrine's mouth pulled into a tight line, her eyes filled with new tears but they shone with bitterness. 'Do you have to be so bloody graphic?' Corrine jerked out of her hold, folded her arms and looked away.

Jodie felt a buzz of success. She'd made Corrine mad. It might've been better if she was pissed off at Kane and Travis instead of her – but angry was angry. She prised Corrine's hand from her folded arms, positioned the nailfile so the sharp end pointed from the base of Corrine's palm, closed her fingers around it in a fist. 'Do it like this.' Jodie lifted her own hand, swept it downwards in a stabbing motion. 'If you can, aim for somewhere soft. Try to hit hard. Make it hurt. You got it?'

Corrine snatched her hand back. 'Yes, all right. I got it.'

Jodie looked at Hannah. She held the scissors loosely in one hand, the other was clasped to the collar of her shirt, her face turned away. 'You too, Hannah.'

Hannah didn't move.

'Hannah?' She couldn't tell if she was blank-faced again or just cross and ignoring her. 'Are you with me?'

'Yes,' she answered quietly, without turning her head.

Jodie was torn between shaking her and hugging her. 'Come on. Don't do this. You have to look after Lou.'

'I *am*.' Hannah's eyes flashed briefly to Jodie's before she dropped them to Louise. 'I am looking after Lou.' As if to prove it, she released the collar of her shirt and pushed a lock of Lou's curly hair from her forehead.

Jodie saw the anger had gone. The blank look wasn't there either, at least not like before. Now she just looked stunned. Her eyes, her whole face. Overwhelmed by it. Cowed and embarrassed by it. Hannah's tough, bossy persona had taken a hit. She didn't like what shock had done to her. Get over yourself, Jodie wanted to tell her. This was not the moment to wallow over a fright response. There wasn't the time for molly-coddling, either.

'For God's sake, Hannah. Hold the damn scissors like I said and show me you can use them,' Jodie snapped. It had the desired effect – Hannah looked up, a flash of ice in her eyes. But she was going to need more than that. 'Is that it? You're just going to sit there and play with Lou's hair? Come on, Hannah, you've always got plenty to say. Why stop now?'

Hannah threw the scissors to the floor. 'I don't *want* the scissors. We should just do what they say.'

'No,' Jodie said. 'They want to hurt us. Pick up the scissors.'

'No. I won't fight them. If we don't fight, they might just let us go.'

What the hell was she thinking? Jodie picked up the scissors, shoved them at Hannah. 'Take them.'

Hannah pushed her hand away. 'I know what happens. I've nursed rape victims. It's always worse for the ones who fight. Much worse. We should just do what they want.'

The thought made Jodie's stomach lurch. *You fought real hard, Angie.* '*No*, Hannah.'

Corrine drew her arms across her torso.

Above them, Matt swore quietly under his breath, dragged on the second rail with more urgency.

'They've got a *gun*,' Hannah said. 'They can shoot us if they want to.' She looked at Corrine, then back at Jodie, spoke firmly, 'I just want to go home.'

Jodie shook her head. They'd all seen the rape in Kane's eyes when he'd pawed Corrine. But Travis had held a gun to Lou's head and shot her. She'd be dead if Matt hadn't come through the glass. Rape was on the agenda but that wouldn't be the end of it. Jodie grabbed Hannah's hand, slapped the scissors into the palm. 'You've only seen the rape victims who *survived*.' She curled Hannah's fingers around the scissors, held them there until Hannah finally took them. 'No one is getting on their back for those animals.'

Jodie sat back down, breathing hard, watching as Corrine slid the nailfile into the back pocket of her jeans. She saw Angie again, her lovely face screwed up in pain and terror. Her killers hadn't bothered to strip her naked. They'd wrestled her out of her jeans and underwear, ripped off her shirt and pushed her bra up under her arms. 'No, put it in your bra. You too, Hannah.'

'But ...' Corrine said.

'Just do it!'

She turned as Matt groaned with effort and saw him pull the second rail from the wall. At the same moment, the crashing from the lounge room stopped and as the rod ripped its housing from the wall, the loud crack of breaking plasterboard seemed to echo in the sudden silence.

They stopped, waited. Matt held the rod with both hands inches from where it had hung. All five of them watched the door. Beyond the room, there were muffled sounds, voices, soft thuds, not the footsteps Jodie had expected to hear storming down the hallway. A door banged. They flinched as one. Then it was quiet.

It was so quiet, Jodie could hear herself breathe. She picked up the rail and the stiletto-heeled boot and propped herself against the door on the floor next to Corrine. 'Do you want me to be the keeper of the light now?' She didn't have to ask twice. Corrine crawled quickly across the floor and huddled in the corner.

Matt limped to the other door, braced himself against it and slid to the floor next to her, his bad leg straight out in front. Jodie could see he was in pain but he hadn't leaned on the wall for support this time. That had to be good. He ran a hand through his hair and settled his eyes on hers. 'What the hell is going on?'

27

J odie licked at dry lips. A distant thud told her Kane and Travis hadn't left the barn altogether. She wanted to move, do something useful but short of surgically removing the bullet from Louise's shoulder, there was nothing to do but wait.

'I have no idea,' she said. 'At first, I thought they were here to hurt us but if that's all they wanted, we wouldn't be sitting here, right?'

Matt nodded as though he'd already come to that conclusion.

'Who are they?' Hannah said. Her voice was firm, a little too loud, as though she was making up for her earlier silence. Beside her on the floor, Louise opened her eyes and waited for Matt's answer.

He looked at each one of them then took a long moment to examine the metal rod in his hand. Jodie's stomach tightened. What didn't he want to tell them?

'They're small-town thugs,' he said at last. 'Born and bred in Bald Hill. No mother, brought up by an abusive, alcoholic father. They spent time in juvenile together after they beat up a kid behind the school. Later, Travis joined the army and Kane did two years in maximum security for aggravated assault. Six months after Kane was released, Travis was back. They've been back here ever since.' It

sounded like a police report. He looked like he had more to add but
didn't.

'What else?' Jodie said.

His eyes met hers. She could see him deciding what to tell.
'They're vicious but you already know that.' He lifted his hand and
passed a rough thumb gently across the bruise on her cheek.

The unexpected tenderness made her eyes tingle with the threat
of tears. She blinked hard. He knew more. 'What else?'

'Nothing else.'

Hey, bro, we should leave him something this time. 'They know you.'

'Yeah.'

'What happened between you and Kane?'

His pupils moved fractionally from side to side. He was thinking,
fast. 'Cop stuff.'

'Is that why they're here?'

'No. It happened a long time ago. How did they get in?'

Jodie paused. Why had he changed the subject? Hannah spoke
into the silence.

'They said they used to live here and wanted to take a look at the
renovations. We showed them around.'

'They seemed really nice,' Corrine said defensively.

'So what happened?' Matt said.

Corrine pointed at Jodie. 'She started yelling at them.'

Matt turned to Jodie, a question on his face.

'No, it started before then,' Hannah said, as though she was
piecing it together for the first time. 'Jodie just caught on faster than
the rest of us.'

Jodie raised her eyebrows. *Caught on?*

Corrine was shaking her head. 'If Jodie hadn't been rude ...'

'Let it go, Corrine,' Hannah cut her off. 'We need to focus on what
to do *now*.'

Jodie frowned at Hannah in the harsh light. She was over her
shock, that much was clear. There was even a little colour on her
cheeks. And she sounded like the real Hannah. The one who'd told
Jodie she was having a breakdown. The one who stood her ground in

an argument. Resentment lodged in Jodie's throat. She pushed up her sleeves and wiped perspiration from her top lip. Her shin and hand ached. It was hot in the wardrobe now. The air was thick with the smell of blood, damp with sweat and fear, and heavy with the silence of unspoken words. They needed to be angry at the two animals on the other side of the door, not each other, Jodie thought.

'Where are your car keys?' Matt said.

Jodie shook her head, reined in her thoughts. 'On the floor in the lounge room somewhere. But there's a spare under the chassis above the front wheel on the driver's side.' The uninjured half of Matt's mouth turned up just a little. He was impressed with her contingency planning, Jodie thought. The man had no idea. 'Have you got a spare?'

He shook his head. 'I was in my brother's car. It sits in the garage most of the time. I doubt he keeps a key in it.'

'Where is it now?' she asked.

'Down on the road. If I can get to it, I can hot-wire it. Where is their car?' He cocked his head towards the lounge room. 'I only saw yours out front.'

Jodie frowned. 'I didn't see a car either.' She looked at Hannah and Corrine for an answer.

Corrine shook her head.

Hannah shrugged. 'They didn't come in a car. At least, I didn't hear one.'

'They didn't have a car last night either,' Jodie said. Matt's eyebrows sat up. 'They were here *last night*?'

'Hannah and I spoke to them outside,' Jodie said. 'I didn't recognise Kane. It was too dark and Travis did all the talking. They said they were camping over the ridge. I think they broke into the barn earlier today, too.' She looked at Hannah, who didn't meet her gaze. Would it have made any difference if they'd called the police this afternoon instead of yelling at each other? Would a police officer turning up have scared the Andersons off? Jodie frowned, remembered something Travis had said about the way she'd gone into town in a hurry. 'I think they've been watching us.'

Matt said nothing but his eyes narrowed and a frown slowly deepened between his brows.

'What?' she said.

His eyes did that tiny side-to-side movement again. 'Nothing.'

Her fingers curled tighter around the clothing rail. 'You know something.'

The thinking had stopped. His eyes were flat and decided. 'No. I don't.'

Her anger flared. 'Don't lie to us, Matt. You know something. I know you do and you've got no right keeping it from us.'

'I don't *know* anything.'

'Then tell us what you *think*. Whatever those two bastards are doing out there, they're not planning to leave us in this wardrobe for the cleaners to find. They intend to come back. We need to know what we're up against.'

His eyes moved to Corrine. Jodie followed his gaze. She was huddled in the corner, horror on her tear-stained face.

'Look, Corrine's freaking out because she's never had a sadistic bastard put his hands all over her. Give her some time. She'll surprise the hell out of you.' She saw the doubt on his face and grabbed his arm, pulled him around to face her. 'Don't make assumptions about what we can handle. You have no idea what we can handle. You don't even know us!' She saw his eyes drop to her stomach. The scars were covered by the sweater now but he'd seen them. He'd had a good long look at them when he was untying her. Plenty of time to decide she wasn't up to an awful truth. Was it too late for him to understand about the cold, steeliness inside her? Or was he like everyone else? Would he try to shield her? Had he already decided one trauma was all she was engineered for?

His eyes lifted to her face. 'Okay. Tell me what time they were here last night.'

Right response, Matt. Ten points. Go to the top of the class. 'It was just after we arrived. We were still unpacking the car. Eight-thirty, nine o'clock maybe.'

'And there were lights outside later,' Hannah said.

Jodie frowned a question at her.

'Jodie saw them,' Hannah said to Matt, as though it had never been in question. 'And there was a car during the night.'

'Is that right?' Jodie said. 'You sure it wasn't just thunder?'

Hannah attempted to look indignant. 'Well, I wasn't sure before but it makes sense now.'

Makes sense, Jodie wanted to shout but now was not the time to have it out. Leave it. Just forget it. The only thing that mattered now was getting home to their families. Jodie could argue with her about it later. Over a glass of wine.

She turned to Matt. His eyes were already on her, as though he'd seen her struggle, was saying 'hang in there, you're doing fine'. 'I saw lights outside the barn around eleven-thirty,' she told him. 'Two, like two people walking around with torches. Close to the verandah, out the back. Then there was a big, souped-up car driving around the barn at three this morning.'

'Your poachers pointing torches at the wildlife?'

Jodie nodded, thinking back to their conversation in the park. She'd thought she was going nuts but apparently it was just the world going nuts around her. Then she remembered what they'd talked about on the way to the park, the police cars in the street, and a couple of dots connected. 'Have they got something to do with that murdered man?'

'Murdered?' Corrine said.

'What man?' Hannah asked. At her side, Louise lifted her head and winced in pain.

'It's possible,' Matt said tentatively.

'Wait,' Jodie said. 'After they tied us up, they argued a couple of times. Travis said something about the cops. And something about not wanting to go into town with the police there.'

'That's right,' Hannah said. 'Travis told Kane he'd hand him over to the cops if he didn't do what he told him.'

Matt ran a hand through his hair. 'The detective on the case was asking about the builders at John's house. Kane and Travis were working there. It doesn't mean they did it but . . .' His lips flattened into a tight line. 'But they are both capable of it.'

A quiet whimper came from Corrine's corner of the room. Hannah closed her eyes and put her hand in Louise's. Jodie thought about Kane at the pub, the dark splotch on his collar, the rusty smear on his neck. The muscles in her legs twitched. She wanted to run – fast, long strides that would carry them all to safety.

She wiped her hands on her jeans. 'But why would they come here? Why wouldn't they hide or hit the road or, or . . .' What did murderers do? 'He went to *the pub*. Kane killed a man then went to the pub. He was drinking beer and trying to pick me up. Bloody hell, I pitched him across the hall!' She rubbed a hand around the back of her neck. 'Is that why they came here? Because of me?'

'Jodie.' He held his hand up like a stop sign. 'It might not have been Kane who did it.'

She shook her head. Come on, you told him you could handle it, don't make a liar of yourself. And think. This can't be just about you. 'Okay, hang on. Travis made Kane go outside and look for something. They both went out. At different times.'

'I saw Travis outside. He was in the garden at the back,' Matt said.

'In the garden? Kane had dirt on his hands when he came in. Before that, he said something about getting their stuff. I can't remember exactly.' She looked at Hannah but it was Louise who spoke.

'It was Travis and it was just before he hit you the first time.' Lou's eyes were open and her voice was weak and breathy but she licked her lips and went on. 'He said 'a meal isn't too much to ask, is it? Then we'll get our stuff and get out of here'.' She winced as she shifted her head a little. 'After they tied us up, he said, 'Now we check it out properly'. Said they should start out the back, that they'd wasted enough time making nice with the wine. Then later, when we were in the kitchen, he told Kane they'd do what they came for, 'shut the bitches up and hit the road. In that order.'' She closed her eyes and opened them again in a slow blink, gave Jodie a small smile. 'Impressive, huh? Who says you need shorthand to quote accurately?'

Jodie returned her smile. 'How are you doing?'

'It only hurts when I breathe.' Lou looked at Matt. 'What did you say the murdered man's name was?'

'John.'

She pressed her temple with the tips of her fingers. 'Kane said Kruger was a prick. Travis told him he should've waited till they were paid before he beat the shit out of him. Is that the man's name, Matt? John Kruger?'

Matt turned his face away, stared into the empty corner of the wardrobe. 'Yeah. It's John Kruger. And he wasn't a prick. Not even close.'

Louise's eyes were closed when she spoke again, as though she was too tired to open them, but her voice was firm, assertive. 'So what's their connection to the barn, Matt?'

He stood up. Suddenly. Well, the movement was sudden but it took him a few seconds to deal with his bad knee as he got to his feet. Jodie watched as he tested his weight on it, made a couple of attempts to bend it. Was he deciding if he could walk or was he stalling?

'Matt?' Jodie repeated Louise's question. 'What's their connection to the barn?' She jumped as he slammed both hands against the door. She wanted to say, 'hey, it's okay'. She wanted to tell him to stop making so much damn noise. 'They said they lived here when they were kids,' she said. 'Is this their place?'

He turned around, leaned against the door. 'This place was never anything but a barn. It was probably already derelict by the time they were born. The pair of them squatted here before Travis went into the army.' His eyes moved around the room, as though he couldn't believe it was the same place. Jodie watched as he closed his eyes, took a breath and let it out. When he looked down at her, his eyes were dark and narrowed and she wondered if she really wanted to hear what he was about to tell them.

'A teenage girl went missing seven years ago,' he said. 'We thought they were involved. We searched this place. Just about tore it apart. Would've got a bulldozer in if the damn heritage people had let us. We searched the whole area.' He lifted his eyes to the wall opposite, stared at the blank space in front of him as he spoke. 'Kane killed her. I have no doubt about that. Travis either helped or helped him cover it up. We never found anything we could pick either of them up on. About a month after she went missing, Travis decided he was a patriot and joined the army. Not long after, Kane used a knife on a guy in a pub brawl and ended up in jail. Kane finished his sentence, Travis was dishonourably discharged. Now John Kruger's dead and they're here, smashing the place up and it makes no sense.'

28

The four of them stared at Matt for a long, silent moment. Jodie didn't know what the others were thinking but she couldn't get the image of that teenage girl out of her mind – trapped in this isolated barn with Kane and Travis.

The brothers had scared the hell out of her before but now, knowing they'd killed, probably twice, made her pulse hammer against her eardrums.

'Why was Travis dishonourably discharged?' Lou said into the silence. Jodie looked at her, surprised it was that fact that had bothered her.

'I've spent some time with military people. You don't get kicked out easily. Did he hurt someone else?' Louise asked.

'His crimes got more sophisticated in the army. He was in on some big weapons racket,' Matt said.

She lifted her head a little, winced as she did it. 'The one out of the training bases?'

'Yeah. Why?'

'I did a freelance job on that story. My old paper was investigating missing weapons and called me in because of my military contacts from Afghanistan. It was a massive cover-up, we couldn't get anyone to talk on record.' She stopped, licked her lips. 'It was rifles, wasn't it?'

'Yeah. About a hundred and fifty of them.'

She nodded. 'About ten grand a pop on the black market. The guys just drove them off the bases in their cars, one or two at a time, handed them over to the officer running the scam for a wad of cash. The brass was scared shitless some terrorist group had them. I thought they all got sentenced.'

'There wasn't enough evidence against Travis.'

Lou closed her eyes, shifted awkwardly. 'He seems to be good at that.'

Jodie looked at her friends, at Matt and realization drummed in her ears. They'd all seen Travis and Kane, knew who they were. 'We're *evidence*.'

No one said anything. They didn't have to. She wanted to yell and scream for help, pound her fists against the door. Then she heard a noise that made her thoughts stop dead.

Thunk.

Since the crashing sounds had ceased, there had been irregular distant thuds. But this one was close. Probably from the lounge room. Not as loud as before but loud enough to let them know Kane and Travis were close by.

Jodie's head snapped up. Someone gasped. Lou groaned quietly.

You already knew they could kill, Jodie told herself. Nothing she'd heard had changed that. The clock was still running. She didn't know how long they had left to play but the game wasn't over yet.

'Okay, listen,' she said. 'There are five of us and only two of them. And they only have one gun. They can't hold it on all five of us all the time. So if you get a chance to run, do it. Take the first exit out of the house and run like hell to the bush. Stay down, don't go out in the open and don't come back inside. Not for anything. Okay?' She waited until all three of the girls nodded. 'If you think you can make it to the front of the barn and down the hill without using the track, go to the house at the bottom and call the police. And don't come back until they get here. Okay?' As they nodded again, there was another thud from the lounge room. She got to her feet, leaned against the door to keep the light on, clutched Corrine's boot in one hand, the metal rod in the other. There was still nothing to do but she couldn't sit any longer.

She looked around the small room. Corrine was in the back corner, furthest from the doors, knees pulled to her chest. Hannah was propped in the other corner, Louise curled up on the floor between them. Matt was on his feet too, leaning on the door. If she couldn't see his eyes, she'd think he was lounging. His arms were folded across his chest, the other metal bar hanging loosely from his fingers but his eyes were alert, watching the way she stood there, the clothing rail in her hand, the boot, her face.

'Jodie,' he said. His voice was low. He dipped his head for a private kind of chat. She stepped over and leaned close, felt the warmth of his cheek where it almost touched her face. 'Don't try anything in here.'

She looked up at him. The brown flecks in his green eyes glowed under the light from the bare bulb. 'I'm going to take whatever chance I can get,' she said.

Outside the room, something banged against a wall. Jodie flinched. The sound was closer than before. Not in the bedroom. Maybe the hallway.

He grabbed her arm. 'But not in here. There's not enough room to swing a cat here, let alone that rod in your hand. And if a gun goes off, there's going to be a lot more blood on the floor.'

She glanced quickly around again. He was right. There was barely enough room to walk between the bodies huddled on the floor.

Footsteps in the hall.

'Jodie,' Matt said. 'If you do anything, do it somewhere else. And make sure they don't get up.'

She nodded, her heart in her throat. Then someone was at the doors. Whatever was holding them closed was being moved about. Matt jerked away and the light went out. Corrine let out a terrified sob.

Matt pulled Jodie against him. It wasn't a tender, protective move.

It was fierce and urgent and insistent. His hand was tight around her upper arm, his torso hard against hers and in the pitch darkness, she could sense the way he loomed forcefully over her. 'Take your own advice, Jodie. Run if you can. Get out of here. Don't wait for anyone.'

Then the doors opened and light flooded the room.

'Get back from the door.' It was Travis. He had the gun in his hand, raised and ready to fire.

Jodie took two small steps back. That was all there was room for. She felt Hannah try to shuffle out of the way behind her. Matt stepped in beside her, his arm out like a tollgate in front of her, the elbow locked straight.

'Planning a sword fight, huh? Guess what. Gun beats pissy piece of pole. Drop them,' Travis said, waving the gun at their clothing rails. Jodie tossed hers to the floor and it clattered against the timber boards with Matt's. Travis looked around. 'You got anything else in here you want to try against a *gun*?' His eyes stopped on Jodie. 'You, tough bitch?'

She felt the heel of Corrine's boot in her hand behind her back, shook her head, let it fall to the floor.

'How 'bout you, Wiseman, you want to be a hero?'

The muscles in his arm flexed before he answered. 'No.'

Travis moved the gun about in his hand, scanned the room. He was sweating, she could smell it, see it damp on the short strands of hair around his face and the wet stains under his armpits. His sleeves were rolled to the elbows and his forearms were specked with dark grains of dirt. His eyes stopped on Corrine. 'You. Blondie. Get up.' Corrine whimpered and shrank further into the corner. 'Get up!' She slid slowly up the wall, her mascara-smudged eyes brimming with tears again. 'Throw them into the other room,' he ordered, indicating the metal rods. Corrine did as he said, limping on her sprained ankle, then backing up into her corner again. 'Not so fast,' he told her. 'You're coming with me.'

Corrine clasped her hands across her chest. 'No. Please, no.'

'And you, too,' Travis said, pointing the muzzle of the gun at Matt.

Travis swung his head back at Corrine, who was frozen in the corner. 'Now. Move.'

One loud beat of Jodie's heart drove movement to her legs. She stepped forward, into the path of the gun. 'No.'

'Get out of the way.'

'No.'

'Move, Blondie.'

'No,' Jodie said again. She could hear Corrine sobbing behind her. A hand was on the back of her calf, she guessed Hannah had reached out across the space between them. Jodie wasn't sure if she was holding her back or pushing her on. 'She can't. She's hurt her ankle. She can't walk far.'

Travis's dark eyes shifted slowly to Jodie. The gun followed them. 'You then.'

She took a deep breath. 'No. We stay together.'

His mouth turned up in a nasty grin. 'Nu-uh. Two of you come with me. Him,' he cocked his head at Matt, 'and one of you.'

Fear gripped her chest. She looked at the pistol, licked her lips. No one stays behind, Jodie. 'We stay together. All of us or none of us.'

The grin disappeared. 'Him and one of you. You choose or we see who's left standing after I let off a couple of rounds.' He inched the gun to Jodie's right, angled it down, pulled back the cock. Hannah's hand fell away from the back of her leg.

'No, wait!' Blood pounded in her veins. They had to stay together.

'Who is it?' Travis said.

'Wait. *Wait*.' Panic rose in her throat.

'Just take me.' Matt stepped up to Travis, got in his face, pushed the gun away from Hannah with his body. 'Leave the women here. You've got no business with them. This is between us now.'

No, Matt, don't. They needed to stay together. All of them.

'Fuck off, Wiseman.' Travis stepped sideways, aimed the gun at Corrine and roared. 'Choose now or I will!'

There was no choice in the end. Corrine was a mess, Louise was injured and Hannah needed to stay with her.

'Me.' Jodie pushed the word out as forcefully as she could. 'I'll go. Leave them alone. Take *me*.'

MATT KEPT himself between Jodie and the gun as Travis hustled them through the hallway. A cold wind blew down the narrow corridor from the lounge room. Through the door, he could see furniture had been shunted around. Two sofas were butted against each other at odd angles in front of the fireplace. What had they been doing out there? And where was Kane? If he was waiting to jump them on the other side of the door, Matt wanted to be the first through. But he was limping and Jodie had marched ahead, back straight, arms stiff, like she was making a statement – you want me out here, then get on with it. Guts of steel.

She took a single pace through the door to the main room and propped. The way she did it, like she'd been halted in her tracks, made his heart beat faster. He reached the door, stepped quickly around her, looking for Kane. Then stopped and stared.

There was a huge hole in the floor. Boards had been smashed, ripped up, tossed aside. It explained the crashing sounds. Bearers and joists had been chopped out, leaving a jagged-edged, rectangular gash big enough to drop one of the sofas through. It was about halfway between the front door and the kitchen, just to the left of one of the old tree trunks supporting the ceiling.

'Get over there,' Travis said.

He shoved Matt between the shoulderblades with the pistol, kept on his heels until Matt was on the edge of the hole beside Jodie, looking down on bare earth. It was dark as pitch down there and the smell of dirt and damp wafted up like cold, foul breath. Jodie's arm shuddered against his. Yeah, I'm with you there, he thought. He put an arm across her shoulders, pulled her to him. Her body was rigid with tension but she leaned into him a tad – not letting go of her fear, just taking comfort.

'Climb down,' Travis said.

He was standing opposite them now on the other side of the hole, gun pointed at their mid-sections. It was the first chance Matt had had to take a good look at the older Anderson. He'd forgotten how much he was like Kane. Except for the hair and eyes, they were cut from the same chunky slab of rock, heads like boulders, all rough lines and angles. Both as tough and hard as they looked. But Travis wasn't crazy like his brother. He was no brain surgeon either but he was calculating and cold. Seven years ago he was somehow involved in the disappearance of that girl and he'd kept his cool, kept his brother in line, stayed out of prison, joined the army when it was time to get out of the way. He'd made corporal, worked in the armoury. He didn't have the smarts to organise that weapons racket and the lack of evidence against him suggested he was only a low-level grunt on the job – but he was cunning enough to be involved. Whatever he'd done with his cut of the proceeds, he hadn't attracted undue police attention since then. He'd been getting work and making like an average Joe.

Back there in the wardrobe, he'd barked out orders like a drill sergeant on a power trip. Out here, the smugness was gone. Now he just seemed ticked off. And Matt was acutely aware that standing over a hole at the messy end of Travis Anderson's gun was not a comfortable place to be.

'Move it, for Christ's sake. Are you both fucking deaf?'

Matt dropped his eyes to the hole. He didn't want to get down there. Instinct and training were in sync on that. It was probably the only way in and out. Why bother smashing through the floor if they could get under the barn any other way? It must be why they checked the garden earlier, for a way in under the verandah. Which meant any chance of escape would have to be through a well-lit hole in the middle of the floor. It was the wrong way to go but Travis had the gun and Matt didn't.

He moved first, dropped his legs into the hole, lowered himself down. He ducked under the timber boards and felt the drop in temperature as he took a quick look around. He thought there'd be some sort of lighting – a gas lamp or an electric bulb strung up – and Kane waiting for them. He thought wrong. Light from the room above illuminated a circle of earth directly under the hole. The rest was a solid mass of blackness.

He stood up again, his head and shoulders above floor height. 'Come on,' he said to Jodie and held out a hand.

She squatted on the edge and sucked in a deep breath like she was planning to swim underwater. Her fingers were icy and shaking, and as she dropped into the hole, she kept a hold on his hand – not a lightweight finger grip but a solid, full-fisted grasp. It seemed to settle the shaking. It didn't hurt him, either.

As Travis climbed down, Matt ducked under the floor again, pulling Jodie into the darkness with him. He wished she wasn't there. Wished she was somewhere safe. The moment they'd stepped into the hole, Jodie and her friends' chances had taken a dive. The hostages were separated and that made getting them all out a whole lot more complicated. Doing it from under the barn with a gun to his back and Kane God knows where, was a major setback. Worse still, if Travis had brought them down here to kill them, or if he just lost his cool and killed them anyway, the hostages' chances were zero. And Matt would have failed four more innocent victims.

Beside him, Jodie slid a hand inside his jacket and gripped the back of his shirt. She was cold and there was trepidation in the way she held him but there was also a fierceness about her. Maybe he was imagining it. Maybe he needed to for his own resolve. But he hoped he wasn't because if they had even the faintest chance of getting out, they'd need every ounce of fierceness they could get. If she fell to pieces, neither of them would make it.

Travis reached into a well between the floor joists, pulled out a torch and flicked it on. The beam cut through the dark, revealing uneven bare earth that sloped away towards the back of the barn. Square towers of brick piers stood in rows all around them, at least four bricks too short for standing room.

'Over there,' Travis said. He had the gun in one hand, the torch in the other, lighting the path he wanted them to take.

Matt had to bend almost double to avoid knocking himself out on the overhead beams. He limped awkwardly, picking his way in the dark, following the light, only sure Jodie was at his back by the hand holding his jacket. 'So where's your low-life brother?'

'Just shut up and walk.' Travis was breathing hard. And not from exertion. The kind of breathing you do when you want to hurl something.

'Left you to handle the hostages on your own, huh? I don't know how you put up with him. He's an arsehole.'

'Don't get cocky, Wiseman. He'll be back.'

'Left you to clean up his shit again, right?'

The light swung around, hit Matt in the eyes. He couldn't make out Travis in the dark behind it, could only see his hand on the end of the torch, but his reply came out loud and clear. 'Keep your mouth shut, Wiseman. And *walk*.'

Matt put a hand in front of his eyes. 'Can't see where to go with that thing in my face.'

Travis did some more heavy breathing, let the light hang on Matt for a couple of seconds, then pointed it ahead again.

They moved further into the darkness, grit and stones scuttling about as their feet slipped on the loose dirt. Behind him, Jodie's breath sounded loud and forced.

'Okay, stop,' Travis said. The hole in the floor was twenty metres behind them. They were well under the centre of the barn, heading towards the back. Travis held the gun on them as he waved the torch left and right looking for something. Then the light illuminated a pile of dirt beside a freshly dug pit.

It was too dark to see Jodie, but Matt heard her. Her feet scrunched on the dirt as she moved around him. She gasped. There was a thud on a beam overhead and she stumbled into him. It must have hurt but it wasn't the whack on the head she reacted to.

'No. No way.' Her voice was loud, a yell. 'If you want to put me in a damn hole, you can do it yourself, you *bastard*. I am not digging my own grave.'

29

Travis swung the torch around. 'Not yet, tough bitch. I've got another job for you.' Matt squinted at Jodie in the sudden glare. She was wild-eyed, breathing hard.

'Get over there,' Travis ordered and they were in darkness again, the torch pointing to the pit.

Even as Matt found Jodie in the dark and wrestled hold of her arm, his brain was ticking over. She tried to pull away but he held onto her. If she didn't come with him, he'd never find her in the dark. And he wanted to see what was in that pit. Travis and Kane came here to dig it. They were either burying something or digging something up. And they'd gone to a lot of trouble to do it. More than a lot. They'd shot a woman, locked five people in a wardrobe and smashed a hole in the floor.

Why do that to bury something? The barn was surrounded by bush. They were in the middle of farming land. They could bury something anywhere out there.

He remembered Louise quoting them. *We'll get our stuff and get out of here.* So they were digging something up? They'd lived here, they'd both been back in Bald Hill for a few years, they had plenty of opportunity to bury a bunch of stuff. If Matt was right, and Travis and Kane had killed John Kruger, what was important enough for them to hide from the cops for a day waiting for a chance to dig it up?

As he and Jodie moved past a brick pier, Matt saw where the torchlight extended beyond the pit. Saw there were two more freshly dug pits. They looked just like the first one – about the size of your average backyard barbecue, maybe knee deep. He hesitated a moment. Cold fear stiffened his spine.

Maybe they were graves.

No, they weren't big enough. He straightened a little, looked at Travis and Kane's handiwork. Three piers in a row, three rectangular pits in front of them. Travis pointed with the torch to the next row of piers.

'Get over there and dig. One hole each,' Travis ordered.

Matt looked at the light bouncing off the piers and wondered about the positioning of the pits. He checked left then right. He couldn't see a thing but he could smell the vague sandiness of the brick and mortar in the piers all around them. It was a big barn, it needed a lot of piers. After standing derelict for years, maybe the renovators had had to add a few more to prop up a sagging floor.

Matt felt his swollen lip turn up at the side. It would be hard to find one particular pier in the blackness. Especially if you hadn't been down here in a while.

He started to move forward but Jodie pulled on his arm.

'Matt, no,' she whispered. 'That's five holes. There are five of *us*. I'm not digging a grave.'

'Move it! Now!' Travis shouted.

Matt caught her under his arm, hauled her forward. 'It's okay.'

She struggled against him, twisting her shoulders as she tried to break free. 'No. We have to run. Now.' Her leg banged into his bad knee and he grunted in pain but he held onto her. Travis had the gun and the torch. Now was not the time to run for it. The torch swung around, lit them up like a spotlight.

'Get over there,' Travis yelled, walking towards them.

Matt gripped Jodie by both shoulders and shook her. 'Keep it together.'

'We have to *do* something.'

'We *do* what he says. Both of us.'

Then Travis was on them. He ripped Jodie away, flung her to the ground and put the pistol to Matt's forehead. 'I said dig, Wiseman.' He looked down at Jodie. 'Get up!' Travis watched as she got to her feet then turned back to Matt. 'Keep her under control or I'll beat the shit out of her. Now *move*.'

Before she turned and walked, Jodie gave Travis one last glance, her eyes dark with loathing. When she looked at Matt, her mouth was a harsh line and her shoulders were rigid with hostility. Let it brew, babe, Matt thought, and warned himself to keep out of the firing line when she let it go.

He checked the first pit as they moved past. There was nothing in it. He guessed there was nothing in the others, either. Guessed that's why they were starting two new pits. A couple of pickaxes were propped against the first brick pier.

'So what've you lost?' Matt said. 'Your pocket money?'

Travis shoved him in the back with the gun. 'Get a pick and dig.'

Matt lifted one, felt the weight of it in his hands. Nice hefty handle, chunky metal head. Gun still beat pick. 'Your dad's good citizen medals? Oh, that's right. He didn't get any. Used you for punching practice then beat up some other guy and went to prison.'

'Shut up and dig!'

The floor was a little higher above their heads here but Matt still couldn't stand upright. He raised the axe awkwardly over his shoulder and drove it into the earth. Pain stabbed his knee but he wasn't going to let Travis know. 'Or maybe you lost your best marbles down here, huh? Heard you were pretty good at those in juvie.'

'Fuck you, Wiseman.'

Travis stood a couple of metres back from them, forming the top point of a wide triangle, holding the torch high to cast light near both piers. Jodie looked at Matt as she raised the pick to her shoulder. No surprise she knew how to swing it.

'Or maybe it's that mangy dog you used to drag around,' Matt said. Rumour back then was that the father had taken to the mongrel with a brick. 'You want to dig it up so you can buy it a nice head-stone?' As the last word left his mouth, the old barn flashed across his memory. How it was seven years ago. Broken windows, holes in the roof, an intact floor.

No verandah. Matt's pulse quickened. He lifted the pick, drove it deep. No, it didn't make sense. Why would they come back for her? A sudden urgency made him attack the soil at his feet. The dirt was dark, friable farming soil but dry and hard packed. A sweat broke out on his back as he widened the hole, dug deeper. How many secrets had Travis and Kane buried?

One pier over, Jodie stopped digging. As Matt looked up, she straightened her legs and bent a little lower to peer into the pit. Her trench was maybe half the size of Matt's, probably ankle depth if she was standing in it. She turned the pick head on its side, scraped away some dirt.

'What?' Travis said.

She backed off a step, glanced briefly at Matt, her eyes puzzled and wary. Travis started towards her as Matt sent his pick into the dirt again. The thunk of metal that sounded under his axe made Travis swing the torchlight around.

'Clear the dirt away,' he ordered. He stomped over, aimed a bright circle of light into the bottom of the hole. 'Hurry up! I haven't got all night.'

Good to know, Matt thought. He'd had enough of having a gun at his back. He pulled clumps of dirt up and out of the pit, exposing the top of a large, flat, rectangular object. When there was only a loose layer of earth left, he dragged the long edge of the pick head across it. The hollow, scraping sound it made seemed to linger in the darkness. Travis's circle of light grew brighter and sharper as he stepped closer. It illuminated a painted metal surface scored with rusted scuff marks.

A scatter of loose dirt made Matt lift his head. Over Travis's shoulder, in the dim light thrown up from the pit, he saw Jodie's pale face and the sleeve of her white sweater as she twisted her body to the side. A second later, there was a meaty thud and Travis jerked forward, stumbling into the pit. Matt pulled back a fist, ready to knock him to the ground, but Jodie followed Travis in and whacked him hard across the back with her pick handle. Travis's head hit the brick pier with a crack. He crumpled to the ground and the torch went out.

Blackness closed in around them. A snapshot of Jodie – face determined, body in full thrust – stayed lit on Matt's retina. Action figure Jodie. He could hear her stumbling around close by, slipping and gasping as she tried to fumble her way out of the pit. He grabbed for her, closed his hand around her sweater, pulled her out and away. She was shaking, breathing hard. He wanted to crush her against him.

'Where is he? Where is he?' she hissed.

'Out for the count.' As he spoke, a double beam of light sliced through the darkness from under the front verandah. The gurgle of V8 twin exhausts broke the silence of the night. He remembered Jodie had heard a car in the night. This morning she'd thought it was The Beast. 'Kane's back. Find the gun.' Matt dropped to his knees, bumped shoulders with Jodie as she crawled about. He patted at the earth, felt around Travis's still body.

'I killed him,' Jodie said.

'No, he's just out cold.' Matt had no idea whether he was dead or alive but he didn't want Jodie freaking out about it. Not now. Kane's headlights turned, pointed directly at the verandah, lighting the underfloor of the barn like a football field.

'Shit,' Jodie said. She was on all fours, looking up at him from the other side of Travis's body. The lights went out. She gasped. 'We need the torch.'

'There's no time to look.'

'I can't see a damn thing.'

'Head for the hole in the floor.' Matt heard her move. He followed suit, crawling on hands and one knee, dragging the bad one behind him.

'Where are you?' she whispered.

A car door opened and the faint glow of the interior light was enough to see her. She had her back pressed into a brick column, one pier over and one ahead.

'I'm behind you,' he whispered.

She looked back with huge eyes. Then the light went out and they were in blackness again.

Trying to remember where she was, Matt got to his feet, limped as quickly as he could across the darkness, arms straight out in front. A hand grabbed him by the shoulder of his jacket and pulled.

'Come on,' she whispered.

His other shoulder slammed into a pier, flung him sideways. 'Shit.'

'Move.'

'I'm moving.'

'Faster.' Her voice was gravel in her throat. Her feet were scrabbling in the dirt but she held onto him. Then their heads were pressed to the underside of the floor at the jagged edge of the hole, just outside its ring of light.

A thud sounded on the front steps.

'Go.'

'Now.'

Matt stood to full height, his head and shoulders in the lounge room, the light blinding after the darkness underneath. He cupped his hands in front of his thighs. Jodie took a huge stride, stepped into his palms and hoisted herself cleanly up into the room. As heavy footfalls sounded on the stairs, he heaved himself up on his hands behind her. Jodie grabbed at his jacket, dragging him over the lip of the floor, pulling at his arm before he had both feet on the timber. He was running before he was upright, taking long, loping steps, following her, trying to ignore the pain in his knee. Outside, the footsteps got louder as Kane hit the verandah.

Jodie yanked Matt sideways, heading for the bedrooms.

He hauled against her, the smashed glass door in his sights. 'This way,' he hissed.

'We have to go back for the others.'

He caught her wrist. 'No.'

The footsteps stopped. Jodie's head swung to the door, swung back to Matt. She took his forearm in a double-fisted grip, heaved against him. A tug of war and he was the rope.

'*No,*' he said again.

The door rattled and as it started on its inward arc, Jodie broke the tension on his arm so fast, he stumbled backwards. Then she was suddenly dragging him towards the back door.

The front door crashed open against the wall. They were halfway across the room. A voice roared behind them.

Kane.

Matt willed his knee to work. Ground bone against mashed cartilage. Jodie was ahead of him, running almost side on as she pulled him through the wreckage of the room. Kane's boots thundered on the floor behind them.

They made it to the smashed door, thumped across the verandah. Jodie hit the steps first. She was halfway down when Matt reached the top one. He should have shuffled his good leg to the front. He should have gone down two at a time, dragging his bad leg behind. But he didn't. And his knee collapsed underneath him. He fell like a sack of apples. His shoulder hit the timber, his forehead followed, then the rest of him rolled over the top. The howl of pain as his knee twisted under him shattered the night.

30

Jodie didn't pause. She just hauled on his arm.

In the lounge room, Kane was skidding on broken glass. Something heavy was sent flying. He was cursing them, shouting for his brother.

'C'mon!' Jodie yelled.

Matt was on his back in the dirt. His knee was one long, screaming pain. He tried to move it, to push himself up but the message wouldn't reach his leg. He was going to get her killed. 'Go, Jodie. Run.'

She flung his arm away, straddled his chest, grabbed the lapels of his jacket in both fists and dragged him to a sitting position.

'Run,' he said.

'Get up, damn it. *Get up!*' She stepped back, heaved some more. She was adrenaline-fuelled. She lifted all six-foot-two of him to his feet.

Matt got his good leg under him, tried to walk. The bush was twenty metres away. He was never going to make it. 'Run. Save *yourself.*'

She jammed a shoulder into his armpit, wrapped an arm around his waist, got a grip on the top of his jeans. '*Shut up and move!*' She didn't give him a choice. She was a steam train on a track, hauling him forward, taking his weight, keeping him moving and upright.

Kane's feet pounded onto the verandah. His voice was like thunder. 'I'm going to fucking shoot you.'

Travis had the gun. Travis was under the house.

Matt heard the distinctive crank of a pump-action shotgun. He hunkered over, pushed Jodie's head down as he did.

'Get down,' he said.

'Run,' she said.

Kane said nothing. He let a shotgun do the talking.

A single boom rolled down the slopes of the hill and ricocheted around the dark valley. Jodie screamed without breaking step. They were ten metres from the bush, light from the house fading behind them. Matt was going as fast as he could but he was holding her back, slowing her down. His leg was agony and he didn't know how much longer it would hold his weight. If it gave up, he couldn't hop the distance and there was no way she could carry him. On current performance, she'd try – and she'd probably give it a good go. She was strong but she wasn't The Hulk.

'I'm gonna to kill you, Wiseman.' There was no lunatic menace in Kane's roar. It was just brutal, resentful fury.

Matt didn't know how good a shot Kane was. With the spray of pellets fired from a shotgun, he didn't have to be any kind of marksman. And right now, Matt couldn't afford to bet against him. Right now, Matt, you're the guy who's going to get Jodie killed. Who gets to live this time, Matt?

He put his hand on the centre of her back, tried to push her ahead of him, already feeling the relief that would come with turning around and facing the arsehole on the verandah. 'Run for it, Jodie.'

Her response was a war cry. A guttural blast of sound that seemed to rise from way down deep inside. Her arm around his waist became a front-end loader, not pulling anymore but pushing. Pressing him relentlessly forward, heedless of his useless knee. Man, she was unstoppable. He was a weak, pathetic bastard and Jodie *was* The

Hulk. On steroids. Any second she was going to tuck him under her arm and carry him away.

'Fuck you, Wiseman. Fuck the both of you.'

Gunfire roared into the night again. A metre ahead, leaves were shredded as shotgun pellets tore into the bush. Two more steps and they were at the edge of dense native bush that looked like a solid chest-high hedge in the dark. They went in headfirst, arms outstretched to fend off the branches that scraped at their faces. Behind them, Kane's boots pummelled down the steps then fell silent as he hit the dirt.

They dropped to the ground, Matt landing heavily across her thighs. She pushed at him, rolled out from under. They were in darkness again. Not as dark as it was under the barn but still too dark to make out much more than the mass of shrubbery around them.

'Stay down and head left,' Matt whispered. He heard her take off, move quickly away and attempted to follow. But his knee was hopeless in a crawl and he dragged it behind as he clawed his way through the dirt and undergrowth.

'You two are dead. You hear me?' Kane yelled, his voice still too far away to be at the line of bush.

Matt tried for a forty-five degree angle away from the barn, moving deeper into the brush while aiming for the lounge room end of the building. There was a rustling nearby, slightly ahead and a little further into the scrub. He hoped it was Jodie and not some sharp-toothed nocturnal animal ready to defend its patch.

Kane's voice was closer this time. Maybe close enough to be at the edge of the bush. 'I can see you. You're going to be dead in a second.'

There was no way Kane could see them, Matt told himself. The direction of his voice was too far to the right but his scalp tingled with alarm anyway. He wanted to get up and run. Find Jodie and charge deep into the bush, not stop until they were in the valley below. For a second he tried to tell himself his tortuous limping would be faster than crawling around blind. But that was what Kane was hoping he'd do – give him a head to take a pot shot at.

He stopped instead, lay flat on the ground. The nearby rustling stopped too. Good decision, Jodie. Stay down. The smell of euca-lyptus filled his nostrils, crisp dry leaves cut into his face, dirt and stones grazed his hands and knees. Over the sound of his own breath-ing, he heard the soft thud of footfalls on grass. Coming their way. If Matt could hear Kane's footsteps on the cleared ground, any move-ment in the bush would be like holding up a target.

'I'm lining you up for a head shot so get ready to die.' Kane was close now, the menace creeping back into his voice, like he was starting to enjoy the hunt.

There'd been no bush-rustling from Kane's direction so he was probably walking along the perimeter of scrub, hoping to catch sight of them before charging in. Matt had no idea how deep into the bush they were but he guessed it wasn't far enough to outrun Kane. Defi-nitely not outside firing range. If he stood up, gave Kane something to shoot at, it might give Jodie a chance to run.

Then what? Even if she got away, there were more hostages in the barn. A stockpile of them. Saving one out of three wasn't good enough.

Matt looked off to the left. Jodie was ahead of him. It was possible Kane was guessing the direction when he'd walked their way. Maybe it was time the guy had something to shoot at.

Matt skimmed his palms across the dirt, patting at lumps of clay and small stones until he found what he wanted. Then he rolled on his back, aimed high and wide, crossing his fingers the chunk of sandstone didn't ricochet off a tree straight back at him.

It landed with a thunk and rustle of underbrush a good ten metres away. Matt had no idea if it fooled Kane, didn't bother to consider it when he heard Kane hit the bush at a run. As foliage thrashed behind him, Matt pushed off the ground with his good leg and loped towards the last place he'd heard Jodie, hoping she'd taken off already and found somewhere safe to hide. Hoping he'd find her again.

'I've got you, you fuckers.' Kane was trying to sound triumphant but the grunting and puffing as he tore through the undergrowth took the edge off it. So did the direction of his voice. He was heading away, shouting abuse, not listening for them.

Matt kept moving forward and to the left, standing higher than he should, daring to call out to Jodie in a loud whisper.

Behind him, the bush fell silent and Matt hit the ground again.

'You think you're smart, don't you, Wiseman?' Kane was out of breath, moving slowly through the scrub now. 'You're not. You're an arsehole.'

Takes one to know one, Matt thought, crawling again, trying to go quietly, grimacing in pain as he lifted his leg instead of dragging it. He heard a soft rustle not far ahead. Keep going, Jodie. He picked up his pace, heading towards the sound, feeling his way. It was so dark, Kane would have to be almost on top of them before he saw them. Then the bush was crashing about again. Kane had picked up his pace, was heading their way.

When Matt saw Jodie, fear tightened his throat. Her white sweater glowed like a streetlight in fog. She was on her hands and knees, crawling under the overhang of a bush – and Matt could make out every inch of her sweater.

'I can see you. Get ready to die,' Kane yelled.

The guy had a limited repertoire but he wasn't blind, Matt thought. And he was close. Too close. All that sweater needed to make the shot easier was a big, red circle. Damn the noise, he thought as he drove to his feet and ran. Bent almost double and limping like his leg was hanging off, he dived through the undergrowth towards her. He hear the pounding of Kane's boots over the thrashing of the bush, saw Jodie look behind, rise to a crouch. No! If she took off running, he'd never catch her.

He braced himself for the pain in his knee and launched himself at her. She was on her feet when he reached her, half revolved towards him, hands pulled back ready to strike. He got both his arms around her thighs, turned his face away but she still landed a solid hit to his collarbone as he pushed her to the dirt. He heard her breath whoosh out, felt the momentary stunned stillness as she hit the ground, took the advantage and scrabbled over her, cupping his hand across her mouth. He'd apologise later. For now, he had to stop her bucking around. She drove hips and knees at him, scratched at his face, whipped her head about. Her eyes were open but she wasn't seeing. He found her ear, pressed his mouth against it.

'It's me. It's Matt.'

He held her head still, one hand over her mouth, the other with a handhold of hair, forcing her to look at him. He felt bad about it but it was better than letting her scream. When recognition hit, her eyes went wide, her body fell still and the hands that had been pushing him away grabbed at his shirt and pulled ferociously at him. He took his hand away from her mouth and she pressed her face into his shoulder, breathing hard. Yeah, Jodie, I feel the same way.

Kane was moving around nearby. Matt tugged at the front panels of his jacket, tried to cover Jodie's sweater with it. She tucked her arms inside his coat, slipped her hands around his back, leaving cold palms flat on his shoulderblades.

She was out of breath, puffing loudly and trying not to, burying her face in his neck, moving her lips against his stubble as she gasped for air. He eased down a little, taking the pressure off his arms, felt her chest heaving against his, her neat, round breasts pushing against his rib cage. She was lean and toned and soft in all the right places. She was tough and strong and she'd just saved his unworthy arse. It was like a cruel joke. He gets his dream woman in a clinch hold thirty seconds before a bullet through the head.

'Hey, tough bitch. You ready to die?' Kane's voice was right above them.

Jodie froze. Foliage whispered, leaves shuffled under boot. A branch snapped. Her mouth on his neck stopped moving, her chest stopped heaving. Matt's heart was a mallet at the back of his throat.

'How 'bout you, Wiseman? You ready to spill your brains?'

A voice boomed and echoed in the night. 'KANE. Where the fuck are you?' Travis was yelling from the barn.

'Wiseman and the tough bitch are out here. Bring the torch.' Kane's voice had moved past them. Matt took a slow, quiet breath. Felt Jodie do the same.

'There's no time for a search party. I found it. Get your arse back here,' Travis yelled.

'I want Wiseman and the bitch on a spit.'

'Fuck that. You got three more up here.'

Jodie's body went rigid. Matt grimaced as her fingernails dug into his shoulder. There was silence except for Kane's breath rasping in and out.

'*Now*, Kane. Get up here and help or I leave without you.'

The foliage overhead shook violently. Kane was flaying about, cursing his brother. Jodie seemed to be struggling for air. He tried to take more of his weight on his arms but she pulled him tighter against her.

'Hey, Wiseman.' The scrub stilled. 'I'm coming back for you. You hear? I'm gonna to beat your brains out and cut you up in little pieces. I'm gonna dig a hole and put you in the ground.'

Matt stiffened. *Like the holes under the barn?*

Leaves swished and swayed against each other as Kane started walking away.

'You and your tough bitch and all her friends,' he yelled.

31

Matt was heavy. He was crushing her. But he was the only thing holding her together.

Kane was going back to kill her friends.

The bush fell silent as he reached the clearing. He must have turned around because his voice came at them loud and clear, amplified by the crisp night, sounding cold and hard and cruel.

'And I've got the perfect spot for you, Wiseman. Right next to that slut you never found.'

Above her, Matt turned to stone. Then, without warning, he pushed his palms flat to the dirt, lifted himself clear of her. She knew in an instant what he was doing. He was going after Kane. And Kane would shoot him. She grabbed him in a bear hug, locked her legs around him.

'No!' she hissed in his ear.

Matt pushed against her, trying to break free. Her arms were weak from hauling him across the grass and she wanted to hit him for trying to be such a hero back there, for telling her to run like he had any right to make that decision, but she just held on for dear life. He was going to survive this thing whether he liked it or not. The battle seemed to ease some of her crazy, uncontrollable shaking. Or maybe it was just being wrapped around his warm body that did that. He was tall and strong and determined – and he was protecting all of her with all of him. There wasn't much more she could ask of a man. Then just as suddenly, the tension left him, as though he'd slapped the book closed on that idea. His weight settled on her again. She let her arms go slack, breathed into his neck, filled her nostrils with his sweaty, dirt-covered man smell. Felt a whole lot less shaky.

Kane's footsteps landed heavily on the timber steps, stomped across the verandah. He was shouting as he went through the door. Travis shouted in answer. Jodie squeezed her eyes shut. She should have made it down the hall. She should have gone back to her friends.

'Are you okay?' Matt whispered. He was close enough for her to see most of the detail of his face in the dark. There was a new bloodied scratch down his cheek, a match for the graze on the other one.

'What was with the crash tackle?' she said.

'Your sweater was glowing like a light bulb. Kane was right behind me.'

She pushed him off her, sat up, suddenly freezing without his body heat. 'What the hell did you think you were doing back there? I told you to run and you sat on your butt.'

There was a beat before he answered. 'I couldn't get up. My knee . . .'

'What about later? You were up on your feet, running just fine.'

'I was trying to save your life.'

Anger and fear burned in her throat. She wanted to put her arms around him, hold onto him tight but instead she poked a finger into his chest. 'I don't need a *hero*. I need you to stay alive.'

He looked down at her finger. His eyes narrowed a little. She couldn't tell if he was annoyed or amused. Maybe he was both. 'Come on. We need to move,' he said.

Jodie got to her feet, watching Matt move awkwardly, favouring his bad knee. How far would they get?

She looked at the barn over the top of the bush. Its high, A-frame roof and towering facade dwarfed the lounge room's long span of windows. Light seemed to bulge through the glass into the almost moonless night, illuminating the verandah from the kitchen to the right-hand corner of the old building. The pale curtains looked undisturbed except for the stretch missing from the centre where the pane had been smashed. Jodie could see into the room through there – the big table askew, a couple of toppled dining chairs, a lounge and a corner of the island bench. Travis was further inside the room, standing side-on. The half of his face she could see was covered in blood. He was shouting, throwing his arms around. Somewhere out of view, Kane was shouting back. She couldn't catch the words, just angry, guttural barks of sound. An argument. The other end of the barn looked dark and ominous. Fear gathered like a fist in her stomach. She moved towards the clearing.

'This way.' Matt grabbed her arm and pulled her in the other direction.

She shook off his hand. 'No. We have to go back for them.' She swung her head to the barn. Lights were coming on inside. Quickly, as though Kane or Travis were running down the hall, flicking the switches in the rooms.

'Come on.' Matt dragged on her arm. 'We have to go.'

'We can't leave them.'

'Come on, Jodie. Now.' As he said it, lights started coming on along the verandah, too. Two at a time. Starting at the lounge room then past the kitchen, the bathroom, around the bedroom end. Two seconds later, the deck that ran behind the fireplace lit up. The verandah was a solid square of light.

Kane's voice boomed from the house. 'I'm gonna get you, Wiseman.'

A powerful floodlight on the roof at the bedroom end of the barn opened up. The stretch of grass from the verandah to the scrub was lit like a prison yard, the top of the bush beyond it silhouetted in the glow. Another came on at the rear of the barn. The clearing to their left lit up. The scrub beside them switched from darkness to reflected low light.

'*Jodie.*'

She looked at Matt. He had her by the wrist, half turned away as he tried to pull her with him, his head above the foliage line. 'Get down,' she hissed, dragging at his hand as she ducked below the scrub.

Suddenly the texture of the darkness around them changed. The sky went from black to deep purple and through a silhouette of branches, the clearing glowed a ghostly green.

'*Move,*' Matt said.

He didn't need to pull this time. She took off behind him, bent low, her arm outstretched where he still held her wrist. Branches thrashed around them. A shot thundered into the night. She held her breath, expecting to feel the bite of a bullet in her flesh.

They crashed on through the bush until the light was well behind them and they could stand up straight without being seen as they pushed further through the scrub. The piercing cold of the night finally reached through her adrenaline rush and the sweat on her skin felt like ice. Corrine's sweater could have been mesh for all the warmth it gave her. The sky was huge and star-filled with a white sliver of moon that gave off no light. Matt's hand had slipped to hers and she held on tight, not wanting to lose him in the dense scrub. Close as he was, he was just a darker shape in the darkness.

'Where are we going?' she asked.

'Somewhere we can see more of the barn.'

'We have to go back.'

'You want to go ask Kane to let you into the wardrobe?'

'No, but we have to help my friends.'

He said nothing, just pushed on through the bush. They'd changed course, no longer moving deeper into the scrub but parallel with the barn, heading towards the bedroom end.

'What did you dig up?' he asked.

She remembered the bristle of apprehension she'd felt when her pick hit softness. 'I don't know. It looked like some kind of thick fabric. Felt, maybe. Like maybe it was wrapped around something.'

Matt's hand tightened on hers. 'Was it red?'

'I don't know. It was too dark to see colour. It wasn't pale and it wasn't black. In between. Yes, it might have been red. Or brown.' *I'm gonna dig a hole and put you in the ground.* Something worse than apprehension scuttled like a rat down her spine. 'What's red, Matt?' He held a branch back, stopped it from slapping her in the face as she walked past. His hand was so tight on hers it was starting to hurt. 'Matt. What's red?'

'Tina had a red coat.'

She swallowed hard. 'Who's Tina?'

'The girl that went missing.'

Jodie stopped walking. She felt sick. She'd dug up a body. A teenage girl. In a red coat. Bile burned at the back of her throat. 'Jesus, Matt. I . . . Was she . . .?'

'Keep moving, Jodie.'

She stumbled on, not watching where she was going, letting Matt pull her forward while her heart banged in her chest. Kane and Travis killed a teenage girl called Tina. They'd buried her in her red coat. They'd made Jodie dig her up.

Matt stopped. 'This is good.'

They were in line with the back corner of Hannah and Corrine's bedroom with a view down one side of the barn to the kitchen and along the other to where the French doors opened out onto the verandah.

Louise and Hannah and Corrine were up there. Locked in with killers.

Jodie thought of the other holes under the barn and felt hot and cold at the same time. Had they made Tina dig her own grave? But Jodie hadn't been digging a grave. She'd been digging Tina up. She looked at Matt in the darkness. He'd squatted on the ground, was looking up the slope towards the barn, his mouth a hard line, his jaw clenched. Jodie knelt down beside him. 'What did you dig up?'

He didn't take his eyes off the barn, barely moved his lips. 'A box.'

A box?

A coffin kind of box?

Jodie closed her eyes, swallowed hard, forced herself to breathe.

A roar of gunshot cracked open the night.

The noise came back to her a dozen times as it echoed around the valley. In her head, she saw Louise and Hannah and Corrine huddled in the wardrobe, terror on their faces. And she was on her feet, the sound of her gasp like a rush of wind in her ears.

Her eyes were on the bedroom. Her legs were already moving as a second shot shook the darkness. Oh, God, no. The adrenaline rush that hit felt like a starter's gun. She took off and was three paces into a sprint, just picking up speed, when Matt reached her. One arm went around her waist, pulled her off course, spun her away.

As they fell, crashing through foliage, a third shot rang out.

'No. No. No,' she cried.

She wanted to scream it but Matt had crushed the air from her. She wanted to yell and punch and kick, tried to as they hit the ground but he held her tight, arms locked to her sides, his body like a wall at her back. He was saying something, over and over, but all she could hear was the fourth blast, filling her up, making her head spin and her body shudder and her eyes spill over with tears.

They were dead. She'd left them and they were all dead. Louise and Hannah and Corrine were dead. And Angie. Four friends. Four shots. One for each of them.

Matt wasn't talking any longer. Just breathing. Loud, laboured breathing. His chest heaved against her spine. His arm around her stomach was like a seatbelt on crash lock. Jodie squeezed her eyes shut, tried to block out the bloody images that were forcing their way into her head.

'I'm sorry. Jodie, I'm so sorry,' Matt breathed into her ear.

A tear ran sideways across her cheek, leaving a cold trail on her face.

'Hey, Wiseman!'

Jodie went limp with fear. It was Kane, shouting. Footsteps thumped on the timber verandah, walking the length of the barn.

'Try being a hero now, Wiseman. See if you can make it past the lights. I wanna do some pig huntin'.' He hooted like a madman.

There was a pause in Matt's breathing. When it started up again, it was still laboured but slower, more controlled.

'Hey, pig,' Kane bellowed.

Matt pulled his arm away, put a finger to his lips. On the verandah, the thud of Kane's footfalls became a double beat. Travis was out there, too.

'Make a run for the bitch's car. See how far you can get on shot-out tyres, pig.' Kane's feral laugh hung in the darkness.

Jodie's head snapped up. Shot-out tyres. Four tyres. Four shots. Not Louise and Hannah and Corrine. Kane hadn't shot them. He'd shot the tyres. If he'd shot them, he'd be bragging about it.

They weren't dead.

She looked at Matt, wanting some kind of confirmation that she hadn't got it wrong. He'd closed his eyes and a muscle on his jaw moved in and out as he clenched and unclenched his teeth. Then he met her eyes in the darkness and she knew she was right. A wave of relief crashed over her. She sucked in a breath that seemed to go on and on forever, as though her lungs couldn't get enough oxygen. As though she was breathing for her friends as well, keeping them alive in the wardrobe. Matt hooked an arm around her neck and pulled her to him, held her against his shoulder, his face in her hair. She clung to the front of his shirt.

They were alive, Jodie. Locked up in a wardrobe, bleeding and terrified but not dead.

The double footsteps moved away, fading to a single beat before they disappeared, as though one brother was walking along the back of the barn while the other watched the front.

Matt took her by the shoulders. 'You have to go for help,' he said quietly.

We've got to run, Angie. Jodie's own voice from eighteen years ago was as clear and as loud as if she'd just spoken.

'Jodie? Did you hear me? You've got to get some help.'

'No.' She pushed away from him. Gunfire echoed in her head and ricocheted around in her skull. She forced herself to breathe, to look at him.

He kept his voice low. 'There's a stock trail through the bush. There's no chance they'll see you from the barn.'

No, no. She'd have to leave them. She'd promised herself she would never do that again. Dread pulsed through her veins. Her heart was racing. She could hear it in her ears. Pounding like a death beat.

'It'll take you all the way down to the house on the road.'

The road's just through the trees. I can run that in under a minute. Flag someone down. Get help.

She squeezed her eyes shut. She was puffing, hard, like she was already running. Through the dark. Through the trees. Running as fast as she could. Not fast enough. Never fast enough. 'No, no. I can't.'

'You can. Just get down to the house and call the cops. Tell them gunmen have taken hostages. Then wait there for them, make sure they find the driveway.' He took her by the chin, tilted her face to him. 'You can do this, Jodie. I know you can.'

She shook her head. It was roaring. She was seeing it all. Louise bleeding, Corrine crying, Hannah frozen in shock, Angie's eyes in the dark, a teenage girl in a red coat, holes in the dirt. The images were careering around, smashing into each other. '*No.* I'm not leaving them.' She pushed his hand away. '*You* go. *You* do it.'

'Jodie.'

'I have to stay with Angie.'

32

J odie put her hand to her head. Don't lose it now. 'No, no, not Angie. It's too late for Angie. I . . . I . . .'

Matt's face dawned with some sort of realisation. He sat back, pushed both hands through his hair. 'Okay, Jodie. It's okay.' He stopped, took a breath. 'Look, I know you've been through something terrible. I've seen the scars. I don't know what happened but I know it was bad and I know you're scared. And I wish this wasn't happening right now. But it is. So listen to me.' He reached out, put his hand on her arm, then let it slide down to her hand and twisted his fingers with hers.

They were warm and reassuring. He thought that's what she needed. He thought she was scared, that she needed reassurance she'd be safe out there in the bush. He was wrong. He'd seen scars but only the ones on her skin. He thought she was frightened of having a knife plunged into her belly again. She wasn't. That thought didn't even rate.

'Are you listening?' he said.

Jodie looked away. He was going to try to convince her. She didn't want to be convinced.

'Your friends need help. They need the cops to come and get them out. I'm not the person they need. I'm not. I can't do it. And I won't make it down to the road on this knee. You have to go. There's no other way.'

Sweat was cold on Jodie's face. Her lungs were so tight she could hardly breathe. She looked up towards the barn. Tears welled in her eyes.

Run, Jodie. Before they come back.

Oh God, God, God. She'd promised Angie. She'd vowed she would never, ever leave a friend behind again. Now Matt was telling her she had to. There was no other way.

Her head was spinning, roaring. Part of her wanted to leap up and charge through the bush, run like a banshee down to the house on the road, call the police, cars and cars of them with sirens and lights that would scream up here and save her friends. Just like Matt said.

But she heard herself, too. *The road's just through the trees. I can run that in under a minute. Flag someone down. Get help.* She shook her head, an aggressive back and forth, trying to shake out the memory that pierced her like a knife. The knife that had cut Angie's throat when Jodie had run eighteen years ago.

'You can do this, Jodie. You're fast. I've seen you. You'll be there in ten minutes. Twelve max. Don't think about it. Just run.' He took hold of both of her hands, made her look at him. 'Just run, Jodie.'

She sat on her haunches, heard his words again in her head, felt as though a hypnotist had snapped his fingers. One second her head was spinning and roaring. The next there was silence.

It wasn't shock and she wasn't deaf. It was just cool, calm silence. Matt had said the words she'd feared the most – *Run, Jodie* – and everything dropped into focus. He'd done her a huge favour. She felt better than she had since they'd run off the road on Friday night. As though she'd reached beyond her fear and found herself again. She took a long breath of cold night air and felt steely resolve settle in her bones.

'I'm not leaving my friends. I'm staying here and we're going to find another way to get them out.'

. . .

MATT WAS ANGRY. He was totally in awe of her and mad as hell at her. 'Don't *do this*, Jodie. You have to go. You can't be here.'

He'd watched her struggle through what could only be intensely painful memories. He'd thought that whatever she'd gone through to get those scars would make her want to get out of the firing line – and he'd have one hostage home free. But now she was putting her hand up and asking to stay. He felt the edge of panic stir in his chest. Her guts of steel were going to be a lead weight around his neck.

They both stiffened as footsteps sounded on the deck again. First one set, then the second. Both brothers.

'Wiseman! You're a chicken shit,' Kane yelled. 'Get out here so I can put you out of your misery.'

His high-pitched laugh was overlaid with Travis's lower, abrupt words. 'Fuck you, Wiseman.'

Matt turned to Jodie. Kane and Travis were going to run out of things to yell soon and he wanted Jodie gone by the time they changed tack.

'Get the hell out of here,' he hissed at her. 'Let me get at least one of you out alive.'

She narrowed her eyes. 'We're *all* getting out.'

'No, we're not.' He made it sound like a statement of fact. Meant it to scare the crap out of her.

She shoved him hard in the chest. 'You bastard! You've given up on them.'

Anger blazed from her eyes. She wasn't going to go. He could see it. She was dug in, defiant, stubborn as hell. And now it was back to four lives in his hands.

'Fuck, fuck.' He spat the words into the darkness. He raked his hands across his head, kicked viciously at the dirt. He needed to get up and stalk around, throw something, but he couldn't, not with Kane and Travis on the verandah waiting for a head to shoot at. Not with *four* lives he could fuck up.

Jodie said nothing. What *could* she say? The guy she thought was going to save her friends was falling apart. She thought he was some kind of goddamn hero. And now she'd put herself in his hands. She didn't know it but he was the guy voted most likely to get her killed.

'Hey, tough bitch. Do you a deal.' It was Travis this time. 'Get up here and I'll let your friend go. The one that's bleeding. She looks real bad, you know. Don't think she'll last much longer. You better get out here.'

Jodie rose to a squat, like a sprinter on her blocks. Matt glanced at her and in that half a second everything got a whole lot worse. Because in his head, he saw her cooking that steak. He saw himself eating the damn thing. He saw her naked, wrapped around him, watching him with those amazing eyes. And it made everything worse. Because he wanted to be in that picture. Because he had no weapon. Because he could barely walk. Because he'd spent the last six months avoiding anything remotely cop-like. All he had now to keep Jodie and her friends alive was his instincts.

His fucking, fucked-up instincts.

'Listen to me,' Matt whispered. She had to know. 'I haven't given up on your friends. But I'm not who you think I am. People died because of me. I don't want your blood on my hands, too. I need to know you're safe. You've already done more than most. You saved my life. I won't forget that. Now get out of here. Please.'

'Shut up, Matt.' She looked at him with hard eyes. 'It'd take the police half an hour to get here on a good night. My friends will be dead by then. And I'm not going to wait down on the road just to hear that piece of news. Not *again*, you got that?'

Again? She had other murdered friends? Whatever had happened to her, it'd turned her into a raging tiger. And right now, she was making him ashamed of his own fear.

She pointed a finger at him. 'You have no idea what I've been through. I am not most people. And I don't care how safe you want me to be. Last time I ran for help, my best friend was murdered. This time I'm not leaving. If people died because of you, then you need to do better this time, Matt. Because I have no idea if this is the right decision but it's the only one I can live with. So get over it and give me some options for what we're can do here now.'

Man, she was something else. She had more guts than most of the cops he knew and she was going to make him stare his own history down. She wasn't giving him a choice. She wasn't taking any excuses. 'Okay. Tell me about the barn.'

Over their heads, Kane and Travis took turns shouting obscenities while Jodie told him everything she knew about the building. Seven years ago, it had been one big room so she walked him through the new layout. She had great recall, knew what was worth noting – which way doors opened, what was in cupboards, places to conceal a person.

'Ever thought of being a cop?' he said.

'I've seen what they have to do. No, thanks.' She paused. 'Look, Matt. I just want to get my friends out. I know you want justice for that teenage girl. I do too. I want it for all of us. But I think we should let Kane and Travis dig up what they came for and leave. Keep them away from my friends and let the police hunt them down when we're all out safe.'

Matt thought about the holes in the dirt under the barn, wondered what else the Anderson brothers had buried there. Tina, for sure. A large metal box. Was there more? He wanted Jodie's friends out. That was a given. But he wasn't going to leave it up to a police roadblock to find Travis and Kane. They'd lived in this area most of their lives, they knew how to get away without being found. No, Matt was determined to make sure they were stopped this time. 'Absolutely.'

THREE MINUTES LATER, Jodie stood and warmed up her legs for the run.

'No heroics, Jodie. Just like we talked about, okay? Then come straight back.'

'That goes for you, too.' She narrowed her eyes, tried to look stern but he could see the fear in them. 'Don't be a hero.'

'Absolutely,' he said again. She was stretching her quads, standing right in front of him. He wanted to take hold of her, tell her if she never saw him again, she should know he was grateful to be doing something. He just looked at her instead, in her dirty sweater with her funky short hair and her huge dark eyes.

She stepped forward and kissed him. Not a peck on the cheek. Nothing remotely like that. Not even long and lingering, the way he'd have done it if he'd had a better time and place to kiss her for the first time. She took his face in her hands and kissed him fast and hard and desperately. Her fingers were freezing and her mouth was hot. It was a sensational combination. He caught her around the waist as she pulled away, hauled her against him and kissed her right back. He ditched the fast bit but stayed with hard and desperate, cupped her face with one hand and held her against him with the other. It was a damn fine first kiss.

When they were done, she stepped away and looked him over again. She smiled a little. 'Don't forget I promised you that steak.'

'You cook. I eat. It's a deal. Now shut up and run.' He turned away from her so he wouldn't change his mind and drag her back. Watched over his shoulder as she disappeared into the dark bush.

He checked his watch. She'd said six minutes.

But it was five minutes too long.

33

A minute after Jodie left, Matt heard screams from inside the barn. Female voices. Then just one female, screaming as she moved through the barn. The sound got suddenly louder, as though a muffler had been removed. She was outside, somewhere around the front. And she was wailing. It sounded like a siren, and it made Matt's hair stand on end.

'Wiseman!' Kane shouted. 'Get out here or I'll put a bullet through her.'

Matt hobbled through the bush towards the front of the barn. Five minutes sitting on the cold earth and his knee was already stiff. He stopped adjacent to the corner of the verandah, looked through the foliage along the deck. Saw Kane and Corrine. His arm was around her throat and he had a pistol at her head.

Matt checked his watch. Jodie wouldn't be close yet. Maybe it didn't matter now.

'I mean it, pig. I got no problem putting a hole in her.' Kane was moving slowly along the verandah, with a wailing Corrine pinned to his chest. He was getting closer to Matt but looking up and down the length of the deck. Kane had no idea where Matt was.

'Got two more bitches inside. Be fun to do one now.'

Matt limped closer to the clearing. Don't be early, Jodie. He rubbed his knee with both hands, trying to get some heat into it, hoping Jodie didn't lose the plot when she saw Corrine or heard her cries. That she just did what they'd planned and came straight back.

'Get out here, Wiseman.' Travis's bellow was distant. He was somewhere around the other side of the barn.

And that was bad news. Matt checked his watch again. Jodie had been gone two minutes. She'd be running through the bush along the rear of the barn by now. She wouldn't go too deep into the scrub. It was denser there and she needed the glow from the floodlights to see where she was going. If she got too close to the clearing, Travis might see her. Matt took a deep breath.

'I'm here,' he shouted. Loud enough for the sound to reach the other side of the barn. 'Let the woman go.'

Through the trees, he saw Kane's head snap around. 'He's out here, Trav.' Kane pushed Corrine ahead of him along the verandah a couple of steps. 'Move into the light.'

'I'll move into the light when you let her go.'

'You got nothing to bargain with, pig.' It was Travis's voice and he'd moved. Matt loped along the edge of the bush a little further to get a wider view of the verandah. Saw Travis just beyond the front door, a shotgun horizontal at his waist. It wasn't a great situation, both brothers armed and waiting for him, but at least Travis had his back to Jodie now.

'Get out here, Wiseman, or I shoot the blonde,' Travis barked. 'Then I go get another one and shoot her if you don't come out. I got three hostages. How many are you gonna make me kill?'

There was an edge to Travis's voice now. He'd had enough. He meant it.

How many, Matt? He took a deep breath, stepped into the lit clearing. 'I'm here.' Kane looked at him over Corrine's shoulder.

Travis swung the shotgun around. 'Where's the tough bitch?'

'Don't know. She took off.'

'Bullshit.' Travis raised his voice, bellowed into the night. 'Get out here, tough bitch.'

'She won't hear you. She took off. Last I saw, she was heading that way,' Matt hooked a thumb over his shoulder. Travis and Kane scanned the dark bush behind him.

With any luck, Jodie was already around the other side of the barn. 'She's gone,' Matt said. 'Forget her. She ran like a scared rabbit.'

Kane laughed like a hyena. Travis said, 'Put your hands in the air, pig, and start walking. Up here. Nice and slow.'

Matt kept his eyes on the shotgun as he moved across the clearing. Corrine was still wailing but the sound was thin and tremulous now. As Matt approached the end of the deck, Travis came forward to stand next to his brother. His face was smeared with trails of blood from a wound on his forehead. Jodie's handiwork.

'Stay in sight,' Travis said. 'Climb over the railing.'

Matt did as he was told, kept his movements slow, looked at Corrine as he swung a leg over the handrail. The gun was at her temple, her eyes were wide and she was breathing in short gasps. He wanted her to look at him, needed her to calm down.

'Corrine?' he said as he dropped both feet to the timber deck. 'Are you okay?' She looked at him but she was too scared to focus.

'Shut up and get your hands in the air,' Travis said. He stepped forward and patted Matt down one-handed.

Matt looked at Corrine over Travis's shoulder. 'Are you okay, Corrine?'

'I said shut up.'

'Just making sure your hostage doesn't freak out. Could get messy for all of us. Especially while your arsehole brother is standing behind you with a gun.'

Travis paused a beat as he patted down Matt's leg then stood and backed off all the way to Kane's side. The brothers looked at him for a long drawn-out moment. Kane grinning like a lunatic, holding a whimpering Corrine. Travis was pissed off, that much was obvious. He was eyeballing Matt with barely contained fury but it wasn't some macho staring competition. He seemed stalled. Like he hadn't planned this bit and he was deciding what to do next. That could be good or bad, Matt thought. Unplanned meant they wouldn't be organised, which could be good. Or it might make Travis reckless, which could be very, very bad.

Travis suddenly lowered his shotgun. 'Get them inside,' he told Kane then turned, stomped along the verandah and went into the barn.

'Corrine,' Matt said quickly, before Kane had a chance to start in on him. 'Hang in there, Corrine.' She looked at him like he was crazy.

'Move.' Kane motioned Matt forward with his head, keeping the gun to Corrine's temple and pulling her backwards. She stumbled and her hands flew up to grab Kane's forearm, the one around her throat.

Any time now, Jodie, Matt thought. He walked slowly forward, watched the panic on Corrine's face grow as she stumbled again, dragging against the arm that was tight around her neck. 'Just do what you're told, Corrine,' Matt said.

She nodded.

'Just like Jodie said.'

She squeezed her eyes shut and nodded again.

He hoped Jodie was right about her. That Corrine was going to be angry enough when she needed to be because right now she looked a mess. 'Corrine.'

'Shut up, pig,' Kane said.

Matt pushed the heel of his hand into the upper left side of his ribs, like maybe he was in pain, and lowered his eyes to Corrine's chest. 'Remember what Jodie told you. Just do what you're told.'

Two big tears ran down her cheeks.

JODIE REACHED the edge of the bush and dropped to a squat opposite the chimney on the lounge room end of the barn. She was out of breath, her shin where Travis had kicked her was pounding and her feet were in agony. Her leather-soled boots weren't made for running – she had blisters on both heels – but at least they'd stopped her turning an ankle on the rough ground.

The shouting had stopped now. She'd heard it over the thrashing of the bush as she'd charged through the scrub. No distinct words, just angry noises. Now everything was quiet. She didn't like it. She had no idea what it meant but she didn't like it.

The bush didn't wrap around this end of the barn the way it did outside Hannah and Corrine's bedroom. She'd gone as far as she could under cover of the bush but there was still a big, open stretch of cleared, grassy land between her and the front corner of the verandah.

The shortest distance was a straight run to the chimney end of the deck. There was a window on either side of the bricked-in smoke-stack and both sets of curtains were pulled wide. If she took that route, she'd be a sitting duck under the floodlights – unless she climbed the handrail, stayed close to the wall and ducked down below the window casement. She ran her eyes along the verandah, saw a crate of firewood, a wicker chair under the power box and a small coffee table. No, too many obstacles.

She turned her head to the corner of the deck, estimated the distance at forty or so metres. Further if she ran it like a right-angle bend to stay out of the light for as long as possible.

How long would she be exposed? Running in a crouch in her bad shoes – probably longer than thirty seconds. Maybe less than a minute. Plenty of time to get shot.

She fingered the rock in her hand. Matt had found it before she left. It was bigger than a tennis ball, smaller than a baseball, heavy like a cricket ball. It had kept her company on the run around the barn. Reminded her what she was doing. That she wasn't just running. She had a job to do.

She flexed the fingers of her right hand, pulled her arm over her head and stretched the triceps. It felt tight but it would have to do. She was out of time for any serious warming up. She took a couple of deep breaths, filled her lungs with oxygen, bent to a crouch and took off across the clearing as fast as she could.

She skidded into the garden like she was making first base, let her feet slide right in under the deck, held her breath, listening to make sure no one was after her. Voices came from around the front. She lifted her eyes over the edge of the timber, saw she had ended up just shy of the front wall of the barn and couldn't see around the corner. She inched forward, keeping low, craning her neck. When she finally saw someone, anger fired in her chest.

Matt, you bastard. She'd left him for five minutes and he'd jumped straight back into the danger zone. What did he think he was doing?

He was halfway along the deck, over near the handrail, his hands up – elbows bent, real casual. And he was walking. Towards her – but not to her. To something out of her view.

She slid a little further forward and the anger turned to fear. Matt was walking towards Kane.

The crazier Anderson brother was close to the wall, walking backwards, moving awkwardly, like maybe he'd been injured. From where she was crouched, Jodie could only see half of him but the half she could see had the pistol and was holding it up high near his shoulder.

Matt was talking quietly. She could hear the deep rumble of his voice over the shuffle of their shoes on the decking. Then she heard something else. Something higher pitched. As she edged forward for a better look, Kane turned and put his back to the wall.

Jodie's blood froze. He had Corrine. And the gun was pointed at her head.

Jodie ducked out of sight. Shit, shit. What now? Her fingers tightened around the rock. She could hit a target from ten metres. She never missed. It was a pointless skill. Until now. Now she couldn't afford to miss.

She looked over the edge of the timber again, guessed Kane was about ten metres away, give or take. She turned her head. Her original target was in range, too. It was meant to be a diversion. Was it going to be enough now? She looked at Matt again. He was two paces from Corrine. What had he said before? *People died because of me.*

Angie had died, too. Now she was here. And so was Matt. They both knew the cost if they got it wrong.

She steadied herself on one knee, pulled back her arm, took aim and flung the rock through the darkness.

It shattered the front passenger window of her car. A split second later, the car alarm ripped open the silence of the night. She didn't waste time admiring the shot, just rolled straight under the overhang of the verandah. A scream shrieked above the howl of the alarm.

Corrine. Jodie gripped the edge of the deck, squeezed her eyes shut. Blood pounded in her head. Look, Jodie. She's your friend. You have to look. She lifted her head above the ledge.

Her car's indicator lights were flashing on and off in sync with the siren, the colour bleeding over the barn lights, turning the verandah intermittently orange then white then orange. Like lazy disco lights. With some kind of slow-mo dance being performed in the glow. Corrine and Kane and Matt were moving – Kane pushing the gun against Corrine's temple, Corrine's hands coming up, Matt lunging towards her.

Corrine screamed again. Not the high-pitched wail Jodie had heard a couple of seconds ago. It was a flat-out yell. Then one hand came down fast. Her fist slammed against Kane's thigh. He bellowed, dropped his gun hand from her head, grabbed at his leg.

'Go!' Matt shouted.

Jodie watched in horror as Corrine turned to Kane and flapped her hands at her sides.

Corrine, run.

Then she did. She took off across the width of the deck, galloped down the steps and ran, limping, a crazy hopping and scrabbling on her sprained ankle across the grass into the dark.

Jodie looked back along the verandah. What she saw made her rise to her feet, made the breath catch in her throat. Matt's fist connected with Kane's cheek but even from the other end of the deck, Jodie could see it was too late. Kane's hand was already up, the pistol aimed straight at Matt.

34

The gunshot roared over the sound of the car alarm. The impact drove Matt backwards. His hip caught the handrail. The momentum pushed him over the top. And he disappeared into the garden under the verandah.

Oh, God, no. Jodie gripped the bottom rung of the handrail, watched as Kane walked to the edge of the verandah and looked over.

'What the fuck . . .?' It was Travis. Standing at the front door, blood on his face, shotgun in his hand.

Kane hooted, raised a fist in the air, shouted, 'I got Wiseman. I fucking killed the cop after all.'

Jodie sank to her knees, bent double in the dirt under the deck. Oh, no. Not Matt. She'd made him go back a second time for her friends. And Kane had killed him. Pain clawed at her chest. She pushed her forehead into the soil. She couldn't breathe. Her chest had turned to stone. Angie was dead and now Matt was dead. Twice her fault. Two lives she owed.

'Get the other two and find the tough bitch,' Travis yelled. He was angry, his voice bellowing over the siren. 'We get the stuff, get them sorted and get out of here.'

A shotgun blast rocked the night. Jodie felt herself scream but the sound was drowned out by the explosion echoing off the roof of the verandah and rolling around the hills. When it was over, the car alarm had stopped and the silence felt like deafness.

Travis's voice cut through it like a chainsaw. *'Just do it, you fuck-up!'* Jodie listened from under the deck as Travis's boots crossed the verandah. Sound was amplified in the new silence. Kane swore under his breath. Travis took half-a-dozen steps inside, made a brief shuffling sound on the timber, a grunt and a scrape. Then the footfalls disappeared. She sat up. Travis was in the hole.

She looked over the edge of the verandah again. Kane was leaning against the wall, bent over his leg. There was a wet, bloody circle on his jeans, something sticking out of it. The nailfile she'd given Corrine. Anger churned in Jodie's gut.

Kane had held a gun to Corrine's head and he'd killed Matt. And now he was going back for Louise and Hannah.

Angie's face swam in her head. Not the one from that dark night. The other one. From the hockey pitch. The one that knew Jodie would always take the shot, the one from out wide. The long shot.

Do it, Jodie.

The game wasn't over. It was getting close but it wasn't done yet.

Up on the verandah, Kane yelled as he ripped the nailfile out of his leg. Okay, Jodie. Think.

You have to help Louise and Hannah.

It wasn't a long walk for Kane to the bedroom end of the barn. She couldn't beat him there no matter how fast she ran. So she had to stop him before he got there.

Adrenaline hummed inside her. Her brain stepped up a gear. She saw everything at once. The light circling the barn like a shield, the front door wide open, the two windows either side of the chimney.

She rose, looked through the closest window. A curtain billowed in the breeze through the smashed glass door and furniture was scattered randomly about the room. Out on the deck: the crate of timber, the wicker chair. The power box.

She heard footsteps on the timber, swept her eyes back around the corner, saw Kane moving away from her. He was going to the bedroom via the verandah, not in through the front door.

Jodie pulled off her boots and moved swiftly along the garden in her socks. When she was level with the chimney, she slipped under the handrail, took two long strides to the wall, lifted the cover on the power box and flipped switches.

Darkness closed around her like a solid object. It was suffocating, claustrophobic. Her heart raced and her breath came short and fast. She blinked hard, saw nothing but black. *Now, Jodie.* If she couldn't see, neither could they.

She ran in her socks on the balls of her feet, feeling her way along the wall, around the corner to the back of the barn. Kane was swearing from somewhere around the front. There was silence inside. She dropped to her hands and knees, crawled along the timber deck, one shoulder to the glass wall. At the smashed panel, she stopped, squatted in the doorway.

She couldn't see a thing. Kane was outside cursing, calling Travis, clumping about like a damn wind-up toy with a missing leg. She inched around the doorframe, listened for noise from under the floor. Then she saw it. A flash of pale light on the wall near the front door.

It was Travis. With the torch. He was still under the barn.

Jodie jerked up to a crouch. Was halfway through a step before she pulled herself back. Her legs wanted to run, to charge down the hallway to the wardrobe. But that would be stupid. In the darkness, the lounge room was an obstacle course of furniture and broken glass, and Travis would hear her. She wouldn't make it to the hall. Her muscles ached to take off but she forced herself to step slowly, quietly over sharp nuggets of shattered glass.

Hands outstretched, she found her way to the island bar, held onto it as she dropped to a squat again, hunkered down behind it and listened.

Kane was tramping around on the deck, still yelling for Travis, too loud for her to hear anything else. She lay down, put an ear to the cold floor, thought she heard a faint shuffling underneath. As she sat up, another flash of pale light flipped across the ceiling. He was definitely still down there.

She felt her way around the kitchen side of the island bench, waited at the other end. Kane was making a shushing noise along the wall, as though he was running his hands over it. Maybe looking for the power box. Maybe trying to find the front door to get back inside. Her heart pounded. Her hands shook. Don't stop now.

She stuck her head around the bench, looked right towards the hole in the floor. It was so black, Travis could be standing right in front of her and she wouldn't know it. The thought made the hair on her head stand up and she put a trembling hand out. There was nothing. She turned the other way, rose to a crouching stand and stepped into the darkness.

She moved cautiously, found the wall then the doorframe, slipped across into the hall, pressed her back against the wall and waited. Her pulse sounded like a drum. It was all she could hear. She wanted to suck in a lungful of air, gasp and pant, but in the silence of the barn, a breath like that would reverberate like a wave crashing. She closed her eyes for a moment, opened her mouth and breathed slowly in. Listened for the shushing sound out on the verandah and heard a noise that made her body go rigid.

It was a creak. The kind of creak a floorboard makes. She looked back towards the lounge room, saw a torch beam slice through the darkness.

She pressed her hands to the wall behind her, tried not to make her own shushing sounds as she scuttled sideways down the hall. The light flashed into the corridor, made a yellow circle on the wall opposite. Fear filled her throat. Travis must have heard her. The urge to bolt felt like a hand in her back, throwing her forward. Hold it together, Jodie, or you're dead. And so are your friends.

Her hand found a doorframe. Her bedroom. She rolled around, pressed herself into the corner between the wall and the built-in wardrobe. Listened.

She couldn't hear Kane. Couldn't tell if he'd stopped moving around or the sound didn't carry through the walls. She closed her eyes, held her breath, strained till her ears hurt.

A thud. Soft. Somewhere near the hall, not actually in it. At least she didn't think so.

She moved to the edge of the wall and turned her face towards the black space that was the doorway. Listened some more.

The other bedroom was just a couple of steps further down the hall. Three at most. Two steps to get out of the doorway, three to the end of the hall, two more and she'd be standing in front of the walk-in robe. Lou and Hannah were seven steps away. Come on. You can make it, Jodie.

She took a deep breath. And another one. Held the doorframe with one hand, took a step.

Torchlight speared the dark hall. Shaky, moving up and down, searching. It burned a circle into the paintwork opposite, roved across the open doorway at the end of the hall. Kept travelling right.

Jodie thrust backwards towards the centre of the room, watched in horror as the light hit the doorway she'd been standing in, spilled onto the floor, illuminated the navy blue toes of her socks. Then moved away.

There was a noise in the hall. A shuffle, a faint scrape. Travis was there, moving towards the bedrooms. The light got closer, brighter, continued its searching movement.

Jodie took two long strides to her bed. Dropped, pressed herself to the floor. Fuck, fuck. This was such a dumb place to hide. The bed was too low to slide under. The quilt too short to cover her. One look with the torch and he was going to see her. She curled into a ball, made herself small, slid along the floor, pushed her head into the wall.

Something cold and hard shifted behind her. It felt like a block of ice against the bare skin between her sweater and the top of her jeans. She reached around, gripped it in her fist and felt it fill her with strength.

The tyre iron. She'd never returned it to the loan car. She'd left it under the bed. And now she had a weapon.

The source of light was close now. She could hear Travis breathing. She propped her back against the bed, gripped the tyre iron with both hands and waited.

Torchlight jumped about the room, from the window, to the other bed, around the walls. Then left.

There was a footfall outside the door. Jodie looked under the bed, saw Travis in the doorway, shining the torch straight ahead into the other bedroom.

Stay away from my friends, you bastard. Anger brought Jodie to her feet and gave her the courage to move. She stepped quickly, quietly across the room, tyre iron out in front as she watched Travis. He stopped in the doorway at the end of the hall, let the torch fill the other bedroom with a dull glow. He was a silhouette framed by the door. A target now. But Jodie waited. There wasn't enough room to swing the tyre iron here. She waited and prayed he didn't turn around.

He didn't. He moved into the bedroom. One step. Two. At three, she moved. Slipped around the doorframe, stepped in behind him, pulled back the tyre iron like a baseball bat. Maybe he heard her. Maybe he was giving up and leaving. He turned, saw Jodie as she started her swing. Jerked away.

She tried to adjust the fall of the tyre iron but it was too late. She'd aimed for his head. Got him hard across a shoulder. A walloping chop that threw him sideways, knocked the torch from his hand. But didn't knock him down.

He spun around, too fast for Jodie to reverse the thrust of the tyre iron. He shouldercharged her, slamming her against the wardrobe door. Air gusted out of her lungs. The tyre iron fell from her hands and she doubled over, gasping for air. Inside the wardrobe, Louise and Hannah screamed.

Keep your eyes open, Jodie. The torch was on the floor but there was enough light to see him take half a step back. She pushed off the door, drove her knee up. Missed his groin but got him high on the thigh. Not a great shot. Not enough to cripple him but enough to make him stoop and grunt. She pulled her hands in tight to her chest, lifted her elbow like a wing and twisted hard at him. Swung her whole body into it, just like she taught her students. Made contact with his jaw, snapped his head around. He stumbled away, still on his feet.

She could hear Lou and Hannah shouting on the other side of the wardrobe door. *You've nearly got them out, Jodie. Don't stop.* She closed the distance to him as he straightened up, slammed the heel of her hand under his chin.

As he fell, a light came on.

Not the room light. It came from outside. Bright, white light coming in through the bedroom window. Jodie looked up and squinted in the sudden glare. That was her big mistake. Travis grabbed her ankle, pulled her leg out from under her. She hit the floor hard, kicked out at him as he tried to grab her feet, scrabbled frantically backwards.

But he kept coming, clawing his way up her body, eyes narrowed and angry in his blood-smeared face. She kept lashing out, striking with her feet, her knees. Must have made contact somewhere, felt him fall away. She rolled over, scratched at the floor, slipped in her socks, pulled herself up to her feet, made the door, slammed into the doorframe. He was behind her, she could hear him, he was yelling, cursing, still getting to his feet. *Run, Jodie!*

She was in the hallway, past her bedroom door, almost out. Then skidding, trying to stop, sliding in her socks, legs wheeling on the slippery timber. Oh, God, no. Kane was at the other end of the hall. A silhouette in the door like his brother had been. Only she could see his face, see the 'gotcha' look. And knew there was no way out.

35

K ane's fist came at Jodie like a freight train. She had time to duck a fraction, probably saved her cheek from being crushed, but the impact on her forehead drove her across the hall and slammed her into the wall.

Her knees turned to rubber and she slid down the wall, tipping drunkenly to one side. She felt movement before she saw it, curled instinctively into a ball, took Kane's first kick on her thigh. There wasn't time to register pain. Just time to wrap her arms around her head, roll away far enough to protect her ribs and take the second kick on her hip. Kane was lifting his foot high, slamming down with the rubber sole, trying to crush her like a beetle. He had a hand on the wall above her, crowding her in. There was no escape. She tucked her head in, tried to get her strongest bones under him, felt anger form a hard, hot, solid mass inside her.

She wasn't going to die. Not yet.

Not in a damn hallway. With Matt dead outside, with Louise shot and bleeding and trapped with Hannah in a wardrobe.

As she flinched for another blow, Kane was knocked away and Travis's voice bounced off the walls. 'Get her out of here.'

'I'm gonna kill the fucking bitch.'

'You're gonna do what you came here for first.'

Between the arms curled over her face, Jodie watched Travis shove his brother again. This time, Kane came back at him. She kept her head down as they heaved each other around, throwing punches, their feet catching her painfully. It was Travis who brought it to an end, stopping Kane in a chokehold against the wall.

'Get her out of here and get under the barn or you can sort your own shit out.'

Jodie heard nothing but heavy breathing for a long, tense moment. She closed her eyes, prayed Kane would do as he was told. Someone grabbed the neck of her sweater, started dragging her along the floor.

Travis had saved her life – for now.

Matt bit down on the cuss at his lips. His shoulder was on fire. Blood was slick on his arm, seeping through his sleeve, running into his hand. The bullet had ripped right through his triceps, left a wide gash on the underside of his upper arm. He fingered a painful, hardening lump on his temple. He must have hit his head on the way over the verandah. Knocked him out. He didn't know for how long – or for how long he'd dropped in and out of consciousness. He just knew he had to get moving.

He gripped his shoulder with his other hand, rolled off the mound of shrubbery he'd fallen into, laid in the dirt under the lip of the verandah for a moment, waiting for the dizziness to subside.

Jodie was unbelievable. She'd been two minutes late. He'd just about given up on her. Didn't think she'd pull off the shot while there was a gun to her friend's head. But she had. Smack through the car window. And then she'd managed to knock out the power. They'd talked about that before she'd left. She hadn't been a hundred per cent sure where the box was but they'd agreed if it was where she thought it was, if it was safe, she'd kill the lights too.

And she'd been right about Corrine. The blonde had slammed that nailfile home. Buried it deep in Kane's thigh. Just as well because she couldn't run for shit. She'd needed every second she had to get out of the light. With any luck, she was now stumbling about in the bush towards the road, heading to a phone. Matt needed help up here. And he wanted Kane and Travis in custody. Handcuffed, locked in the back of a van, facing down life in prison. They deserved to suffer for the things they'd done.

Both brothers were inside now. Matt had seen Kane turn on the roof-mounted spotlights on his truck. It was the blinding light that had finally forced him into full consciousness. He'd heard Kane's limping stomp across the verandah and now he and his brother were shouting at each other inside the barn, slamming doors.

It was time to move. While they were at each other. Before they turned on the other two hostages. Get them back to Jodie in the bush then get them all to safety.

Matt pulled himself into a sitting position, his head spinning like a barrel, clambered about in the garden until he found a way out. His knee was bad and his arm was useless and he was bleeding badly. He needed to get this done fast. He checked the verandah, made sure he was alone, then ran low and limping across the grass to the bedroom end of the barn.

It was darker around there. Just enough light from the car to see what he was doing. He crept across the deck, slipped through the French doors, folding them open against the wall behind him. One of the brothers was talking loudly at the other end of the barn, the sound muffled through the closed bedroom door. In the eerie light from outside, he could see dark circles of his own blood on the floor, a tyre iron in front of the wardrobe – and the spade still securing the handles.

He quietly removed the spade, eased one door open, looked inside. The light didn't penetrate to the back of the walk-in robe and it took a second for him to see them. The two women were huddled in the far corner, the injured one, Louise, lying down, her knees curled up, her head on the lap of the nurse, Hannah.

As he approached them, Hannah braced both arms protectively around Louise, in a way that made Matt think she'd spent her time in the wardrobe pulling herself together. She seemed to have moved on from the sheer terror that had pinned her to the wall before. She was frightened now, that was obvious in the wide-open eyes, but she looked bolder, more resolute.

'It's okay. It's Matt,' he whispered as he knelt beside them. 'How is she? Can she walk?'

He spoke to Hannah but Louise answered. 'If you can get me on my feet, I can walk.'

Matt couldn't see her face clearly in the dark but her voice was determined. She needed to be. It was a long walk to the bush and he couldn't carry her. Not now.

'Where's Jodie?' Hannah said.

'Tie her to the post,' Travis ordered.

Kane dragged Jodie to her feet, shoved her face first at one of the big, old tree trunks holding up the roof of the lounge room. As he pulled her arms around either side of the trunk, bound her wrists tight with electrical tape, the double-edged knife tattooed on his forearm swam sickeningly across her still woozy vision. Travis stood back and watched, wiped at the blood on his face and glared at his brother. He was out of breath from the fight in the hallway but his heavy breathing seemed to be more about reining in his fury. Fury that wasn't just aimed at Jodie.

When Kane was done, he pulled on her hands, dragged her hard-up against the trunk, got in her face. 'I'm gonna enjoy you, bitch.'

'Get the fuck under the barn,' Travis yelled at him.

Kane spun around, looked ready to charge but stopped when he saw the gun in Travis's hand. He held the pistol low at his side, muzzle pointed to the floor.

'You gonna use that thing on me?' Kane's growl was a challenge.

'You gonna get under the barn or make me think about it?'

Jodie watched from behind as Kane folded his arms across his chest. When he spoke, his voice was filled with venom. 'You wanna be the old man now?' He took a threatening step forward.

Travis raised the gun.

Kane roared, 'Who the fuck do you think you are?'

'I'm the one with the *gun*.'

Neither brother moved for a second.

'You leave her for me,' Kane said.

'She's is all yours.' Travis's first words were spoken calmly then he raised his voice to a bawl. '*So do something useful and get under the goddamn barn.*'

'Fuck you!' Kane shouted but gave up the fight.

Travis watched in silence as Kane dropped his legs into the hole and disappeared under the floor. He turned, focused on Jodie for a brief, tense moment then walked to the kitchen.

Jodie closed her eyes, swallowed at the bile in her throat. She was pressed up close to the gnarly surface of the tree trunk, the dried remains of the bark rough against her cheek. She was still in her socks, dirt crusted on the knees of her jeans, Corrine's white sweater torn and filthy. Her face hurt. Her head felt like it wasn't sitting properly on the top of her neck and she had large patches of tender new bruising along the right side of her body. But her anger was intact. Travis was leaving her for Kane and her anger felt great. It felt like a weapon. The only weapon she had.

Off to her left, a tap was turned on in the kitchen. She moved her head, rested her other cheek against the trunk, saw Travis at the sink cleaning blood from his face – some of it fresh from the fight, some of it dried and crusted from when she'd smashed his head into the brick pier.

She smiled a little at the memory of that. She'd been terrified down there, had been terrified since she'd walked through the front door this afternoon, but as she watched Travis, she realised she felt no fear now. Kane and Travis were going to kill her. They were going to kill Louise and Hannah. She was never going to see her beautiful children again. There was nothing she could do about it. But fear wasn't what she felt.

What she felt was hotter and sharper and filling her up, infusing every artery, every vein, every muscle.

She thought about how it might go. When Kane was finished under the barn, Travis was going to let him get his kicks spilling their blood. Travis had been using Jodie and her friends as a bribe all night. Like bribing a child with chocolate to make him clean his room, only Kane got a thrill kill if he did his job. But he had to do his job *first*. Travis was worried about time, worried that if Kane got started before they were ready to leave, they were going to run out of time. Which meant whatever Kane did to get his thrills, it wasn't quick. His warning to Matt came back to her.

I'm gonna beat your brains out and cut you up in little pieces.

Jodie looked at the hole in the floor, at Travis wiping his face on his shirt, felt the heat inside her rise.

She was *not* going to die in fear. Too much of her life had been spent fearing the evil of others. Fearing the pain that could be inflicted. The screaming and the blood and the loss and the powerlessness. Well, she'd been there. Done that. And she was over it. Fucking over it.

'JODIE'S WAITING for you in the bush,' Matt said as he eased Louise upright and let her rest against the back wall of the wardrobe.

'They got her,' Hannah said.

'No, she's in the bush, waiting for us.'

'You saw her?'

He hesitated a second. 'Yeah.'

Hannah put her hands to her face, pulled in a shuddering breath. 'Oh, God. I thought they got her. I thought it was too late.' She looked up at him again. 'What about Corrine?'

Matt wrapped Louise's arm around his neck. 'She jammed Kane with the nailfile and ran for her life.'

Louise smiled weakly.

Hannah gasped. 'She did? Is she okay?'

'She made it to the bush. Safest place to be right now. That's where we've got to get you two. Hannah, you're going to have to help me.'

Louise slid her arm across his shoulder, lifted her hand quickly. 'Matt! You're bleeding.'

'Yeah. Come on. We've got to go.'

He stopped them at the door, checked the bedroom, put a finger to his lips then pointed to the French doors. He was worried about the noise of their shoes on the timber floor. Impossible to drag an injured woman across a room without making a sound. But they made it to the doors, inched through sideways, half carried Louise across the verandah. Pain filled his arm, spilled into his chest, made his lungs spasm. He was gasping for breath as they took the steps but he couldn't afford to stop. He had to get the women across the clearing as fast as possible. It was dark but not pitch. Kane or Travis could make a mess of them firing the shotgun from the verandah. He couldn't hear them now. Could only hear his own rasping breath, Louise's agonised wheezing, their feet pounding on the grass in rhythm with his heart.

The twenty metres to the scrub felt more like twenty kilometres. When they were through the first line of foliage, he lowered Louise to the ground, looked back up at the barn and tried to work out where he and Jodie had sat in the dirt. Where Jodie would be waiting for them.

'We need to get further into the bush,' he whispered.

'Where's Jodie?' Hannah asked.

'She's waiting for us further in. Can you keep going, Louise?'

She didn't answer for a second. Her breathing was shallow, uneven, as though it hurt to draw in air. 'Yep,' she finally managed.

Matt helped her to her feet again, grimaced at the pain in his shoulder, wiped the blood that had run down to his hand on his jeans. He walked them another five metres, found a small clearing, let them stop. There was enough light for them to see each other, barely, not enough to see much further. Jodie could be anywhere out here.

'Jodie?' he called softly. He held his breath in the silence. '*Jodie.*'

'Where is she?' Hannah asked.

Matt pressed the digital display on his watch. It glowed like a torch in the darkness. Eight-fifty-four. Twenty-five minutes since she left. He closed his eyes. It took her eight minutes to throw the rock, give her two more to kill the lights. That's fifteen left to hightail it back here.

'Matt? Where is she? Where's Jodie?' Hannah said.

'Not here.' Damn it, Jodie. Where are you?

Beside him, Hannah was starting to panic. Flinging her hands around, talking to herself, stumbling in the bush. 'Jodie!' she cried, too loud for comfort.

'Be quiet!' he hissed.

'They've got her, Matt. We heard them. They've got her.' She was crying now and he could hear the dread in her voice.

It was all he could do to stop her fear from running rampant inside him. He looked at the dark scrub, at the distant light from Kane's car. Maybe she couldn't get back to the bush without being seen and was hiding under the verandah. Maybe she fell, sprained her ankle. Maybe he got the wrong spot and she was waiting for them thirty metres away.

Maybe she was in the barn. With Kane and Travis.

Hannah's words came back to him and he turned to her. 'What do you mean you heard them?'

'She was in the bedroom. Just before you got there. And Travis. We heard them fighting. Then they were gone.'

She was in the bedroom? He told her to come straight here. She was never meant to go inside. He squeezed his eyes shut. She'd been out of it. She'd been out of the barn, away and safe, and he let her go back. What have you done?

He thought of her, before she left. Stretching her quads, warming up, kissing him. She'd been totally in control in those few minutes. Frightened but determined. *Last time I ran for help, my best friend was murdered. This time I'm not leaving.*

No one could have stopped her.

If people died because of you, then you need to do better this time, Matt.

Matt looked up at the barn again. 'No hostages are dying tonight, Jodie.'

'What?' said Hannah. She was crying.

He took off his jacket, winced at the pain. 'I'm going back.'

'They'll kill you, Matt.'

He ripped off his torn sleeve, held it out to Hannah. 'Bandage my arm.'

'Oh God, are you shot?'

'Make it tight to stop the bleeding.'

She held his sleeve in her hand like she didn't know what to do with it.

'Now, Hannah. Then you and Louise get moving.'

'What about Jodie?'

He looked at Hannah's frightened eyes, at Louise at his feet on the dirt. 'She won't be long now.'

36

'What's under the barn?' Jodie figured if she was going to die, she may as well know what for.

'Keep your mouth shut,' Travis said. He was at the sink, didn't look at her when he spoke.

Jodie smiled to herself. He was going to kill her but she was going to piss him off first. It was the least she could do. 'It must be pretty impressive.'

He ignored her, took off his blood-smeared shirt, tossed it on the marble bench. He was wearing a filthy white T-shirt, part of a tattoo showing below the sleeve of his right arm – it looked like half a coiled snake.

'I mean, you've gone to a lot of trouble here,' she said, her voice growing in force. He grabbed the bottle of bourbon off the bench, unscrewed the cap.

'Hacked a bloody great hole in a perfectly good floor. Assaulted a bunch of women minding their own business.'

He looked across at her with narrowed eyes, smears of blood on his face, an open wound on the bridge of his nose. He tipped the bottle for a long drink.

'Pretty daring stuff, Travis. You're a real hero.'

He slammed the bottle onto the marble. 'I told you to *shut up!*'

She went on talking as though he hadn't said a word. 'Oh yeah, you shot a cop, too. At least that fuck-up brother of yours did. Whatever it is down there, it'd want to be pretty damn impressive for that.'

He lifted the bottle and hurled it at her. A wide arc of bourbon curled into the air as the bottle flew across the room. She turned her face away as it hit the other side of the tree trunk and smashed on the floor. At least the pistol hadn't been the closest thing to hand. It was tucked into the back of his jeans. Out of sight, out of mind, she hoped. She looked back at him, flinched as he swept one outstretched arm across the island bench. Glassware, crockery, cutlery and the unwashed frypan crashed to the floor.

A flash of victory shot up Jodie's spine. She'd got to him. She watched him smugly as he stalked back and forth across the kitchen. It was a dangerous game but she was enjoying inflicting some misery on him. He deserved worse, a lot worse, but aggravation was the best she could do from where she stood.

'Is it more impressive than that body down there? The one you made me dig up. *Tina.*'

He slammed his hands down on the marble bench, leaned against it like he wanted to push it through the floor. His back was to her but in the light from the truck, she could see his T-shirt straining as he breathed hard.

He was angry. She was impatient. This night had gone on long enough. Jodie looked down at her feet, saw the remains of the bourbon bottle had fallen clear of her trunk. She pushed off her dirty socks. 'Is it more impressive than killing that man in town yesterday? *John Kruger.* It'd want to be if you're risking getting caught by the battalion of cops out looking for you.'

His body stiffened. Jodie watched, waited, as he took another breath. He shoved himself away from the bench, lashed out at a cupboard with his boot, stalked through the kitchen to the hole in the floor. 'Kane!' he bellowed. 'Get your arse *moving!*'

Jodie heard a muffled shout from under the barn. She looked at Travis leaning tense and taut over the hole and suddenly saw it. How it worked between Travis and Kane. Why Travis hadn't killed her when he could in the hallway, why he was shouting at Kane right now instead of beating her up, why the gun was still in his waistband when he could turn around and shoot her.

'It's Kane, isn't it? Kane's the killer. And you keep him on a leash like a rabid dog.' Travis threw a look at her over his shoulder, one that said he'd unleash him on her if she didn't shut up. Nothing new there. 'So what happened yesterday, Travis? Did you let your psycho brother loose on that man in town? Did Kane beat him to death or cut him in pieces for *you*?'

Travis came at her then. Closed the distance between them in three long strides. He raised a fist and she braced for its impact. But it didn't come. He pointed his index finger at her face like the pistol he'd held there before. 'John Kruger had nothing to do with me. Kane did that. And he shot Matt Wiseman. Not me. You remember that, tough bitch. *I* haven't killed anyone.'

He was near enough for his bourbon breath to wash over her face, for her to see the black streaks in his dark irises, the red veins in the off-white globes of his eyeballs. She wanted to spit in them but was too dry in the mouth to pull it off. 'Yeah, you're a real pacifist, Travis. You haven't done a thing. Just promised me and my friends to your psycho brother. Well, guess what? That makes you as psycho as him.'

He grabbed the back of her head in one meaty palm, crushed her cheek into the trunk. 'I'm *not* a psycho. I didn't put those girls down there.'

Her nostrils filled with the stench of his sweat. Her quickening pulse thumped against the old tree. Girls? There was more than one? 'You put *something* down there.'

He mashed her head harder against the rough trunk. 'Insurance. That's what I put down there. For when Kane fucked up so bad I'd have to leave for good. I never *killed* anyone.'

Anger burned in Jodie's veins. He knew about the girls, knew his brother had killed them. Travis was as guilty as it got. 'You shot Louise.'

'That was *your* fault. Yours and Wiseman's. I wasn't going to shoot her. I was trying to scare her.'

No. She was not taking the blame for him. She was done with carrying the guilt for other people's violence. 'You held a loaded gun to Lou's head. You pulled the trigger. It's your fault. *You* shot her.'

Travis grabbed the trunk with one hand, shoved the flat of his other hand into the centre of her back, pushed her hard up against the post. 'Listen, tough bitch.' His voice was a growl, his breath hot and sour on her cheek. 'The cops have got nothing on me and I plan to keep it that way. So me and my brother, we're going to get my stuff and piss off out of here, go where no one will find us. And if you keep your mouth shut like I told you, quit your screaming for ten fucking minutes, it might not be the last ten minutes of your life. Got it?'

Jodie didn't move. *Not* kill them? Is that what he meant?

His hand moved up to the back of her head again, forced her face around to him. 'So keep your fucking mouth shut.'

Something fragile and cautious stirred deep in Jodie's belly.

Hope.

And it scared the hell out of her.

Travis was offering to give her life back. Hers and Lou's and Hannah's. All she had to do was be quiet. Hold her anger inside. Keep her hate to herself.

She wanted to believe him with every cell in her body. But that would mean trusting him. The man who shot Lou. Who thought it didn't count because she wasn't dead. Who sanctioned his brother's murders. Who used Jodie and her friends as bait.

If he was lying, if she let her hate get watered down by hope and it turned out to be some kind of sadistic joke, it would break her. If she was compliant, made it easier for them and they killed her anyway, it would be the death she'd always feared – powerless and screaming.

She kept her voice low, spat the words in his face. 'You're full of shit.'

His eyes narrowed briefly, a quick contraction of the lids. 'Listen, for fuck's sake. It's the screaming that gets him going. I've been telling you all night to shut up.'

'And you've been telling your brother he can *do us* all night.'

He changed his grip on her head, closed his fist around a handful of hair, pulled it tight. 'I've kept him off you and your friends this far but once he's done down there, I won't be able to hold him back if you don't keep your mouth *shut*. He loves the fighters. Even better when they scream. He keeps it going for as long as they make a noise.'

He stopped talking, screwed his lips together. The muscles in his jaw tightened, his Adam's apple jerked up and down. Jodie squeezed her eyes shut, waited for the globule of saliva he was working up. When it didn't come, she opened her eyes again. What she saw on his face took her breath away.

Revulsion.

Travis was revolted by his brother.

Hope stirred in her belly again. Maybe Travis was telling the truth. Maybe they had a chance after all.

He let go of her head, flicked a glance over his shoulder to the hole. 'I don't give a shit about you and your friends. He can slice you up or not, I don't care. I just want to get the hell away from here without my name on one of his bodies. I'm not getting done for this. I'm *not*.'

He thrust away from her, walked a tight circle, pushed both hands into the front of his blood-matted hair. 'Fuck! This was meant to be easy. Get in, get my stuff, disappear.' He looked at her. 'I had to bring him.' He said it defensively, like he needed to explain. 'Kane's a fuck-wit. He went to the pub after he killed John Kruger, for Christ's sake. The cops would've picked him up before I had a chance to get my stuff. Then they would've come for me. They always do. Like we're a fucking double act.' He pointed at her again. 'Well, we're not. Killing those people is his sick hobby, not mine. I just do my job – clean up after my useless little brother and keep him out of a prison cell.' He let his arms drop, swung his whole body around to the hole, stood for a second, hands on his hips. Then, like he'd felt a breath of fresh air, he lifted his head, straightened his shoulders and turned towards the front window of the barn, the headlights from the truck outside illuminating narrowed eyes, a hard mouth. 'Fuck Kane. Fuck him.'

A bead of sweat broke out on Jodie's lips. Travis looked over at her, his eyes moving from her bare feet, to her tied hands, to her face that ached from being jammed against the post. Was it indecision or a long last look before he left her to die? She couldn't tell, figured she didn't have time to work it out.

'If you leave Kane here, he'll kill us. You know he will. And the cops will come after you. They'll know you were here. Your DNA is all over the barn – and me. You may as well sign your name on my forehead.'

He hesitated, mouth open, eyes unsure.

Jodie took a chance. Quietly, she said, 'I'll keep my mouth shut about you if you take Kane with you. We all will. We'll tell the cops it was Kane. Not you. We'll say Kane was here first. That you came and got him. You stopped him hurting us, made him leave us alone.'

There was movement under the barn. A thud. A scrape.

'Take him with you, Travis. Leave him somewhere for the cops to find. They won't go after you if we say it wasn't you. Just don't leave him here.'

Loose earth scattered beneath them. Kane grunted. He was close. He was almost done.

Travis stepped over to the hole in the floor and looked down.

Jodie felt panic rise in her chest. She wanted to survive. Wanted Lou and Hannah to live. Tears welled in her eyes. 'Please, Travis.'

Kane was right under them now. She could hear him. Almost feel him under her feet.

Travis ran his hands through his hair again, kept his eyes on the front window as he did so.

Jodie's legs trembled. He wasn't looking at her anymore. She was out of his plans now. He was going to save himself. He was going to leave his brother behind. 'Then cut the tape on my hands, Travis. At least give me a chance against him.'

He turned his eyes on her then. It wasn't a yes. But it wasn't no, either.

'*Come on*, Travis. He won't have to know. Just cut it enough so I can tear the rest. You've got to get your stuff out to the truck. Make Kane help you with it. I can get out through the back of the barn. Get my friends out. We can hide in the bush. He'll never find us in the dark. You can leave him here for the cops. I'll tell them you saved us. They won't even look for you.'

Travis jammed his hands onto his hips and let fly with a guttural, near-whispered torrent of abuse. His whole body jolted and strained as each word was driven out of him. It wasn't directed at Jodie. Or at the hole in the floor. Just spat into the room like the afterburner of a jet.

He turned, stomped to her, bent quickly, straightened again. A snicker of sound made Jodie look down. There was a blade in his hand, must have been pulled from a holster on his ankle. Short, narrow like a talon, a bone handle tucked neatly into his fist. Her stomach tried to force its way into her throat.

He held it up to her face. 'I'll handle my brother. You keep the cops away. You don't, I'll come back for you. And I'll have no problem using this on you.'

She looked at the short metal blade and had a sudden urge to laugh. To gag on the ludicrousness of the moment. Her salvation rested on a knife edge. Who came up with that cruel joke? 'I'll make you sound like a bloody hero, Travis.'

She twisted her head around the trunk, watched him lower the blade and felt some kind of macabre charge at the cold touch of it on her wrist.

'What the fuck are you *doing*?' Kane's voice was a growl. Travis turned his head, lifted the knife, left the tape uncut.

37

Not now, Kane. Not yet. Jodie's breath jammed in her chest. She looked past Travis, saw Kane's head and shoulders in the room. The rest of him was still under the barn.

'You thought you'd start without me. Is that it?' Kane put his palms flat on the floorboards, lifted himself up and out of the hole, stood to his full height. 'Or did you think you were going to keep her for yourself?'

He was sweating and dirty, stripped down to the blue singlet, a dark stain on his trousers from the wound in his thigh, his face and arms shiny in the light from the car outside. The sight of him made Jodie's limbs go loose. He'd made girls scream. Murdered them. Buried them under the barn. She breathed hard, pushed air in and out of her lungs. Cut the tape, Travis.

Travis turned to her, looked down at her hands, up at her face.

She pleaded with her eyes, stretched her wrists towards him. *Now*, Travis.

He lifted the knife, made a show of folding it closed, pushed it into his back pocket.

'Nah, bro. Just getting her started for you. She's going to fucking scream her lungs out.'

. . .

MATT SKIRTED around the edge of the bush towards the rear of the barn. The same path he'd taken hours earlier when he hadn't trusted his instincts, when he'd felt like a stalker for checking up on Jodie. His instincts had been right on the nose. Now he hoped they stayed there.

He paused opposite the glass doors, the ones he'd smashed with the wrought-iron table. The car lights shone right through the lounge room, casting a glow on the deck and beyond into the garden. Matt watched elongated shadows move about inside, hoping for some sign it was only Kane and Travis in there but the eerie shapes were too distorted to identify. He bent low and limped across the grass clearing, stopping in the garden below the kitchen. He listened, heard footsteps, an aggravated male voice. No clear words but it was Kane. Then Travis. They were both on the other side of the big room.

Matt flexed his injured arm. The bandage was tight enough to cut the circulation in his hand but the blood had stopped running. Now it just hurt like hell.

Not as much as losing another hostage.

Not as much as losing Jodie. Not now that he knew who she was, what her courage had done for him.

He lifted himself onto the verandah, scooted to the wall and peered around the edge of the glass door. The sight of Jodie tethered to a post turned his stomach sour. He snapped his head away, closed his eyes. How did she end up get there?

You should have taken out Kane on the verandah, his guilt yelled. You should have taken him out seven years ago. But Jodie's words rang louder.

Do it better, Matt.

She'd wanted him to do it better for her friends. Now her life depended on it. So do it better, Matt.

Get the hostage out. Stop the bad guys. Do your *job*.

He took a deep breath. And another. Then rolled his face back around the edge of the glass.

Okay, what do you see?

Ahead of him was the separate kitchen bench. To the right, debris was scattered across the floor – glass from the shattered door, broken crockery, the wrought-iron table he'd used to smash his way in, a dining chair upturned. Further into the room, two of the big lounges were pushed haphazardly together, forming a barrier across the centre of the room. Beyond them was Jodie. The post she was tied to was so wide, she looked like she was hugging it. Her body was pressed up against it, rigid and tense, her head turned to one side with her cheek laid against the timber. Somewhere out of sight, between the kitchen bench and the front door was the hole in the floor.

There was no easy way in but where he was squatted at the back door was probably the worst entry point – a minefield between him and his target, and no clear view of the room. And he still had no weapon.

Matt took a long look at the half of Jodie's face he could see, felt a flare of admiration. Lit up by the spotlights outside, she was deathly pale, there was a trail of blood under her nose, and she looked as mad as hell.

One of the Andersons let out a roar. There was a thump and Matt felt the verandah shudder under him.

Kane appeared from behind the kitchen bench, rising up as though he'd been squatting on the floor. He was dirty, sweating and moving with the exaggerated motions of someone who was mightily pissed off. Matt looked at Jodie. She was pulling away from the post, one shoulder wedged back as though she was trying to get as much distance from Kane as she could. But her face was angled down to the hole in the floor.

Matt dropped to his knee, found a clear line of vision between the bench and the lounges, to where the floorboards had been ripped up. Kane was bent over, using both hands to take hold of something in the mouth of the hole. He heaved and a large metal chest rose up and out onto the floor.

It had to be the box Matt had dug up under the barn. Same

colour, same rectangular shape. About a metre long, half a metre high. In the light, it looked military green. Kane used his foot to push it along the floor. Whatever was in there, whatever it was they'd come back for, was heavy.

Kane stood up, smiled like a snake at Jodie. Matt saw her body stiffen. She shifted her weight on her feet like she was getting ready for a fight.

'You ready for me?' Kane said.

Jodie lifted her chin, said nothing.

Kane laughed, a high-pitched crazy sound.

Matt took one last look at Jodie. Her lips were pressed together, her was body taut, her tethered hands were in fists, arms locked around the timber. Hold on, Jodie. Don't let go yet. Then he slid quickly, quietly across the verandah, dropped into the garden and took off as fast as his injuries would let him.

JODIE WATCHED the feral smile on Kane's face as he moved towards her. Fear tightened around her chest. She wanted the hate back, wanted to feel it boil and hiss inside her. But hope had taken the heat out of it.

She swung wild eyes to the hole. Where was Travis? He was going to handle his brother. He'd slid a thumb and index finger across his lips before he'd dropped into the hole behind Kane. Zip your mouth. And she had. She'd kept silent. She'd held onto the trunk, listened to her own ragged breathing as Kane and Travis hauled up the metal chest. She'd done what he'd told her, let hope grow like a tumour in her gut. So where the hell was he?

Kane circled the post, stopped behind her, did nothing for about thirty long seconds. Jodie's heart boomed. Then he grabbed a fist of hair, yanked her head so far back her mouth gaped open. He pushed his face into her field of vision, grinned as he walked two fingers across her throat.

'You're gonna be good.' His foul breath filled her mouth, her nose. 'Hey, bro, you gotta watch this time.'

'You're not finished yet,' Travis barked.

Jodie saw Travis on the edge of the hole. Relief and hope welled in her throat, came out like a gasp.

'Bullshit,' Kane said. 'I got your chest out. Now I get the tough bitch.'

Travis grabbed him from behind and hauled him away. 'You get her when I say you do.'

Kane wrenched out of Travis's hold, just far enough for Travis to throw an elbow into his brother's face. Kane's head snapped back a second before he dropped to one knee.

Travis stood over him. 'I keep telling you, you fuck-up, you don't get to call the shots.'

Jodie watched Kane. Light from the window glowed like a halo around his short-cropped hair, throwing his face into shadow. It hid his eyes, his mouth, but she didn't need to see them to recognise his anger. Slowly, his face turned towards her. On the floor near her feet, his hands curled into fists.

MATT LIFTED the tyre iron in his uninjured hand. It felt solid, heavy, not even close to being a gun but the best weapon he could find at short notice. He'd had to move it away from the wardrobe door when he came to get Louise and Hannah, had no idea how or when it was left in the bedroom, just pleased he'd seen it.

He lifted his head at sounds from the front of the barn. Footsteps on the timber deck. More than one set of feet. He moved silently through the bedroom to the French doors, listened again as the foot-steps moved down the front stairs. He limped as quietly as he could across the verandah, down the set of steps beyond the bedroom, squatted in the garden. The footfalls were soft scuffles now on the gravel parking pad at the front of the house. It might have been the distance, the muffling effect of the barn between him and them, but it sounded like the steps were laboured. Not the solid crunch of feet walking easily over gravel. Not a dragging. More an uneven shuffling. As though the walkers were moving with difficulty. With weight.

The metal box.

Matt moved to the corner of the verandah, inched his face around. The first thing he saw was the blinding flood of light from the top of the truck. Two huge, mounted spotlights cast a dazzling V of bright, white light that lit up the entire front face of the barn like a stage, leaving everything around it in blackness.

The next thing he saw was one of the Andersons. He was standing near the truck, maybe a metre in front of the left-hand spotlight, just within its arm of light. He was half turned, crouched forward, more back view than side view and from that distance, in the glare, Matt couldn't tell whether it was Kane or Travis.

The third thing he saw was the box. It was at Anderson's feet, half of its khaki length clearly visible, the rest lost in the darkness behind the spotlights. It was open, its metal lid tipped back against the truck.

Matt stood slowly, pressing himself against the verandah railing, hoping the height would give him a view inside the chest. It didn't. Then it didn't matter.

Anderson shouted, the 'Fuck you!' carrying clearly in the cold night air. Matt tensed as the man lunged aggressively into the darkness behind the truck. He heard the distant ping of a stone hitting the metal. Then a sound that even at twenty metres away rocked through Matt's body. A rifle shot.

Matt looked up at the barn. Where was Jodie?

He dropped to his knees again as Anderson moved into the light. The same Anderson. He was holding a gun now. Short stock, long barrel. Unmistakable, even at this distance. It was a Steyr. Standard-issue military rifle. Where had that come from?

Civilians couldn't buy them. The only way to get one was to steal it.

Travis. It had to be. The weapons racket. He'd kept one for himself. And now the brothers were armed with a powerful, automatic killing machine.

Matt watched Anderson stride to the barn, the sound of his boots on the parking pad making Matt's pulse pick up pace. Solid crunches in the gravel this time. No hesitation, no looking over his shoulder.

Whatever had just happened, Anderson wasn't worried about turning his back to it.

Matt looked at the darkness behind the truck and felt fear explode in his head. Who was behind the truck? Don't let it be Jodie.

How long had it taken Matt to run around the barn, get the tyre iron, land back in the garden? Long enough for Jodie's tethers to be cut, to make her lift one end of the box and carry it to the truck? Yeah, plenty of time for that.

As Anderson reached the verandah, Matt limped out into the darkness that surrounded the bright V of spotlight. Shot didn't mean dead, Matt.

Shot was bad.

It didn't have to be dead.

JODIE STIFFENED against the tree trunk as the amplified clap of gunfire rang out. Travis had shot his brother? Travis had to be the shooter. He had the pistol tucked into his waistband when the two of them went out with the chest.

She stared at the front window, horror dry in her mouth. Is that what Travis had meant when he said he'd 'handle' his brother? What kind of messed-up, dysfunctional family were they? But the disgust didn't last long. Big, fat tears welled in her eyes and relief crashed through her.

Kane was handled. Whatever that meant, he wasn't arguing the point or yelling in pain. So he had to be dead. Or unconscious. Or quietly bleeding to death. She should feel bad about that, but she didn't. He didn't deserve her compassion. And right now all she cared about was getting the tape off her wrists, getting Lou and Hannah out of the wardrobe and getting away from this fucking barn.

She braced her feet around the base of the trunk, dragged back on her wrists, felt the tape pull tight. Come on, tear. Footsteps sounded on the gravel parking pad, thudded onto the front stairs. Travis was coming back to release her. No reason for him to leave in a hurry if Kane was out of the picture. Jodie lifted her eyes to the open door, impatient to see him. Desperate for the night to end.

As his shadow moved into the doorway, Jodie felt a swell of emotion. It was over. In ten seconds, she'd be free. Thirty seconds, she'd have Lou and Hannah out of the wardrobe. A minute and they'd be out of the barn, going home.

Then Kane walked through the door.

38

M att carried the tyre iron low at his side, took loping strides in a deep arc behind the brilliance of the spot-lights. He guessed it was a forty-metre straight run across the front of the barn to the truck. With his detour behind the light, call it sixty. It felt like a marathon.

The clearing in front of the barn was anything but clear. In the dark, it was a minefield of loose rocks, old tree stumps and ankle-breaking divots and he stumbled and struggled to stay upright on his bad knee. The pain was unbelievable – like a hacksaw working off his kneecap, his arm trapped in a fiery vice. The only plus was the stage lighting on the barn. It guided his way, turning the Andersons' truck and Jodie's car into sharply defined silhouettes, like late-stayers at a drive-in movie.

Matt ran until he hit the gravel on the parking pad, trod cautiously across the rubble beyond the truck then dropped to the ground, keeping the body of the vehicle between him and the front door. Aside from his own lungs gasping for air, the night was silent. No sound from the truck. No sound from the barn.

He crept closer, eyes straining in the dark. He was five metres from the truck when he saw it. A dark shape on the ground. On the other side of the truck. Still, quiet, lifeless.

Matt swallowed hard. Worked down the dread that was trying to climb its way into his throat.

Shot wasn't dead. Don't be dead, Jodie.

THE HOPE that had blossomed inside her shrivelled like a bud in a bushfire. Jodie's knees buckled.

She was going to die.

It was already a fact. It couldn't be changed.

Kane had shot his brother. Now he was going to kill her. And she was going to wish she was dead long before her heart stopped beating.

'We got the place to ourselves now, tough bitch.'

Kane stepped further into the room, grinned at her as he held up a rifle by its barrel.

'Won't be needing this now.' He tossed it to the floor. The sharp crack as it landed on the timber made Jodie flinch as though he'd swung at her. Kane pulled the pistol from the front of his waistband, held it with a finger through the trigger guard. 'Won't be needing this, either.' He flipped it onto the floor with the rifle, laughed. The same feral laugh she'd heard all night. Her skin felt like it was trying to crawl off her bones.

He walked to her then, stopped in front of the tree trunk. Just stood. Panic rose cold and hard in her chest.

'Got nothing to say now, tough bitch?'

Jodie kept her mouth shut, frightened of the scream that was gathering in her lungs. Frightened of the screaming, powerless death that would await her if she let it out.

Kane's hand snapped out, grabbed the back of her head and slammed her cheek into the trunk. 'Come on, bitch. Say something nasty. While you got the chance. Before you *scream* for me.'

Pain bit into her face. Her head filled with the stench of his sweat, the tang of blood from the wound in his thigh. And anger sparked in her belly. She had no chance of beating him. Not tied to a tree. But she was *not* going to scream for him. She lifted her eyes to his, said nothing.

His grin turned hard. 'What? You want your friends out here to watch? How 'bout I go get them, make them watch you bleed? Would you talk dirty for me then?'

Jodie saw them. Just a flash, a freeze-frame. Louise bleeding in Hannah's arms. And the hate returned. Hot and angry and heaving. She wasn't going to get them out. They weren't going home to their families. Kane was going to kill them all. '*Fuck you!*'

He let her go, pushed away from the post, smiling like she'd waved a white flag.

'Oh yeah. That's the tough bitch I wanna mess up.'

Hate burned inside her like a furnace, hissing and glowing, forging a will of steel. And as she watched him swagger away from her, strutting like a pimp, like he had a goddamn audience, she waited. Back in the place she'd never, ever wanted to be again – waiting to die, waiting for her friends to die. But this time, she wasn't going to fear the man who wanted to hurt her. She wasn't going to give him that power. This time, she was going to make him work hard for his thrill. She was going to fight him every step of the way. She was going to hurt him before he was finished.

And she was going to hate him. She was going to stare him down and hate him to her last breath. It would be her final act of will.

Kane rounded the marble bench, walked through the kitchen to the back wall. To the knife block. It hadn't moved from where Jodie had seen it earlier. A chunk of pale timber near the stove, a sharpening tool on one side, the two long blades missing, one stainless steel handle jutting out from its slot. He pulled the paring knife, half turned towards her, made sure she could see as he used his thumb to test the blade.

He shook his head theatrically. 'Nothing worse than a blunt tool, hey, tough bitch?'

Bile rose in Jodie's throat. She wanted to squeeze her eyes shut, put her hands over her ears, block out the world around her. But she forced herself to watch him, to listen to the grinding sound as he pushed the blade in and out of the sharpening tool – and nursed her hate.

When he was done, he turned, sauntered back across the kitchen. Instinct made her pull against the tape on her hands, lean away from the tree trunk, try to shield herself behind it.

There was no point, of course. He was free to move wherever he wanted. She was at his mercy.

And there was going to be no mercy.

He stopped beside her and held the point of the knife to the tree trunk.

'You want me to carve your name in the tree? How about 'tough bitch bled here'.' He laughed as he flipped the knife over, held it in a reverse grip, rammed it into the wood.

He was showing her how clever he was, how he could ram that thing into her like she was nothing but a piece of wood. She was meant to whimper, to shriek in terror.

Eighteen years ago she'd been stabbed six times in the abdomen. She never saw the knife. Hadn't known she was cut and bleeding until after she'd fought off her attacker, run to the road and the head-lights of an oncoming car had illuminated the waterfall of blood streaming from her.

She'd had plenty of time to think about knives since then. To see them in her dreams, to wake in fear of the touch of another one. Every time she took off her clothes and saw the horrific scars.

Until this moment, she'd have said without hesitation or shame that the sight of Kane holding the knife he planned to drag across her throat would have crushed her in fear.

It didn't.

She looked at the point buried in the timber. The gleaming, sharpened edge. The filthy, brutal hand holding it. The double-edged blade tattooed on his arm. The blood-lust in Kane's eyes. And a flame flared deep inside her. It fed like a starving child on her hate. Grew big and strong. Filled her with a scorching, aching, all-consuming rage.

Kane pulled the knife from the tree trunk and held the edge of it against Jodie's cheek. 'You worried yet, tough bitch?'

She locked her eyes on his, let the hate pour out of them. Rage pounded in her head. She made herself smile. 'Of you?'

He moved quickly, shoved her hard up against the trunk and held her there with the weight of his body, pressing the knife to the side of her neck. 'How 'bout this?'

His knees dug into her thighs, his breath was hot in her hair, she was surrounded by his stink. And he was too damn close for her to throw her head back and break his nose.

'Thought you were the kind of guy who'd want to do it from behind.' She braced herself, hoped she hadn't pushed it too far, that he didn't just plunge the knife into her throat before she could hurt him.

She flinched as he drove the blade into the timber next to her face, pushed away from her.

'Want it rough, huh? Wanna watch while I cut you up, huh? That can be arranged.' He strutted to a pile of tools by the door, found the electrical tape he'd tied her with earlier.

'Just so you know,' he said, coming back, talking to her from the other side of the tree, 'I like a woman to flail around. Nothing like a good fight to get the blood flowing.' He held the knife against her wrists, sliced through her binds in one clean cut.

Jodie's lungs heaved in and out, her pulse pounded in her throat. It was better than she'd hoped.

He held both her hands in a crushing grip. 'Try anything and I'll slice clean up your arm.'

She pulled one arm from around the tree, held it out to him, watched with a ghoulish sense of satisfaction as he wrapped them both up in tape again.

MAYBE IT WAS THE DARKNESS, maybe it was Matt's desperation, but he was almost to it, already starting to drop into a slide to take him right to the body, before he processed it.

The body was too big, it wasn't in a white sweater. He skidded to a stop on one knee, rolled the body over, saw Travis's throat ripped apart by a bullet and a pool of thick dark blood seeping into the gravel around him. Matt spun back to the light.

Jodie was in the barn.

With Kane.

He was on his feet before he'd thought about it, breathing hard, adrenaline tingling in his veins. He looked down at the tyre iron in his hand. Big stick versus rifle.

A shadow moved in the front window, something crashed to the floor. He threw himself across the gravel, pressed his back to the side of the truck. Saw the open chest next to him and bent closer.

It wasn't just one Steyr.

The chest was full of Steyrs.

Twenty or more.

And a magazine of ammunition sat on the top like an afterthought.

Anger stiffened his spine. This was about guns? They'd shot a woman, shot a cop, were threatening to kill all five of them – for rifles? Were they complete fucking maniacs?

No. Kane was. Not Travis.

The facts, the few he had, hurtled through his head. John Kruger was murdered yesterday, beaten to death with a piece of timber. Not a robbery. The work of someone out of control. Travis and Kane were the builders. They were hiding from the cops. They should be on the run but they weren't. *Or I leave without you.* Not yet.

This wasn't about guns.

It was about money.

Travis's chest of stolen, illegal, automatic rifles would sell for a small fortune. Plenty for a couple of country boys to hide out on. Enough to get them as far from Bald Hill as they wanted.

But now Travis was dead.

And Jodie was inside with the Anderson family psychopath. And she was screaming.

· · ·

JODIE LOOKED down at the straight splice across the sleeve of Corrine's sweater and the blood spilling over its edges. Kane had cut her. It hurt but she'd hurt him first.

He'd teased her with the knife. Tipped her head back, run the blade teasingly over her chin, her throat, her breasts. She'd refused to react. Had stared him down, welcomed the rage pulsing through her body – and waited for a chance. It didn't take long.

He yanked on the tape binding her hands. She saw the intent in his pale eyes as he hauled her in. He wanted to get in her face, make her feel small, victimised, overpowered. She went with the momentum and drove her forehead at his face, her rage spilling over in a primitive scream.

The knife had sliced through her sweater above her wrist as he ricocheted away. She looked at the result of a wound that barely hurt. Looked up at the blood streaming from his nose and smiled.

He spun her around, wrapped an arm across her chest, used the other hand to hold the knife blade to her throat. She could hear him dragging air in through an open mouth. He turned his face, spat on the floor. 'Try that again and I'll cut your throat.'

She should have been terrified. She should have been pleading for her life. She was going to die. In a lot of pain.

But all she felt was the rage.

It crashed through her, wiping out any sensation but sheer fury. Kane had hurt her friends. Killed Matt. Murdered a teenager. A girl like Angie. And he was about to deny her children their mother.

Rage cleared her mind, opened her eyes, made her strong. Made her a gladiator.

The tree trunk was to her left. The hall door to the right. The island bench directly in front. Which meant the hole in the floor was right behind them.

ane was at her back, one beefy, muscular arm trapping her against his chest. They were bound together. Wherever they were going, they were going together.

She lifted her hands over the forearm pinning her to his chest, found the hand holding the knife and dragged on the wrist.

'No, please no,' she cried.

She struggled in his arms, strained against him, tried to haul herself away from his hold. She dragged down with her legs, thrust her hips forward, shook her shoulders, felt the blade digging into the soft flesh of her throat. Until she felt his weight shift.

He leaned back a fraction to keep his balance, to stop her from pulling him over. As he did, she released the tension, reversed her effort, drove backwards. Hard, gripping the floor with her toes, pushing through her legs. He took a step to stop from falling. She went with him, trapped his other foot under hers, leaned into him. Felt him stumble. Leaned some more. Another step back. Then Kane lost control and they were staggering away. Two, three steps.

They must be close. Jodie squeezed her eyes shut, dragged down on his knife hand. It was going to hurt. The fall itself could kill her. Or the knife, if she couldn't keep it away from her throat.

She felt his leg go slack as he stepped into clean air. She pressed backwards with her shoulders, pulled both knees up, tried to ride him like a cushion to the earth under the barn.

It felt like falling down a well. The light from the lounge room disappeared overhead and they were dropping into darkness. Kane was shouting, flailing and the arm that pinned her chest flew out, looking for a handhold. She fought the urge to do the same, hung onto his wrist, prayed she was strong enough to keep the knife clear.

The impact was like being slammed by a Mack truck. Her head jolted backwards, hit something hard. She felt a crack underneath her, inside Kane. He roared in pain. She was dizzy, loose-limbed but his free arm was moving.

She threw her head forward and bit down on his knife hand. He struggled. She hung on, tasting blood, grinding his tough flesh between her teeth. He grabbed a handful of her hair with his free hand, tried to drag her away but it was too late. His fingers opened and the blade fell out of reach.

As she opened her jaw, he pressed his palm to her face and pushed. He forced her head back, driving her chin up, pulling her hair with the other hand, trying to break her neck. She twisted her shoulders, dug an elbow into his broken ribs. He shrieked, let go of her hair. She pushed down on his chest with the point of the bone as she rolled off him, to her feet. He was thrashing about, rocking back and forth, trying to get away from her. He was in pain, having trouble breathing but she didn't give a shit.

She lifted a foot, slammed her heel into his ribs. Watched in the dim light from the room above as he writhed in the dirt. Listened as his howl echoed inside her and fed the rage.

The knife blade caught the light. She bent, picked it up two-handed and turned it towards her. One quick slice was all it took to cut the tape around her wrists then she crouched beside him, held the point to his cheek, pressed it hard enough to make a dent in the skin, spoke clearly, calmly.

'Fight me and I'll slice you open.'

He stopped moving, looked at her over the top of the knife. His face was smeared with blood and dirt.

'Get up, you animal. *Move.*' She kept the blade on his cheek as he sat. 'On your knees.'

He moved awkwardly, wincing in pain, breathing noisily. When he was there, he turned, smiled. 'You Jack the Ripper now, tough bitch?'

She looked him in the eye. Three minutes ago she thought she was dead. Now she was standing and Kane was on his knees at her feet. She had nothing to lose. 'Oh, yeah, I'm Jack, all right.'

'You ever seen a knife wound? So much blood it'll make you puke.'

'Tell me about it.'

He grinned. 'You think you're real tough, don't you? You'll never do it.'

'Try me.'

He made a grab for her hand. She pulled the knife up high, out of his reach, drove it straight down into his thigh.

It took no effort at all. The knife slid through his flesh, stopped when it hit bone. He yowled in pain. She pulled it out and looked at the blood on the blade. She was surprised at how easy it was. How good it felt to hurt him.

Kane moved fast. Locked his meaty hand around her fist, the one holding the knife. He was a big man, probably twice Jodie's weight, a head taller. Even with broken ribs and a deep thigh wound, she would never beat him in an arm-wrestle. She was already on her feet but he was dragging her towards the ground. She kicked out hard at his injured thigh. He let out a scream, threw himself at her, knocked her backwards onto the loose earth.

If he got on top of her, she wouldn't have a chance. She pulled her knees up, pushed out with her feet as he came at her, managed only to topple him sideways. He took her with him, crushing her hand under his as he hauled her over the top of him, threw her to the earth on the other side.

Then he was straddled over her hips, still holding her fist in his hand, crushing the bones of her fingers around the knife handle. She gasped for breath and his ugly face split into a smile.

Slowly, like a game, a battle of wills, he pushed down on her hand. She locked her elbow but he was too strong. She couldn't hold out against him. He forced her arm to bend, forced her hand around until the knife pointed at her like an arrow. She strained against the pressure on her arm, twisted her face away, as though she could escape him.

She squeezed her eyes shut as the cold point of the blade came to rest on the soft skin under her ear.

Kane laughed. 'You didn't know you were going to cut your own throat, did you?'

She turned her eyes to him, kept them there, burning with hate, as he increased the pressure on the knife. As something trickled down her neck.

Her breath was loud in her ears. Her head pounded in rhythm with her heart. She watched Kane and thought of her children, of Louise and Hannah and Corrine. Matt. Angie.

The light in the room above dimmed. No, Jodie. Do *not* pass out. You're going to look this bastard in the eye to the end.

He nodded at her.

No, not a nod. His head tipped forward. The grin slid off his face.

'Drop it, Anderson.'

MATT KEPT the muzzle of the rifle jammed hard up against the base of Kane's skull, watched from the floor above as Anderson lifted his arm, released Jodie's hand. The knife tumbled to the dirt.

He saw the blood then, the thin, dark line running into the neck of Jodie's sweater. Another second and she'd be bleeding to death. His grip tightened on the rifle. He wanted to put a bullet through Kane's head, put him down like a rabid dog.

He felt the trigger under his finger. One small movement would blow the arsehole away. He sucked in air. Blew it out. Don't do it, Matt.

'*Get your hands up!*' Matt yelled. He lifted his finger from the trigger, telling himself there was no justice for anyone in a quick, painless death.

'Get off me!' Jodie screamed. Her eyes were wild, her chest heaved in and out. '*Get off me.*'

Matt kept his voice loud, aggressive. 'Keep it slow, arsehole.'

As Kane lifted his weight from Jodie's hips, she scuttled out from under him, rolled away, came up on her feet, in a crouch, with the knife in her hand. She pointed it at Kane, held it firm, unwavering, slashing distance from his face. She touched fingers to her neck, saw the blood, closed her hand into a fist and punched him in the face.

It was an impressive shot. Thrown full force from the shoulder, catching him square on the cheekbone, knocking him back on his haunches. Her knuckles were going to hurt later but right now she didn't look like she was feeling a thing. No fear, no intimidation, nothing but some kind of seething fury that was pouring right out of her.

'Jodie, are you okay?' Matt asked.

'He cut me.' She didn't take her eyes off Kane. Matt wasn't even sure she knew who he was.

'Jodie?'

'He fucking *cut* me.' She swung at Kane with the knife.

As Anderson ducked back, Matt jammed the rifle in his ear. He had a stream of blood running from his nose, a crazy woman with a knife in front of him, the cop he shot behind him. He looked like an unhappy man. Suck it up.

'Jodie?' Matt said again. She didn't move. 'Jodie. I've got a gun on him.'

She shot a brief look up to where Matt was leaning over the edge of the hole. Took a little longer the second time, let her eyes focus on him before she turned them to Kane.

'Matt?' she said.

'Yeah.'

'He shot you.'

'Yeah.'

'I thought you were *dead*.'

'I'm not. You can put the knife down now, Jodie.'

She kept the knife where it was as she wiped at her face with the heel of her other hand. 'He was going to kill me.'

'I know. I've got him now. Put the knife down.'

'No.'

'Jodie.'

'*No!*' She moved closer to Kane, touched the blade to the underside of his chin, forced his head back, slid the point down to the hollow at the base of his throat. The skin puckered under the pressure of her hand. Kane didn't move, looked like he didn't dare.

'You worried yet?' she said.

Matt felt a new kind of fear for her then. Bitter experience had taught him a brief moment of revenge didn't make cold-blooded cruelty any less brutal. Having a killer's blood on your hands didn't change the outcome, didn't heal any wounds. Didn't reverse your mistakes. Just made you the same as the thing you destroyed. No, if there was any chance of justice – for tonight, for Jodie and her friends, for Tina – Kane Anderson would rot in a prison cell for the rest of his life. 'Put the knife down, Jodie.'

She kept her eyes on Kane. 'He was going to kill my friends.'

Matt swung his legs into the hole, kept the gun to Kane's head as he dropped his feet to the earth. 'Your friends are safe now. Give me the knife.'

'He was going to *kill me* and then he was going to *kill my friends*.'

'Louise and Hannah are safe. I got them out. Like we planned.' He reached out to her, put his hand on top of hers, let his fingers slide forward onto the handle of the knife.

'Look at me, Jodie.' She slid her eyes to him. 'They're all safe. You saved them, Jodie. Let me have the knife.'

He held her gaze for a long moment, tried to make them tell her that he understood. That it was over now. That it was never going to be over for Kane. He didn't know if she understood but her fingers finally softened and he pulled the knife from her grip, threw it far into the darkness under the barn.

He drew her to him then, away from Kane, kept his eyes and the gun on Anderson, let his mouth brush over her hair. It was gritty under his lips. She was rigid, wary, covered in dirt, bleeding and bruised. The best thing he'd ever seen.

'Where's his brother?' she said.

'Outside.'

'Dead?'

'He's not going anywhere. Can you climb up?'

She straightened into the gaping, broken hole in the floor, half in the barn, half under it. She gazed around the spotlit room as though she'd forgotten what it looked like. She nodded.

Matt watched her as she braced her hands on the timber boards and hoisted herself up. The adrenaline must still be flowing. She seemed as strong as she ever did, no hint of the shakes. Maybe shock would hit after she'd seen her friends alive and safe.

'Give me the gun,' she said, looking down at him.

He thought of her with the knife in her hand, hesitated.

'So I can keep it on him while you climb up. It's okay. I've used a rifle before.' He checked her eyes. The fury he'd seen before seemed under control now. He passed it up to her. Beside him, Kane moved for the first time since Jodie had held the knife to his throat. He turned his head, looked up at her, something unreadable in his pale eyes. She propped the butt of the gun against her shoulder like she'd done it a hundred times, pointed it at Kane.

'You next,' she said.

It was the right move, Matt thought. If Matt climbed out first, Kane could duck back under the boards and disappear into the darkness. But something about the way Jodie said it made him uneasy.

Kane took it slow. He was breathing through his mouth as though his bloodied nose no longer worked, he kept one elbow pulled in tight to the side of his body and he was bleeding a lot from a second thigh wound. Matt pushed him up with a hand under his foot. Up above, Jodie had both bare feet planted firmly on the floor, her eyes never leaving Kane.

'Move away from the hole,' she ordered when he was up.

Matt heard Kane chuckle. 'You GI Jane, now?'

Jodie's response was loud, explosive, aggressive.

'*Don't talk to me!*' she screamed and Matt realised he'd made a mistake.

40

Jodie knew now what it was like to be Kane. Knew how it felt to want to hurt someone. She wanted to make Kane scream in agony. Wanted him to feel trapped and terrified and in fear of his life. And she wanted to watch him to the end, until he couldn't take another breath. Until he got what he deserved.

She nestled the rifle into her shoulder, glad of the hours she'd spent at the gun club in the first years after Angie died.

'I made you bleed, tough bitch.' Kane stood on the edge of the hole, hands loosely at his side, grinning through the blood on his face like he'd scored some kind of prize.

The rage was a wild animal inside her. It beat against her ribs, clawed at her belly, bellowed in her head. 'Shut up!'

'One second longer and your blood would've been gushing all over me.'

'*Shut up!*'

'I could've taken a swim it.'

Jodie moved her finger to the rifle's trigger.

'Jodie!'

It was Matt. Still in the hole. She'd thought he was dead. Thought she'd lost him before she even had him.

'Help me up, Jodie,' Matt said.

Without taking her eyes off Kane, she dropped one hand from the rifle, leaned down, grasped Matt's as he hauled himself into the lounge room. When he let go, her hand was sticky with his blood.

Kane had made him bleed. She looked into the bastard's freaky, pale eyes, saw the arrogance and cruelty inside them.

'Give me the gun,' Matt said.

'No,' she said. 'Move,' she told Kane. 'To the door.'

She stayed on his heels as he walked to the front door. Matt was at her side all the way, edgy, looking like he wasn't sure who he should be covering – her or Kane. As far as Jodie was concerned, it was an each-way bet who was more dangerous right now.

Kane put a hand on the doorjamb, squinted in the brilliant light from his car, looked back at her with a sly grin. 'You ever used a gun like that before? The recoil will break your shoulder before you hit anything.'

Jodie pointed the gun at his thigh. 'You want to try me again?' She smiled at the uncertainty in his eyes. 'Move. Out the door.'

The spotlight blinded her as they stepped outside. She couldn't see anything beyond the front steps. She glanced both ways down the verandah, felt the rage gather strength when she didn't see what she was looking for.

'Louise?' she shouted. 'Hannah? Corrine?' She swung accusing eyes on Matt.

'Where are they? You said you got them. *Where are they, Matt?*'

'I took Louise and Hannah into the bush. They're safe. Give me the gun.'

'Where's Travis?' she demanded. She'd thought he was dead but she'd thought Matt was, too.

'Jodie.'

'You said he was out here!' she yelled at him. 'Where is he?' She shoved Kane with the muzzle of the gun, pushed him towards the steps. 'You better start praying I see your brother out here or I'm going to make you scream until he shows himself.'

Kane cupped his mouth with one hand, lifted his voice. 'Hey, bro, where are you?' He made like he was shocked, like he hadn't already pulled a trigger. 'Wiseman killed him. *He* killed my brother.'

She pointed the gun at his face. 'Good.'

'Give me the gun, Jodie.' Matt pulled on her shoulder as she moved towards the top step.

She shoved him off, pushed Kane ahead of her as she stormed down the stairs.

'*Where?* Where's Travis?' Then she saw him, in the dim reflected light behind the beam of the spots, on his back, arms spread wide, blood staining the gravel around his head.

There was a sudden flash of movement beside her. She turned, saw Kane make a move towards her, saw Matt dive at him, swing an elbow into his ribs. Kane doubled over, gasping painfully, making hoarse sucking sounds as he tried to breathe in.

'Get on the ground,' she shouted at him. 'On your knees. Hands behind your head.' She watched and smiled in brutal satisfaction at his pain.

Matt was in pain, too. She could see him clutching his upper arm. Fresh blood was oozing out of a makeshift bandage, starting to run down his arm.

Kane had shot Matt. He'd held a gun to Corrine's head. He'd locked up her friends. She felt again the press of the knife he'd held to her throat.

The wild thing inside her beat itself against her ribs again.

'This was *my* place for the weekend. You chose the wrong weekend to come here.' She walked to Kane, put her foot on his chest, pushed him. He screamed, grabbed at his bloody thigh as he fell to his back.

She stepped over him, aimed the muzzle of the gun at his face. 'You cut me.'

'Felt good, didn't it, bitch?'

Blood roared in her head. '*You cut me.*'

'No, Jodie.' She could hear the pain in Matt's voice. It made her fingers tingle with the urge to pull the trigger.

'Do it, bitch,' Kane said.

She nestled the gun tighter into her shoulder, looked at Kane's ugly, bloodied face along its length.

Matt moved into the edge of her vision, on the other side of Kane. 'It won't change it, Jodie. Killing him won't undo what he's done.'

'*He cut me.*'

'I know what it's like to want revenge, Jodie.'

'Shut up, Matt. Just shut up.'

Kane suddenly reached up, grabbed the end of the rifle with both hands. Jodie flinched, almost pulled the trigger.

He yanked on the gun. He was angry now, agitated, holding the weapon with tight fists. '*Come on*, tough bitch. *Do it.*'

She wanted to. Her finger was on the trigger. One squeeze and Kane Anderson wouldn't hurt anyone ever again.

He wanted it, too. He wasn't playing her. She could see it in his eyes. He wanted her to pull the trigger. He wanted to die.

And that's what made her hesitate.

'*Come on,*' he yelled.

She smiled down at him. 'How bad do you want it?'

'Fuck you.'

She lowered her eye to the rifle sight.

'Jodie,' Matt said quietly.

'No,' she answered.

'Just letting you know if you shoot him from there, you'll get his brains all over you.'

Matt's unexpected, casual, shootin' the breeze, tone of voice shifted something in the haze of her rage. She got a picture of it then. Not of the violent, appalling act she was about to commit. But a sudden, gruesome, Technicolor image of Kane's brain matter splattered over her jeans. She saw herself trying to get out of her clothes with his thick gore clinging to her. She smelled it, felt it warm and slippery on her skin. And knew she would never escape that. She would see it every time she closed her eyes. Like she saw her own blood when she looked at her scars, heard Angie's screams in her sleep. She would never be free of Kane.

She swept the gun above her head and fired into the night. As the crack and boom ricocheted and rolled around the valley, she lowered the rifle and slammed the butt into Kane's head.

41

J odie woke in crisp, clean sheets, her body heavy and lethargic from the drugs she'd been given to sleep. She swallowed in a dry mouth, took stock of her injuries.

Stitches in her forearm, one high on her throat. A taped and bandaged hand. An array of tender bruises on her face, down her right side, on her shin. Blistered feet. Strained muscles. Not bad considering.

'Oh, you're awake,' Hannah said.

Jodie rolled her head painfully on the pillow, saw Hannah and Corrine sitting on the bed next to her. The hospital had cleared a four-bed ward room for them, made them all stay the night.

'How's Lou?' Jodie looked across the room to where curtains were closed around her bed.

'Still sleeping,' Hannah said.

Lou and Hannah had waited in the bush until the shouting stopped before cautiously emerging. Jodie had clung to them, sobbed with them but their questions about what had happened went unanswered. One man was dead, another was unconscious and both she and Matt were bleeding – but all she could bring herself to tell them was that she was alive, she was okay, it was over. By then, Matt had tied Kane's hands and feet and left him facedown in the dirt near the brother he'd murdered. Fifteen minutes later, a convoy of police cars turned into the long driveway, thanks to Corrine. She'd managed to negotiate her way through the dark scrub to the cottage on the road and made a triple-O call.

Jodie had sat dazed and in shock on the front steps of the barn as police swarmed around the hill. She'd wept with relief as Lou and Hannah were loaded into an ambulance but as Kane was stretchered into another van and driven away, all she'd felt was a cold, detached hollowness. She didn't actually see Matt leave. He'd refused to go until she'd been taken down to join Corrine in the cottage. Seemed he had some code about not leaving before the hostages. No reason to argue with that.

It was after midnight before she and Corrine finally made the forty-minute trip in the ambulance and arrived at the nearest hospital. Louise was already in surgery, Matt was waiting his turn and despite the late hour, a cast of thousands had gathered. Family, police, reporters, camera crews and photographers. She was desperate to see Adam and Isabelle, to hold her children after almost losing them forever, but when she spoke to James on the phone, she asked him not to bring them in. She'd caught a look at her face in a mirror and didn't want to upset them more than they needed to be.

'How are you?' Hannah asked, helping Jodie to sit, plumping her pillows.

'Sore. Alive. Pleased to see you guys sitting there.' Jodie tenderly fingered the bruise around her eye. 'Actually, pleased doesn't cover it.'

Hannah and Corrine smiled but they both looked uneasy with it, as though they weren't sure smiling was the right response.

'Are you really all right, Jodie?' Hannah said suddenly. 'Your face and your . . .' She touched her hand to her throat, lowered her voice. 'Did they do that?'

Jodie looked at the bandage on her arm. The wound wasn't deep, it would heel quickly. But there was no dressing for what she felt on the inside. It was as though the rage that had coursed through her had burned her, left her raw and inflamed. 'Kane did. But I did worse to him.'

'He's here in the hospital,' Corrine said. 'On another floor.'

'There's a police guard on him,' Hannah said.

Jodie raised an eyebrow. 'Is that to protect us or him?'

Hannah gave her the uneasy smile again.

Corrine said, 'Reporters want to talk to us. They called me a hero on the news this morning. Well, they didn't say my name. They said the one who escaped and ran down to the road and got help.'

'You should talk to them,' Jodie said. 'You were really brave and people should know that. And you're going to need to remember that yourself later.'

Corrine squeezed her eyes tight for a second. 'I was really scared out there.'

'Same,' Jodie said.

'What happened, Jode?' Hannah asked. 'At the end?'

Jodie saw Kane's face along the length of the rifle again, looked away from her friends, out of the window to a gorgeous, sunny winter's day. 'It doesn't matter now.'

Hannah said, 'The hospital's organised a counsellor to come and see us.'

Jodie shook her head. She didn't want to tell them her version of events. Not yet. They would have their own nightmares to deal with. She didn't want to add her images of knives and guns to the mix. Or what she did to reunite them with their families. That was her own burden. And her salvation. And she wasn't sure she could explain that to them.

'I'm going to pass on the therapy.'

Hannah nodded. She looked like she wanted to say something but didn't.

'I'll get there but not today. There's something else I need to do before I go home to my gorgeous kids.' Jodie slid carefully off the bed, winced at the pain in her body as she moved.

Hannah put her hand out as she passed. 'Wait. I need to say something.' She lifted her chin, took a shaky breath. 'I'm sorry, Jodie. For not believing you. For what I . . .'

'It's okay,' Jodie said.

'No, it's not. I *have* to say this. What I did . . .' she stopped then started again. 'When we heard you on the other side of the wardrobe, I couldn't believe you'd come back. Then Travis was beating you up, right there on the other side of the door.' She swiped at a tear on her cheek. 'I thought I knew better than you and it almost got us killed. I don't deserve . . .'

'No, stop.' Jodie went to them, wrapped an arm around each one and pulled them close. 'We're friends. We're all here and believe me, that's all that matters.'

She took a shower, dressed in clothes Hannah's husband Pete had brought in, stood in front of the bathroom mirror and examined her face. One big, purple, mottled bruise covered her forehead, right eye and cheek. Her lips were puffy and cracked. Her hair was a nightmare. She sucked in a breath, blew it out and thought about Matt.

Last night she'd invented the whole damn romantic delusion. Then she'd put a gun to a man's head and almost blown his brains out. She figured that ugly, unhinged moment had blown a crater right through any chance she might have had with Matt, but she wanted to explain it anyway. Needed to. What he thought mattered to her.

She knocked on the door to his room, hesitantly poked her head in. He was sitting on top of the bed in fresh clothes. His face was worse than hers. He had a black eye, grazes on both cheeks and his bottom lip was swollen. One arm was in a sling and he had a metal brace on his bad knee. She felt guilty and grateful in equal measures.

'Can I come in?'

'Sure.' He turned off the tiny TV hanging from the ceiling, kept the remote in his hand and his eyes on her as she walked across the room. Not pleased to see her, not unhappy either.

Jodie sat in the chair next to his bed. 'You look good.'

He raised an eyebrow. 'You too.'

She ruffled her hair, touched a finger to her tender cheek. 'Yeah, I think the new look is working.' She laughed.

A small smile played across Matt's mouth as she did. Then he moved on, got to business. 'Have you spoken to the police this morning?'

She nodded. 'They didn't tell me much. I said I'd go up to the barn this afternoon to walk through what happened.'

'You don't have to do that, you know.'

'I want to,' Jodie said. 'I want to see the place in broad daylight. To replace the night-time images I keep seeing when I close my eyes.'

He watched her a second, tapped a finger on the remote. 'You should know something before you go. In case you want to change your mind. The preliminary searches have turned up three bodies under the barn.'

Jodie's stomach tightened. 'Is that teenage girl one of them? Tina?'

'They won't confirm it until they've checked the old case records but, unofficially, her name was found sewn into the back of the coat you dug up.'

Jodie remembered the thick fabric she'd uncovered with the pick-axe, swallowed hard on the acid taste in her mouth. 'What about the guns?'

'The army is saying they're part of a cache of weapons stolen from military training bases. The same gun scam Louise knew about. They've estimated the black market value of the stockpile from under the barn at around a quarter of a million dollars.'

'Travis's insurance,' Jodie said. His face flashed in her head. She closed her eyes, fought back the image.

'Are you all right?' Matt asked.

'Yes and no. I won't be turning the lights off any time soon.' She took a deep breath. 'Matt, what happened at the end . . . What I did . . . I . . . All I could think about was hurting Kane before he killed me. Then the gun was in my hands. I didn't plan it. It just happened.'

'You don't need to make excuses.'

'I'm not making excuses. I want you to understand. I'm not ashamed. I *wanted* to kill Kane. I admit that. But I *didn't* kill him.'

'I know what happened.'

The resolute way he said it and the unwavering look on his face as he did, told her what he thought. She would have killed Kane if he hadn't stopped her. And there was no changing it.

Still, she couldn't leave it there. 'But don't you see? You saw me at my worst. At the worst moment of my life.'

'No, you're wrong.' His voice was firm, decided. 'Last night you saved your friends. You saved me. And you pulled yourself back from the brink of a nightmare. It wasn't your worst moment, Jodie. It was your *best*.'

She couldn't speak for a moment around the lump in her throat. 'Thank you,' she finally whispered. It didn't come close to covering how she felt but it was all she could say without breaking down and sobbing on the edge of his bed.

And she saw then that maybe she hadn't blown her chance. She ran a hand through her hair, took a breath. 'Okay.' She was bad at relationships. She had trust issues, didn't like to take chances. But she'd already crossed those bridges with Matt – no point beating around the bush now. 'I'm not sure exactly how to handle this so I'm just going to say it. Getting to know you has been intense and, well, weird. And what happened between us, in the bush, well . . .' She stopped. He wasn't looking at her anymore, was gazing past her, like he'd lost interest. 'What?'

He shrugged. 'It's okay. I know what you're going to say.'

'What?'

'That it was just the heat of the moment. That it was nice to meet you but it'll be better if we go our separate ways. Don't worry about it, Jodie. It's fine.'

Oh, jeez. Maybe he was the one who'd been swept up in the heat of the moment and in the cold light of day . . .

Then she remembered the way he'd kissed her last night. 'Actually, I was going to ask you to come home with me.'

That made him look at her.

She shrugged. 'My boss has given me two weeks off so with you rooming with your dad and the fact I'm not ready to be on my own just yet, I thought we could keep each other company.'

'Jodie, you don't need to . . .'

'Don't tell me what I need.'

Irritation sparked in his eyes before amusement slid in over it.

'Look, the way I figure it,' she said, 'we both know what we're capable of. It could be a good place to start.'

He watched her a second, one side of his mouth slowly turning up, like he was considering it. 'So, your place then?'

She laughed. He seemed to like the way she did it. 'Don't get too excited. I'm thinking: you on the sofa bed, me in my own bed, and about eight or nine hours of uninterrupted sleep. Then maybe we can get to know each other, see if we still like each other.'

'Are you going to laugh like that?'

'You don't like the way I laugh?'

'Oh no, your laugh is great. It's a very cool laugh.'

She liked the way he looked at her then, as though whatever she did was going to be just fine. 'There's something I promised myself last night.' If she got another chance. She sat on the edge of his bed, looked at his bruised lower lip. 'I'm sorry if this hurts but, hey, a promise is a promise.' She leaned forward and kissed him. Long and slow. Closed her eyes as Matt wound his one good arm around her and pulled her against him.

When she was done, when he let her go, he raised an eyebrow. 'Any more promises you want to make good on?'

She smiled. 'There's one more. How do you like your steak?'

ACKNOWLEDGMENTS

Beyond Fear wouldn't have been finished without the determined support of my sister Nikki. Thank you for the well-timed text messages, the coffee consults and the insistence that being tied to a computer was a worthy way to spend my time.

Thanks to my agent Clare Forster of Curtis Brown (Aust), and Random House Australia, especially Beverley Cousins and Virginia Grant, for giving my author life a start.

Sam Findley for sharing his knowledge of Australian police operations, police officers and his own experiences – it was invaluable and cool, too.

A huge thank you to the Turramurra Women's Fiction Critique Group: Isolde Martyn, Christine Stinson, Kandy Shepherd, Elizabeth Lhuede, Simone Camilleri, Carla Molino, Melinda Seed and Caroll Casey. And to the many author friends who have contributed words of wisdom, encouragement and advice, both technical and creative, including (but not limited to) Fiona McArthur, Michelle Douglas, Cathryn Hein, Wendy James, Louise Reynolds, Rachel Bailey and Kaz Delaney. Also Romance Writers of Australia for providing author support, networking and a great conference.

For encouragement, reading and support over the ten years it took to get this book onto shelves, many thanks to: Gwenda Fulford, Julia Nalbach, Cath and Grant Every-Burns, Tracy Hewson, Fiona Honson, Joan and Brian Hankinson, Sylvia and Phil Cox, Bradley Wilson, Paul and Victoria Murphy, Kyle and Denise Loades.

My biggest and most heartfelt thanks goes to my fabulous family: my husband Paul for the walking and talking and an unexpected skill in fight choreography, my son Mark for the brainstorming and logistics sessions, and my daughter Claire for her powers of insight and listening skills. Thank you most of all for letting me follow my dream.

KEEP READING FOR A SNEAK PEEK OF
THE NEXT JAYE FORD THRILLER ...

Scared Yet?

CHAPTER I

'Talk to you tomorrow, honey. I love you.'

'Love ya, Mum,' Cameron said.

The ghost of a smile played on Liv's lips as she dropped the phone into her handbag and listened to the crack of her high heels echo through the quiet car park. God, she missed him.

She stepped out from the lighting on the pedestrian ramp into the dimness of the third level and hesitated. This afternoon, the lot had been full but it was after seven-thirty now and all but deserted. Dark and ominous was the only way to describe it. Huge slabs of concrete on the floor and ceiling, massive shadowy columns, intermittent pools of dull light from the overhead fluorescents. Metal cages around the fixtures reminded her there were people who got cheap thrills smashing up places like this. She dug the bunch of keys from her jacket pocket, clutched the one for her car like a dagger and started across the tarmac.

Her car was on the far side, past five lanes of nose-to-nose allotments. She took a wide berth around a lone van in the second row, keeping a cautious eye on it as she passed.

You're fine, Liv. Keep walking.

As the light grew dimmer and traffic noise from the street more distant, she picked up the pace, struggling for speed in her Italian snakeskin pumps. They were a leftover from when she had money to spend on frivolous footwear but with her straight skirt, they were hopeless for moving fast and her heels rang in sharp, staccato claps that ricocheted back at her. Somewhere on a lower level, a bang went off like a shot from a gun and she jumped, skittering awkwardly off an ankle, adrenaline tingling in her fingers.

Just a door closing, Liv. Calm down, get to the damn car and go … home.

Half-a-dozen echoing steps further into the murkiness and her feet slowed as the hairs on the back of her neck stood up.

Something had moved.

Over there, by the column near her car.

Her eyes searched the shadows. No. Just her imagination running wild. She glanced warily back at the ramp. It seemed ludicrously well lit now, making her feel as though she was marooned in blackness. An engine roared to life on a floor below. There were layers of concrete between it and her but it felt like it was going to burst through the floor and swallow her up.

She took off fast, moving in short, flat-footed steps, trying not to lose a shoe or twist an ankle. Aiming the key at her car, she heard the high-pitched beep, saw the tail-lights flash and silently cheered with relief. She felt ridiculous running like a crazy woman but her legs had a will of their own and her brain was already imagining her high-speed exit from the parking lot.

Her arm was out as she rounded the bumper, her fingers reaching for the doorhandle as she saw her reflection in the driver's window – and a brief movement behind her.

Then a hand slammed over her mouth.

What came next happened too fast for thought. A strong arm thumped across her chest. Fingers gouged her upper arm, pinning it to her side. Knees dug into the back of her thighs. And she was hauled backwards, feet slipping and scrabbling in her heels.

She wanted to scream but her jaw couldn't open under the pressure of the hand crushing her lips. Desperate, smothered, gasping sounds came from her throat. Fear shrieked inside her.

Then she heard him.

'You're mine, slut.'

It was spoken in her ear. Muffled, as though there was something over his mouth. Not angry. Not panicked. Just full of intent.

Cameron's lovely, freckly, eight-year-old face flashed in her mind and something switched inside her.

She tightened her fingers, felt the long, slim shank of her ignition key protruding from the base of her clenched hand and drove down hard. Something soft and resistant took the impact. There was a grunt and a flinch. She did it again. Again and again until a knee moved from behind her thigh. Anchoring a foot beneath her, she thrust back with an elbow and as the body behind angled away, she twisted towards it, aiming high with her other fist. It found the sponginess of his throat and the hand fell from her mouth.

She wasn't frightened now, wasn't feeling anything. She just wanted to get out of his hold. She stabbed with the key, swung elbows and fists.

He didn't let go but his grip loosened.

If she'd stopped to think, she might have shoved away from him and run for her life. But she didn't think. Or run. Just rammed bunched knuckles into his gut. It was a good, solid punch with the hand holding the keys and it knocked him back a step.

A second chance to run – but now there was an angry, determined, red-hot burning behind her eyes. And, with a muscle memory she thought was long forgotten, she followed through with a left to his ribs. Air whooshed from his lungs. She kicked off the one shoe she was still wearing, lifted her hands in a boxer's stance and when his head came up, she swung at his face with her right.

Sharp pain shot through her hand as he reeled away. She saw then he was covered in black. Black clothes, black gloves, black balaclava. This wasn't a spur of the moment thing. He'd planned it. He'd dressed for it. He'd waited in the dark for her.

'*Bastard!*' She lunged at him.

He was prepared this time and came back with his own fist. It was more sound than pain when it hit, like a train crash in her head. She was hurled against the car. Then he was hitting her, slapping and grappling, crushing her against the chassis, tearing at her clothes. She couldn't get a hand up to defend herself, even to cover her face. He was breathing hard inside his balaclava and the tang of his sweat filled her nostrils. She twisted her head, pulled air into her lungs and screamed.

She didn't see the roof of the car before she hit it. Just felt the crack in her neck as her head slammed sideways, the cold, rigid metal on her face then . . .

CHAPTER 2

Liv was on her side. Lying on something hard and cold. She smelled rubber and exhaust fumes. Her face hurt. And her hand. Someone said her name.

She opened an eye, focused through the veil of hair over her face, saw she was on concrete, looking at the underbelly of a car. It might have been hers. It was hard to tell from just wheels and an exhaust pipe.

A warm hand touched her arm and she jolted upright. Her vision was blurry, her head spun and the light was murky, but she could see the unmistakable shape of a man crouched next to her. Christ, he was huge.

The fight instinct flared again. She rolled onto her hip, lashed out with a knee, hit him in the ribs. As he tipped and righted himself, she scrabbled backwards, scraping her bare feet on the concrete, grazing her hands, retreating until a car tyre was jammed between her shoulderblades. She held out a hand like a stop sign. 'Stay back.'

He held up both of his and spoke. She couldn't make sense of the words, wondered if he was even speaking English. His dark hair was so short it was almost stubble and his eyes were like black holes in his face.

He was talking again. She forced herself to focus.

'. . . Daniel Beck. I work in the office across the hall.'

Who? What? Her chest heaved. Her hand burned.

'Livia?' His shirt was pale blue and his tie was striped. Okay, he was wearing a tie.

She licked her lips. 'Yeah.'

'Are you injured?'

She didn't know, she couldn't tell. Her hand was still out, holding him back, but it was shaking now. She touched it to her bottom lip, felt something damp and sticky there. The other hand, the one in pain, was clenched around the wheel arch at her back and as she released it, a hot poker shot through the middle finger. She swung her eyes briefly to it then held it out to the huge man. 'I broke my finger.'

It was misshapen and already swelling around the middle knuckle. He didn't say anything, just produced a suit coat and laid it over her legs. Oh, jeez. Her skirt was ripped to the top of her thighs and her legs were bare and splayed. But at least she still had her knickers. The man in black hadn't got that far.

'I'll call an ambulance,' he said.

'My finger snapped on his cheekbone.'

He pulled a phone from his shirt pocket, tapped the screen. 'You were lucky. It could have been worse.'

'It was a good right hook.'

He raised his eyes.

'I punched him. Here, here and here.' She used her other hand to point to her cheek, ribs and solar plexus. 'When the cops pick the bastard up, they can identify him by the bruising.' The tough-girl atti-tude felt good. Like something from her past. Didn't sound anything like the storm of emotion going on inside her.

The guy looked a little surprised by it. His eyebrows lifted slightly and he said nothing for a good couple of seconds, only turned away to speak into his phone.

Liv pushed hair off her face and glanced around. She was dazed and confused but she could see she was still in the car park and it was her own car she was leaning against. The third floor looked just like it had when she'd walked across it – shadows and columns and eerie pools of light. How long had she been lying there? And where was the bastard in black?

'I want to move you to somewhere more comfortable,' he said. 'Can you walk?'

He cupped a hand under her elbow and she snapped it away. Thirty seconds ago she thought he was going to kill her. She wasn't ready to let him near, so she held onto the car and staggered to her feet. Upright, he was even more startling. Liv was tall and he had a head on her. He was broad, too, all shoulders and arms in his business shirt. She stayed close to the car, tugging at the hem of her skirt. The sleeve of her jacket was ripped and her blouse was torn down the front. She pulled at the ragged edges, trying to cover the lacy bra underneath. The big man draped his coat over her shoulders. She couldn't remember his name now, just eyed him cautiously as she wrapped it across her chest.

He must have seen her wariness and kept a pace or so between them as she moved along the side of the car. At the rear corner, she noticed the debris on the ground – her purse and phone, sunglasses, her little digital camera, a lipstick. The keys. One of her snakeskin shoes was on top of her shoulderbag, the other was two parking spaces away. She remembered it then, the hand on her mouth, the thud on her chest and the memory knocked the breath from her. *You're mine, slut.* She reached out to steady herself, gasped as her wounded finger made contact with the car.

'Oh, God,' she heard herself say, nothing tough at all in her voice now.

She put a hand to her mouth. Her stomach lurched but nothing came. She stood bent in the middle, trying to breathe, trying to stop the spinning in her head. He caught her around the waist as her knees folded. She grabbed for his shirt, felt solid muscle, a brick wall, underneath it. Then tears spilled over her lids. She'd been ready for them but not the raw cry that burst from her throat and the uncontrolled outpouring that accompanied it. Without meaning to, she clung to him, her legs loose, her uninjured hand pulling his shirt into a fist, her lungs gasping for air. And he let her, just stood there until she was done.

It didn't take long. When her head cleared, the closeness of him unnerved her. She didn't know him from Adam. Didn't know who else was here.

'Where is he?' She pushed away.

'Who?'

'The man who hit me. The bastard in black. Is he gone?'

'I think he ran when he heard me.'

She wiped her eyes and nose with the back of her good hand, looked around to confirm it.

'Come over to the passenger door. You can sit in here.' He opened it, watched patiently as she sat down gingerly and fingered a painful lump on the side of her face.

He wasn't going to hurt her. She'd figured out that much. 'What did you say your name was?'

There was a tiny lift to one side of his mouth before he spoke. 'Daniel Beck. I work in the business across the hall from you. We've met a couple of times.'

Had they? She couldn't remember. Then a thought jagged. Teagan giggling, something about him filling a suit like a leather jacket. Oh, Daniel Beck. 'Right, right. Sorry.'

'Can I call someone for you?'

Who, Liv?

'A husband?'

'No.'

'A partner? Boyfriend?'

'God, no.'

'What about your business partner? Kelly, isn't it? What's her number?'

She saw Kelly in her mind, the face Liv had known since she was five years old – the green eyes and the contagious smile. Kelly and

Jason deserved a break from her disastrous bloody life. She pulled in a breath. Come on, you can handle this. It's a sore hand and a bump on the head. You don't need to dump more late-night shit on them. She combed fingers through her matted hair, rolled her lips together like she was fixing her lipstick. 'Yes, it's Kelly. But you don't need to call her. I'm okay. I just hurt my hand.'

As she said it, red and blue lights flashed across the car park from the street below.

ABOUT THE AUTHOR

Jaye Ford is a bestselling Australian author of five chilling suspense novels. Her first thriller, *Beyond Fear*, won two Davitt Awards for Australian women crime writers (Best Debut and Readers' Choice) and was the highest selling debut crime novel in Australia in 2011. When she needs a break from the dark stuff, she writes romantic comedy under the name Janette Paul. Her novels have been translated into numerous languages and recorded as audio books. Before writing fiction, she was a news and sport journalist, the first woman to host a live national sport show on Australian TV and ran her own public relations consultancy. She now writes fiction full time from her home in Newcastle, NSW, Australia where she loves to turn places she knows and loves into crime scenes.

To sign up for Jaye's newsletter click the link here, or visit her website the join up at www.jayefordauthor.com

Or connect on social media:

www.facebook.com/JayeFordauthor

www.instagram.com/jayeford50

DON'T MISS JAYE FORD'S NEXT THRILLER ...

Scared Yet?

When Livia Prescott rights off a terrifying assault in a deserted car park, the media hails her bravery. After a difficult year – watching her father fade away, her business struggle and her marriage fall apart – it feels good to strike back for once.

But as the police widen their search for her attacker, menacing notes start arriving – and brave is not what she feels any longer.

Someone has decided to rip her life apart, then kick her when she's down. But is it a stranger or someone much closer to home? In fact, is there anyone she can trust now?

When her family and friends are drawn into the stalker's focus – with horrifying consequences – the choice becomes simple. Fight back or lose the people she loves most ...